Also by Paige Tyler

SWAT: Special Wolf Alpha Team
Hungry Like the Wolf
Wolf Trouble
In the Company of Wolves
To Love a Wolf
Wolf Unleashed
Wolf Hunt
Wolf Hunger
Wolf Rising

X-Ops
Her Perfect Mate
Her Lone Wolf
Her Secret Agent (novella)
Her Wild Hero
Her Fierce Warrior
Her Rogue Alpha
Her True Match
Her Dark Half
X-Ops Exposed

WOLF
RISING

WITHDRAWN

PAIGE
TYLER

sourcebooks
casablanca

Published by Sourcebooks Casablanca, an imprint of Sourcebooks, Inc.
P.O. Box 4410, Naperville, Illinois 60567-4410
(630) 961-3900
Fax: (630) 961-2168
sourcebooks.com

Printed and bound in Canada.
MBP 10 9 8 7 6 5 4 3 2 1

With special thanks to my extremely patient and understanding husband. Without your help and support, I couldn't have pursued my dream job of becoming a writer. You're my sounding board, my idea man, my critique partner, and the absolute best research assistant a girl could ask for.

Love you!

Prologue

Gulfport, Mississippi, 2013

SHERIFF'S DEPUTY JAYDEN BROOKS HAD JUST DRIVEN PAST Bayou High School when the call about a suspicious person came across the radio. Someone had reported a big man lurking around the school's gym with a knife. Mill Road was deserted at this time of night, so he pulled a U-turn across the median and raced back in the other direction, flipping on his lights as he called his response in to dispatch.

By the time he got to the gymnasium parking lot less than three minutes later, a dozen high school kids were running out of the building. Based on the day of the week and the limited number of vehicles there, it was probably the tail end of volleyball practice. It was late, but schools in this part of the country were serious about their sports.

Cursing as a group of four more teens ran out of the building, some with blood on their clothes, Brooks shoved the car in park and jumped out. On the radio clipped to his shoulder, other Harrison County deputies were calling in their ETAs to his location. Sounded like he was on his own for at least the next five minutes. But that didn't stop him from racing toward the gym. It didn't take his eight years of experience on the job to know there was something bad going on in the school.

Brooks caught the arm of the first kid he crossed paths with. A girl about sixteen, she was tall and slender with blond hair.

"What happened?" he asked.

It took several long, excruciating seconds for the girl to focus on Brooks. Her hazel eyes were wide and so filled with terror, Brooks thought she might pass out. "We were finishing up practice when this big, scary guy with these crazy eyes and a knife came into the gym. Coach Ellis got between him and the rest of us and told us to run." The girl's eyes filled with tears. "She hasn't come out yet. I-I think he hurt her."

Shit.

"Where's the guy now?" Brooks asked.

"He went after Cassie." More tears came, spilling down the girl's cheeks. "She's the captain of the volleyball team. I think she was trying to get him to follow her so he wouldn't come after us."

Brave, but crazy, Brooks thought.

"More cops are on the way," he told the girl. "You and your friends get out of here, okay?"

She nodded, her bottom lip trembling. "What about Coach Ellis and Cassie?"

"I'll find them," he promised.

Taking his Glock from the holster on his hip, he sprinted toward the gym. The cold air fogged in front of his face, and his right knee immediately started to throb. It always did when the temperature dropped quickly like it had tonight. He'd torn some ligaments playing college football, and while it had healed well enough for him to become a cop, it hurt all the time.

Two teenage girls came out of the school just as he

was going in, a woman he assumed was Coach Ellis between them, her arms draped over their shoulders, blood on the front of her shirt.

"Which way?" he asked, moving past them without slowing.

Despite being injured, it was Coach Ellis who answered. "Down the hall, then turn left. There's a door that leads to the football field. Cassie led him that way a few minutes ago. Hurry. He's crazy."

Brooks nodded and ran, his boots pounding on the floor and echoing off the walls. He radioed dispatch on the way, giving them an update and requesting an ambulance. When he got to the door the coach had mentioned, he shoved it open, swinging his weapon and his flashlight in a wide sweep into the darkness behind the school.

He moved as cautiously as he could but picked up the pace within a few feet. His gut shouted at him that Cassie didn't have time for him to waste being careful. From the sirens in the distance, backup was on the way, but Cassie could be dead long before they arrived.

The gate that led onto the field and the bleachers was locked with a big looping chain. Brooks looked up in the darkness, wondering if the girl—and the man chasing her—had climbed over. The fence was at least twelve feet high with two strands of barbed wire atop it. He didn't know about the psycho with the knife, but there was no way the girl would have gone up and over the thing.

He looked left and right, past the small ticket booths and food stands, toward the other small outbuildings and occasional row of pine trees farther along the fence line. He cursed. The girl could have gone anywhere.

Brooks shone his flashlight one way, then the other,

looking for some indication of which way to go. He was about to give up and pick a direction at random when a cracking sound from his left made him spin in that direction. Any country boy who'd spent time in the woods would recognize that sound. Someone had stepped on a big stick and snapped it underfoot.

He headed in that direction, keeping the fence to his right as he moved toward the noise. When he rounded the corner of a small food stand, he swung his flashlight over the woods behind it. He would have missed the girl if it wasn't for the soft squeal of fear she let out as his light swept over her hiding place behind a large pine tree.

Thank God.

Slim with curly red hair pulled back in a ponytail, she was huddled down on her knees in the pine needles, blood running down her leg from a deep gash in her left thigh even though she had both hands clamped over the wound. She was shaking, but Brooks couldn't tell if it was from the cool night, fear, blood loss, or a combination of all three.

Brooks threw a quick glance over his shoulder to check for the crazy guy with the knife, then dropped down on one knee beside the girl, checking her for other injuries while calling in their location to dispatch and trying to keep an eye out for the psycho at the same time.

"Cassie, I'm Deputy Brooks," he said when he got off the radio. "I'm going to get you out of here, but I need to know where the guy who hurt you is."

She sniffed and shook her head. "I don't know. When I ran over here to hide, he was right behind me, but then he just disappeared."

Brooks looked around again, but there was no sign of the maniac with the knife. Maybe the sirens had scared the guy away. From the chatter streaming across his radio, it was obvious the other first responders weren't going to make that same assumption. He could hear his shift supervisor calling out orders to establish a perimeter, for three-officer teams to move in and start methodically clearing the school, and for EMS to maintain their position outside the barricades.

Cassie moaned and rested her forehead against the tree she was still kneeling behind. Despite the chill in the air, she was soaked with sweat, and her face was pale. Cursing silently, he shoved his weapon in its holster. The girl didn't have time to wait for EMS. She was bleeding out by the second.

"Hey," he said softly, resting his hand on her shoulder. "Stay with me, okay?" When she nodded, he continued, "Can you try to hold my flashlight so you can guide us out of here while I carry you?"

She took one trembling hand away from her bloody leg to take the flashlight. "I think so."

Picking her up in his arms, Brooks quickly started back the way he'd come. By the time he reached the main sidewalk heading to the gym, he was almost running. His heavy boots pounded loudly on the concrete as he raced to get the girl to the paramedics, which was probably why he didn't hear the second set of footsteps until it was too late.

He jerked his head toward the sound in time to see a huge man hurtling out of the darkness, the dim moonlight coming through the trees glinting off the edge of a blade.

Time slowed, and for reasons that didn't make a lot
of sense, Brooks found himself taking in every detail
of the big man. The long, wild hair. The maniacal grin.
The wide eyes that seemed to glow in the moonlight.
And most of all, the wickedly sharp machete whistling
through the air as he swung.

Brooks tried to backpedal, but it was too late. And
with Cassie in his arms, going for his weapon wasn't an
option, either. So he did the only thing he could think of.
He twisted his body around to protect the girl.

He'd hoped his tactical vest would stop the machete,
but when a ribbon of fire sliced through his lower back
and right side, he knew the man had hit him below the
edge of the Kevlar vest. The guy had hit him in the one
area the protective gear didn't cover.

Brooks tumbled forward as pain tore through him. He
tried to hold on to Cassie, but she flew out of his arms
anyway. She hit the ground with a scream…then kept
screaming as she realized what was happening.

Brooks rolled the second he hit the pavement, ignoring the ever-increasing pain and the wetness running
down his side as he pulled his weapon. Somehow, he
managed to get the gun pointed at the man. He couldn't
get a good look at the guy's face from this angle, but
from the growl of rage he let out, it didn't take a genius
to figure out he was psychotic…or on drugs.

"Sheriff's Deputy! Drop the knife or I'll shoot!"
Brooks yelled.

He'd never had to pull the trigger on someone in
his entire career in law enforcement, but when the man
came at him again, Brooks didn't hesitate. The .40
caliber weapon bucked twice, the bullets hitting the guy

right below the sternum. Dark spots of blood immediately stained the front of the man's T-shirt.

It should have been enough to put the man down, but he didn't even slow.

Brooks tried to fire again, but his attacker was impossibly fast. Snarling, the man swung the machete again, catching Brooks across the chest and right forearm. His tactical vest protected his chest, but his arm wasn't so lucky. The tip of the machete bit in deep, making his whole arm from elbow to wrist go numb with pain. His Glock fell from his hand, disappearing into the darkness of the concrete.

The big man stood over him, growling like a wild animal. His eyes seemed to glow blue in the moonlight, making him appear barely human. Brooks had no doubt the guy was drugged out of his mind. He had no idea if it was coke, heroin, or meth, but the guy was riding something hard.

Brooks was still trying to figure out how to take the psycho down when the man strode off and headed for Cassie, machete in hand. The girl screamed and tried to drag herself away, shoving at the ground with her good leg.

Gritting his teeth against the pain, Brooks rolled to his knees. He had to get to the man before he reached Cassie. As enraged as he was, the lunatic would kill her in seconds.

Brooks swayed as he got to his feet. He only had a minute or two before blood loss made him pass out—or worse. He had to finish this before it was too late.

Taking a deep breath, Brooks charged the man like he was still playing fullback at LSU. At the last second, he lowered his shoulder and slammed into the center of the man's back. The impact jarred every bone in Brooks's body, making the deep cut in his side burn like it was on fire as he drove the man to the pavement. But it got the madman away from Cassie, and that was what mattered.

The guy squirmed in his grasp like a greased eel with 'roid rage. As they rolled around on the ground, Brooks managed to get one hand on the base of the machete, successfully keeping the weapon away. But that left him open to the man's fists. The son of a bitch seemed to take great pleasure in punching him in his injured side.

Cursing, Brooks pulled out his Taser with his free hand and shoved it against the man's bare neck, then pulled the trigger. There was the familiar clicking sound as the nonlethal weapon pumped fifty thousand volts into the man. That would have been enough to incapacitate anyone else, but Mr. 'Roid Rage simply dropped the machete and wrapped both hands around Brooks's neck like he hadn't even felt the electricity course through his body.

Brooks tossed his Taser aside. One, because it wasn't doing crap. And two, because he needed to protect himself. But as he ripped the man's hands away from his neck and tried to restrain him, his vision began to swim. *Shit*. He was maybe thirty seconds from passing out. If that happened, he was dead. So was Cassie.

Balling his hand into a fist, he punched the man in the throat. Mr. 'Roid Rage grunted in pain and let go of him. Before the man realized his mistake, Brooks slammed the heel of his hand into the big guy's nose. The crunch was loud and gratifying, but Brooks knew even that wouldn't be enough to finish this.

Grabbing the man's long hair in both hands, he got

a firm grip to hold him still. With blood running down from his shattered nose and eyes blazing with that crazy blue, drugged-out glow, the guy looked like a frigging monster. His teeth even seemed to be longer than a normal person's, and for a minute, Brooks thought he might actually try to bite him. Brooks didn't give him the chance. With a growl of his own, Brooks slammed his head forward and smashed it into the guy's face.

Bones crunched, and bright lights flashed in his eyes. But even though it hurt like hell, Brooks headbutted him again and again until the man's face was a bloody mess. Even that didn't take the fight out of Mr. 'Roid Rage. Somewhere in between the third and fourth headbutt, he grabbed Brooks by the shoulders and flung him away like a rag doll.

Brooks hit the ground hard, air exploding from his lungs as ribs cracked. Groaning, he opened his eyes to see the man coming toward him with that damn machete in his hand.

Ignoring the metallic taste of blood in his mouth, Brooks struggled to push himself onto his hands and knees, stunned when he saw his Glock on the ground in front of him. With something between a laugh and a sob, he wrapped his hand around the gun and found the trigger with his finger.

But Mr. 'Roid Rage was already swinging the machete.

Brooks could barely feel himself squeeze the trigger, much less know where he was aiming. He got off three shots before the guy slammed down on top of him, those impossibly long teeth inches from his neck.

Sure the man was going to rip out his throat, Brooks threw his arm up to block the blow. But then everything stilled as the guy stopped moving. With the little strength he had left, Brooks shoved the man off him. There were three bullet holes in the man's chest.

Too tired to even care anymore, Brooks fell back on the concrete, pain radiating through every inch of him as he fought for breath. He was dimly aware of Cassie crying somewhere nearby, then bright lights were in his face as officers and paramedics moved in. He knew most of them, had worked with some of them for years. But it was the face of his shift supervisor, Sergeant Jack Walker, that he focused on.

Even though Jack had been doing this job for a long time, his face still betrayed how bad it was. That was okay. Brooks had already known.

He tried to smile as his old friend grabbed his hand and gave it a squeeze, but wasn't sure he managed. The older cop wasn't merely a coworker and friend. He was like a second father to him. Jack had been there when Brooks's real dad had been killed in a gang shooting more than a decade ago and had been in his life ever since.

"We got you, kid," Jack said, eyes misty with tears.

Or at least that's what Brooks thought he said. His ears didn't seem to be working very well. It didn't seem like his eyes were working right, either. Everything was dull and muted around him.

Brooks smiled anyway. Jack was the only person in the department who ever called him kid. Hell, there weren't many who'd even use his first name. They'd always been too intimidated by his size to be that casual with him. That had never been a problem for Jack, though.

Jack leaned in close, encouraging Brooks to keep fighting. Brooks had no intention of giving up, but it probably wouldn't matter. He had a gash in his side big enough to park a bus in. No amount of fight was going to change that.

While the paramedics worked to save his life, he turned his head to look at the man he'd killed. As he watched, the bizarre blue glow that had been in the guy's eyes throughout the fight slowly faded away. Stranger, the fangs—for lack of a better word—were also fading, retracting until they looked like normal teeth. Brooks frowned, shocked that no one else seemed to notice the monster in their midst. But everyone was focused on trying to save his life.

As everything around Brooks began to get fuzzy and the pain disappeared, he knew their efforts weren't going to matter. He hoped that none of them blamed themselves. He'd died doing his job and protecting people. A man couldn't ask for more than that.

Chapter 1

Dallas, Texas, Present Day

"WE'RE MOVING INTO POSITION NOW."

Brooks motioned the four members of his SWAT team toward the back of the warehouse on the east side. At his signal, fellow werewolves Diego Martinez, Connor Malone, Trey Duncan, and Remy Boudreaux quickly ran across the sunlit street and soundlessly disappeared into the shadows of the building on the other side.

"Roger that," Sergeant Ray Porter said over the radio in Brooks's ear. "Just watch yourselves back there. I haven't heard anything from my CIs, and it's starting to worry me."

"Understood," Brooks said as he followed his teammates.

Ray Porter was one of the most experienced officers in the Dallas PD Gang Unit and was damn good at his job. Which was why he was running the joint gang, narcotics, and SWAT task force the brass had put together to deal with the recent increase in gang-related heroin showing up in the city. But while Ray was a good cop, he was an even better person, and those confidential informants in there were kids he'd worked with for years. It was obvious he was worried as hell about them. That was something Brooks understood and respected.

Even though his nose and ears told him there wasn't

anyone behind the warehouse to see them, Brooks wasn't thrilled with the idea of hitting the place in broad daylight. There were too many things that could go wrong. But if the intel they'd gotten from narcotics was right, there could be as much as two hundred pounds of high-grade heroin in that building, along with some high-level gangbangers from several of the biggest gangs in the city, all coming together to figure out how to move the drugs. Multi-gang operations like this were unheard of in Dallas, but Ray's CIs had said a new boss with money and muscle had moved in and was actively consolidating most of the east side gangs. Nobody knew who this guy was or if he could pull something like this off, but if he did, it meant crime in the city was about to get a lot worse than it already was.

So while the operation was risky, it would be worth it if they could keep the heroin off the streets. Taking down the gangs and their new boss would just be gravy on the biscuits.

Normally, their squad leader, Mike Taylor, would have taken lead for an operation like this, but he was helping the newest member of their SWAT team with in-processing. A werewolf SWAT cop from Chattanooga, Rachel Bennett, had shown up on their doorstep a week ago saying she'd heard about people hunting werewolves in Dallas and that she wanted to help. To say they'd all been thrown for a loop was an understatement. Usually, their commander, Gage Dixon, went out and brought new werewolves into the Pack after carefully vetting them to make sure they'd be a good fit. This was the first time a werewolf had joined the Pack on their own. It was kind of weird.

Brooks didn't mind running the operation in Mike's absence, but he'd be lying if he said he wasn't concerned about this raid being risky, especially considering they had no idea how many gangbangers were in there or how well armed they were. That was the kind of info he'd hoped Ray's CIs could give them, since both of them were active members in the gangs involved, but the older cop hadn't heard from either kid in two days. Which was why Ray was worried. If someone figured out those kids were working with the cops, they were dead.

"Civilians along the front of the warehouse," Ray said in Brooks's ear. "Entry on hold. All personnel, maintain your positions until my order."

Brooks bit back a growl as he joined the rest of his team behind a Dumpster surrounded by piles of wood pallets and cardboard boxes. Another sniff told him the back side of the warehouse was still clear, but they were pressing their luck hanging around like this.

The original plan had been for Ray's gang unit, along with officers from narcotics and K9, to converge on the front of the warehouse while Brooks and his SWAT team went in through the back. The idea was to execute the raid before anyone saw them coming. The longer they waited, the greater the chance of something screwing that up.

Beside Brooks, Connor's eyes flashed gold, a sure sign his inner wolf was trying to get free. On the other side of him, Diego, Trey, and Remy started to get a little fired up, too. Even though Brooks had complete control of his animal side, at times like this, he had to admit he felt the urge to let the wolf out.

He blamed it on the hunters. It had been more than

three weeks since the run-in with those assholes when they'd almost lost one of their pack, Zane Kendrick. Since then, the Pack had been on full alert waiting for the next attack, and they were all feeling the strain.

Brooks resisted the urge to extend his claws and fangs and focused on getting his team back under control.

"Take it down a notch, guys," he growled at his pack mates. "Between hunters trying to kill us, somebody in the DPD trying to sell us out, and a city full of werewolves depending on us for protection, we're already dealing with enough shit. The last thing we need is some gangbanger's video clip of one of us in midshift going viral on the internet."

His teammates immediately got it together at the mention of that. Even Connor, the least experienced werewolf among the five of them, reined himself in. Brooks hated reminding them about all the negative crap going on lately, but one little mistake on any of their parts, and a lot of people were going to pay the price. They'd handled the hunters this last time, but now that there was someone inside the Dallas PD working with the assholes, this fight was only going to get worse before it got better.

"We're cool," Remy murmured in his N'Awlins accent.

"Good," Brooks said. "Then let's move."

They were out from behind the Dumpster and moving toward their positions without another word, M4 carbines locked and loaded. Diego, Trey, and Remy peeled off and headed for the loading ramp entry at the far end of the warehouse while Brooks and Connor moved toward the big double doors on the opposite end of the building. As he kept an eye out for anyone coming around the back of the warehouse, Brooks heard Ray issuing updates over the radio, letting everyone know there were still civilians loitering around the front.

"I get the feeling you and Ray have worked together before," Connor remarked as they slipped behind a row of A/C units and crouched down.

Brooks nodded. "I worked in the gang unit with Ray when I first started at the DPD before joining SWAT."

Connor did a double take, his hazel eyes filled with surprise. "No shit. I assumed Gage brought you straight onto the team since you had prior police experience."

Brooks shook his head, remembering the day Gage Dixon, the Dallas SWAT commander, had shown up at the sheriff's department in Gulfport and told him he was a werewolf. A lot of things had changed for him—fast. But getting onto the Dallas SWAT team hadn't been one of them.

"Nah. HR was still making it hard for him to bring new people straight in, so I started in the gang unit while Gage worked the system to get me into SWAT."

Connor frowned. "That must have been rough. Being away from the Pack when you were still a new werewolf, I mean."

"I still hung with the Pack on my off time, which helped me wrap my head around the whole werewolf thing."

Good thing, too. If Gage hadn't found him when he had, Brooks probably would have thought he was having a mental breakdown. Or turning into a monster.

"We're in position," Trey whispered over their internal SWAT frequency on the radio.

Brooks glanced over his shoulder to see Diego, Trey, and Remy crouched below the concrete loading dock.

They were doing a damn good job of making themselves as small as possible. Which was a hell of a trick for three guys who weighed over 250 pounds each.

He radioed Ray to tell him they were ready, reminding him that their asses were hanging in the breeze. Ray instructed him to sit tight for another minute, saying there were two civilians still in the way. Brooks cursed silently. While he didn't like the idea of being back here with minimal cover, clearing the area of people could alert the gangbangers inside to their presence. Then things would get ugly real fast.

Brooks frowned as he suddenly picked up a scent he couldn't place. He turned to ask Connor if he smelled it too, and was shocked to see a sleek black cat rubbing up against his teammate, looking happy as hell to find him there.

"What the hell is that?" he asked.

Connor looked at him like he was an idiot. "It's a cat."

Brooks wasn't sure he agreed with that. Unlike dogs, cats hated werewolves. Besides, that slinky thing weaving back and forth through Connor's legs had the weirdest scent he'd ever picked up from a cat. Like she'd spent an entire weekend trapped inside a Bath and Body Works at the mall.

"Okay, better question then. What the hell is she doing here? We're about to kick in the door in a minute. Now isn't the best time to make a new friend."

Connor ran his hand over the cat's fur. The animal immediately leaned into his touch and purred. "Hey, it's not like I'm doing anything to attract her attention."

In his ear, Ray announced the coast was clear and that he was getting his team ready to move. Brooks gave

Connor a pointed look. "Well, get her to go away before the situation gets tense."

He could just imagine the cat trying to follow Connor inside the warehouse and into the middle of a firefight.

Connor gently nudged the cat farther down the alley with his hand, but the graceful feline turned back around and rubbed up against the leg of his cargo pants. He gave Brooks a sheepish look. "I don't think she wants to leave."

Brooks lifted a brow. "You're kidding me, right? You're a two-hundred-and-fifty-pound werewolf with claws, fangs, and a bite that's even worse than your bark, and you're telling me you can't figure out how to get the cat to leave. Seriously?"

Connor looked at him blankly for a moment before realization dawned on his face. Turning to the cat, he growled low and menacing, his eyes flashing gold as he bared his fangs.

Brooks expected the animal to jump ten feet in the air, then go running like she'd seen a ghost. Or a werewolf. But instead, she regarded Connor with an expression that clearly indicated she hadn't been impressed. Then she turned and casually walked away, her head and tail held high. A few moments later, she disappeared around the corner of the building.

Connor glanced at Brooks. "I think that cat just rolled her eyes at me. I can't figure out if I should be offended or not."

Brooks chuckled. "I'm not sure offended is the word I'd use. Maybe embarrassed might be better. Or ashamed. Mortified even. But if saying you're offended that a cat punked you works for you, have at it."

Connor muttered something under his breath about not being a cat person, but Brooks ignored it. It was time to focus on the job they were here to do. Over the radio, Ray announced they were entering the building in two minutes.

The words were barely out of his mouth when shouts came from inside the warehouse, immediately followed by shooting. A lot of it, too. Rapid-fire pistol mixed with automatic weapons fire.

Shit.

"Ray, we're going in," Brooks said into his mic.

"Hold until I give the word!" Ray shouted. "There are only five of you. I don't want you going in there on your own."

Brooks cursed. His gut was telling him to kick in the damn door, regardless of what Ray said, but he forced himself to obey the order, knowing he'd give the same command in the other cop's shoes. That didn't keep him from growling in frustration as the shooting continued. People were dying in there.

In his ear, Ray shouted orders on the radio, moving his people up to the front door. José Rodriguez from narcotics yelled back, saying they were in position.

"Okay, Brooks," Ray said. "Go!"

About damn time.

"SWAT going in," Brooks announced.

Lifting his leg, he kicked in the back door, slamming it against the wall. Down near the loading dock, Trey did the same.

Dozens of scents hit Brooks as he and Connor worked their way down the hallway that led to the main part of the warehouse. Blood and sweat mixed with the acrid stench of gunpowder amid the maze of pallets and boxes, but none of it masked the pervasive smell of an opioid drug. Fentanyl probably.

Brooks was wondering why the scent of drugs was so strong, since the stuff was usually sealed in plastic bags, when a dark-haired guy in a T-shirt and jeans darted out in front of them. The gangbanger immediately lifted the submachine gun he held and pointed it in their direction.

"Dallas PD! Drop the weapon!" Brooks ordered, aiming his M4 at the guy even as Connor did the same.

For a moment, Brooks thought the gangbanger might comply, but a split second later, bullets sprayed around them. Brooks dropped to the floor and rolled right while Connor rolled left. They came up on their knees together, both of them returning fire.

A part of Brooks winced as the gangbanger—who was barely out of his teens—fell to the floor, his weapon spinning across the concrete. But Brooks quickly forced the thought aside as he and Connor moved quickly toward the front of the building where the other members of the task force were. Brooks sensed Trey and the other two members of his pack off to the left, heading in the same direction.

Gunshots and automatic weapons fire continued to echo in the building, but it had slowed drastically. In its place, he heard cops shouting at people to drop their weapons and get on the floor. It sounded like some of the gangbangers complied, but most didn't. He and Connor crossed paths with three more bad guys on the way. Two put their guns down and their hands up, but the third guy refused, instead putting three rounds from his submachine gun into the wall inches from Connor's head while he was cuffing the others.

A bullet to the head would kill a werewolf just as dead as a normal person, and Brooks quickly took the guy out before he could get another shot off.

As they got closer to the middle of the warehouse, the scent of drugs was so strong, it made Brooks's nose sting. That was when it hit him.

"Ray, call back the K9 teams!" he shouted into his mic. "This whole place is filled with loose fentanyl."

But even as he said the words, Brooks heard the sound of dogs running and out of control barking. *Shit*. If the K9s stepped in any of those drugs, they were going to be in trouble. Fentanyl—synthetic heroin—could soak through skin on contact. That included the pads on a dog's feet…or nose.

Brooks and Connor sprinted toward the source of the odor. They got there just as Ray, several cops from the gang unit, and a K9 team ran up.

Brooks skidded to a stop. While he was still concerned about the drugs and where the hell they were, he couldn't ignore the five dead men slumped in their seats along one side of a rectangular table. From the empty chairs on the other side and bullet casings littering the table, it seemed like the gangbangers had been ambushed by whoever had been sitting across from them.

He cursed as Ray moved over to take a closer look at the men. He recognized every one of them from the photos Ray had pinned to the briefing board back at headquarters. Two of them were Ray's confidential informants. The other three were leaders in the east side gangs who'd been invited to the warehouse to discuss working together with the new boss to distribute drugs. Instead, it looked like he'd wiped out the competition.

Ray dropped to his knee beside his dead CIs, tears in his eyes. The two kids looked like they were eighteen or nineteen, twenty tops. It didn't take a genius to know where Ray's mind was headed. Brooks moved closer to the table, opening his mouth to tell his friend that what happened to those kids wasn't his fault, but Trey's voice cut him off.

"Brooks," his pack mate whispered from halfway across the room, his voice so low, only another werewolf could hear it. "You and everyone else need to back out of that area. Carefully."

Brooks glanced at his teammate. Trey was standing with the rest of the guys, their faces intent and filled with concern. Brooks wasn't sure what Trey was trying to tell him until his pack mate looked pointedly down at the floor in front of Brooks, then back at him.

Brooks looked down, cursing silently when he realized he was standing in the middle of a pile of white powder that was scattered all over the floor near the table. He'd been so intent on the dead bodies, he hadn't even seen the damn stuff. Werewolves could handle getting a few grams of the junk in their bloodstreams without going down, but for a human, a trace amount of powder on their skin could put them into immediate overdose—or worse.

"Ray, there's loose fentanyl all over the place, including the floor where we're standing," Brooks said. "We need to get a hazmat team in here to clean up before we do anything else."

The older man looked at him in shock, then cursed.

"Okay, everybody. Walk out of here the same way we came in. Nobody touches anything."

Nervous looks on their faces, they all did as Ray instructed, moving slowly and cautiously. Brooks thought they might get out of there unscathed, but then Kyber, the Belgian Malinois K9 who'd come in with Ray, stumbled and fell. A moment later, his handler, Officer MacIlwaine, collapsed too.

"Connor, grab Kyber," Brooks ordered. "Trey, we need all the Narcan you have out front. Now!"

Tossing his M4 over his shoulder by the strap, Brooks scooped up an unconscious MacIlwaine and sprinted for the front of the warehouse. Connor was right beside him, Kyber in his arms. Fentanyl could kill a dog even faster than a human. Behind him, Ray was calling for EMS, telling them to get ready for two overdose patients on the way out.

Trey hit both MacIlwaine and Kyber with two nasal doses of the opiate antidote Narcan before the Dallas Fire & Rescue paramedics could get out of their vehicles. EMS hit the officer and his K9 partner with another dose before loading them in the ambulance and hauling ass for the nearest emergency room. Brooks watched them go. Even with multiple doses of antidote, both of the cops in that vehicle weren't out of the woods yet.

Even though Brooks was fine, he went through the motions of letting the paramedics check him for fentanyl contamination anyway. Beside him, Ray did the same. All they could do was sit on the back of an ambulance and watch as members of the task force escorted out the gang members who'd been arrested and others helped fellow cops who'd been injured. EMS went in to treat the ones who couldn't walk out on their own. Rodriguez had reported over the radio that there'd been no law enforcement fatalities, but nobody seemed to have an idea how many gangbangers had been killed or injured. However many it was, it was too many, considering the original plan had been to arrest all of them without a shot being fired.

"They set up this meeting to be an execution from the start," Ray said softly from beside him, his gray eyes filled with anguish. The paramedics had finally finished checking them out, and they were alone. "How did we not see this coming? How did my CIs get it so wrong? How the hell did they end up dead?"

The lines around Ray's eyes seemed deeper and more pronounced than they'd been before the raid, making him look older than his sixty-some years. Brooks knew why he was so devastated. Ray's relationships with his CIs were different from most cops. His informants were kids he'd personally befriended, teens he'd run into on the street and had gotten out of trouble. Hell, almost all of them had become CIs as a way to repay Ray for everything he'd done for them.

"I don't know." Brooks sighed. "All we can hope is that this new guy who's running the gangs is one of the people we arrested—or shot."

"I wouldn't hold my breath," Remy drawled as he and Diego came over to join Brooks and Ray. "We tracked a group of gangbangers out through a service tunnel under the warehouse. The trail dead-ended in a parking lot about two blocks from here, where they probably had vehicles waiting. There were six of them, and one was probably the new gang boss who set the meeting up in the warehouse because he knew there was an escape route if he needed it."

Ray eyed Remy like he was insane. "You…tracked them?"

"Officer Boudreaux grew up in the swamps of Louisiana," Brooks interjected before Remy could answer, because he was afraid of what might come out of his mouth. Remy was unpredictable like that. "He's very good at tracking people."

Remy snorted. "He's trying to say I'm a coonass. If it moves, I can track it."

"Regardless," Brooks added, throwing Remy a pointed look. "It seems that the guy we're really after got away."

Ray muttered a curse. "So my CIs died for nothing. This whole raid was for nothing!"

Brooks rested his hand on his friend's shoulder. "Maybe not. We arrested a lot of gangbangers today. One of them has to know who the new boss is. All we have to do is get them to talk. Then we go after this guy and make sure he pays for what he's done."

Ray's mouth tightened. "Damn right, he'll pay."

He probably would have said more, but before he could, a loud alarm tone blared from the radio, cutting across the channel they'd been running the operation on. A moment later, dispatch called for Brooks and his SWAT team to get to Terrace Grove High School. There was an active shooter and hostage situation in progress, suspected gang involvement.

Damn, this crap never ended.

<hr />

Selena Rosa sat on the edge of her desk, listening to sixteen-year-old Ruben Moreno carefully work his way through the second act of *A Christmas Carol*, reading the story of Scrooge and Marley aloud to the rest of her Terrace Grove classroom. The dark-haired boy read slowly, never lifting his head to look at her or the other students around him. He was way too self-conscious to ever do that. Which was probably a good thing. Because if Ruben looked up and saw someone smirk at the way he had to stop and sound certain words out before saying them, he would have stopped reading completely.

She'd tried to tell him that he shouldn't let what other people think bother him. His reading had improved drastically over the course of the past school year, and she was extremely proud of him. But Ruben was a teenager, and by definition, teens worried extensively about what other people thought of them—especially when they were people he desperately wanted to impress.

Like Marguerite Mendes, the curly-haired girl in the back of the class he had a crush on. Or his friend, Pablo Garza, a.k.a. Wheels as he preferred to be called these days. Selena was pretty sure the new nickname had something to do with cars, either stealing them or acting as a getaway driver in one. It was hard to tell which, since the Terrace Grove Locos, the gang Pablo had joined recently, were involved in both chop shop operations and hitting convenience stores. Along with drugs, prostitution, theft, carjacking, and any of a dozen other major criminal endeavors. The Locos were bad people, and Pablo was doing everything he could to get into their good graces.

As if on cue, Pablo snorted, making sure everyone heard him as he cracked on Ruben about reading the old Christmas story like a first grader. Ruben stumbled to a halt like Pablo had almost certainly known he would. Pablo, who'd been Ruben's best friend since the two of them were seven years old, wasn't in Selena's English class today to learn. Or to listen to his friend read Charles Dickens. He was there to harass his fellow students and try to convince some of them—especially Ruben—to leave with him. Pablo was there on a recruiting mission for the Locos.

"Knock it off, Pablo," she said sharply, stabbing the boy with a sharp glare. "You'll get your chance to impress us with your reading talents. If you decide to actually hang around long enough."

Pablo glowered at her, clearly not liking that she'd challenged him in front of the other students. But Selena had been dealing with gangbangers her whole life. She'd grown up in a part of the city tense with gang activity. She'd watched them take her father and older brother away and chase off her mother. After that, she'd learned one very powerful lesson. Regardless of whether you walked through the neighborhood or taught in the classroom, you could never let them think they had you scared. That was something her brother had taught her, and she'd never forgotten it.

"Keep reading, Ruben. You're doing well," she murmured, her eyes still on Pablo.

The fact that Pablo didn't look away worried her. Pablo had always been one of those kids who refused to let anyone get close to them. She'd tried to reach out to him several times, but he'd refused her help. Back in November, he'd gotten into a fight with some other kid because he didn't like the color of the boy's shirt, claiming they were gang colors. The fight had gotten nasty, and Pablo had been suspended for two weeks. He hadn't come back afterward. Selena had tried to keep in contact with him, had even checked in with his mother, but it had been useless.

Selena had been hopeful when he'd walked into her classroom less than an hour ago, but that had been short-lived. Pablo had changed drastically in the time he'd been away. There was an edge to him now that hadn't been there before, a look in his eyes that told her it was too late to reach him.

She'd been fighting to keep her students out of the gangs since she'd become a teacher. Terrace Grove was right on the border of two rival gang territories, the Locos on the east side and the Hillside Riders on the west. The kids at the school were under constant pressure to go one way or the other, with both gangs actively recruiting right out in the open. Boys were expected to become soldiers or dealers while girls were used as mules...or worse. And trying to stay on the sidelines was even harder than choosing sides.

Selena refused to shy away from the problem. She determinedly put herself into the middle of her kids' lives, fighting for anyone who'd reach out and take her hand. If a kid didn't give up, she wouldn't give up, making both gangs go through her to get to any of her students. But no matter how hard she fought, there was only so much she could do. While most days it felt like a losing battle, it was worth it if there was a small chance she could keep even a single kid out of the gangs.

Ruben was one of those kids. He was big for his age, already over six feet tall and thick with muscles in the shoulders and arms. The school wanted him for the football team, but the Locos wanted him for their gang... and they wanted him badly. They came at him a dozen different ways, threatening him, offering him girls, drugs, cars, even money. Ruben didn't want any of that stuff. Well, okay. Yeah, he wanted girls. What hormonal teenage boy didn't? But it wasn't a stretch to say he wasn't interested in the kind of girls the Locos were throwing his way.

The one thing Ruben really liked, the one thing that was beyond the comprehension of most gang members, was books. And that love of books was what kept him out of the gangs. At least it would as long as he was able to handle the ridicule thrown his way by people like Pablo, who thought real men didn't read books—at least not books that didn't involve naked women.

Ruben picked up the Charles Dickens story again, reading it out loud in his slow, deep voice. He had trouble with some of the words, but he had a way of reading that made people want to listen. Heck, some of the girls in the room got dreamy-eyed when he really got into a story.

He was getting back into the rhythm of the words, moving into the third act as the silent spirit showed Scrooge the future that awaited him, when Pablo stood up and kicked over his desk.

Selena stood, too. "Pablo, you need to leave. Now."

"Fuck you," he said, walking over to give Ruben's desk a shove that almost tipped it over. Then he tore into his one-time friend, letting out a long string of curse words in Spanish, calling his old friend a coward, a loser, and a wimp. Those were Selena's translations, of course. The actual words were much worse.

Pablo spun around to take in the rest of the class, his face red with anger. "And the rest of you are no better. You're a bunch of weaklings, sitting here reading whatever this bitch teacher puts in front of you. Stupid stories by people who've been dead a thousand years. You're all cowards, doing as you're told so the teachers will pet you on your head and call you a good doggy."

"That's enough!" Selena snapped.

It was times like this she wished the school board had funded those panic buttons the principal had wanted to put into each room. She could grab her cell phone and call the front office or one of the other teachers, but that would take too long. She needed Pablo out of there now.

She crossed the room toward Pablo, intending to physically push him out of the classroom if she had to. But then she caught the rage in his eyes, saw the way the veins in his temples were actually pulsing as he ignored her and went back to berating Ruben for wanting to read a stupid book when he could have been out with the Locos making more money than he knew what to do with. This was going to get uglier than it already was.

Ruben must have finally had enough, because he rose to his feet and got in Pablo's face. "I'm not going anywhere with you. You're a chickenshit who gave up and fell in with the Locos, and now you want me to fuck up my life, too. Well, screw you!"

The rest of the class was out of their seats now. Most of the students had backed into the walls, but some had added their voices to the cacophony of angry shouts. So much for having to worry about getting a call out on her cell phone. With all this shouting, the teachers on either side of the classroom would be calling for help soon enough. If they hadn't already.

She was moving in to separate everyone when she caught sight of a movement that nearly stopped her heart.

Pablo had dropped his right hand behind his back, resting it on a bulge under his T-shirt, right there at the waistband of his jeans.

Crap.

He was carrying a gun.

"Pablo, please don't do this," she said, not mentioning the fact that she knew he had a gun but still slipping between him and Ruben anyway. "There's no way this ends well unless you do the right thing and get the hell out of here."

She'd said the words as calmly as she could, but he spun on her with a vicious expression. A split second later, he brought his hand out from behind his back, pointing a big automatic pistol first at her, then fanning out toward everyone else in the class. There were gasps and screams as every one of her students freaked.

Pablo turned and pointed the gun straight at Selena's head for a long moment before moving to the side a little so he could aim it at Ruben. The weapon was so big, it barely fit in his hand. She couldn't begin to guess how many bullets the thing held.

"I'll get the hell out of here the second my homeboy walks out with me," Pablo sneered.

Ruben looked her way, his expression questioning, like he was wondering if he should simply defuse the situation and go with Pablo. That definitely wasn't a good idea. Now that Pablo had flashed a gun, the cops would get involved. They'd go after Pablo, and if Ruben was with the newest member of the Locos when the cops found him, there was no telling what might happen. Selena wouldn't let Ruben put himself in the middle of that kind of trouble.

"Pablo," she said, moving to put herself firmly between him and Ruben again. "I'm not going to let Ruben go anywhere with you. I can't."

Pablo pointed the weapon at her again, then stepped forward until the barrel was pressed up against her forehead. Selena thought for a moment that her heart actually did stop. He smiled slowly at her, but there was absolutely no humor in that expression. It fact, there wasn't much of anything as far as normal human emotions. It was like she was staring into the eyes of a dead man. Selena had faced a lot of bad situations in her life, but this was the first time she ever remembered thinking she was about to die.

She'd spent her whole life trying to fight the gangs. Now the gangs were going to kill her for that. And after Pablo killed her, he was probably going to get Ruben killed and maybe other students as well. While she was terrified at the thought, she was also mad as hell.

"You know, I never liked you," Pablo said, pressing the big weapon harder against her forehead. "You always act like you're the shit, bossing us around, telling us to study hard, do our homework, stay away from the gangs. Like anything you have to say matters. But you're not my teacher anymore. You're not anything to me. So I'm going to take Ruben with me when I leave. Right after I shoot you in the head."

Her students screamed, some begging Pablo not to shoot her, others pleading with him to leave, but everything around Selena faded into the background. All she could hear was the beating of her heart...and the metallic click as Pablo pulled back the hammer on the weapon.

Chapter 2

TERRACE GROVE HIGH SCHOOL WAS IN CHAOS BY THE TIME Brooks and his teammates drove up. Local cops and teachers were doing their best to get the students out of the building, but the kids seemed more interested in snapping pictures on their cell phones than being somewhere safe. Add in media with cameras and concerned parents running around desperate to find their kids, and it seemed like the whole situation was seconds away from total meltdown.

Spotting the SWAT operations truck parked near the front of the school, Brooks headed that way, jumping the curb with his SUV and parking on the lawn by the flagpole. Trey and Diego pulled up right behind him.

"Think we should help out with crowd control?" Connor asked as he and Brooks jumped out.

Brooks hesitated. School lockdown situations were tough to get a read on, but when they went bad, they went really bad. On the way over, dispatch had reported shots fired, which meant there was a good chance his team would have to go in soon. If so, he didn't want to waste time getting them together. But if a kid got shot because the cops weren't able to clear the school property, that was bad, too.

"Do what you can to help with the students," he told his teammates. "But stick close, and be ready to go in."

His guys nodded and took off while he turned and ran for the operations truck to get a situation report, although *truck* was kind of a misnomer. It was an RV that had been converted into a mobile command post, so instead of couches and beds, there were whiteboards, computers, and television monitors. Gage was inside, along with Zane, one of the team's hostage negotiators as well as Brooks's best friend. There were a man and a woman there, too. Probably some kind of school officials. Brooks gave them a nod as he closed the door behind him. They were both so focused on the television monitors, they barely glanced at him.

Zane sat in front of one of the monitors, calmly talking to someone on a cell phone in his soft British accent. No doubt whoever was holding the kids hostage. That assumption was confirmed a moment later when Zane urged the person on the other end to put down the weapon and come out of the school on his own. Zane was one of the best hostage negotiators in the entire police department. If anyone could talk someone into giving himself up, it would be him.

Gage took his eyes off the drawing of the floor plan of the school on the whiteboard to glance at Brooks. Tall with dark hair and brown eyes, he wasn't only the commander of the SWAT team, but the alpha of their pack of alphas as well. "You're here. Good." He gestured toward the concerned-looking man and woman sitting near the opposite wall. "This is Eva Gilbert, the principal of the school, and Hugh Kennedy, the vice principal. Senior Corporal Jayden Brooks."

Brooks gave them another nod. This time, they returned it.

"What's the situation?" Brooks asked, turning back to Gage.

His commander jerked his thumb at the television monitor closest to him. "Pablo Garza, the kid with the gun, recently joined a local gang and showed up today to recruit some of his classmates. Fortunately, a teacher saw him flash a weapon when he got on campus and called 911 before he even stepped foot in the classroom. We were able to establish communications with him just in time to keep him from shooting his teacher, Selena Rosa, in the head. Since then, he's dropped all the window shades and locked the only door into the room. He's threatening to kill everyone, starting with Ms. Rosa. Pablo seems to have a real issue with her. Probably because she won't back down from his threats."

Thanks to the team's resident tech guru, Eric Becker, they'd gotten multiple camera views inside the classroom from three direct angles. Pablo was standing in the middle of the room by himself, armed with what looked like a Desert Eagle .50 caliber automatic that he swung back and forth from one side of the group of students huddled against the wall to the other, making them cower in fear.

Zane once again calmly tried to convince Pablo to give himself up. That must have been the breaking point for the kid, because he took the cell phone away from his ear and slammed it against the wall, shattering it.

"Dammit!" Zane tossed his own phone onto the table, then reached out and flipped the switch on a box near the TV, filling the RV with screams, shouts, and sobbing from the classroom. "Pablo already shot out the school intercom, so now all we have is the audio feed Becker rigged up. It's only one way, though, so the kid can't hear me. Not that it matters. Pablo isn't interested in negotiating. He doesn't want anything beyond proving he's tough. The way he sees it, the best way to do that is to stay in there and kill a few people, even if it means he dies in the process."

The screams and sobs only seemed to push Pablo closer to the edge. He cursed in Spanish, screaming that he was going to kill everyone in the room, starting with the teacher and ending with a kid named Ruben.

Someone stepped away from the group near the wall, one hand out in front of her in a placating gesture. She was so petite, Brooks thought she was a student at first, but when she deliberately put herself between Pablo and the other kids, he looked more closely and realized she was the teacher.

As a werewolf, Brooks had excellent vision, but he stepped nearer to the monitor to get a better look at Selena Rosa anyway. Now really wasn't the time for this, especially considering the danger she was in, but he'd be lying if he said he didn't notice how beautiful she was. Even though she was slender, she had some serious curves beneath the black slacks and red sweater she wore, and while her dark hair was pulled back in a bun, something told him it'd probably reach halfway down her back when it was loose.

But, he thought again, now wasn't the time. That kid Pablo was half a minute away from pulling the trigger and killing her. The reality of that suddenly had Brooks's inner wolf howling to get out, and he balled his hands into fists at his side to keep his claws from coming out.

"Brooks, move your team into position," Gage said,

yanking Brooks's attention away from the monitor and Selena, who was still trying to talk sense into Pablo. "Three of you go through the windows, while the other two take the door."

"Roger that," Brooks said.

The principal jumped to her feet, her dark eyes filled with fear. "There has to be another way. Going in there could get those students killed!"

Gage pinned her with a hard look. "And not going in there could get them killed, too. Our goal is to make sure no one ends up that way today." He looked at Brooks. "Go."

Brooks was halfway to the door when Zane got to his feet.

"I'll go with you," he said. "Those kids along the wall are going to go barmy when the glass starts breaking, and you could use an extra body."

Brooks threw a quick glance Gage's way, hoping for Zane's sake their boss would say yes. But Gage shook his head. "I want you in here on the monitors feeding Brooks and his team details as they go in. They'll need that more than another body going through the door."

Zane opened his mouth like he wanted to argue but closed it again. Jaw tight, he nodded and turned back to the TV monitor, but not before Brooks saw the anguish in his dark eyes. The bullet laced with synthetic wolfsbane he'd taken to the arm courtesy of the hunters during the attack a few weeks ago had left him all but disabled, and knowing he couldn't help the team because of it was ripping Zane's guts out.

If the regret on Gage's face was any indication, their alpha was having just as hard a time with Zane's injury. Unfortunately, it wasn't likely to get better anytime soon.

But while he felt their pain, Brooks forced himself to compartmentalize it. A teacher and a classroom full of kids were depending on him to do his job. If he didn't, somebody innocent was going to die, and there was no way in hell he was going to let that happen.

"Go!"

Brooks shouted the order before the echo of the gunshot from inside the classroom faded. He prayed Trey and the other guys on the roof had gotten their ropes in position, or this hostage rescue operation was about to go really bad, really fast. The plan had been to wait for Zane to let them know when Pablo was facing away from the door, because it would give them the element of surprise, but now that was off the table. No matter how much he tried to focus, Brooks couldn't keep the horrible image of the beautiful dark-haired teacher lying dead on the floor a few feet away out of his mind. A growl slipped from his throat as his fangs extended. Anger he hadn't experienced since his first change boiled over inside him, threatening to consume him, and he kicked in the door of the classroom so hard, it split down the middle.

He charged into the room, Connor at his heels. To his right, the students were still huddled against the back wall, wide-eyed looks on their faces. Selena stood protectively in front of them, her gaze locked on Pablo as he pointed his gun at her. While she was putting up a good front, Brooks knew she had to be terrified.

The windows on the far side of the room suddenly exploded as Diego, Trey, and Remy rappelled in, hitting the floor in a spray of shattered glass. Trey and Remy rushed toward the students, seeking to get as many of them down on the floor as possible, while Diego trained his weapon on Pablo, shouting for him to drop the gun.

But Pablo's finger was already squeezing the trigger.

Brooks snarled and launched himself at the teacher. Even as he left his feet, he knew he was too late. The boom as the huge .50 caliber gun went off was over-whelming, drowning out every other sound in the room.

He slammed into Selena, sending her flying through the air. A bullet buzzed past his head as he wrapped his arms around her and held her close, praying he'd be able to roll when they hit the floor, or he'd break every bone in her small, perfect body.

But then a bullet punched him in the lower back, and the pain from it made coordinated movement nearly impossible. The best he could do was twist a little, coming down on his left shoulder and arm instead of directly on top of her, then sliding across the floor and through a row of desks.

As they came to a stop, he felt something wet spread across his stomach. Fear ripped through him as he real-ized the bullet had gone right through his tactical vest and him, too.

There was a loud popping sound behind him as an M4 went off. It was immediately followed by a shout of pain. Screams filled the room, but they were quickly followed by sobs of relief, and Brooks knew Diego had gotten Pablo. The kid was still alive, but Brooks couldn't find it in him to care at the moment. All he could do was worry that the bullet that had gone through him had hit Selena.

He shoved the desk beside him out of the way, sending it sailing across the room. Then he carefully rolled her over as gently as he could. His heart stopped when he saw the blood on her sweater, only to start beating again when he realized it was his, not hers.

He opened his mouth to ask if she was okay, but then he stopped himself. Selena might not have gotten hit with that bullet, but something was obviously wrong. Her breathing was coming fast and shallow, her skin was pale, and her eyes were glazed and unfocused. His gut told him it was more than simply shock. Had she broken or torn something when he'd tackled her to the floor?

Brooks slipped his arms under her, picking her up as gently as he could as he got to his feet. As he headed for the door, he caught sight of Trey treating a bullet wound in Pablo's right shoulder. They'd bring the kid out soon, and he wanted to have Selena in an ambulance and long gone by then.

He moved as fast as he could down the locker-lined hallways, making sure not to jostle her too much. When she let out a soft moan, he glanced down and almost stumbled into a wall locker as he found himself captivated by her beautiful, dark eyes. He stopped, leaning in a little to tell her she was going to be okay and that she was safe, but the moment he got close, her scent hit him full force, and he forgot whatever he'd been about to say.

He didn't even realize he'd stopped walking until a paramedic clapped him on the shoulder. "We got her from here."

Brooks looked up in surprise to see that the paramedic and her partner had rolled a gurney up to him. He'd worked with Fletcher and Barnes before, so he knew they were good at their jobs. He couldn't help but stare at them in confusion, though. How long had he been standing there lost in Selena's eyes?

At the paramedics' urging, Brooks gently placed Selena on the gurney, but when he tried to pull back, her right arm had somehow found its way around his neck and refused to let go. Their eyes locked again, and for a moment, time seemed to stop.

Until the female paramedic gently took Selena's arm from around his neck and carefully placed it on the gurney beside her.

By the time Brooks recovered, Fletcher and Barnes had already shoved the gurney down the hallway and out the door, asking Selena where she'd been shot as they went.

He hurried after them so he could tell them Selena hadn't been hit but got outside in time to see the doors of the ambulance slam shut and the female paramedic hauling ass around to the driver's side door. The ambulance pulled away just as he reached it, lights and sirens coming on and the tires squawking on the asphalt of the parking lot.

For one crazy moment, he had an incredibly powerful urge to shift into his wolf form and chase after the vehicle so he could be with the woman whose scent still filled his nose.

What the hell was up with him? He couldn't shift in broad daylight in front of a couple hundred people, not to mention all the reporters and camera crews that had shown up. As he watched the bright red emergency vehicle disappear around the corner, he wondered what it was about Selena Rosa that had him so rattled.

He was still trying to figure that out when Diego and Remy brought Pablo out and put him in another ambulance. He absently noted the short discussion with one of the paramedics but didn't bother to listen in as Remy hopped in back to ride to the hospital with the teen.

"You okay?"

Brooks jumped. *Shit*. He hadn't even heard or smelled Trey come up behind him.

"Yeah, I'm good," he murmured.

Maybe he should jump in his SUV and follow the ambulance to make sure Selena got to the hospital okay.

"Good, huh?" Trey said, walked around to stand in front of him, hazel eyes thoughtful. "So, that blood on your shirt and running down your arm isn't a big deal?"

Frowning, Brooks glanced at his arm. Damn, Trey was right. His arm *was* bleeding. He had a hole the size of his little finger drilled right through the inside of his right forearm up near his elbow. Unlike the one that had hit his stomach, this bullet didn't look like it had gone through and through.

One of the team's two medics, Trey grabbed his arm, probing and squeezing with well-practiced fingers, then grunted. "The bullet is still in there, wedged between the radius and the ulna. You honestly didn't feel it?"

Brooks shook his head. "I guess not." Even as he said the words, his arm began to burn and tingle. "But I'm definitely feeling it now. Can you get it out?"

While werewolves could recover from just about any wound, except one to the head or the heart, foreign debris inside the body slowed down the healing process, not to mention hurt like hell.

"Yeah, I can get it out," Trey said. "Good thing the

paramedics didn't see this, or you'd be taking a ride to
the hospital along with the teacher and our gangbanger."

"The paramedics must have thought all the blood
on me was from the teacher. They never looked at me
twice."

"Thank God for small favors." Trey regarded him
curiously. "You sure you're okay? Your eyes are a little
glassy. Plus, it's weird that you couldn't feel the bullet
in there until I mentioned it."

"Yeah, I'm fine," Brooks said.

But as they headed for the operations truck, Brooks
wasn't so sure about that. Why hadn't he felt that bullet
in his arm? And why the hell had he been standing in
the middle of the school parking lot for who knew how
long watching an ambulance disappear down the street?

He didn't have an answer to either of those questions, and right then, he couldn't waste any more time
on them. After Trey got the bullet out, he needed to help
get witness statements. Even though Pablo'd had a gun
and was going to use it, this situation was going to get
messy. They needed to make sure everything had been
done by the book.

That didn't stop him from looking back at the road
the ambulance had driven down. Selena was probably
halfway to the hospital by now, yet he still had this crazy
urge to run all the way there to check on her.

Chapter 3

"DR. PHAM WANTS TO KEEP YOU FOR OBSERVATION FOR A few hours." The blond nurse tucked the blanket around Selena, covering up the hideous hospital gown they'd given her to replace the blood-soaked clothes she'd shown up in, then added, "Maybe overnight."

Selena sat up in bed and pushed the blankets down, not even trying to hide her agitation. "Why would I need to stay here overnight? I'm fine. Heck, I've never felt better in my life."

In fact, she felt more energized and alive than she could ever remember. But the nurse—Melinda—merely arched a brow and gave her a dubious look before glancing pointedly at the bank of monitors on the cart beside the bed. The instruments were beeping and blinking, which meant absolutely nothing to Selena but apparently everything to the nurse.

"Ms. Rosa, your heart rate is still dangerously elevated, and so is your blood pressure," Melinda said, sighing like she was talking to a kid. "Your temperature is insanely high, you're soaking wet with sweat, your oxygen saturation is so far above normal our equipment can't even read it, and you haven't stopped shaking since you were brought in."

Selena clasped her hands together, trying to stop the worst of the trembling the nurse was talking about. Even though everything the nurse said was probably true, she had a crazy urge to argue with her. She hated it when people told her what to do, where to go, or how she should feel in any given situation. Pushing back came as natural to her as breathing. But in this case, she realized there was something else going on.

Simply put, she was terrified.

She'd been scared when Pablo had started waving that gun around in the classroom and even more freaked when the gangbanger had taken a shot at Ruben. But then the whole classroom had exploded around her, men with guns crashing in through the door and windows, a huge body slamming into her just as Pablo had tried to kill her.

She remembered that moment like it was trapped in time.

But while she'd been afraid, she'd been angry, too—furious even. The idea that Pablo had come into her classroom, her private sanctuary from the whole ugly gang world out there, and tried to hurt her and the students she loved made her want to scream.

Then, when the big cop had tackled her to the floor, everything had gotten hazy. All kinds of unfamiliar sensations and raw emotions had assaulted her, overwhelming and terrifying her. Something had happened to her in that classroom, and it scared her that she couldn't understand what it was.

"Am I going to be okay?" she whispered.

The nurse's expression softened, perhaps sensing how agitated Selena was right then. "You'll be okay. The doctor is a little worried you might have a concussion from getting tackled by that police officer. From the way you described him, it sounded like he was huge."

Huge? Now that was one hell of an understatement.

"But could a concussion cause all these weird symptoms?"

"It's possible." Melinda gave her a small smile that was probably supposed to be reassuring. "I'm sure it's nothing more than that."

The nurse looked away just long enough for Selena to somehow know she was lying or at least deliberately exaggerating the truth.

"Dr. Pham will be in to talk to you soon," the woman added, still not looking at Selena as she busied herself with the blankets again, then the instruments on the cart. "He'll explain everything then. Until he gets here, relax and don't worry. Everything is going to be fine."

Melinda left shortly after that, once again telling her this was all very normal. It took everything Selena had in her not to laugh. The whole day—and everything that had happened in her classroom—had been anything but normal.

Selena lay back on the pillow and replayed the moments after the cop had saved her life. Getting tackled by a guy who probably outweighed her by over a hundred pounds had definitely hurt, but getting shot would have been worse.

Maybe she'd gotten a concussion then. That would certainly explain the confusion and blurry vision, along with the memory of how the impossibly handsome dark-skinned cop had so easily picked her up and carried her out of the classroom like she was a kitten.

Then there was the blood. The skewing of reality that came with a concussion might also explain all the blood she'd been covered in. Or at least why she couldn't remember where it had come from.

She'd first noticed it in the ambulance on the way to the hospital. When the paramedic—Trent—had pushed up her sweater to check her for injuries, she'd told him she hadn't been injured. He'd paused, then said the least calming phrase she'd ever heard in her life.

"Ma'am, please don't be alarmed, but you're bleeding."

Yeah, that hadn't worked. She'd freaked out when she realized her sweater and slacks were covered in blood. They'd quickly figured out the blood wasn't hers, which had only upset her more, because she couldn't remember where it had come from.

"Was the cop who carried me out wounded?" she'd asked, inexplicably frantic at the thought.

The idea that he might have been shot was simply too painful to consider.

"No way. Not with the way he was carrying you," Trent said. "He definitely wasn't hurt. He would have said something if he was."

Trent had suggested it might be Pablo's blood, but that hadn't seemed right, either. Even as addled as she was, Selena was sure Pablo hadn't been anywhere near her after the shooting started. The rest of her students had been even farther away. There didn't seem to be any explanation for where the blood had come from.

Selena was still sorting through the limited possibilities while waiting for the doctor to come in when a tall, slim redhead with fair skin and freckles came into the room. Rebecca Young had a big gym bag in her hand that Selena prayed held the jeans and top she'd called and asked her friend and fellow teacher to bring, but before she could say anything, Becca charged the bed and hugged her fiercely.

"I was so scared when I saw them bringing you out on that gurney." Tears welled up in Becca's green eyes. "I thought Pablo killed you."

Selena returned Becca's hug, trying to comfort the woman who'd become her best friend over the past five years they'd been teaching together. "I'm fine. Everything's okay."

"But you were bleeding." Becca pulled back a little to look at Selena, making a face that suggested she wasn't sure Selena was telling the truth. "I saw it from where I was standing on the far side of the parking lot."

Selena smiled. "It wasn't my blood."

Becca eyed her doubtfully for a moment, then sighed in relief. Her expression quickly turned serious again as she took in the medical equipment around the bed. "If it wasn't your blood and you're not hurt, then why do they have you hooked up to all this stuff?"

Selena waved her hand. "It's nothing. The doctor is concerned that my pulse and blood pressure are a little high. He's monitoring it. That's all."

Becca looked like she wanted to throw a BS flag on that, but after a few moments, she finally relaxed. "After the day you've had, I'd be shocked if your blood pressure wasn't high. I know mine is, and all I had to put up with was seeing Pablo walk into the school showing off that gun."

Selena blinked. "You saw Pablo before he got to my classroom?"

"Yeah, I saw him and knew he was up to no good. I considered finding the nearest fire alarm and pulling that but was worried the commotion would provoke him to do something rash. Instead, I ran straight to the office and told Eva. She called the police, then I helped her and the other teachers evacuate the school."

Selena smiled. Hearing Becca talk so casually about the best way to handle an armed intruder at the school, then evacuating students for their own safety, it was difficult to believe she'd grown up in the ritzy University Park zip code with a family that had made its fortune in the oil business. It was even harder to believe the only reason Becca had started teaching at Terrace Grove was because she'd refused to let her family pay for her college education.

The school was part of the state's student loan forgiveness program, and Becca had once told her that she'd only planned to stay at Terrace Grove long enough to get some of her loans paid off. But then she'd fallen in love with the challenge of teaching kids who really, really needed her. Five years later, here she was talking about guns and clearing the school like it was the most normal thing in the world.

Selena was about to point that fact out, but Becca interrupted her. "I heard your students talking after the shooting. They said that big cop threw himself in front of you to save your life, then carried you out in his arms like a puppy. Is that true?"

"Yes, he saved my life," she said, smiling again. "Though I don't know if I agree with the last part. The details are a bit blurry, but I'm pretty sure he carried me like a person, not a puppy."

Becca laughed. "I saw him coming out after the paramedics loaded you into the ambulance. He certainly seemed big enough to pick you up like a puppy. Hell, he looked big enough to pick up the ambulance."

Selena thought back, remembering what it had felt like to be in his muscular arms. She'd felt safe there, like nothing could hurt her.

"He's definitely a big man," she admitted. "Strong, but gentle, too."

Her friend's eyes danced. "Sounds like the details aren't so blurry after all."

Maybe they weren't. In fact, she distinctly remembered gazing into his beautiful blue-gray eyes when he'd set her down on the gurney and feeling the strangest sensation she'd ever experienced. In some way, it was like there was a part of her deep inside that recognized the cop as special. She didn't understand it, and she couldn't explain it, but it was still there even now.

"Like I said, I was all the way across the parking lot when I saw him," Becca continued, a smile curving her lips. "But even from that distance, I could tell he was hot. If tall, dark-skinned, handsome, incredibly well-muscled men are your thing, I mean."

"Aren't they everybody's thing?" Selena asked with a laugh.

Okay, truthfully, she giggled. But that was because Becca brought it out in her, always getting her to comment on guys they saw, asking if she'd swipe right or left on them.

Becca grinned. "So, what's his name?"

Selena stared at her friend for several long moments, at a complete loss for words as she pictured the man who'd saved her. While she might know every line and curve of his face, she was stunned to realize she had no clue what his name was. In all the time she'd been in his arms, she'd never even considered looking at the name

tag on his uniform—if there was one—much less asking
what it was.

"You don't know his name, do you?" Becca asked.

Selena shook her head. "Things were so crazy after
the shooting, and I really wasn't in a condition to talk.
Then by the time I was…well…it was too late. I was
already in the ambulance on the way here. The guy
risked his life for me. I think I should at least thank him."

"It shouldn't be that hard to track him down." Still
smiling, Becca mimicked dialing a phone and holding it
up to her ear. "Hello, Dallas PD? This is Selena Rosa. I
was rescued by an incredibly attractive, muscular, dark-
skinned Adonis from your SWAT unit who likely makes
a habit of saving damsels in distress. Could I get his
name and number so I can thank him in person?"

"That's all I have to do, huh?"

"Sure." Becca shrugged. "How many guys like him
could they have working there?"

Selena had to agree with her friend on that. The man
would definitely stand out in a crowd. But while she
honestly wanted to thank him for what he'd done, she
couldn't really see herself calling the police department
and asking for his name and number.

"If you get his contact info in time, maybe you could
bring him as your date when you go out with Scott
and me," Becca said, the words coming out in a tone
just a bit too nonchalant. "We're going to the club on
Wednesday, remember?"

At first, Selena was worried maybe Dr. Pham was
right about her having a concussion. She didn't have
any idea what her friend was talking about. But then
she remembered a conversation she and Becca had had

last week in the break room about how disappointed her parents were with her relationship status.

"Hold on. You're not serious, are you?" Selena sat up so quickly, she was worried she'd get dizzy. Thankfully, that didn't happen. "You're really going on the blind date your parents set up for you?"

Becca winced. "You don't have to make it sound so horrible. They're just concerned because I haven't met anyone yet and that none of the men I date seem to be interested in long-term relationships. They're worried their dreams of spoiling their future grandkids are going to disappear in a haze of dull, infrequent, meaningless first dates."

Selena sighed. She knew what Becca was saying. Finding a good man in this town was tough, but finding one when you spent almost every night grading papers, writing lesson plans, or checking in on troubled students made it even harder.

"Hey, I'm not throwing rocks," she said, holding up her hands. "My social life is too crappy for me to even consider that. But still, going out with a guy your parents found on a dating site? I mean, have you even talked with him yet?"

Becca shook her head. "We haven't talked, but we've texted. His name is Scott Llewellyn and he's a tax accountant. He seems nice, and considering how classy my last few dates have been, I'm willing to give nice a chance."

"You think he's nice?" Selena said dubiously. "But you still want me to go with you?"

Her friend gave her a sheepish look. "If you don't mind. I mean, he might be great, but I can't help remembering that documentary I saw on Jeffrey Dahmer where all his neighbors described him as nice. I think I'd like to have some backup with me when I first meet this guy, just in case."

Selena couldn't fault her friend for that. "Okay, I'll go. But no promises about bringing the cop with me—if I even find him. He could be married for all I know."

They were still planning their midweek date when the doctor showed up. He checked Selena's vitals again, flicked his flashlight in her eyes a few times, and asked how her head was feeling. Selena said she felt fine with no lingering effects from the attack at all. That wasn't exactly true. She still felt really out of it. But she wasn't going to mention that to him.

After seeing that her pulse, blood pressure, and temperature had dropped to relatively normal levels, he declared she could leave. Selena immediately yanked the blanket off and got out of bed, almost hanging herself with all the wires attached to her. Dr. Pham quickly stepped forward to put a restraining hand on her arm, then unhooked her from the equipment.

"Your vitals are better, Ms. Rosa," he said. "But you've been through a major traumatic event. You're going to need to take it easy for the next week or two."

Selena nodded and promised she would. After a lengthy lecture on getting some counseling for post-traumatic stress, he sent the nurse back in with the necessary paperwork for Selena to sign. The moment she was done, she took the clothes Becca had brought and quickly put them on, then got the hell out of there. She appreciated the doctor's concern, but she hated hospitals, and other than being a little woozy, she felt fine. Besides, she had a lot of stuff to do.

Even though she wasn't looking forward to it, the first thing on the list was to go back to her classroom and see how much damage had been done. That place wasn't just her sanctuary. It was her students', too. After everything that had happened today, her kids were going to need the feeling of safety now more than ever.

"This can't wait until later?" Brooks asked.

He had to work hard to keep the anger out of his voice as he followed Zane toward the front of the admin building at the SWAT compound. In the bullpen, the rest of the Pack was discussing teammate Max Lowry's last-minute wedding plans. The SWAT werewolf and his soul mate, Lana Mason, were getting married that weekend after knowing each other barely a month. Finding *The One*, that person who loved and accepted you for being a werewolf, sounded great to Brooks, but still—soul mate or not—getting married after a month together struck him as a little fast.

Zane shook his head. "No. We've been trying to get that damn hunter to talk to us for nearly a month with no luck. His lawyer called and said his client has agreed to a meeting, but only with the two of us, and only if we do it tonight."

Brooks bit back a growl. For hours, he'd been trying to slip away to the hospital so he could check on Selena to make sure she was okay. But everything involving the classroom raid, from clearing all the students out of the school to waiting for the K9 teams to check the place for explosives, had taken ten times longer than it should have. Then, when he'd gotten back here with Diego to wrap up the paperwork, he'd found Zane waiting for him so they could go down to the Coffield Unit prison. The place was almost two hours away. Visiting hours at the hospital would be long over before they got back.

"Why the hell would he want to see us now?" he demanded.

Zane stopped to look at him. "I'm not really sure. I asked the same question when Gage told me Oliver's lawyer called. The only thing we could come up with is that the hunters have decided to dangle him in front of us as bait."

Brooks frowned, crossing his arms over his chest. "Bait for what?"

Seth Oliver was the only surviving hunter from the attack on the Pack last month. Until now, he'd refused to talk to anyone, but if they could get him to tell them where the hell the other hunters were, they might be able to stop the next attack before it happened.

If Oliver was bait, as Zane suggested, that implied the man had been in contact with the people who'd sent him to Dallas to kill werewolves. Oliver had been on 24/7 lockdown the entire time he'd been in prison at Coffield. He shouldn't have been able to talk to anyone. But in truth, it was ridiculously easy to get information in and out of prison, especially if you had the right people on the outside to make it happen. The hunters were obviously the right people.

"Intel probably," Zane said in answer to his question. "The hunters may have knocked us out the last time we fought, but in return, we pretty much wiped them out. Whoever is in charge is probably trying to figure out how that happened. They seem to operate like a militia organization, which means they'll want to learn more about us. The easiest way to do that is get us to talk to Oliver."

"Okay, I get that," Brooks said. "If they assume we'd be stupid enough to tell them anything. But why the two of us? Why not Gage? He's the Pack alpha. Wouldn't they want to talk to the man in charge if they're looking for information about how we operate?"

Zane snorted. "You're assuming they have a clue what an alpha is. They only care about two things— tracking and killing our kind. The idea that we're anything more than animals is probably something they've never considered. They most likely don't know there are even different kinds of werewolves. To them, we're all the same—except for size. Which is probably why they want to talk to you. They probably assume you're the apex predator since you're so bloody big."

Brooks could see Zane's point. The hunters were damn good at finding werewolves and also coming up with weapons to kill them. They'd filled their bullets with a potent synthetic wolfsbane, which acted like a nerve agent on werewolves but had limited effect on humans. That showed a shocking level of sophistication. But at the same time, they didn't seem to understand anything about how werewolves lived or their pack structure. In fact, the biggest reason they'd come after Lana last month seemed to be an obsessive fascination with getting a chance to hunt down a female werewolf. Apparently, they hadn't seen very many.

"If they arranged this meeting with me so Oliver could get a look at the werewolf they think is their biggest physical threat, what's their angle with you?"

Brooks asked. "They just curious about a British were-wolf living in Dallas?"

Zane let out a harsh laugh and pointed at his injured arm. "More likely, they want him to get a look at this so they can figure out why I'm still alive. I'm there for battle damage assessment."

"Battle damage assessment" sounded like something a military person might say, which wasn't surprising, considering Zane had served in the British Special Air Service before joining SWAT. Still, it sounded harsh for him to refer to his injured arm that way. Like it wasn't even part of him anymore.

"You think it's a good idea to let them see how bad they messed you up?" Brooks asked softly.

He knew the minute Zane's eyes flashed gold that it'd been the wrong thing to say, but it was too late to take it back.

"What, you think I'm so wretched I can't even sit in a chair across from that wanker and look normal?" Zane growled, his British accent deepening and the tips of his fangs showing.

Before getting injured, Zane had rarely lost his cool, but ever since the hunters had nearly killed him, it happened all the time. Brooks didn't say anything, instead giving his friend a chance to get himself together.

When Zane's eyes resumed their normal brown color, Brooks reached out and gave his shoulder a brief squeeze. "You know that's not what I meant. You said yourself the whole reason Oliver wants you at this meeting is so he can assess the damage their poison ammo inflicted. The last thing we want to do is encourage them to come after us again with that stuff."

Zane let out a breath. "I know you didn't mean anything. It's me. I'm not dealing with this well."

Brooks was going to tell him everything was going to be okay, that he'd get through this. But Zane cut him off with a look.

"I know what you're going to say, and I'd rather not get into it." He threw a quick glance at the bullpen area. "Not here."

"That's cool," Brooks said. "But we are going to talk about this. Soon."

Zane nodded and started for the exit again. "And don't worry about me slipping up and revealing how close the hunters came to killing me. I'll do whatever is necessary to make Oliver think their poison had no effect on me at all."

Brooks didn't doubt it. But was meeting with him worth the risk?

"You think we'll get anything useful out of Oliver?" he asked. "I mean, it's not like we can get this guy a reduced sentence. They're looking at him for six murders already in addition to what he did in Dallas. Even if he does talk, anything he tells us about the hunters will likely be a lie. Especially if he is still in contact with them."

"I know, but there's always a chance we can trip him up and get him to reveal something critical without him even realizing it." Zane looked at Brooks. "As long as we play along and let him assume we're nothing more than dumb animals."

That might work. Zane knew how to work people. It's what made him a good negotiator. Besides, right now, he needed something to make him feel like he was still a useful member of the Pack.

As Zane shoved open the door leading out to the parking lot, Brooks picked up a strange but familiar scent. He glanced down to see a slinky black cat stroll into the building like she owned the place. Tail high in the air, she disappeared into the bullpen, then came back into the main part of the building and jumped onto the couch, where she promptly made herself comfortable.

Gage suddenly appeared in the doorway of the bullpen, a confused look on his face as he gazed at the animal. After a moment, he looked at Brooks and Zane. "That is a cat, right?"

"That's a cat," Brooks confirmed.

Gage studied the cat for a bit, then shook his head and walked back into the bullpen. On the couch, the cat regarded Brooks and Zane with big, green eyes. She might look like a regular kitty, but she didn't smell like any cat he'd ever sniffed before. Fortunately, Connor, Trey, and Remy chose that moment to walk in the door Zane held open, giving Brooks something else to focus on instead of the cat.

While Connor and Remy stopped, Trey mumbled something about needing to do paperwork, glanced once at Zane, then strode away.

Brooks bit back a curse. As a medic, Trey was trained not only on how to save people but werewolves too. Unfortunately, there'd been no training to prepare him for what happened when that hunter's bullet had hit Zane. It had been the most horrible thing Brooks had ever witnessed. Zane had writhed and screamed in pain, begging Trey to cut off his arm as the flesh rotted right before their eyes. Trey'd had two choices. Wait and see if Zane's werewolf healing powers stopped the poison from spreading before it killed him, or cut out the infected muscles.

Trey had done what he'd had to do, but that decision had come with a hefty price.

Even though Zane had never said it, Brooks knew there was a part of him that blamed Trey for crippling him. Worse, Trey blamed himself. As a result, Zane and Trey didn't talk to each other much these days. Brooks wished he could say something to change that, but he couldn't think of a single damn thing.

Instead, he looked at Connor. "You brought the cat back here with you?"

"I wouldn't really say I *brought* her back here." Connor shrugged. "She jumped in the SUV of her own accord before we left the warehouse and refused to get out."

"Jumped?" Brooks lifted a brow. "And you couldn't…I don't know…shoo her out?"

Connor shrugged. "Why would I do that, since she obviously wanted to go with us? She probably figured we were going to a nicer neighborhood than that area around the warehouse. She isn't wrong."

Brooks was still working his way through that logic when he realized exactly what Connor had said. "Wait a second. Are you saying you left a cat inside your vehicle the whole time we were at Terrace Grove?"

Connor didn't even have the sense to look chagrined. "Well, yeah, I let her stay in the vehicle. It's not like I was going to toss her out to roam around the school. She could have gotten hurt. I left the windows down, and she sat on the center console and watched us work."

Brooks opened his mouth, then closed it again, speechless.

"And on that note, I'm out of here," Remy said, mouth twitching as he made a beeline for the bullpen.

"We need to get moving," Zane murmured, his tone reminding Brooks there was something more important than Connor's sudden feline infatuation.

Brooks started to follow Zane out the door, but then a thought struck him. Of a particular pit bull mix walking into the place and finding a cat in her compound. "Have you even thought about the fact that we already have a Pack mascot? And that Tuffie and the cat might not get along?"

Connor glanced at the cat, who meowed at him. "They'll get along fine. You worry too much."

Brooks shook his head. "Right. Because it's not like dogs and cats have ever not gotten along."

As he and Zane crossed the parking lot, a brown four-door sedan pulled through the front gate and slipped into one of the reserved visitor spaces in front of the admin building. A moment later, Chief of Police Randy Curtis stepped out of the unmarked patrol car. As he approached them, Curtis's gaze swept over Brooks, Zane, and everything else within view as if nothing quite measured up, including them. Brooks didn't take it personally. Curtis disliked anyone and anything that had even the slightest chance of derailing his political ambitions.

"Senior Corporal Kendrick. Senior Corporal Brooks," Curtis said, extending his hand.

Brooks didn't have any choice but to shake it, though he felt greasy as hell afterward. Curtis may have been a cop before he came to Dallas to take over as chief, but since then, he'd turned into a politician. It was tough to like a man when you knew he viewed everything through the lens of what it meant for his own career.

"I heard you and your team did real good at that school shooting today," Curtis said. "But I also heard our gangbanger was a student there. Is this going to come back as a clean shoot?"

Brooks bit his tongue so he wouldn't say anything he regretted. Curtis didn't care in the slightest whether the students, teachers, and even officers on the scene were okay. Hell, he didn't even care how badly the suspect had been injured. All he wanted to know was if anything negative was going to come back on him. That made sense, since Curtis made no secret of the fact he was looking to make a run for mayor. The worst part was that most of the good press the man had gotten lately was because SWAT had taken down a lot of bad guys. Between organized crime figures, psycho killers, major drug dealers, and a corrupt councilman, SWAT had made a large dent in the Dallas crime statistics, and Curtis was taking credit for all of it. If he got elected mayor, it would probably be because of SWAT.

That was a horrible thought.

"There's video and audio of the entire operation from start to finish." Brooks glanced at Zane. "Senior Corporal Kendrick was the on-scene negotiator who tried to talk the suspect into giving himself up, but when the teen took a shot at one of the other students in the classroom, we had to go in. Officer Martinez entered through a window and tried to get him to drop the gun but was forced to take the shot when the suspect turned his weapon on the teacher."

Curtis's gray eyes narrowed the moment Brooks said

the word *video*, and his interest only increased when Brooks added details. When the chief turned his attention to Zane, Brooks could practically see the gears turning in the man's head. "You're the officer who was injured last month at the medical clinic, right?" When Zane gave him a reluctant nod, he continued. "Injured in the line of duty and already back out on the street trying to convince a gangbanger to give himself up. That's good. Really good."

Brooks didn't think anything about the situation was really good. Neither did Zane. But they kept their opinions to themselves. It was obvious Curtis only cared about how the shooting would play out with the media.

"Where is Officer Martinez?" Curtis asked. "I'd like to get his perspective on the shooting. Maybe get him in front of the cameras at the press conference."

"You'll need to get in line, sir," Zane said. "Detective Coletti from Internal Affairs is currently with him. Following normal DPD procedure, he'll likely be placed on desk duty until the investigation is complete. He won't be able to make any public statements during that time."

While Brooks and the other guys hadn't fired their weapons at the high school, they had at the warehouse, so Vince Coletti had talked to them as well. While the IA detective definitely still took his investigations seriously, he wasn't nearly the asshole about it that he had been before falling for a beta werewolf who'd recently moved into the area.

"Of course. IA has their job to do," Curtis said. "Where are the two of you headed? It would look good to have you both with me at the press conference I'm holding later."

Brooks bit back a growl. Like hell they would be

there. "We'd really like to, but we're on our way to Coffield Unit. The suspect from the shooting at the medical center asked to talk to us. We're hoping he might tell us who he was working with."

Brooks expected Curtis to ask why SWAT would interrogate a murder suspect, since they didn't normally investigate cases. But the man didn't even blink an eye. "I understand. I believe there were several SWAT officers at the scene, so I'm sure Sergeant Dixon has someone he can give me for the press conference."

Brooks sure as hell wasn't going to volunteer anyone, even though he probably should have thrown Connor under the bus for bringing the cat back here. But he'd never do anything like that. None of his pack mates liked being in front of a camera.

"Good luck down at the prison," Curtis said. Giving them a nod, he headed toward the admin building.

Zane climbed behind the wheel of the SUV before Brooks could offer to drive. They hadn't gone more than a mile before Zane looked his way with a quizzical expression.

"What's the story behind you and the teacher you rescued?"

Brooks frowned. "What do you mean?"

Zane shrugged. "You seemed cross you couldn't go see her."

"Nah, man. I saved her life and just wanted to make sure she was okay."

"Right." Zane glanced at him. "So that's not why you almost growled at Curtis just now? Or why you've been acting distracted as hell ever since the shooting? Or why you didn't want to go down to Coffield with me?"

Brooks opened his mouth to say Zane was way off the mark but then snapped it closed again. He hated lying to a friend, especially when that friend was right. Selena had gotten into his head—fast.

"It's complicated," he said.

Zane chuckled. "She's a woman. That makes the situation complicated by definition. The real question is, what are you going to do about it?"

Brooks stared out the window at the mile markers slipping by. "I have no idea."

Chapter 4

"YOU PROBABLY SHOULDN'T GO IN THERE, MA'AM." THE young police officer standing outside the doorway of her classroom gave her an apologetic look. "It's bad."

Selena glanced at the officer's name tag. "I only want to grab my purse out of my desk, Officer Webber. And I really should clean up, since tomorrow is a school day."

The blond-haired cop shook his head. "Ma'am, I don't think you'll be having any classes in that room for a while. Like I said, it's a mess in there."

Selena found that difficult to believe. She vaguely remembered there had been some broken glass from the windows and that some of the combination chair/desks had been pushed all over the classroom, but hopefully the young officer was exaggerating the extent of the damage, and she'd be able to clean up the place quickly. It had been a long day, and she was exhausted beyond belief. She definitely needed to get some sleep before facing the kids tomorrow. And today was only Monday. She'd be ready to drop by the end of the week.

She put on her best teacher face—the one she used when her kids got unruly—until the cop finally relented and moved aside. "Okay, I'll let you in there, but only so you can grab your purse and look around. This is still technically a crime scene, even if the CSIs are already done with it. Just be careful, okay? I don't want you to get hurt."

Selena didn't think that was a possibility until she

noticed the door was completely gone. There was nothing left but a broken frame and some twisted hinges. She hesitated a moment, wondering if Officer Webber was right. But then she took a deep breath and forced herself to keep moving. There was no amount of damage a little hard work couldn't fix.

But when she stepped into the classroom, she stopped cold. *Crap*. It was even worse than the officer had suggested.

Broken desks were everywhere, chunks of the fake wood tops strewn about. There were bullet holes in the walls, and the entire row of windows along the outer wall of the classroom had been shattered. Glass shards spread from one side of the room to the other. The nice wood blinds she'd paid for with her own money were smashed and hanging in pieces from their rods. The breeze blowing into the room made what was left of them sway and clatter against the frames, sounding nearly as desolate as Selena suddenly felt.

Even the little Christmas tree she'd put up in the front of the room near the corner looked saddened by what it had witnessed today.

Moving farther in, she saw what could only be pieces of the door lying halfway across the room. She couldn't even begin to understand how they'd gotten there.

But worse than any of the broken glass and furniture was the blood. So much blood.

She expected to find it where Pablo had been shot. But the largest spatters of the reddish-brown stuff were in the middle of the floor, where she'd been tackled by that big cop. She frowned, trying to understand where the blood there had come from.

She replayed what had happened in her head, distinctly remembering Pablo pointing the gun at her, recalling how angry she'd been with him. After that, the windows had come crashing in, then the cop had tackled her to the floor. Even now, Selena could almost feel his muscled body shielding her as the sound of booming gunshots filled the air.

Had Pablo moved closer to them after he'd gotten shot? It didn't seem possible.

She closed her eyes and forced herself to replay the scene again, even though it made her heart thump harder. She almost snarled as she realized how close Pablo—another kid ruined by the gangs in this city— had come to killing her and Ruben.

But no matter how many times the events flashed through her head, no matter how hard she dug for something she might have missed, Selena couldn't come up with an explanation for how all that blood had gotten from where Pablo had been shot to the place she and the cop had been lying. How it had ended up on her was even more of a mystery. The only thing that could have possibly explained it was if one of the cops had been hit.

More precisely, one particular cop.

"Was the officer who saved me injured in the shooting?" she asked, turning to look at Officer Webber.

He stood a few feet away, looking around at all the destruction like he was as stunned as she was. "You mean Senior Corporal Brooks from SWAT?"

"Is he the big, good-looking black guy with all the muscles?" she asked.

Webber laughed. "I can't really speak to the

good-looking part, but yeah, that's him. It's kind of hard to miss those muscles. He's a really big man. But as far as him being injured, I don't think he got a scratch on him during the shooting."

That didn't make sense. There had been blood all over the both of them, and there didn't seem to be any way it had come from Pablo. And it sure as hell hadn't come from her. "Were you here during the shooting? Did you see him after I was taken away in the ambulance?"

The cop shook his head. "No. I got here about ten minutes after everything went down. But I saw Corporal Brooks several times after that and talked to him before he left. There were definitely blood stains on his uniform, but there's no way it was his."

Selena sighed. Was she ever going to figure out what had happened in this room?

"Do you happen to know where his office is located?" she asked the cop.

It was nearly impossible to live in this town and not have heard about the team of elite police officers in SWAT, but while she'd seen a few video clips of their exploits, she'd never had an opportunity to meet one in person.

"They have a training compound on the southeast side of town off Highway 175," Webber said. "You can get the exact address online if you need it, though."

Selena nodded, already pretty sure she knew where it was. She thought she'd seen a sign out that way the last time she'd driven to Athens to see some friends.

She was about to ask Webber what Brooks was like and what other cops thought about him and whether he was married, but the young officer held up a hand as a string of chatter came over his radio. She had no idea what all the codes and cop speak meant, but Webber obviously did.

"I gotta go," he said. "They need me out front. You can grab your purse, but don't try to clean up, okay? This is still a crime scene."

Then he was gone, leaving her in the middle of the mess that was her classroom. He didn't need to remind her it was a crime scene. That much was obvious.

Selena was digging her purse out of the big desk positioned in the front of the room when she heard the crunch of shoes on glass. She looked up, expecting to see Webber, and was surprised to see the principal and vice principal, relief on their faces.

"Selena," Eva said, coming over to wrap her in a warm hug. "I tried to get the hospital to tell us if you were okay, but they wouldn't release any details. I feared the worst."

"I'm fine," Selena said as she pulled back.

The hug reminded her again how bruised her body was. She'd noticed the purplish areas coming up as she'd been getting dressed at the hospital. They hurt like hell, but bruises were better than the alternative of getting shot.

"The doctor kept me for a few hours. He was concerned about a concussion," she added, wanting Eva to know there was nothing wrong with her. "But I passed all the tests, so they said there's no reason I can't go right back to work."

Eva smiled, the corners of her dark eyes crinkling a little behind her glasses. "I'm glad. We were all worried about you."

While Selena didn't doubt the older woman was concerned about her health, Eva's husband happened to be one of the school board's lawyers. Sadly, that meant almost everything that came out of Eva's mouth had something to do with school liability. At the end of the day, Eva was probably more worried Selena's injuries might end up costing the county somehow.

"Can I get some help cleaning up after the police are done with it?" Selena asked hopefully.

Hugh stepped forward. "This place is going to need more than a quick cleaning, Selena. I have people coming over to board up the windows, but they won't be able to replace them until later in the week. I'm still working with the county office to find someone who can clean up the blood. There are only so many companies who specialize in that."

Selena was shocked at the wave of anger that surged through her. She felt like punching a wall right then… or at least screaming. But she couldn't do either of those things with Eva and Hugh there. So instead, she closed her eyes and took a deep breath, letting the frustration and rage flow over her.

"I guess I can use the library. Or the gym if I have to," she finally said.

It would be a pain in the butt for sure, but nothing she couldn't deal with. Then she saw the look that passed between Eva and Hugh, and her stomach twisted up. There was something they weren't telling her.

"What's wrong?" she asked.

Had somebody gone after Ruben or her other students because he wouldn't go with Pablo?

"Nothing is wrong," Eva said. "But you won't be

teaching any classes this week. You and your students went through a horrible ordeal, and the superintendent wants to make sure all of you get the help you need to process everything that's happened today." She exchanged another look with Hugh. "We've given the students who witnessed the shooting the rest of the week off so they can see a counselor for post-traumatic stress. We've also gotten a substitute for you so you can get counseling."

Selena stifled a groan. The woman sounded like Dr. Pham. "Eva, I don't need counseling, and neither do my kids. What they need is to be in school instead of out there on the streets. In here, I can keep them out of trouble. Out there, they're completely on their own. They're never going to get counseling, and you know that."

She didn't know why she bothered. Eva and Hugh were the kind of people who thought schools were there to teach kids and nothing else. They refused to even consider that for kids like hers, school represented safety from alcohol, drugs, gang violence, abusive parents, and a hundred other things that could screw up their lives. Weekends and summer breaks were bad enough, but a week away from this school after everything they'd seen today was the worst possible thing for her students.

She kept trying anyway, hoping to sway Eva, even attempting to get Hugh on her side, but in the end, it was no use. The lawyers and the school board were doing what they thought was the right thing. There would be no arguing with them.

Selena returned to her desk to grab her purse, mentally putting together a list of which students she'd need to check in on first when Hugh spoke. "Selena, Eva and I were in the SWAT vehicle watching the video when Pablo tried to kill you. And while I know you aren't the kind to seek out professional counseling for yourself, I hope you'll take this time off to talk to someone. A friend, your family, a priest. Hell, you can talk to Eva and me if you want. But please, talk to someone. Don't try to do this alone."

She opened her mouth to tell him that he needed to spend more time worrying about the kids and less about her but bit her tongue. Hugh was just trying to help. It had been a long, crappy day, and her frustration was getting the best of her. So she nodded and thanked Hugh for his concern, then murmured a few noncommittal words about talking to a friend as she left.

The sun had set while she'd been inside, and the parking lot was now lit with nothing more than a few of those fuzzy orange streetlamps, which was why she almost missed the guy standing beside the car near hers as she approached. Selena slowed, her heart beating faster. She was just wondering if she should go back inside, but then the man stepped into the light. She sagged with relief when she saw it was Ernesto. She hadn't recognized his car, because it was a new one.

"Hey there, Little Sis," he said with a grin as he walked over to meet her. "What are you doing messing around with the gangs? Don't you know that's my job?"

Selena laughed, her mood immediately lifting as her very best friend in the world pulled her into a hug. While she wasn't really his baby sister, that had never stopped Ernesto Lopez from treating her like one. Or kept her from accepting him as a stand-in for the real older brother she'd lost a long time ago.

"What are you talking about?" She pulled back to take in his fancy suit, not to mention the shoes that looked like they cost more than her car. "You don't hang with the gangs anymore. They're bad for your image."

Ernesto chuckled. "True." He gazed down at her, his expression suddenly serious. "I was scared to death when I found out about what happened to you. Are you okay? I came as fast as I could."

Based on the suit, Selena guessed Ernesto had been in one of his business meetings, maybe even something with the city. He used to be in the gangs years ago and had worked as a high-level lieutenant along with her brother, Geraldo. When Geraldo had gotten killed, that had been the last straw for Ernesto. He'd gotten out, turned his life around, and become a successful businessman. These days, he ran a chain of custom car franchises that stretched all the way from Dallas to California. More than that, he'd become a role model for other gangbangers, showing them it really was possible to get out of the life.

And he'd done it in large part for her. To become the brother she'd lost.

She hugged him again, even if she had to hide a grimace of pain as Ernesto squeezed her. "I'm fine. A little bruised up, but nothing I can't deal with."

Ernesto's eyes hardened at her words, reminding Selena that while he hadn't been in a gang for nearly a decade, there was still a sense of danger lurking under the surface.

"How did you find me?" she asked, trying to distract Ernesto before he got wound up and started in on his overprotective older brother routine. He'd made a promise to Geraldo, swearing he'd never let the gangs hurt her. He took that promise seriously.

Ernesto frowned, completely aware of what she was

doing, but then he flashed her that charming smile he always had for her. "When I got to the hospital and discovered you'd been released already, I figured you were either at your apartment or at school. I came here."

Selena returned his smile as she tucked her hair behind her ear. "I guess I'm predictable, huh?"

He shook his head. "Not really. I just know you. Even after one of your own students attacks you, the first thing you're going to do is worry about the other kids in your class."

Selena could read the disapproval on Ernesto's face. He'd been trying to get her to move to a different school for years, telling her over and over that it wasn't her job to save these kids all by herself.

She sighed, really not in the mood to argue tonight. Especially after the day she'd had. "Well, you'll be happy to know you have nothing to worry about. Not only is my classroom a complete wreck, but the school board has decided I need counseling…along with my entire fourth period class. I've been shut down for the rest of the week."

Ernesto was nice enough not to cheer, but it was obvious he was pleased at the outcome. "I know you don't want to hear this, but you could have been killed today. You need time to deal with that. You can't help those kids if you don't take care of yourself first."

She frowned, not having a counter to that argument. The truth was, Ernesto was right. She had almost died. She simply wasn't ready to think about it right now. She wasn't sure when she would be.

"What are you going to do with all that time off?" Ernesto asked.

She shrugged. "I'm not sure. I guess I'll hang out at my place and catch up on some TV while I work on lesson plans."

In reality, she'd spend most of the week checking in on her at-risk students, but she wasn't going to tell Ernesto that. He'd lose his ever-loving mind if he found out she was planning to plant herself right in the middle of some of the worst gang neighborhoods in the city. Then there was her plan to track down that cop who'd saved her life. She doubted Ernesto would like that idea, either. He might be on the right side of the law now, but that didn't mean he liked cops.

"You could hang out at my place if you want," her surrogate brother said. "I could take some time off. We could play video games, binge-watch *Game of Thrones*, or do anything else you want to do."

Ernesto had an awesome place in Arlington, out past the stadium. It had a ridiculous number of bedrooms, heated pool, movie theater, and all kinds of toys to keep her distracted if that was what she was looking for.

But it wasn't.

"Thanks," she said, really appreciating the offer. "But you have a business to run, and this isn't something another person can help me with—even you. I need to work through it on my own."

Ernesto opened his mouth to argue but then shook his head as he stepped close and pulled her in for another hug, this one even more gentle than the first. "Okay, I get it. Like I said, I know you. Nobody's ever going to get you to do something you don't want to do. But just so you know, my offer stands. If you need a place to get away or just need to talk to someone, I'll be there."

She hugged him back, feeling blessed to have someone like Ernesto in her life. He'd been the rock that had kept her sane after losing her brother, and she had no idea where she'd be without him.

Selena watched him drive away, waiting until his taillights disappeared out of the parking lot. Then she turned with a heavy sigh and headed for her car. She reached for the door handle, when she caught movement over by the corner of the school. She looked that way and was surprised to see Ruben standing there, his big shoulder resting against the brick, his expression unreadable.

Something told her he'd been hanging around the school to talk to her. She started across the parking lot, when a police car came around the far side of the building and headed toward her. The vehicle's appearance startled her, but instead of stepping back in fear, a snarl of anger escaped her lips.

She forced herself to take a deep breath and calm down as the cruiser pulled up beside her. Officer Webber leaned out of the driver's side window to smile at her.

"I thought you'd already be gone," he said. "Everything okay?"

She returned his smile, but just barely. Most of her attention was wrapped up in trying to understand why she'd reacted so strangely to seeing his car. If she didn't know better, it seemed like she'd been ready to attack the damn thing, which was absolutely insane. She glanced over at Ruben, but he was nowhere to be found.

"I was just getting in my car when you came around the corner," she lied.

She doubted the officer would be thrilled if she

mentioned one of her students was wandering around
school property at this time of night.

The cop nodded, his smile broadening. "Okay, have a
good evening. I hope everything works out getting your
classroom back together."

Selena nodded absently as he drove off, looking
around for Ruben again before getting in her car. But
like she'd expected, he was gone. She sighed, knowing
he wouldn't have been out here if there wasn't something seriously wrong. She hoped it wasn't something
involving the Locos. With the way things had gone
down in her classroom, she could see the gang blaming
Ruben for what had happened to Pablo.

She considered driving around for a while, thinking she might be able to find Ruben, but she realized
that would be useless. He could have gone anywhere.
She'd stop by his grandmother's place tomorrow and
hope he'd be okay until then. After that, she'd make the
circuit to see the rest of the students in her class.

"Since we're stuck here with nothing to do while
we wait," Zane said, leaning back in his chair in the
Coffield Unit attorney visitation room, "why don't we
talk a little more about this teacher that has you so tied
up in knots?"

Brooks groaned, wondering how much longer his
friend was going to keep nagging him. During the
whole drive to the prison, Zane had peppered him with
questions, and now that they were forced to sit on their
hands, waiting for the guard to bring in Seth Oliver, he
was at it again.

"Let's not and say we did."

Beside him, Zane snorted. "Come on. You can't expect me to just drop this. I saw your face when you carried her out of the classroom. She got to you."

Brooks looked at him in surprise. "You saw me?"

Zane nodded, the smile that had been on his face earlier fading a bit. "Yeah, on the video feed. I saw you throw yourself in front of her and saw the bullet hit you. When you rolled her over, I thought for sure she'd been hit."

Brooks swallowed hard, remembering how scared he'd been. "Me too. Even after I realized it was my blood on her sweater, I was still worried she'd been hurt. She looked really out of it."

"She was in shock," Zane pointed out. "One of her students tried to kill her. That's enough to mess anyone up."

"Yeah, I guess," Brooks murmured.

He couldn't shake the little voice in his head that kept trying to tell him there was more to it than that. The way she'd looked at him as he'd carried her out…it was like…well…he didn't know what it was like. But he'd seen lots of people go into shock before, and it hadn't looked quite like that.

Zane hooked his thumbs in his equipment belt. "She wasn't the only one who looked like they were in shock. You looked rattled, too."

"I was worried we'd lost a hostage. That's all."

"Brooks, we've been friends since the day you walked into the SWAT compound four years ago. If you want me to mind my own damn business, that's fine. I won't push. But if you think I believe that rubbish about you only being worried about a hostage, you're bonkers."

"I'm not trying to be a jackass about this, but the truth

is, I don't know what's going on." Brooks sighed. "All I can say is that when I looked into Selena's eyes, something weird happened. I'm still trying to process it all."

Zane dropped the front legs of the chair he was balancing to the floor with a thud. "What do you mean... weird? Are you suggesting she might be—"

"No!" Brooks said, quickly interrupting Zane before he could get the words out.

Werewolves in the Pack had been stumbling over their soul mates left and right throughout the past year, but he had a difficult time believing that was going on here. He'd know it if Selena was *The One* for him... wouldn't he?

"Selena is beautiful, I'll give you that," he added. "She was in danger, and that got to me. That's all I'm saying right now."

Zane regarded him in silence for a moment, a smile tugging at the corners of his mouth. "Okay, I won't go there—for now. Instead, for the sake of argument, let's say you and Selena have a *connection*. Are you planning on seeing her again?"

Shit. He felt like he was going through a cross-examination on the witness stand. "It'll be too late for that by the time we get back. Even if she's still at the hospital, visiting hours will be over."

Zane lifted a brow. "Seriously? You're a cop. You have her name, and you know what she looks like. It shouldn't take you more than a few minutes to pull her address out of the DMV database."

Brooks had already thought of that but wasn't sure that was the best thing to do. "Doesn't that seem kind of stalkerish?"

His friend considered that. "Okay, I see your point. Some people don't see the inherent romance in knowing how easy it is for Big Brother to track them down. You could always stop by the school in the morning before class."

"That could work, although I think I'll wait a couple days. You know, give her some time to deal with everything that happened."

Even as he said the words, something inside him revolted at the idea of waiting. Before he could examine it, the door opened. Instead of the guard escorting Oliver, a distinguished older man in an expensive suit walked in, a briefcase in his hand. Everything about the guy screamed lawyer.

The man gave him and Zane an appraising look as he sat down across from them. "William Cohen, attorney for Seth Oliver. I have a few things we need to go over before you talk to him."

"What kind of things?" Brooks asked.

Opening his briefcase, Cohen took out a document and a pen, then slid both across the table toward them.

"This meeting was scheduled at the insistence of my client and against my professional advice," Cohen continued. "For whatever reason, he's decided to talk to the two of you without me present. The only way I'll allow it is if you agree to everything in this document and sign it."

"Or?" Brooks prompted.

"Or I'll get one of my favorite judges on the phone and have my client committed for a psychiatric evaluation. If that happens, you won't be able to talk to him for a very long time—if ever. Because I think we all know Mr. Oliver is a deeply disturbed young man, and if he goes into the mental ward at the North Texas State Hospital, he's not going to come back out anytime soon."

Exactly how much did Cohen know? Brooks was confident in saying Oliver didn't hire the man, which meant Cohen almost certainly worked for the hunters. Did that mean he knew about werewolves? Considering how calm the man sitting across from them was, Brooks didn't think so.

"What are we signing?" he asked, sliding the document closer and scanning it.

Cohen gave them a small smile. "You're agreeing not to record this meeting or any that follow. In addition, you won't take notes of any kind, nor will anyone else be allowed to listen in from the observation room. And finally, any statements my client makes during this or any other meetings will be considered hypothetical, and nothing said in this room can be used against my client in a court of law in any way."

Zane's eyes narrowed. "Why would we agree to any of that rubbish?"

Cohen shrugged. "I have no idea. But my client assured me you would. Was he wrong?"

As a cop, Brooks knew he shouldn't sign it. But as a werewolf desperate for information on the hunters, he had no choice. They needed to know what was coming their way, and he'd pay any price to find out.

Biting back a growl, he signed the document on the line above his name, then handed Zane the pen. Zane hesitated but, after a moment, put his name to paper, then shoved it across the table to the lawyer. Cohen put the document and the pen back in his briefcase, then snapped it shut. Sliding back his chair, he got to his feet.

"Gentlemen." Giving them a nod, Cohen left, closing the door behind him.

"I'd feel better if we had something we could hold over Oliver's head when we talk to him," Zane muttered.

"I'm with you there," Brooks said.

Unfortunately, Oliver hadn't gotten into much trouble growing up in Rapid City, South Dakota. He had played sports in high school, then did three years in the army infantry, where he'd gone on deployment to Iraq. He had gotten out of the military shortly after that with an honorable discharge, then bounced around a few oil field and mining jobs before falling off the radar, only to show up in Dallas with a group of hunters.

"It would be even nicer if we could find a connection between Oliver and whoever is working with the hunters inside the department," Brooks added.

It was bad enough there were people who wanted to kill werewolves simply because of what they were. It was even worse knowing somebody in the Dallas Police Department was helping them. But when they'd attacked the medical center, Lana had overheard a phone conversation between one of the hunters and a man who knew where Zane was being treated, that she was there, and exactly how long it would take SWAT to move on the clinic. The only person who could know all that stuff was a cop.

But after weeks of digging into the background of every cop and department employee who'd ever looked at the team sideways, they had nothing to show for it.

They couldn't find a link between anyone in the department and Oliver or any of the hunters who'd been killed during the raid.

"It doesn't help that the feds are investigating the murders now," Brooks continued. Of course, they didn't know the victims were werewolves. They thought Oliver was a run-of-the-mill serial killer. "Becker is digging as deep as he can into Oliver's background, but he has to be careful not to let the FBI know what we're doing."

"So what, we play it safe and hope the next time the hunters show up, they don't kill one of us?" Zane snarled. "Or maybe we'll get lucky again, and they'll only cripple someone else."

Brooks didn't answer.

Beside him, Zane cursed. Lifting his good arm, he ran his hand through his dark hair. "Sorry. I'm just cross. I don't mean to take it out on you."

"Don't worry about it. We're Pack. I'm not going to patronize you and say I understand what you're going through, because I don't. None of us do. But your arm is going to heal. You just have to give it time."

Zane looked dubious but didn't argue. If he had, Brooks might have punched him. He and the rest of the Pack weren't giving up on Zane, and Brooks damn sure wasn't letting him give up on himself.

The thump of footsteps approaching the door put an end to any more conversation. Both he and Zane got to their feet as the door opened. Two beefy guards came in, leading Seth Oliver between them. Tall and wiry, Oliver had grown a beard since the last time Brooks had seen him, but he still had that same hatred in his eyes.

The guards moved him over to the table positioned

in the center of the room, then sat him down in the chair and attached the handcuffs he was wearing to the shackle point bolted on his side of the table. One of the guards yanked on it a few times to make sure it was secure, then looked at Brooks and Zane.

"The prisoner stays in cuffs the whole time," he said. "You aren't to give him anything. By anything, I mean no gum, no water, no pencils, no pens, no good luck charms—nothing. Understood?"

Brooks nodded. He and Zane didn't spend a lot of time talking to suspects in prison, but it wasn't like they were planning to get friendly with this guy. It was much more likely Zane would get mad and rip Oliver's head off. If that happened, Brooks would make sure to point out that the cuffs and shackles had stayed on throughout the process.

"We'll be down in the office at the end of the hall if you need us," the second guard said.

After giving Oliver's handcuffs one more look to make sure they were secure, the guards left the room and closed the door. Brooks listened to the echo of their footsteps as they disappeared down the hall.

Across from them, Oliver leaned back in his chair, regarding Zane with amusement. "Last time I saw you, you were stuffed in a fancy ice chest like a werewolf Popsicle. I thought you'd be dead by now for sure."

Zane growled, his eyes flashing gold as he half rose from his seat. Brooks reached out and grabbed his shoulder, urging him back down. Zane's entire body was tense, the anger pouring off him. Oliver had just come in, and Zane was already on the verge of losing it.

Not that Brooks blamed him. Zane had been

unconscious during the attack at the medical center, something that ate at him as much as the injury to his arm. Not that he'd had any say in the matter. After getting hit with one of the hunter's poison bullets, Dr. Saunders—the only human who knew enough about werewolves to treat them—had put Zane into a hypothermic coma, dropping his body temperature down to dangerous levels in an attempt to slow his heart rate and limit the effects of the synthetic wolfsbane. It was the only reason Zane was still alive. Even so, he hated the fact that he hadn't been there to fight alongside the Pack during the raid.

On the other side of the table, Oliver regarded Brooks thoughtfully. "We figured you were the top dog of the group. Alpha, I'm guessing. You're the biggest, so it makes sense."

"We?" Brooks asked.

Oliver ignored the question. "We're still trying to figure out how the hell a big pack of you mutts can live and work this close together. All the previous werewolves we ran across were either high-strung, violent loners or small ones living in tiny packs. Then we found out there's a whole SWAT team filled with you freaks. When I saw you crashing through those doors in that clinic, throwing my guys around like they were toys, I knew right away you were the boss. You're the only one big enough to keep these other mutts in line."

Brooks could tell from how steady Oliver's heartbeat and respiration were that the man believed every word he said. The hunters genuinely knew nothing about werewolves. Those high-strung, violent loners Oliver described were almost certainly omegas, big strong werewolves who'd never experienced pack life and therefore tended to possess little control over their behavior and abilities. The smaller werewolves were betas. They weren't as physically strong as the alphas and omegas, but they were completely dialed-in and committed to their packs.

Brooks knew he'd never be able to explain a pack bond or the way that bond could keep even a group of big alphas like the Dallas SWAT team together. Oliver and the assholes he rolled with would never get that Brooks and his pack mates were closer than family.

Not that Brooks would tell the hunter any of that. The less they knew about werewolves the better. Because the truth was, those werewolves he'd talked about running into were probably dead now. Knowing how many innocent werewolves this guy had killed made Brooks want to reach across the table and twist his head off.

"What's this meeting about, Oliver?" Brooks demanded.

Oliver leaned forward, his shackles clinking against the table. "You know exactly what it's about. It's the same reason you agreed to come. We both want something the other has—information. And we both think we can get it without betraying our own."

"Then let's get to the point," Zane said, eyes flaring gold again. "Who do you work for?"

Oliver regarded Zane like he was something he'd scraped off his shoe. "Not the way it works, mutt. Think of this as the scene in *Silence of the Lambs*. I'm Hannibal Lecter, you're Clarice, and we're going to play a game of quid pro quo. You tell me something. I tell you something."

"We already told you Senior Corporal Brooks is the alpha of our pack," Zane pointed out. "That makes it your turn to tell us something."

Oliver's expression didn't change. "We both know I figured that one out on my own. So it's not my turn. But nice try…for a mutt."

Brooks extended his fangs and bared them at Oliver. He wasn't in the mood for this crap. "What do you want to know?"

"No reason to get hostile, big dog. My first question is simple. All I want to know is how the fuck this mutt is still alive?" Oliver gestured at Zane with his chin. "That wolfsbane bullet I put in his arm should have killed him in less than two hours, yet here he is, alive and kicking."

Brooks's claws came out to go along with the fangs. It was a struggle not to leap over the table and rip out Oliver's throat. Beside him, Zane looked like he had the same problem. As for Oliver, the asshole sat there smugly, like he knew they wouldn't dare touch him.

As much as Brooks hated to admit it, Oliver was right about that. They needed information on the hunters, and this prick—as irritating as he might be—had it. But that didn't mean Brooks was going to give a piece of intel this valuable away for nothing.

"And what exactly are you going to tell us in exchange for something this important?" he asked.

Oliver grinned. "You're just gonna have to wait and find out."

Brooks might be willing to play Oliver's stupid game, but he wasn't going to let the man dictate all the rules. Pushing back his chair, he got to his feet, then headed for the door. Zane followed.

"Hunters are sent out in teams of three to five guys," Oliver said, his voice urgent, like he didn't want them to leave. "Most of the teams—like the one I was with—are pretty much hired guns. We're well-paid killers, though we like to call ourselves independent contractors instead."

Now they were getting somewhere. Brooks stopped and turned back to see Oliver looking at him expectantly. He'd give almost anything to know who the hell hired these independent contractors, but he knew there was no chance Oliver was going to tell him something like that right off the bat.

"How many of these teams are there?" he asked instead.

Oliver relaxed, leaning back in his chair. "I can't really give you a concrete answer. The teams get a text or email with the location of a possible werewolf and a dollar figure. If we find the mutt and exterminate it, we get paid. But I've crossed paths with half a dozen other teams over the years. I'm guessing there are probably more." He gestured to the seats across from him. "Quid pro quo, remember? How did the mutt survive that bullet?"

Brooks glanced over at Zane before moving back to the table. His pack mate joined him, his eyes still flashing in anger, but apparently willing to see where this went.

Brooks had no intention of telling the hunter that Dr. Saunders and members of their extended pack had come up with an antidote to the wolfsbane poison. Or that they'd used that antidote to create a vaccine to make werewolves immune to that poison. But considering how little Oliver seemed to know about werewolves, he hoped he wouldn't have to.

"Alphas can cure members of their pack from nearly any affliction, if they're strong enough," Brooks said.

"How?" Oliver demanded.

"I bite them." He let his fangs slide out. "If they survive being turned again, whatever wounds or sickness they had before that point is healed."

While Oliver looked back and forth between him and Zane curiously, Brooks jumped in with his next question before the man could look for holes in the BS story he fed him.

"How did you become a hunter?"

Brooks didn't give a crap about Oliver's life story, but his gut told him he'd get more out of the guy if he worked him slowly.

Across from him, Oliver chuckled and leaned forward, his face lighting up. "That's my favorite story. I used to tell it to my buddies all the time, and it never got old."

Brooks had the feeling he and Zane weren't going to be nearly as thrilled with it. "We're listening."

Oliver grinned. "I was in this bar in Tulsa when this fight broke out between this big ugly guy and a few other dudes. I didn't know it at the time, but that ugly guy was a werewolf. And those other dudes? They were hunters. Gotta tell you, it was one awesome fight. Well, right up to the point when I shoved a broken bottle in the mutt's neck. I remember it like it was yesterday."

His eyes took on a dreamy look, like he was reliving the whole thing as he told them the story in excruciating detail.

Chapter 5

"HAVE WE GOTTEN ANYTHING ON THIS NEW PLAYER IN charge of the gangs yet?" Brooks asked.

He was in the training room at the SWAT compound, along with Diego, Connor, Trey, Remy, Ray, and the rest of the task force. Up until today, they'd held all their other meetings at police headquarters downtown. But with the media crawling all over the shootings at the warehouse, it was impossible to get anywhere near HQ without getting a microphone or camera shoved in their faces.

It had been twenty-four hours since the raid on the east side warehouse, and they were still trying to figure out who was behind the murders.

On the other side of the conference table, Ray shook his head. "Afraid not."

Brooks frowned. "How can that be? This guy had four people executed. And none of the gangbangers we arrested are talking?"

"I took another run at them this morning," Ray said with a scowl. "Nothing."

"What about the streets?" Brooks asked. "There has to be somebody associated with this new guy who'll talk. Half the city should know his name by now."

"You'd think so, but that's part of the problem." Ray spread his hands. "Whoever this new boss is, he's not playing by the normal gang rules. And everyone on the street is lining up to follow his lead. Nobody is talking to us, and the people we arrested are willing to go to prison rather than cross this new guy."

Brooks cursed. Ray was right. Gangs could be vicious and cutthroat in dealing with each other, but none of them liked the cops. It was ingrained into their DNA. No matter how bad it got out on the streets, no matter how many of their fellow gang members got wiped out, few of them would ever turn to the cops for help.

They went around the room, getting updates from each gang unit and narcotics officer present. When it was his turn, Rodriguez mentioned that fentanyl had disappeared off the street overnight.

"So, what the hell are we going to do about it?" Remy asked.

Ray sighed. "Look, I know you'd all love to figure out a quick, simple way to deal with this gang war, but the bottom line is that it's been going on long before we all got on the job and will go on long after we walk away from it. If we want to do something about what happened in that warehouse and catch the guy responsible, we're going to have to figure out who he is and what he's planning. The only way we'll do that is with good old-fashioned police work. Let's get the hell out there and find a lead."

There were grunts of agreement around the table. Rodriguez and the other members of the task force left a little while afterward, a sense of determination about them that hadn't been there at the start of the meeting. Ray always knew how to get his people motivated. But as Brooks stood and watched his old friend slowly wipe down the whiteboard at the front of the room, he couldn't miss the furrow between his brow.

"What's wrong?" Brooks asked after his pack mates

left. "And don't try telling me it's nothing. We've been friends for a long time, and I can tell when something's bothering you."

"Chief Curtis paid me a visit this morning," Ray said softly without turning around. "He's not too thrilled with how things turned out at the warehouse. Times are changing, and the department is under a lot of pressure to somehow fix the gang problem. He suggested maybe it's time for someone else to take over the gang unit. Someone with new ideas."

"Screw him," Brooks growled. "You've got over thirty-five years on the force with a list of citations longer than your arm. He might be the chief, but he can't force you out of your unit without reason."

Ray set the eraser on the tray along the bottom of the board, then turned around to give him a sad smile. "Maybe that's true. If I wanted to fight it."

Brooks stared. "Why wouldn't you fight it?"

Ray pulled out a chair and sat down with a heavy sigh. "Jayden, I've been doing this for a long time, fighting the good fight and all that crap. But no matter what I do or how much I do it, things don't get any better. Gangs are worse than they ever were, and kids are joining them younger and younger, screwing up their lives before they even start."

"What are you saying?"

The man took a deep breath and let it out slowly. "I'm saying I'm tired, Jayden, and I think maybe it's time for me to step back."

That was bullshit. Brooks opened his mouth to tell Ray as much, but Becker stuck his head in the door. "Hey, Brooks. You got a visitor in the admin building."

"Not right now," Brooks said over his shoulder. "I'm busy."

"I know. But you're going to want to see this person."

Brooks spun around to tell his pack mate to screw off, but Ray interrupted him. "Go on and take care of business." He got to his feet. "We can talk later."

"Just don't do anything stupid before we talk, okay?"

Ray slid some papers across the table and stuck them in a manila folder. "Don't worry about me, Jayden. I'll be fine."

Brooks frowned. "Promise me. Nothing stupid."

He gave Brooks a small smile. "You know me, kid. Do I ever do anything stupid?"

That wasn't really an answer, but Ray was already heading out the door.

Brooks glared at Becker. "So, who's this visitor, and why couldn't they wait?"

Becker grinned. "You'll see."

Brooks resisted the urge to growl as he followed Becker out the door. Halfway down the hallway, they ran into Mike and the Pack's newest member, Rachel. Khaki Blake, the team's only other female member, was with them. They were talking about the demanding physical training program Gage ran and how everyone had to share the open-bay showers in the other building.

"The guys always let me go first, then blame me for using all the hot water," Khaki said with a grin.

"They won't have to worry about that with me," Rachel said in a lyrical Southern twang. "I'm in and out of the shower and dressed in fifteen minutes."

Mike glanced at Brooks. "You met Rachel, right?"

"Yeah, but just barely."

Actually, he hadn't done much more than wave in her direction as he'd headed out on one of the gang task force operations. The moment she'd walked in, the single guys had immediately wondered if she was *The One* for someone in the Pack, like Khaki was for Xander Riggs, the team's other squad leader. But Rachel had taken a quick look around, told them they weren't her type, and that was the end of that. She might find her soul mate someday, but it wasn't going to be anyone in SWAT.

"How's the in-processing going?" Brooks asked.

Rachel made a face. "Not bad. I just hate wasting time filling out forms when I could be helping you guys deal with the hunters. Mike told me that you and Zane spent time last night interrogating one of them?"

Brooks winced. "I'm not sure if I'd call it an interrogation. More like a torture session—for Zane and me. Oliver went into great detail about the werewolves he'd tracked down and killed. I think he gets off on telling the stories."

Rachel shook her head. "This guy sounds like a complete chucklefuck. Did y'all get anything useful out of him?"

Brooks wasn't exactly sure what a chucklefuck was, but he was willing to trust her opinion on the matter. "We know the hunters don't know much of anything about werewolves, that most of them are nothing more than paid assassins who care little about who they kill as long as they get paid, and that they get their orders from someone who seems to have an almost endless supply of money."

Mike frowned. "Any idea who they're working for? Or at least where he might be located?"

"No. Oliver is being pretty cagey about what he tells us. We have another meeting with him in two days, so I'm hoping we'll learn more then."

Khaki was saying something about never having the patience to talk to someone like Oliver when Zane stuck his head in the front door. "Brooks, there's someone waiting to see you." He looked at Becker. "Didn't you tell him?"

Becker shrugged. "I told him."

Whoever it was, they must be damn important, Brooks thought. Nodding at his pack mates, he headed for the door.

"Who is it?" he asked Zane as his friend walked into the building as he walked out.

"Go see for yourself," Zane said.

Were his pack mates intentionally trying to piss him off?

Brooks was still steaming when he reached the admin building and jerked open the door, expecting to see some bureaucrat from police headquarters. But the moment he got inside and picked up a familiar scent, he forgot all about the pencil pushers at HQ. He quickened his step, heading for the bullpen, when a certain dark-haired, curvy teacher walked out. Dressed in jeans, knee-high brown boots, and a leather coat belted at the waist, she looked just as beautiful as he remembered. She had her hair up in a ponytail today. He'd been right. It was long.

"Selena?" He stopped where he was, mesmerized by the sight of her. "What are you doing here?"

"I never got a chance to thank you for saving my life yesterday," she said. "I didn't even get to properly introduce myself, though it seems you already know my name."

There was a primal part of him that wanted to pull her into his arms and kiss her until neither of them could breathe. The urge was so strong, he had to ball his hands into fists at his sides to keep from giving in.

"My commander told me your name before I went into the school to rescue you," he said as he unclenched his fist in time to shake the hand she offered. Her hand was small in his, her skin warm and soft against his rough palm, and he didn't want to let it go. "Since you're here, I guess that means you already know my name, too. Doesn't mean we can't do this right, though. Jayden Brooks."

She gave him a smile that made his knees weak. "Selena Rosa. I'd really like to thank you for saving my life."

He leaned closer so he could inhale more of her intoxicating scent. He wasn't sure how it was possible, but she smelled even better than she had yesterday. Then, there'd been fruity flowers. Today, there was a hint of spice thrown in. The scent was like nothing he'd ever smelled before, yet familiar at the same time. He thought at first she was simply wearing a different perfume, but when he took a deeper breath, he knew that wasn't it. He was smelling her pheromones, and his inner wolf was getting drunk on them.

He forced himself to release her hand so she wouldn't think he was a weirdo. "Don't think I'm complaining when I say this, but you didn't have to come all the way out here to thank me. You could have just called."

Selena's dark eyes danced as she held up one finger. "Hold that thought."

Brooks's wolf half wanted to chase her the moment

she turned and hurried into the bullpen, and it was all he could do to stay where he was. Selena came out a moment later, an enormous aluminum foil pan in her hands. He thought he smelled chocolate, but he couldn't be sure, since his nose was still filled with her scent.

"If I hadn't come in person, how would I have brought these?" she asked.

Grinning, she held out the pan. Brooks glanced down at the thick, gooey brownies inside. Selena might look and smell even better than the chocolate goodness she'd brought, but Brooks never turned his nose up at food. She was damn near overwhelming, but brownies were brownies.

And now he had an image of Selena lying naked on a bed with pieces of brownies scattered all over, from those perfect breasts to the juncture of her thighs. He immediately went hard at the thought.

In an attempt to push the mind-numbing vision out of his head, Brooks took one of the brownies—cut adult-sized, not those little kid-sized snack squares you had to eat half a dozen of—and took a bite.

"Wow," he moaned as it melted in his mouth. He'd eaten a lot of brownies in his life, but these were on a whole different level. If he weren't in polite company, he would have shoved the whole thing in his mouth at once. "This is amazing."

Selena laughed, tilting her head back so she could look up at him. It struck him then how petite she really was. She barely reached his shoulder. "I'm glad you like it. I would have made something special, but I thought it was more important to give you a gift of my gratitude now rather than wait until I could run to the store and grab all the stuff I needed."

"Special?" he mumbled as he took another bite. "These seem pretty special to me."

She waved her hand. "These are nothing. I just threw them together at the last minute because I wanted to make sure I got here before you went home."

Brooks didn't know what to say to that. Not that he could have said much anyway, his mouth was so full. If this was an example of what Selena could throw together at the last minute, he couldn't imagine what it would be like when she took her time. Instant foodgasm, maybe?

His head went straight to thoughts of brownies, orgasms, and Selena all at the same time, and he hardened in his uniform pants again. *Shit*. He needed to get his act together before he started humping her leg right there.

He ate the rest of the brownie, then started to lick his fingers before stopping himself. He gave her a sheepish look. "Sorry. I usually don't inhale food like that. But that was seriously the best brownie I've ever eaten."

Selena laughed again. "No apology necessary. I never mind watching a man enjoy himself."

Brooks was considering whether to lick the rest of his fingers clean when the innuendo in her words suddenly dawned on him. He looked up sharply, only to see her regarding him with a sweet, if amused, expression, as if butter wouldn't melt in her mouth. Then he caught a glint in her eyes—a lightning-quick flash of coyness— that had him closing the few feet of distance between them. He truthfully had no idea what he was going to do once he got there, but he'd figure it out.

"So, are you going to share any of those brownies with the rest of us or just hog them all for yourself?"

Brooks stopped in midstep to find pack mate and fellow SWAT officer Landry Cooper leaning casually against the doorjamb of the bullpen, a grin on his face that implied he knew exactly what the hell he'd interrupted. No shock there. Every werewolf in the building had no doubt heard him and Selena talking. Smelled them, too, which was a disconcerting thought, since Brooks had no doubt he was putting off buckets of arousal pheromones right then.

Of course, Cooper was the only one irritating enough to actually stick his nose in.

"I wasn't planning on it," Brooks said, giving Cooper a grin. "Selena only brought enough for me. Too bad, because they're really good."

Cooper opened his mouth to reply, but Selena interrupted him with a laugh.

"Of course, there are enough to share." She gave Brooks a reproving look. "You'd get sick if you tried to eat all these brownies."

Brooks wanted to complain, but it wasn't like he could point out that werewolves could eat anything and everything they wanted without it ever affecting them. Instead, he had no choice but to stand there and watch as Selena took out a brownie, then handed the pan to Cooper.

"Could you make sure the other SWAT officers who were at the school get some of these?" she asked Cooper. "I want to let them know how much I appreciate what they did, too."

"I'll definitely do that. And I'll make sure they know

how much Brooks was thinking about them, too,"
Cooper added, giving Brooks a grin.

Luckily, Selena had her back to Brooks, so she
couldn't see the rude gesture he made in Cooper's direction, which was a good thing, since she'd probably be
shocked. The guy might be like a brother to him, but that
only meant he could sometimes be as irritating as one.
Cooper just made a show of sniffing the brownies and
walked back into the bullpen with a chuckle.

"Don't worry," Selena said, coming over to hand
Brooks the brownie she'd saved. "I can bring you
another batch if you want."

He bit into the brownie. "You can bring me these
things anytime you want."

"If you're planning to come back with more," Cooper
called from the other room, "I'll take a few dozen, if
you're taking orders. I'll even pay you for them."

Selena laughed.

"Want to head over to one of the other buildings?"
Brooks asked. "So we can talk without constantly being
interrupted."

That earned him a chuckle from Cooper and the rest
of his pack mates in the bullpen.

"Sounds good to me," Selena said.

Brooks popped the rest of the brownie into his mouth
as he led her outside, then across the compound into the
training building, hoping Mike, Rachel, and his other
teammates weren't there. Fortunately, they weren't.

The dayroom was big enough for the whole SWAT
team to fit, as well as their extended pack, which was a
good thing, since it was growing in leaps and bounds.
In addition to the two couches and coffee table, there

were beanbag chairs and a sweet big-screen TV. Since it was the holiday season, there was also a Christmas tree with all the trimmings. Brooks gestured to one of the couches, then sat down beside her.

"I'm glad we got a chance to talk in private," she said. "I wanted to ask if you got injured in the rescue but wasn't sure if I should bring it up in front of everyone else. I know guys can get embarrassed when women ask questions like that around other men."

He was so distracted by the sexy curve of her hips as she crossed her legs that he almost missed what she'd said. "Injured? Nah."

"You weren't? Huh." She frowned, confusion clouding her eyes. "There was so much blood on my clothes, not to mention the floor, and when I realized it couldn't be Pablo's, I naturally assumed it was yours."

Brooks's first instinct was to say nothing. That was the standard response anytime someone outside the Pack saw something they shouldn't. But Selena looked so distressed, he had to tell her something.

"Oh, you must mean these." He gestured at the freshly healed scars on his forearm from both the small bullet hole up near his elbow and the larger incision he'd gotten when Trey had dug Pablo's bullet out of him. "I cut myself on a piece of glass picking you up. It was nothing."

Selena studied the scars, her eyes narrowing a little before she looked back at him. Brooks had no doubt she was trying to figure out how scars that looked like they were a week old could possibly have produced as much blood as she'd had on her clothes. When she stared him straight in the eyes for several long moments, he wondered if this was what her students felt like when they'd been caught lying. He held his breath, sure she was going to call him on it.

But instead, she nodded and broke eye contact. "I'm glad it wasn't anything more serious. You could have gotten shot shielding me like that."

He breathed a sigh of relief. "It was nothing. I was more worried about hurting you. I slammed into you pretty hard. I didn't break anything, did I?"

Selena shook her head. "No breaks, thank goodness. The doctor was worried I might have gotten a concussion, though. He could be right. My head was a little wonky last night for sure."

"Wonky?" It was his turn to frown. "What do you mean? Should you be out of the hospital?"

Brooks subconsciously moved closer, his heart beating faster at the thought that he'd hurt her. He was half a second away from sweeping her up into his arms and hauling ass for his truck to take her to the hospital.

Selena must have read his mind, because she stopped him with a smile and a gentle hand on his arm. "I'm okay…really. I'll admit my heart rate was all over the place when I was there, and I had a fever nobody could explain, but thankfully, everything went back to normal. As it turns out, the doctor decided my symptoms weren't related to anything physical."

"What was it then?"

She took her hand away from his arm as she shrugged. "He seemed to think I'm dealing with post-traumatic stress."

A part of Brooks was relieved Selena wasn't physically injured, but at the same time, he was worried. PTSD wasn't anything to mess around with. He'd known a lot of good cops who'd lost their jobs, their families, and sometimes more because they'd gone through a rough situation they'd never been able to get past.

"Have you thought of talking to someone about it?" he asked.

She sighed. "You sound like my principal and vice principal. They want me to talk to somebody, too. In fact, they've essentially kicked me out of my class for the rest of the week, so I can take time off to recover. Whatever the heck that means."

"Selena, this is serious," Brooks said. "Someone tried to kill you. It's normal to be affected by something like that. Normal to feel confused, scared, and freaked out as hell. It's also completely normal to sit down and talk with someone about it."

Her shoulders sagged. "I know. And to be honest, I am a bit freaked out by everything that happened—the parts I can remember anyway. But honestly, I'm not sure who I'd even talk to about something like this. I don't know if I could walk into a therapist's office and open up to someone I've never met. My grandmother is the only family I have left, but I don't want to worry her any more than she already is after what happened yesterday." Selena thought a moment. "I suppose I could talk to my priest, but he's such a gentle soul that I'm not sure I could bring myself to tell him all the things I was feeling in the classroom when Pablo was waving that gun around."

"You could always talk to me," he said softly. "I mean, I know you just met me, but at least you don't have to fill me in on all the details, since I was there with you. And I do a pretty good job of listening, if I do say so myself."

That gorgeous smile returned. "Well, since it seems like I have the rest of the week off whether I want it or not, maybe we could get together and talk over lunch?"

"Lunch would work," he agreed. "But how about dinner instead? If you're comfortable with that, I mean."

Selena didn't answer. *Crap.* Had he completely misread the situation? It hit him then that he'd never even considered the possibility she might have a boyfriend… or a girlfriend, for that matter. But then he heard her heart thump a little harder and realized she was definitely intrigued by the suggestion.

"I'll consider dinner," Selena said slowly, her lips curving in a surprisingly sultry way. "But only if you come to my place."

Brooks certainly didn't mind going to her place, but he was a little taken aback by the invitation. Then he picked up a very distinct scent filling the room. *Damn.* If he didn't know better, he'd swear she was getting aroused. Which immediately got him going, too. The image of him humping her leg came roaring right back.

Down, boy.

"Are you good in the kitchen?" he asked.

Selena gave him a look that suggested she knew exactly what she was doing to him. "I'm good in every room of my place."

He chuckled, loving the unexpected flirty banter, especially when her face heated up, making him think she'd been more shocked by the words than he had. "Well, in that case, dinner at your place it is. Tonight work for you?"

She hesitated, and again he was struck by the idea that this wasn't the way she normally behaved. But then she took a deep breath and nodded her head. "Tonight sounds good. Eight o'clock?"

"Perfect."

They talked a little while longer…and flirted a bit in between exchanging phone numbers, too. Every once in a while, he'd pick up the tantalizing scent of her arousal. But now, it was mixed with the one he'd picked up when he'd first walked into the admin building. He tried to get his head around the amazingly complex aroma. It was equal parts delicate flowers, exotic spices, and something feminine and uniquely Selena.

He couldn't believe how different her scent was today from yesterday. It was almost like he was smelling a different woman.

But no matter what Selena smelled like, Brooks couldn't deny how strongly her scent affected him. Some of the guys in the Pack had experienced this sensory sensation before, and in every case, it involved stumbling across *The One*.

Did Selena's amazing scent mean she was his soul mate, a woman he'd known for all of thirty minutes? His head spun at the idea. Not because he didn't believe in the idea of finding *The One*. It was simply that he'd never expected it to happen. He'd tried a long-term relationship once, and it had failed spectacularly. After that, he'd stopped trying.

But if Selena was *The One*, that would all change, right?

He was still wrestling with those thoughts when Selena stood up. "I'd better get to the store and pick up some stuff for dinner if I'm going have everything ready by eight."

"You know you don't need to do anything fancy, right?" He flashed her a grin as they walked to the door. "I'd be happy with another tray of brownies."

Selena laughed. "You know, I think you mean that. But putting together a good meal isn't work for me. I love to cook. It's what I do for the important people in my life. Like you."

Brooks gazed down at her, suddenly robbed of speech. Selena slowly ran the tip of her tongue over her lips, leaving a moist sheen behind that made his gums tingle as his fangs threatened to slip out. He leaned in to kiss her, when suddenly, the door jerked open.

Brooks shot out a hand and caught Selena before she could fall, but that didn't keep her from blushing as Khaki and Rachel stood there with knowing looks on their faces. There were some introductions, a few apologies, and a lot of laughter as Selena got her feet back under her.

Neither of them spoke as Brooks walked her to her car. When they got there, Selena opened her door before turning to him with a smile.

"I'll see you tonight."

The urge to kiss her was still there, but he held himself in check and returned her smile instead. "I'll be there."

As Brooks watched Selena's car disappear down the street, he replayed the moment right before Khaki and Rachel had opened the door and interrupted them. The thought of Selena's luscious lips had him thinking about all kinds of things a couple normally didn't do on a first date.

"She's nice," Rachel said, coming up behind him. "Y'all going to see each other again?"

Brooks started to answer but then stopped himself as he caught that almost familiar smell again. Even though she'd already left, Selena's scent lingered in the air, surrounding him.

He turned and gave Rachel a sniff, then Khaki. Their scents weren't exactly the same as Selena's, but they were damn similar.

Khaki frowned. "Everything okay?"

"Do you smell that?" he asked. "Selena's scent in the air?"

Rachel and Khaki tipped up their noses, testing the air. Rachel didn't seem to be getting it yet, but from the way Khaki's eyes suddenly widened, she'd picked it up. No surprise there. Khaki had the best nose in the Pack.

"I smell…something," Khaki said, closing her eyes and opening her mouth a little to take short, panting breaths. "She almost smells like one of us, but it's not quite right. The scent is…strange."

Brooks's heart began to beat faster. "It's not just the scent that's strange. When I rescued her yesterday, Selena didn't smell like this. She smelled good—great even—but not like this."

"That's not possible," Rachel said. "People don't change the way they smell overnight."

"Actually, they can," a deep voice said from behind them.

Brooks turned to find Gage standing there. "What do you mean?"

"That extremely subtle but familiar scent you're

picking up is a woman going through the first day of her change."

"Are you sure?" Brooks demanded. "I mean, she didn't get shot or stabbed or anything like that. How could she become a werewolf?"

"You know as well as I do that she doesn't have to go through a life-threatening event. Just a traumatic one," Gage said. "Having one of her own students try to kill her is pretty damn traumatic."

Brooks knew all of that, of course. He just wasn't thinking straight. His head was swimming with the realization that Selena was turning into a werewolf. The beautiful woman he'd almost kissed a few minutes earlier, the same one who smelled so damn good, it was hard to even stand near her without wanting to bury his face in her hair and breathe her in, was going to be a werewolf like him.

He wanted to be thrilled but wasn't. This was the absolute worst time to be a werewolf in Dallas. If hunters found out, she'd be marked for death.

But beyond the fear he felt at the prospect of Selena becoming a target for the hunters, there was something else that struck him even harder. Not ten minutes ago, he'd assumed her scent had his head spinning because she was *The One* for him. Now, he wasn't sure. It was just as likely his reaction was simply an alpha werewolf taking notice of a woman about to go through her change. She probably smelled the same way to everyone in the Pack with a nose good enough to pick it up. That knowledge disappointed the hell out of him. Damn. It had only been for a few minutes, but he'd gone and let himself start thinking she could be *The One*. It seemed he was wrong.

None of this changed the fact Selena was about to go through something that was going to rock her entire world and that it would be tough on her. It had been that way for him and every member of the Pack when it happened.

"How do we handle this?" he asked Gage. "I'm meeting her for dinner in a few hours. Should I tell her?"

"What, that she's a werewolf?" Gage lifted a brow. "Somehow, I don't see that going over very well. *By the way, you're a werewolf. Could you pass the butter?*"

Brooks grimaced as Khaki and Rachel snorted in amusement. Okay, something else he should have known…if he wasn't so frigging addled by all this.

"You're the one who saved her life, Brooks, so you're the best person to tell her," Gage said. "Just remember, there's no need to rush. Since there wasn't a major injury involved, it will take at least a few weeks before Selena starts noticing the effects of the change. That gives you time to break it to her gently. You just need to find the right time—and the right way—to tell her."

Chapter 6

"IT'S NOT A COMPLICATED QUESTION, SELENA," ERNESTO said. "All I asked is whether this is dinner with a friend or a date?"

"Oh, it's definitely a date," Becca murmured. "With a dress like that, it's definitely a date."

Ernesto and Becca had stopped by after work to make sure she was doing okay on her first full day of forced downtime, but the moment they'd figured out she had a date, their interest had been piqued. Since then, they'd been peppering her with all kinds of questions, trying to see where this thing with Jayden was going.

Selena glanced down at the little black dress she was wearing when Ernesto stepped closer, then leaned in and took a sniff.

"I think you're right," he said, glancing at Becca. "She's wearing that expensive perfume you bought her for her birthday, the stuff you promised would make men swoon over her."

"Hey!" Selena pushed Ernesto away with a laugh. "I always wear nice perfume."

Becca gave her a knowing look. "Honey, there's perfume you wear to smell nice, and then there's perfume you wear to smell *nice*. The stuff you have on now is definitely in the second category."

Selena threw her hands up in defeat. "Okay, so I put

on my best perfume and a fancy dress. What's wrong with that?"

The words had come out sharper than she intended, and Selena immediately regretted them. Maybe she did need to talk to somebody about what had happened to her. Because she definitely wasn't acting like herself. Fortunately, neither one of her friends took offense at her tone.

Ernesto smiled. "Nothing is wrong with it. I'm just not sure what I think of my girl going on a date with a cop. It feels like I should be against that idea."

She laughed and thumped him on the shoulder. Even though he was out of the gangs now, he still liked to act like he was a badass from the streets. "Even if he's a cop who saved my life?"

He snorted. "That's the only reason I'm even considering it. But I'm telling you, he better be nice to you, or I'm going to go medieval all over his ass."

Selena was about to tell him that line would have sounded a lot tougher if he hadn't stolen it from a movie. But before she could get the jab out, the doorbell rang. She knew it was Jayden without even needing to look through the keyhole.

"Okay, you two." She gave her friends a warning glare as she headed for the door. "Be nice."

The expressions of mock disbelief they both sent her way almost made her laugh out loud. She stopped herself, focused on answering the door and greeting her date. Yeah, tonight was about having dinner. But her friends had been right about one thing. This was definitely a date.

The sexual chemistry between her and Jayden had

been impossible to miss earlier today at the SWAT compound. It had also been impossible to explain. She'd been around a lot of men she thought of as attractive, but none of them had ever affected her like the big SWAT cop. As crazy as it sounded, she'd gotten aroused from simply being in the same room with him. If he'd actually kissed her, they might still be making out.

Selena almost laughed. Who was she kidding? She'd been ready to rip his clothes off and have mad monkey sex with him right there on the couch in the dayroom. It was like she was a hormonal teenager again.

When she reached the door, she hesitated. She could almost feel Brooks on the other side of it. In some bizarre way, it was like she knew exactly where he was standing, could sense his patience as he waited for her to answer the door. Even weirder, she had a sneaking suspicion he knew exactly where she was standing, too.

Smiling, Selena opened the door, ready to greet him. But the words got stuck in her throat the moment she saw Jayden. He was wearing jeans, work boots, and an untucked button-down, the sleeves rolled up to show off muscled forearms. It was difficult to believe, but he looked even better now than he had in his uniform—and he'd looked hot as hell.

Her gaze worked its way up to his face again, taking in the strong lines of his jaw, outlined with a trim beard to match his mustache, the sparkle of mischief in his blue-gray eyes, and the perfect lips that had almost touched hers earlier today. Her pulse skipped a beat, a little quiver of excitement running through her.

Crap. She'd just met him at the door and already

wanted to jump him. What the holy cheese and crackers was wrong with her?

"Hey, there," he said, flashing her a sexy grin. "I'm not too early, am I?"

"Actually, you're right on time," she said, finally finding her voice. "Come on in."

Selena picked up the fragrance of Jayden's cologne as he stepped inside the entryway, and it was all she could do to keep her hands to herself. How was it possible for a man to smell this good? She was so intent on his mouthwatering scent, she almost didn't see the tall, colorful gift bag in his hands. It was tied at the top with a silver ribbon, the neck of a wine bottle sticking out.

"You didn't need to bring anything," she said as she closed the door. "I invited you here for dinner, which kind of implies I'm responsible for supplying the food and beverage."

Jayden shrugged. "It wouldn't have been right not to bring something. I wasn't sure what you were serving for dinner, but I took a guess and brought a bottle of red. It was either that or go with Cooper's suggestion, and that's never a good idea."

She smiled at the mention of Jayden's roguish teammate from back at the compound. She'd gotten the feeling Cooper was like one of the many pranksters in her class, always causing trouble but usually with the best of intentions. "I hesitate to even ask."

"He thought I should show up with the empty aluminum pan you brought the brownies in today, so you'd get the hint and bring it back full."

She laughed, taking the bottle of wine and motioning him forward where her friends were waiting impatiently in the living room. She made the introductions, then went into the kitchen to check on the dinner. Becca joined her a few seconds later. Her back to Jayden and Ernesto, who were chatting in the living room, she made a show of fanning herself with her hand.

"Girl, he's even bigger up close," her friend whispered. "Do you think he's that big all over?"

Selena rolled her eyes, unable to help laughing. She'd actually been wondering the same thing herself. She just wasn't bold enough to say the words out loud. But man, was her overactive imagination filling in all kinds of details right then.

"I've always thought Ernesto was a big guy," Becca added, looking out at the two men over the island that separated the kitchen and living room. "But Jayden makes him look small in comparison. How do you end up attracting all the big stud muffins?"

Selena snorted as she checked on the taco bake and sweet corn tomalito that were warming in the oven. Satisfied they weren't drying out, she closed the door and glanced over at Jayden and Ernesto. While they were both big, tough-looking guys, Jayden probably had a good thirty pounds worth of muscle on her friend, but Ernesto still had that dangerous street edge to him. Neither were the kind of men anyone would want to mess with.

"For one thing," she said, "Ernesto isn't a big stud muffin. He's a friend. And for another, it's not like I did anything to attract Jayden's attention, other than have someone shoot at me."

Becca stared longingly at the guys for a moment, making Selena wonder whether her friend was seriously considering the value of getting involved in a shoot-out in order to meet someone like Jayden.

"You know, Ernesto isn't dating anyone," Selena pointed out. "There's absolutely no reason the two of you couldn't give it a shot."

Her friend shook her head. "I'm not his type."

Selena opened her mouth to ask what the heck that meant, but the guys wandered over before she could. Jayden didn't look pissed off, so Ernesto mustn't have tried to interrogate him about what his intentions were. That was good. She wouldn't want to have to get in the middle of the two of them going at each other.

"You ready to get out of here, Ernesto?" Becca asked, picking up her purse and coat from the couch where she'd tossed them earlier.

"I guess we don't have a choice," Ernesto said as he helped Becca into her coat. "Unless Selena wants to invite us to stay for dinner."

Becca grabbed Ernesto's arm and pulled him toward the door. "Come on, time to go. If you're that hungry, you can take me out to dinner if you want."

He laughed. "I was just kidding about hanging around. I have a late night planned at the office, so rain check on that dinner?"

Becca shot Selena a look that said *I told you so* as she and Ernesto walked out. Selena sighed. It looked like Becca was just as firmly in Ernesto's friend zone as Selena was. Too bad. They'd make a cute couple.

She turned to Jayden to see him leaning back against the counter, his arms crossed over his muscular chest.

"Something smells really good in here," he said, his low, deep voice making heat swirl in her tummy.

"Yeah, the food is almost ready," she answered.

His dark eyes smoldered. "I wasn't talking about the food."

The heat in her tummy slowly migrated south, pooling between her thighs. Something Jayden was completely aware of, if the smile he gave her was any indication.

"Thanks for helping with the salad," Selena said, peeking around his shoulder and watching him work. "But I'm almost afraid to ask, where'd you learn how to handle a knife like that?"

Brooks chuckled as he peeled another carrot, then made a quick series of julienne cuts to turn it into long, slim pieces slightly bigger than matchsticks. "I'd love to tell you I picked up my knife skills in the CIA or someplace cool like that, but to be truthful, my mom taught me. She loves all those cooking shows on TV and makes me watch them with her every time I visit."

When Selena didn't say anything, Brooks turned his head to see her standing beside him with a stunned expression. "What, did I just blow your whole image of me by admitting that?"

She shook her head. "Not at all. I'm just trying to figure out how you could possibly get any better. You're attractive, heroic, show up for our date on time, bring wine, help me make dinner, and now I find out you visit your mother. It's enough to make a girl wonder what kind of deep, dark secrets you're hiding behind those captivating eyes of yours, because nobody's that perfect."

He could think of one deep, dark secret he was definitely hiding that he'd love to tell her about, but he resisted the urge. Selena wasn't ready for something like that yet. Then again, was she likely to handle it any better after dinner? For that matter, was it going to be any easier for her to take three days from now?

Probably not. But like Gage had said, it was up to Brooks to figure out when and how to tell her. He only hoped he didn't screw it up.

"Trust me, I'm far from perfect," he finally said with a little laugh as he finished cutting the carrot and added it to the salad. "Just ask the other members of my team. They'll be quick to point out all my faults and failures."

Selena leaned her hip against the island, her long hair falling over her shoulder as she gazed up at him with those beautiful dark eyes of hers. "You realize you're just making it worse, right?"

"What do you mean?"

It was kind of hard to think clearly when Selena was this close to him. The scent of arousal that had been coming off her since he'd first walked in the door was captivating. Brooks wasn't sure exactly what was going on, but he assumed it was some kind of subconscious reaction on her part. Maybe her inner werewolf taking notice of him as an alpha.

He'd considered slipping off to the bathroom to send a quick text to Khaki and ask if she knew why a female werewolf would put off pheromones like this but quickly decided against it. Mostly because he had no idea how he could possibly bring this subject up in a text to a woman, even if she was a member of his pack.

Selena continued to gaze up at him, eyes like two deep pools of melted chocolate. For a moment, he thought she might actually kiss him, but then she spoke.

"I've met lots of guys who think they're all that and go out of their way to tell every woman they meet. Yet here I am showering you with compliments, and all you can say is that you're far from perfect. Trust me, women like a man who's both sexy and humble."

Brooks snorted. "I'm not sure if many women out there would agree with you. If they did, I probably wouldn't still be single."

Selena shrugged, the movement doing amazing things to the cleavage exposed by the curve-hugging dress she wore. "I can't say for sure yet, since we just met, but something tells me the reason you're single is that you've been hanging out with women who don't know what they're looking for in a man—or wouldn't know it when they see it."

Brooks considered the single real relationship he'd had and the string of short-term failures and decided Selena was pretty spot-on. Most of the women he'd gone out with hadn't seemed to know what they wanted out of a relationship. Or they'd wanted something completely different than he did. On the flip side, he was man enough to admit he'd rarely known what he'd been looking for in a relationship, either.

Though that seemed to be changing quickly.

"How about you?" he asked. "Do you know what you're looking for in a man?"

Heat blazed up in her eyes, making them glint enough for him to think they might actually be glowing, but Selena leaned past him to pick up the salad bowls before he could be sure.

"I know exactly what I want," she said. "Come on. Let's go eat. You look hungry."

Turning, she headed for the table, her hips swaying hypnotically as she moved, her dress showing off just enough of her shapely legs to tease him. That, along with Selena's words, made him harden in his jeans and pulled a low, rumbling growl from his throat.

Oh yeah. He was hungry all right.

———

"Wait a minute," Selena said, a tortilla chip halfway to her mouth. "You played football for LSU? Were you any good? And don't try to be humble, because you know I'm going to Google you."

Brooks forced himself to tear his gaze away from Selena's luscious lips. The casserole she'd made, as well as the spicy bean and cheese dip, were delicious. But while the food was spectacular, the company was even better. When he wasn't mesmerized by the sound of her voice, he was enthralled by watching her eat. He absolutely loved the way her mouth moved.

"I was okay," he admitted. "I was a blocking fullback, so when I did my job right, all the crowd saw was the running back cutting through a wide-open gap in the line. I never got any of the limelight, but that was okay, and for two amazing seasons, I got to live out my dream. I even had a chance to play in the national championship in my sophomore year."

She gave him a questioning look. "Why two years?"

"Late in the third quarter of the championship game, I got caught up in the pile and completely blew out the ACL and MCL in my right knee. I never played football again."

Selena sat back in her chair, her face full of empathy. "I'm sorry about that."

Lots of people had said the words to him before, but few had genuinely meant it. Like when people said *good morning* without actually caring if your morning was good or not. But Selena was sincere.

He shrugged, reaching for another chip. "Don't be. Even though I lost my scholarship, I was still able to finish my degree. Besides, if I hadn't torn up my knee, I probably wouldn't have become a cop, which means I wouldn't have been there to save you. So, in essence, you owe your life to a bunch of clumsy, three-hundred-pound linemen who couldn't stay on their feet."

Selena picked up her wineglass and leaned forward in a toast. "Here's to fate then…and clumsy linemen. It seems they both worked together to put you in that classroom exactly when I needed you."

He clinked his glass against hers, very proud of himself for keeping his eyes focused on Selena's expressive gaze and not her cleavage. "To fate…and being at the right place at the right time."

As Brooks sipped his wine, he wondered if there was more to all this than fate. Gage always said there was nothing magical about turning into a werewolf. People who had a mutated gene buried in their DNA turned into werewolves if they went through a traumatic event. What kind of werewolf they became—alpha, beta, or omega—was based entirely on the specific circumstances of that traumatic event. Even the process of finding *The One* was probably nothing more than probability, chemistry, and werewolf genetics.

But at times like this, Brooks had to wonder if they were all wrong. Yeah, he'd been at the exact right place at the exact right time to save Selena's life. But it was pushing the boundaries of impossibility to think it had simply been good luck that she had shown up at the compound in time for him to recognize she was going through her change and that she'd need someone to help her through it.

It was enough to make a pragmatic man like Brooks start believing in a higher power, be it God or magic. Hell, maybe those were the same thing.

"What happened after football?" she asked. "How did you end up in law enforcement?"

Brooks didn't answer right away, his attention focused on Selena's mouth as she took another sip of wine. He especially liked the way the tip of her tongue slipped out to trace slowly across her lips, capturing a few stray drops of red liquid…along with his heart. It was possible she was doing it without knowing how sexy the move was. Then again, the sparkle he kept seeing in her eyes suggested she knew exactly what she was doing to him.

She was driving him crazy.

"Actually, being a cop was part of the plan all along. Well, maybe the backup plan." He shifted in his chair in a hopeless attempt to get more comfortable in jeans that were getting tighter by the minute. "Sure, I'd dreamed about making it to the NFL, but I was practical enough even back then to know the odds of that weren't very good. Blocking fullbacks weren't really in demand in the pros, so I was already well into my criminology program when the knee injury kind of made my decision for me."

She smiled. "Okay, so in addition to being strong, heroic, and dependable, we can also add practical to the list of your better qualities. You know, you really are getting more amazing by the minute."

Brooks chuckled. He liked the way she said exactly what she was thinking. It was nice being with a woman who didn't have a filter…or play games. "I don't think I've ever had a woman tell me that practical is a quality they look for in a man. Daring, bold, and confident, but never practical."

Selena lifted a brow, and damn, it was sexy as hell. Then again, she could probably cross her eyes and stick out her tongue, and that would work for him, too.

"Trust me, women like practical more than they'll admit. The first time they date a guy who can't hold a job for more than two weeks at a time or discover the man on the other side of the table at a restaurant doesn't have money to pay for dinner, practical suddenly becomes an extremely valuable trait."

"It sounds like you're speaking from experience," he said, though he had a hard time believing a woman as incredible as Selena would waste her time with deadbeats.

"I am," she admitted. "But we're not talking about me."

"We're not?" he countered.

"No," she said. "We were talking about how you and your practical self ended up in law enforcement. I can see having a backup plan beyond football, but why law enforcement? Is your father a cop?"

Brooks shook his head. "No. My dad wasn't a cop."

When he didn't continue, the smile slowly slipped from Selena's face. She reached across the table and covered his hand with hers. "Hey, I didn't mean to bring up bad memories. We can talk about something else if you want."

"It's okay," he said. "It was a long time ago."

Though sometimes it felt like just yesterday that he'd lost his father.

Selena regarded him with concern. How had they gone from sexy banter to awkward silence so fast?

"Gulfport had a really bad gang problem in the nineties," he said. "Hell, like most cities in this country, they still have a gang problem. But back in the midnineties, the crack cocaine epidemic was in full swing in Gulfport, with gangs selling it on nearly every corner of the projects where I lived. Lots of kids in the apartment building hung out on the corner with the gangbangers just so they could act cool. My parents, especially my dad, didn't put up with that kind of crap, and when he found out that one of my friends had gone down to the corner, he went to go bring him home. I went with him."

Brooks thought back to that night, remembering how his whole world had changed. "It happened so fast. I remember my dad being pissed and telling the gangbangers to get away from our apartment building. But then one of them pulled out a gun. He didn't even bother to threaten my dad. He just shot him in the heart, right there in front of all of us. And just like that, I didn't have a dad anymore." He swallowed hard. "My father died in my arms."

Selena's eyes filled with tears. "I'm so sorry, Jayden."

He nodded, not trusting himself to say anything.

"How old were you when it happened?" she asked.

He took a deep breath. "Fourteen."

The silence stretched out again, and they both turned their attention to the meal. He knew Selena wasn't going to ask any more questions, but he felt like he needed to finish the story anyway. Somehow, it seemed like she would understand.

"The cops showed up, and it was obvious that most of them could care less that there was one more poor person from the projects lying dead on the sidewalk," he said. "They asked a few questions about what happened, but they were only going through the motions, and everyone there knew it. Of course, no one saw a thing. But then Jack Walker showed up, and everything changed."

Brooks pushed what was left of the casserole on his plate around with his fork.

"He was just a county deputy, but the moment he arrived, it was obvious he was different. When he talked to the other cops, they listened. And when he talked to the people who lived in the apartment building, they listened, too."

Brooks thought back to that night and how amazed he'd been to see a cop like that. He remembered how Jack had sat down beside him on the curb and asked him in a serious, matter-of-fact voice whether he wanted his father's life to matter.

His father's death had been a turning point in his life. Meeting Jack Walker had been another.

"He wanted me to tell him exactly what happened and who killed my father," Brooks continued. "I didn't want to, because in my experience, few gangbangers ever went to prison. Even when they did, there was another gangbanger right there to take their place. It never ended, and I didn't want anyone coming after my mom."

"What did Jack say?" Selena asked.

"He told me that my father died because doing the

right thing had been important to him. It was now up to me to decide who I was going to be—the kind of man who looked the other way, or the kind who stood up and tried to make the world a better place. Like my father."

"That's a pretty heavy load to drop on the shoulders of a fourteen-year-old kid."

He shrugged. "Yeah, I guess it was. But sometimes events happen, and people have to grow up a lot faster than anyone wants to. In the end, I led Jack straight to the man who shot my father, then I pointed him out at the trial and sent him to jail for twenty years."

Selena's lips curved. "I probably shouldn't be surprised. It's not like you woke up yesterday morning and decided to be brave and fearless. You've been that way your whole life." When Brooks opened his mouth to argue, she cut him off with a glance. "We already talked about the whole humble thing, remember?"

Before he could agree to disagree—or even wonder how this tiny slip of a woman could shut him down with a single glance—she continued as if she hadn't even noticed the interruption. "I'm guessing Jack is the reason you became a cop?"

Brooks nodded. It felt like he was talking to a woman who'd known him for years instead of hours. "Yeah. He helped my mom find a better job, got us out of the projects, and got me into a better school. He's even the one who talked me into playing football and helped me get that scholarship to LSU."

"He sounds more like a saint than a cop."

"Pretty much," Brooks agreed. "He became like a second father to me. He even got me a job with the Harrison County Sheriff's Department in Gulfport after

I graduated. Ultimately, he's the reason I ended up on the Dallas SWAT team, too."

Selena's smiled broadened. "So, I guess I have someone else to thank for your appearance in my life. Besides a group of clumsy linemen, I mean."

He silently agreed, but now wasn't the time to talk about the other events that had led him from Gulfport to Dallas. Instead, he cleaned his plate, then reached for another helping only to discover they'd eaten every scrap of food on the table. Time had obviously gotten away from them while they'd talked about his journey from the projects of Gulfport to the dark-blue uniform of a DPD cop.

That was when he realized he and Selena hadn't talked about her at all. If he didn't know better, he'd think she'd skillfully manipulated the conversation to keep everything focused firmly on him. He wondered why she'd do something like that. Not that it mattered, since they now had the rest of the night to talk about someone much more interesting than he was.

He wiped his mouth and placed his napkin on the table beside his plate. "Dinner was incredible."

Selena smiled. "Thank you. I'm glad you liked it." She picked up her wineglass. "Why don't we move into the living room and talk about dessert? If you're still hungry, I mean."

Brooks followed her over to the couch, gaze fixed on her perfect ass.

Oh yeah. He was definitely still hungry.

Chapter 7

SELENA KNEW IT WAS HORRIBLE OF HER TO TEASE JAYDEN, but it wasn't like she'd intended to do it. All she'd done was dim the lights in the living room, then get the cheesecake from the fridge and move over to sit beside him on the couch. It wasn't until she leaned back and crossed her legs that she realized how much thigh she'd exposed in the process. If the heat in his blue-gray eyes, not to mention the mouthwatering bulge in his jeans, was any indication, it seemed like her heroic SWAT cop would rather have her for dessert than the dulce de leche cheesecake she'd made.

Not that she would have complained.

Tonight had been the most amazing evening she'd ever spent with a man. Jayden was charming, funny, easy to talk to, easy to look at, and smelled like heaven in a pair of blue jeans. And that voice? Holy cheese and crackers, it didn't even matter what he said. Merely listening to his deep, rumbling tones turned her into one big, gooey puddle of contentment. Seriously. She'd gotten aroused listening to him tell her about blowing out his knee in college. Was that whack or what?

Selena dated now and then, when her commitment to her students gave her time, but to say she'd never been this crazy for a guy was an understatement. If it wasn't for the fact that she'd felt like this from the second

Jayden had walked in the door, she would have thought it was the wine talking.

No way. There wasn't enough wine in the whole world to make her feel this good. This was sexual chemistry like she'd never experienced in her life.

Jayden leaned over and filled her wineglass before doing the same to his. Okay, it was official. He was absolutely perfect. At this rate, she'd be marrying him before the end of the week.

Though he tried to be casual about it, Selena noticed he had to adjust his jeans a little to get more comfortable as he leaned back on the couch. She didn't mean to stare, but her attention was naturally drawn to the bulge in his pants. The sight of it—and everything her overactive imagination did with it—made her breath hitch. She might have been exaggerating about that whole marriage by the weekend thing, but getting Jayden naked by then might be a very real possibility.

She didn't normally jump into things with a guy that quickly, but in this man's case, she'd make an exception. Then again, there was something about Jayden that made her think he was going to have her doing all kinds of things she normally wouldn't.

Selena picked up one of the plates and held it out to him.

"Cheesecake?" she asked, trying to distract herself by thinking of something other than Jayden sitting on her couch with no clothes on.

He took the plate, then loaded some of the rich, creamy dessert on his fork and tasted it. A moment later, she was treated to a moan similar to the one he'd let out at the SWAT compound when he'd eaten the brownies.

"Did you make this?" he asked.

She smiled. "I did."

"Wow." He ate another forkful. "You're an amazing cook. Did your mom teach you?"

Selena supposed her mother did have something to do with her learning to cook, just not in the way Jayden was implying.

"Not really." She took a bite of cheesecake. "I'm pretty much self-taught."

Jayden regarded her expectantly, like he was waiting for her to elaborate. When she didn't, he frowned. "I hope this doesn't come off like I'm trying to interrogate you or anything, but is there a reason you don't like talking about yourself? I kind of noticed I'm the one doing most of the sharing here. Not that I don't like talking about myself, but I'd like to learn a little about you, too."

Selena ran her fork over the fluffy sides of the cheesecake, making ridges there. She didn't know why she was being her normal cagey self. It wasn't like he couldn't learn anything about her past he wanted. He was a cop after all.

"I don't mind sharing," she murmured. "I just usually don't talk about my family. There's not a lot of good stuff to say, especially to someone in law enforcement."

Jayden seemed to somehow understand what she was saying and didn't take offense. But she hadn't expected that he would.

"My dad was into all kinds of drugs and gang crap before I was even born." She ate another forkful of cheesecake. "He was in and out of prison when I was little, and by the time I was eight, he took off. Or he got murdered. Or Mom threw him out. I never really knew for sure, and my mom never told me. Regardless, she hung around for a while after that, but her heart just wasn't in it." Selena shrugged. "Don't get me wrong. She wasn't a horrible mother. She simply wasn't worried about trivial stuff like cooking, cleaning, paying the bills, or taking care of a little kid. Then one day, she went out to the store for cigarettes and didn't come back. My grandma was around, but she was too old to take care of a kid full time, so my older brother—Geraldo—kind of picked up the slack. He was only six years older than me, but he pretty much raised me. He kept me fed and out of trouble, made sure I washed behind my ears, and helped with my homework, even though he was lousy in school. Grandma made sure I went to church, and Geraldo took care of everything else."

Jayden placed his empty plate on the coffee table. "Your brother sounds like a great guy."

She smiled, feeling warm all over at the flood of memories. "Yeah, he was the best. Sort of a brother, best friend, mom, and dad, all rolled into one."

"Was?" Jayden prodded gently.

Her smile faded as the good memories of Geraldo were replaced with ones that weren't so good. "I loved my brother like crazy, but our parents were gone, and our grandma was older, and we needed money."

"So he joined a gang," Jayden surmised.

She nodded, taking another bite of cheesecake. It was creamy and sweet and her favorite thing to make. She'd made it for Geraldo all the time, even before she'd gotten the hang of baking, when she was never quite sure how it was going to turn out. He'd never complained, though.

"When I was younger, I didn't think about where all

the money was coming from," she said, focusing on the texture of the cake and not the words coming out of her mouth. Even now, after all these years, thinking about it could make her cry. And she seriously didn't want to cry in front of Jayden. "But as I got older, I realized what the tattoos meant and who the people he talked to outside the apartment on the curb in the middle of the night were."

"How old was he when he joined the gang?" Jayden asked.

"Sixteen," she said. "He was big enough that most people wouldn't mess with him. It also helped that he and Ernesto were best friends. Gangs talk a lot about loyalty, but what they usually mean is loyalty to the gang, not to each other. Ernesto and my brother were different. Nobody ever came between them, and they always had each other's backs. They were senior lieutenants by the time I was seventeen, and pretty much running things." She looked at Jayden. "Please don't think I approved of what he was doing. I didn't. But I loved my brother. I begged him to walk away from the gang. He never got the chance."

"How did he die?" Jayden murmured.

Selena opened her mouth to answer, then closed it again. Thinking about the day Ernesto had come to the apartment to tell her Geraldo was dead always made her sad. But more than that, it made her mad. Angry enough that sometimes she wished she'd been there with Ernesto that day so she could have fought to protect her brother like he had. She'd found that over time, the edge on the sadness grew dull. But the anger was always there, as sharp and painful as ever, even after all these years.

"A rival gang," she finally said. "Ernesto has always spared me the details, but it came down to jealousy and greed. My brother had everything, and other people wanted it. During a supposed truce talk, a rival gang member shot my brother in the back. Ernesto was shot, too. Geraldo's death was the last straw for him. He ended up getting out of the life a little while later so he could take over the role my brother had played. That's how much Geraldo meant to him."

"I'm sorry about your brother," Jayden said quietly.

It should have been odd to hear a cop talk about being sorry about a gangbanger killed by other gangbangers, but Jayden was different.

"Thanks." She placed her dessert dish on the coffee table, though she couldn't remember when she'd finished it. "But like you said, it was a long time ago. Geraldo has been gone now for over ten years."

"Ten years is a long time," Jayden agreed. "But I'm guessing you're a lot like me, and there's probably not a day that goes by without you thinking about him."

Damn, this guy was good.

"True." She sighed. "But to be honest, I try to avoid thinking about my brother."

Jayden regarded her curiously, like she'd caught him by surprise. "Why don't you like thinking about him?"

She shrugged. "Because for whatever reason, when I think about my brother, I get really furious."

Jayden studied her for a long time, his smoky blue eyes drinking her in like he was reading her mind. "When you get mad, it's not your brother's memory that makes you angry. It's the gangs that took him away from you."

She wondered if he'd minored in psychology in college. "Am I that obvious? I hope not. I've always heard that women are supposed to be mysterious."

He chuckled. "Don't worry. Your feminine mystery is firmly intact. But I saw you in that classroom yesterday standing up to Pablo. I saw the anger in your face. It was the same expression you had just now, when you were telling me about your brother. Trust me, I get it. I know what it's like to hate gangs and everything about them. But take it from someone who knows, you can't keep letting it get to you. You need to find a way to let the hate go."

Selena stared at him. She knew she'd said this to herself at least three or four times already tonight, but without a doubt, Jayden Brooks had to be the most amazing person she'd ever met. He'd known her for a few hours and was already reading her like a book.

"But how do you let it go when every time you go to work, it's right there in your face?" she asked. "When you're doing everything you can, and it doesn't seem to help?"

"You talking about me being a cop or you being a teacher?"

"Is there a difference?"

Jayden considered that. "When I first became a cop, I thought I could somehow fix everything, that I could make the world a better place all by myself. But I was wrong. The world is too big for any one person to have an effect on. So these days, I focus on helping the person right in front of me. I save the world one person at a time. It's that simple. Keep helping the students right in front of you, the ones who are willing to accept your help, one kid at a time, one day at a time.

Stop trying to save the world, and be satisfied saving the people in it."

Selena sat there, gawking at him like he was some kind of heavily muscled Adonis who'd magically shown up on her couch. "Seriously, how the hell are you still single?"

He chuckled, a mischievous sparkle in his eyes. "Guess I haven't met that one-in-a-billion yet. Any idea where I might find her?"

His laugh washed over her, provoking wicked electrical sparks that raced back and forth over her skin before ultimately finding their way to that spot between her legs usually reserved for the tip of her right middle finger—or her vibrator. Then she caught the look in his eyes as he essentially asked her if she was a one-in-a-billion kind of girl. That question—and the heat that followed—had her fighting a crazy urge to yank off her LBD, crawl across the couch, and take a seat in his lap. Because right then, Selena wanted to be his one-in-a-billion girl.

Selena was still thinking about how insane climbing in his lap would be when she felt something thick and solid pressing against the insides of her thighs. She looked down in confusion only to discover she was straddling Jayden's lap, his hard bulge dangerously close to her throbbing pussy.

Oh, thank God, she was still wearing her dress!

She had no idea how she'd gotten to his side of the couch, much less how she'd gotten onto Jayden's lap. She wasn't bold with men, not by a long shot. Even in her wildest dreams, she couldn't imagine doing something this out of control.

But then Selena looked down and saw Jayden gazing up at her, an expression on his face like she was some kind of angel from above, and she stopped caring about how she'd gotten here.

"I have no idea where you might find this one-in-a-billion woman you're looking for, but maybe I can help you search," she whispered, leaning closer.

Jayden gently cupped her face in his big hand. Then he smiled, and from this close up, she swore it was brighter than the sun. Even his eyes seemed to glint gold. But that was probably only a reflection of the colorful lights of the Christmas tree beside the couch.

"I'd appreciate the help," he said softly. "If you're not too busy."

"I'm not busy at all," she murmured as their lips came together with a zap.

Okay, there wasn't really a zap. But she definitely felt the most delicious electric sensation that started right where their lips met and drifted out from there, warming her whole body. The feeling was so amazing, she moaned.

The sound was like a dam breaking, and suddenly they were both kissing each other like crazy. Her tongue slipped into his mouth, and his was right there to greet it. Tangling, teasing, exploring. The taste of his mouth was impossible to describe, but she found herself wanting more of it.

She felt his strong fingers in her hair, felt them tugging and tipping her head to the side, making it easier for Jayden to devour her. Selena couldn't remember anybody ever tugging her hair before. Not since grade school anyway, and that situation had been completely different. Then, she'd hated it. Now, she absolutely loved it.

Jayden kept kissing her even as his free hand began to roam slowly down her back and across her hip until it reached her upper thigh. Her bare upper thigh. That's when Selena realized that in her zeal to climb aboard the Jayden Brooks love train, the hem of her already short dress had gotten shoved up nearly to her waist. And when that big, warm hand of his made contact with the hypersensitive skin at the top of her leg just inches from the tiny pair of panties she wore, her heart began to beat like a drum, and she decided there was a very good chance she'd be getting him naked tonight.

Selena broke the kiss and sat back a little, needing to breathe. But more importantly, needing to get her mouth on other parts of this gorgeous man. The move pressed her panty-covered crotch firmly against the hard-on in his jeans, yanking something that sounded suspiciously like a hungry growl from her throat. Had she really growled? Who the hell did that while making out... besides her apparently? She was absolutely sure she'd never growled in her life.

She felt Jayden's hand slip out of her hair, settling on her other bare thigh, his firm grip gently rocking her back and forth against him. Her whole body was pulsing like mad, but the throb between her legs was at a completely different level. She thought she might come simply from sitting on his lap. That shouldn't be possible. But then again, she'd never gotten this crazy hot before.

"You are one beautiful woman," Jayden breathed.

His eyes reflected the lights from the tree like nothing she'd ever seen, and the adoring expression on his face made her catch her breath. She couldn't remember a man ever making her feel so sexy before.

She leaned forward slowly, her lips coming down for a moment on his before skirting to the side and tracing little kisses along his jawline to his ear. She buried her face there, nipping and biting his earlobe before doing the same along his neck. She was almost overwhelmed at how good he smelled…and tasted. She couldn't get enough of him. It was like she wanted to eat him up.

As she nibbled, her fingers found the buttons of his shirt, undoing them from the top down until she'd exposed a good expanse of smooth muscular chest and broad shoulders. She couldn't believe how aggressive she was, but she didn't want to stop.

She wanted more…a lot more.

Selena pulled back again to look at him, swearing the dim living room had brightened around her as she gazed down at all that manly yumminess. But she ignored that impossibility, instead focusing on the feel of his thick pecs and traps under her fingertips as they skimmed here, there, and everywhere.

She nestled against the junction of his neck and shoulder again, inhaling his scent as his fingers slid farther under her dress, encircling her waist and moving her against him. She licked and nipped at his neck, excited beyond belief.

Jayden groaned, a sound of such pure pleasure, Selena was nearly undone. All she was doing was sitting on his lap, but she knew without a doubt that it was enough to make him so aroused, he was practically losing his mind.

She had no idea why she did it, but right then, she

wanted Jayden more than she'd ever wanted another man before in her life, in a way that was so completely different, she couldn't come close to explaining, so she trailed kisses down to his big muscular shoulder…and bit him.

The sensation was…orgasmic. Her entire body lit on fire, and she swore she was experiencing some kind of climax, just not the one she was used to. It was amazing nonetheless, and she didn't want it to stop.

Then sensations began to filter through her addled mind, distracting her from the pleasure of the moment. She felt Jayden tense, like he was having a climax of his own. She was thrilled at the idea until a metallic taste hit her tongue. The excitement she'd been feeling disappeared in a fuzzy poof.

Blood.

Selena pulled back and looked down in horror, her eyes going wide at the sight of four small puncture wounds on his shoulder, right where his trap muscles met his thick neck. While they were bad enough, it was the blood that really freaked her out.

"Oh, God! I bit you!" she cried. "You're bleeding!"

She tried to climb off his lap, but Jayden's hands tightened around her waist, keeping her right where she was. "Relax," he said softly, his sensuous mouth curving into a smile. "It's not a big deal."

She blinked. "Not a big deal? Jayden, you're bleeding!"

"I know," he said. "Do you see me complaining? No. You got a little frisky and nipped me. It's just a scratch." He ran his thumb over the wounds. "See?"

Selena looked down in amazement. The four puncture wounds weren't bleeding anymore, which was hard to believe. There'd been a lot of blood a few seconds ago. She watched the rivulets now drying on his neck and chest. The wounds were definitely still there, but they didn't look nearly as bad. She'd bitten him hard enough to make him bleed and barely even remembered doing it. That fact scared her more than anything else.

That was the moment she realized all the amazing pleasure that had been throbbing through her earlier had ebbed drastically. Now, all she felt was the satiated feeling she got after really good sex, which was bizarre beyond words. It was almost like she'd gotten off on biting him.

Jayden stood, picking her up at the same time. She instinctively wrapped herself around him, her arms going around his neck and legs clamping around his waist. His big hands slipped under her butt, supporting her easily. While she might have grabbed onto him out of pure instinct simply so she wouldn't fall, she couldn't ignore the fact that this position was seriously sexy.

He carried her to the kitchen, then grabbed a paper towel off the rack and soaked it under the faucet before setting her on the counter and handing it to her. She took the towel without thinking and cleaned the blood off. When it was gone, she allowed herself to breathe again. Maybe the wounds weren't nearly as bad as she'd thought.

"You okay?" he whispered.

His breath was warm on her face as she leaned in close to him. He was standing between her legs, her ankles still locked behind his back.

"Yeah," she said. "Sorry about biting you."

He chuckled, such a warm...real...sound that she

couldn't help laughing with him. She looked up at him as he leaned a little closer, the bulge in his jeans still as evident as ever, and rested one hand on the cabinet above her.

"Don't worry about it," he said softly. "If it will make you feel better, I could promise to bite you back at some point in the future."

She felt a tingle between her legs at that. Most of her might not like the idea of biting, but there was at least one part that was interested.

"So, you're down with a second date," she asked. "Even after all this?"

He nodded, his eyes dancing. "Definitely. And don't worry. I was just messing with you about that biting thing. We can do a normal, old-fashioned date the next time if you want. No biting required or expected."

Selena gazed at him, feeling a little overwhelmed with all the things she was feeling right then. The bite—and the blood—had thrown her for a loop, but she was still crazy about this man. She had a ton of instincts screaming at her right then, telling her he was seriously into her, too. As in the kind of serious that changed everything.

"I'm not sure how normal and old-fashioned it might be, but I sort of committed myself to being a wingwoman tomorrow night for Becca. She's going out with a guy she's never met before, so she's meeting him at a club in the Main Street Entertainment District and asked me to be there for her. You want to come as my plus one?"

It sounded like a god-awful idea the second the words were out of her mouth, but Jayden smiled. "That sounds good to me. You want me pick you up here or meet you there?"

She considered the logistics for a moment before answering. "The plan was for me to ride with Becca, so she could use me as an excuse if she wanted to bail early. Would you mind meeting us there? I'll text you the name of the club as soon as I find out which one it is. If everything works out well between Becca and this guy, I can slip out with you."

He nodded. "Sounds good. I'm looking forward to it."

She pulled his head down for a kiss, wondering how he could get any better. Nobody liked the idea of a double date with a couple they didn't know, but Jayden agreed without a second thought. Their tongues tangled for a while, those crazy tremors starting back up between her legs. It didn't help that she still had her ankles locked behind his back or that his shaft was still as hard as concrete in his jeans.

Jayden was the one who finally pulled back. He traced one long finger down her jawline to her neck, sending a delicious shiver through her. "I guess I'd better go, or I might not get out of here at all tonight."

Selena reluctantly unwrapped her legs from his waist, letting him help her off the counter, then walked with him to the front door, wondering when she'd taken her shoes off. She remembered having them on earlier but found them tossed carelessly aside near the couch.

At the door, he turned to face her. "I had a really good time. Dinner was amazing, and dessert was even better."

She smiled, standing up on her tiptoes to hook her arms around his neck. "I'm glad you had fun," she murmured against his mouth as she stole one more quick kiss. His mouth was seriously addicting. "I did, too."

"Tomorrow night, then?" he asked.

She nodded as she stepped back. "I'll text you tomorrow with the club name and the exact time."

Jayden was half out the door when she caught his arm, making him stop and turn back. "Before I forget. Thanks for telling me about your father. And for talking to me about the gangs. It helped."

He smiled, leaning in for another kiss that almost had her following him out the door. "I'm glad. We can talk more about it tomorrow if you want."

She watched him walk down the hall, only closing her apartment door after he'd disappeared around the corner. Then she wandered back into her place, still a little wobbly on her feet. That had been some date. And he was right. The dessert had been even better.

She considered cleaning up the kitchen but then reminded herself it wasn't like she had anything to do in the morning. Besides, she was surprisingly worn out now that Jayden had left and the adrenaline that had been flooding her body earlier was gone. Cleaning the kitchen could wait, she thought as she headed to the bathroom to get ready for bed.

Her tiny black panties were embarrassingly wet, and she had to rinse them before tossing them in the hamper. Jayden had gotten to her like nobody's business. Even now, ten minutes after he'd left, her body was still humming.

Selena jumped in the shower and rinsed off, resisting the urge to let the spray linger in that one particular spot for too long or to let her mind wander to thoughts of how nice it had been to sit on Jayden's lap. If she started down that road, she wouldn't get to sleep for a long time. And she really was tired. Even more tired than she'd been the night before after her crazy day at the school and hospital. She guessed Dr. Pham had been right. The stress of the shooting had taken more out of her than she thought.

She was brushing her teeth a little while later when she thought about the whole biting thing again. She replayed the moment in her head, remembering how Jayden had smelled, how he'd tasted against her mouth. It had been delectable, but that didn't explain why she'd bitten him. It was a little unsettling to think she could bite hard enough to draw blood.

She smiled at herself in the mirror, peeking through the toothpaste and trying to understand how she'd even done it. There was nothing in the mirror that explained it. Her teeth weren't that sharp.

But as she stood there turning this way and that, looking at canine teeth that weren't nearly large enough to make the holes she'd seen, another disturbing thought occurred to her. The blood had freaked her out, but she'd enjoyed sinking her teeth into the tastiest hunk of man she'd ever met. It was bizarre to think something like that, but it was true. Even now, thinking about the possibility of doing it again had her body tingling like crazy.

She abruptly considered the promise he'd made to bite her back someday. That was when her body started to really heat up. She was going to need another shower—a cold one this time. What the heck was wrong with her? It was bad enough getting aroused at the idea of biting Jayden. Now she wanted him to bite her back?

Maybe she really did need to see a therapist.

Chapter 8

"I'M SURMISING FROM THE STUPID GRIN ON YOUR FACE THAT your date with Selena last night went well?"

Brooks jerked his attention away from the farm they were passing on their way back to Coffield Unit to look at Zane. His pack mate always insisted on driving whenever they went anywhere now, like he thought he had to make up for his injury by proving he could still operate a motor vehicle.

"How do you know I wasn't grinning at the cows we drove past?" Brooks countered.

Zane snorted. "Right. You've had the same dreamy expression on your face since we got in the truck an hour ago. So, unless it's my cologne that's doing it for you, it's a woman. Stop messing about, and tell me what happened with Selena last night. I've seen you date some amazing women before, but none of them have ever left you looking this smitten."

Brooks shook his head. Zane wasn't going to let this go until Brooks spilled his guts. But where did he start? How was he supposed to describe last night's date with Selena?

Amazing?

Unbelievable?

Spectacular?

Mind-blowing?

While all those words applied, they also fell way

short of summing up the evening. Last night had been the best date he'd ever been on. Hell, it might very well have been the best night of his life. Which was shocking considering they'd kept their clothes on for the most part.

He stifled a groan as he remembered how hot Selena had looked in that tiny black dress. And the way it hitched up around her waist when she'd climbed on his lap? *Daaaammn.*

"It was…good," he finally said, trying to keep the smile from his face and failing miserably.

Zane lifted a brow. "Good?"

"Okay, better than good," Brooks admitted. "I went over there with no expectations for the evening and ended up staying half the night."

"That was fast."

Brooks chuckled. "Nothing happened, so get your mind out of the gutter. Yeah, we kissed some. Well, a lot actually. But mostly, we just talked. Selena made this killer Mexican meal, and we hung out and chatted about work and family. I told her about my father and how I became a cop, and she told me about growing up in Dallas. Turns out she lost her parents and brother to gang violence. She refuses to let the gangs win."

"No wonder she wouldn't back down from Pablo when he was threatening her with that gun."

"Yeah. I get the feeling she'd go toe-to-toe with anybody to protect her students."

"I can respect that," Zane said. "Her interactions with the gangs are about to take a drastic turn now that she's a werewolf. If they thought she was tough to deal with before, wait until she has fangs, claws, and enough strength to rip their heads off."

Brooks frowned. "Shit. I never thought of that. When I tell her she's a werewolf, I'm going to have to remember to make sure she's careful not to reveal what she is in front of them—or anyone else. With the hunters and all the other crap going on, that's all we need."

"No kidding." Zane checked his side mirror, then passed a slow-moving farm tractor. "The topic of werewolves never came up, huh?"

"No," Brooks said. "You may find this hard to believe, but as smooth as I am, I couldn't come up with a way to work it into the conversation. But I get the feeling I'm going to have to tell her sooner rather than later."

Zane looked at him sharply. "Why?"

Brooks rested his elbow on the open window. "Because when Selena was on my lap and we were making out, she bit me."

His friend's mouth twitched. "At your age, I didn't think I'd have to talk about the birds and bees, but sometimes when two people are snogging, they can get a bit frisky and nip each other."

"Funny," Brooks growled.

He pulled the collar of his uniform T-shirt away from his neck, showing Zane the four round scars. They were completely closed up but still obvious.

"I'm not talking about a little nip," he said, sitting back in his seat. "We're talking four fangs at least a half inch long."

Zane considered that. "She has fangs within twenty-four hours of going through the traumatic event? And all you two were doing was kissing? That's a little concerning."

Brooks remembered what it had been like when he'd gone through his change after getting sliced open by

that psycho in Gulfport. At first, the only outward sign
he was a werewolf was the fact that he'd survived an
injury he shouldn't have, and he'd written that off to a
good old-fashioned miracle like everyone else had. His
claws hadn't come out until weeks later when he'd been
dealing with a loud, angry drunk. His fangs had shown
up the following week. Was the fact that Selena had
fangs this soon a sign that something was wrong with
her development as a werewolf?

"So, if she bit you, how did the fact that she's a werewolf not come up?" Zane asked.

"She didn't realize she had fangs," Brooks said. "She
freaked out when she saw the blood."

Zane was silent for a while. "Maybe we're worried
about nothing. Maybe some werewolves go through
their change faster than others. Then again, maybe we're
also seeing another result of the hunters showing up. If
Alex was able to learn how to shift fully into wolf form
almost overnight because of the threat the hunters present, maybe Selena can go through her entire change in
days instead of weeks."

Brooks hadn't thought of that. A lot of crazy things
had occurred since the hunters came on the scene.
According to Remy's future mother-in-law—who knew
even more about werewolves than Gage—it was all
because the Pack had an enemy now. Since so many
pack members had found their soul mates, the Pack was
stronger. They were also tapping into new werewolf
abilities no one had ever had before. While Alex Trevino
had learned how to transform into wolf form in the span
of fifteen minutes, Remy had developed some kind of
telepathic link with his mate. The guy could track her

anywhere she went like she had a frigging GPS chip in her. Even more wild, the couple shared emotions, too. If she was happy, scared, or mad, Remy knew it even if they were miles apart.

Looking at it that way, maybe it was possible for Selena to go through her change in a matter of days. Damn, that was a terrifying thought. Turning into a werewolf was hard enough to handle when it happened slowly. If the process sped up, it could end up being too much for Selena to handle. At this rate, she could go full claws and fangs within days. He didn't have time for the slow and careful approach anymore. He was going to have to tell her what she was—soon.

Zane slowed the SUV and took the exit off State Road 287, slipping onto 645, a small county road that led to the prison. As they drove along the narrow back road past brown, dormant fields, Brooks worked through different scenarios in his head, wondering if there was anything close to a good way to broach the subject of werewolves to Selena. He was still trying to come up with something when Zane broke the silence.

"I know you thought I was bonkers when I mentioned it to you the other day, but do you still think Selena's not *The One* for you? Clearly, the chemistry is there. Hell, she started to shift right in the middle of you two going at it."

Brooks had lain awake last night for a long time asking himself this exact same question. "I'd be lying if I said I haven't thought about it. After Gage told me Selena was turning into a werewolf, I told myself my attraction to Selena was because she was going through her change. That maybe my inner alpha was simply worrying about another werewolf in trouble."

"That's the stupidest thing I've ever heard you say. You were hooked on Selena the first time you smelled her, and that was before she started going through the change."

Brooks shrugged. "Yeah, I know. But I still find myself trying to come up with reasons to think she's not *The One*."

Zane gave him a curious look as he pulled into the parking lot of the prison. "Why would you do that? Are you scared of finding your soul mate or something?"

"Maybe," he admitted. "I'd never really thought about it one way or the other, but now that the possibility is right in front of me, I'm worried I'm going to mess it up somehow."

"How in the hell are you going to cock it up?"

"Selena is turning into a werewolf faster than she should, so it's possible what we consider normal is off the table," Brooks pointed out. "What if I screw up helping her through the transition? How do I get her to believe some magical folktale has decided the two of us are supposed to be together if I can't even get her to understand what she's turning into? I could end up losing her…both as a werewolf and as *The One*."

The thought made his chest tighten painfully.

Zane shook his head and put the SUV in park. "Don't even think I'm letting this subject go," he said as he opened his door. "As soon as we're done with Oliver, you and I are going to talk. Because you are overthinking the hell out of this situation."

Brooks snorted as he got out to join his pack mate, not sure what else there was to talk about. Telling Zane what was going on in his head would actually require him to know in the first place, which he didn't.

As they walked across the parking lot, Brooks was nearly overwhelmed by the flood of scents coming from the place. Coffield Unit was a big prison, covering twenty thousand acres of land and holding over four thousand prisoners who were in there from anything as minor as simple drug possession up to assault, rape, and murder. Right then, Brooks swore he could smell every one of them.

They were halfway to the entry building that straddled the northern edge of the prison's perimeter fence when he caught one particular scent that made him slow. The smell was familiar, but he couldn't quite place it, especially with all the other scents mixing with it. Whatever it was, his gut was screaming at him that there was something wrong.

He sniffed the air, letting his feet guide him toward it.

"Where are you going?" Zane said, moving up beside him with a confused look on his face. "We have to go through security to get into the prison."

Brooks didn't answer. Instead, he walked faster, leaving the parking lot behind and heading toward the western edge of the prison's big perimeter fence. He scanned the prison facilities inside the fence as he went, trying to pinpoint exactly where the familiar scent was coming from.

Coffield Unit was one big square, fenced-in compound, with a large central building flanked by two tri-wing cell blocks on either side. The central building held most of the general-use facilities like the library, cafeteria, hospital, and visitors' center, while the cell blocks housed the prisoners. Each cell block had its own yard facilities, but there was no one outside right now, so that couldn't be what Brooks was smelling. Maybe he was picking up the scent of some criminal he'd put behind bars in one of the cell blocks. But his nose kept leading him west, not east toward the main buildings.

As they walked along the western fence line, Brooks noticed Zane lifting his nose to sniff the air like he was.

The only thing in the direction they were heading was the prison's side gate and the small guard station that handled vehicles that moved back and forth between the inner and outer gate. Brooks had seen supply trucks and prison transport buses move through it plenty of times. One gate would open, letting a truck or bus pull into the checkpoint. Once the guards were satisfied everything was clear, the second gate would open, allowing the vehicle to come or go.

There were two big trucks currently inside the double gate area, their engines running like they were waiting for the outer one to open and let them both out. They looked like the kind of trucks that belonged to a laundry or uniform delivery service, but they didn't have names on them.

The closer he and Zane got to the side gate, the stronger and more familiar the scent became. He was already getting a bad feeling in his gut when he finally figured out what the hell was going on. Both he and Zane broke into a run at the same time, yelling and waving their arms to get the attention of the guards manning the side gate.

"Stop those trucks!" Brooks shouted.

Either no one heard them, or they were ignoring them, because the outer gate opened, and the truck in front began to move forward.

"Oliver is in that truck," Zane growled. "He's trying to escape."

"Jeremy Engler and Armend Frasheri are in there, too." Brooks pulled his Sig .40 caliber and ran faster, the muscles in his legs and glutes twisting and reshaping as he went through a partial shift. "There are some omegas with them. They're packed in there together so tightly that their scents are practically merged together into a single smell. That's why I didn't recognize what I was smelling at first."

Jeremy Engler was a deranged cop who'd followed Khaki all the way from Washington State because he'd thought she belonged to him. The man had tried to kill both Khaki and Xander when he realized they were together. Armend Frasheri was a boss in the Albanian mob who had gone after Eric and his mate, Jayna, after Becker had gone undercover in Frasheri's organization and destroyed the whole operation.

How the hell those two had ended up working together with Oliver on an escape was impossible to explain, but Brooks knew one thing—it didn't bode well for the Pack or any of the werewolves in this city looking to them for protection.

He and Zane were still a hundred yards away when one of the prison guards finally saw them. The man hurried toward the first truck, motioning for the driver to stop. Brooks wasn't in a position to see exactly what the driver was doing, but he saw movement behind the windshield, then heard gunshots. A moment later, the guard fell to the ground.

Both trucks sped through the gate, then turned left, racing away even as more guards came out of the security building and fired at them. But it was too late for that, and other than punching a few holes through the back doors of the trucks, the guards' attempts did nothing.

Brooks and Zane were running at Olympic sprinter speed as they hauled ass past the gate and the few guards there. It was stupid to run this fast in public, but they couldn't let any of those assholes get away.

Brooks shouted at the guards to sound the alarm as he and Zane raced past, but he knew it wasn't going to matter. These weren't a few dumb inmates grabbing a random truck and making a dash for the Mexican border. Frasheri had money and endless criminal contacts. Oliver was a man who had traveled the country killing people for years while staying off the grid. It was a guarantee that with those two involved in this, there was a plan in place to make sure they got away.

Brooks and Zane followed the trucks down the narrow road that ran past the prison. Fortunately, the rural farm road wasn't meant for high-speed traffic, so the trucks couldn't do more than forty miles an hour. That meant he and Zane could at least keep the vehicles in sight until they moved out beyond the first turn in the road so the guards at the gate couldn't see them anymore.

As soon as they were clear, he and Zane pushed their shift even further, claws and fangs coming out while the bones in their legs and backs changed shape to let them move even faster. If it had been nighttime, Brooks would have dropped his clothes and fully shifted to his wolf shape. In that form, he would have caught up to the trucks in seconds.

But even on two legs, they were still able to catch up to the rear vehicle. Brooks made a hand gesture to Zane, pointing at the front tires. Zane nodded, slowing a little as he lifted his weapon and took careful aim at the front driver's side tire. At the same time, Brooks veered to the left side of the road and picked up speed, drawing even with the cab of the truck.

Out of the corner of his eye, he caught sight of the driver's panicked expression. Brooks lowered his head, tightening up his right arm and shoulder, then charging in as Zane fired his pistol. The front driver's side tire blew out at the same time as Brooks slammed into the door. That little nudge, along with the blown-out tire, was enough to send the truck out of control.

Brooks already had his feet back under him and was chasing after the other vehicle when the one he'd just tackled slid off the road and flipped over a few times. He and Zane ignored it, both of them more worried about catching up to the other truck.

He was already motioning toward Zane, planning to take out the second vehicle the same way they had the first one, when the back door rolled up, revealing Frasheri, Engler, and Oliver all standing there with automatic weapons.

Brooks wasn't too worried. He doubted any of them were good enough to pull off a kill shot from a moving vehicle, especially as fast as he and Zane were moving.

Bullets sprayed in their direction, slamming into the asphalt around them, sending up the stench of synthetic wolfsbane. Brooks subconsciously slowed, recoiling at the idea of getting hit with one of them, even though he'd been vaccinated against the poison.

But while Brooks flinched a bit when the first few bullets impacted around him, Zane lunged to the side while running at forty miles an hour to avoid them. Brooks heard bones breaking as his friend tumbled head over heels into the nearest field.

Brooks growled in frustration as he slowed to help his pack mate. He fired a few rounds at the fleeing vehicle, but it was useless. The truck had already picked up speed and was pulling away. One of the omega werewolves with them gave him the finger as they disappeared down the road.

Cursing, Brooks turned and ran into the field. He found Zane kneeling in the deep furrow his body had carved out in the dirt when he landed, cradling a right arm that was obviously broken.

"Why the fuck did you stop chasing them?" Zane demanded. "You could have gotten them!"

Brooks didn't answer as he knelt down beside his friend, checking for other injuries. Broken bones were nothing to mess around with. Werewolves healed fast, but if the bones in Zane's arm were misaligned when they did, they'd stay that way, which would only limit his mobility more than it already was.

He heard the sound of approaching sirens as he reset Zane's forearm bones. The area was going to be crawling with cops soon.

"I'm fine!" Zane snapped, pushing Brooks's hands away and standing up. "Let's go check on the inmates in the other truck. Maybe they can tell us where Oliver is heading."

Brooks got to his feet and followed without a word. While the omegas in the truck they'd flipped had almost certainly survived, he doubted they'd be able to tell them anything useful. Frasheri and Oliver were unlikely to reveal critical details to some out-of-control omegas.

As they walked toward the other truck, Brooks pulled out his cell and punched his commander's number. Gage was going to shit bricks when he heard about the escape.

———

Selena drove past Terrace Grove High School, hoping to see Ruben hanging around outside. He wasn't there. Then again, she hadn't expected him to be.

She sighed as she watched the school disappear in the rearview mirror. It was beyond weird not to be in her classroom at two o'clock on a Wednesday afternoon, but it wasn't like she had a choice. Another long argument on the phone earlier with Eva hadn't gotten her anywhere.

So she'd spent the morning doing what she could, visiting those members of her class most likely to find themselves in trouble. Whether it was sitting down and watching TV with them, working through some homework problems, or even talking about the violence they'd seen in her classroom, it was about letting them know she was there for them. She'd even gotten sweet, quiet Marguerite to sign up for a session with the school-provided counselor, so maybe Eva and her damn school board would be of some help in the end.

But while she'd been able to see nearly all her troubled students yesterday and today, it was the one she wasn't able to find who had her the most concerned.

No one had seen Ruben since Selena had caught that one quick glimpse of the boy Monday night outside the school. Ruben's grandmother said he hadn't slept in his bed in two nights, and she was terrified something horrible had happened to him. Selena was worried, too. She wouldn't put it beyond the Locos to go after Ruben in some kind of twisted retribution for what had happened in her classroom. Her biggest fear was that the kid was lying in an alley somewhere, beaten senseless. Or worse.

She turned her car onto a side street off Ferguson, doing a circle around the apartment complex where Ruben and his grandmother lived. Then she went to the next block up and did the same thing. Blindly driving around in circles, hoping to find the kid by chance wasn't the most brilliant of ideas, but it was the best scheme she could come up with.

After fifteen minutes of driving around the neighborhood, Selena began to think she was wasting her time. This was the definition of finding a needle in a haystack.

She wondered if she should call Jayden. He could almost certainly help her track down Ruben. But she quickly dropped the idea. Jayden was a SWAT cop for the city of Dallas, not her personal security service. She would do what she had to do to find Ruben on her own.

Thinking about Jayden brought a smile to her face. That wasn't surprising. He was incredible. Seriously, how many guys would have been as cool as Jayden after getting bitten hard enough to draw blood? Not only that, but he'd agreed to go out with her on a double date with another couple he'd never met. She was pretty sure there weren't many guys like him out there in the world. Actually, she was pretty sure there weren't *any* other guys like him. He was one of a kind.

Selena had been dreading her night out with Becca and Scott, but now that Jayden was going, she was looking forward to it. The club they were going to had some great music—even in the middle of the week—and while Selena's main reason for going was to fly cover for her friend, the thought that she might get a chance to dance with Jayden had her grinning. Something told her Jayden Brooks could dance his ass off.

And who knew? After a night of getting all hot and sweaty on the dance floor, maybe they'd go back to her place and get all hot and sweaty doing something else.

There was a part of Selena that was shocked she'd gone there. She wasn't skittish about sex, not even close. But it was completely out of character for her to think of doing stuff like that with a guy she'd just met. Since last night, she couldn't get Jayden out of her head. She'd even dreamed about him. And it was the wildest, steamiest, most intense erotic dream she'd ever experienced. She'd woke up breathing hard, excited beyond belief, and filled with an almost uncontrollable urge to text him and say, *Was it good for you?*

She hadn't, of course. Instead, she'd gotten out of bed and run for a ridiculous amount of time on the treadmill in the corner of her bedroom, then taken a shower. The combination of exercise and cold water was enough to get rid of all the excess energy she seemed to have built up, not to mention calm her hormones.

The one thing it hadn't done was change her mind about Jayden. She wanted him. He wanted her. There was no reason to act like it wasn't going to happen between them.

Selena was so caught up in thoughts of Jayden—and possibly getting naked with him—that she almost missed the group of people hanging out in the abandoned lot on the corner of Ferguson and Highland behind the discount liquor store and the tire center. She probably would have driven right by them if it wasn't for the one guy standing head and shoulders above the others.

Ruben.

Heart beating faster, she pulled a U-turn and looped back around to slip into a parking space along the side of the shop that specialized in wine, beer, and snack food. Thankfully, it was relatively empty at this time of day, so there was nobody around to see a local high school teacher not only parking in front of a liquor store, but also slipping out of her car to disappear behind the place.

Because that wouldn't look weird at all.

Selena stopped and looked around when she reached the god-awful, smelly Dumpster in the back. They were supposed to build an apartment complex on the empty lot in the future, but for now, it was simply a piece land where the neighborhood kids played tag and sometimes tossed around a football. Older kids and adults used the lot as a playground, too. Unfortunately, their games usually involved drugs.

As she neared the group of people near the privacy fence, she saw there were eight boys and three girls. She recognized all of the girls and two of the boys besides Ruben. Both of the boys and one of the girls had dropped out of Terrace Grove more than two years ago and were involved in the gangs. The other two girls weren't in any of Selena's classes, but she knew they'd started skipping school lately. Unless something changed, those two would end up in the gangs before the school year was out.

When people thought about gangs, they assumed only guys got involved in them. Unfortunately, that wasn't true. These days, girls and women accounted for as much as ten percent of the local gang population, and they were just as involved in crime and violence as their male counterparts. Many times, the women would be stuck carrying the gang's weapons or drugs so when the cops caught them, the women were the ones who ended up going to jail. Even worse, the gangs frequently put their female members out on the street to make money or used them for their own entertainment. In some ways, being in a gang was tougher on the women than the men. But the gangs kept recruiting them, and the girls kept joining.

Selena squared her shoulders and walked right into the middle of the little get-together, ignoring everyone else as she approached Ruben. Out of the corner of her eye, she caught some of the guys regarding her with interest. One hooted, asking if she was there to have a good time. But most of the people in the group looked at her with barely disguised annoyance.

When she didn't respond to the catcalling, the oldest guy among them reached out to grab her arm. Anger immediately surged in her, and she smacked his hand aside as she stopped in front of Ruben.

"What are you doing here, Ruben?" she asked. "Your grandmother has been worried sick about you. I've been worried about you, too."

For a moment, the Ruben she knew, the big kid with the good heart, had the decency to at least look chagrined. But then he seemed to realize he had an audience, and his face changed, taking on a casual, unconcerned expression. "I was just hanging out with my friends. It's not a big deal."

Friends? Since when?

Selena bit her tongue, almost drawing blood as she tried to quell the rising wave of fury rushing through her. She wanted to ask if this had something to do with Pablo, but stopped herself. Of course it did. Ruben had resisted the pull of the gangs for years, but then two days after seeing Pablo get shot, he was standing on the corner with Pablo's gangbanger friends.

More frustration and anger clawed its way up from her stomach, and she had to force herself to take a breath. Her emotions were getting the best of her, dammit. Yelling at Ruben wouldn't do any good.

"Not a big deal," she said. "You stay away from home for two nights without letting your grandmother know where you are, and you think it's not a big deal? Is that the way you treat the woman who took you in and cared for you since you were five?"

She kept her voice soft, but it was difficult. Ruben's grandmother was almost seventy but still worked, because that was the only way she could cover the cost of raising a teenager with an appetite like his. To his credit, Ruben hung his head a little at her jab, and Selena could almost feel the shame rolling off him.

Selena was this close to taking his hand and getting him the hell out of there, but the guy who'd tried to grab her arm before wedged himself in between her and Ruben, forcing her to take a step back unless she wanted him right in her face.

Her body's reaction to the aggressive move was startling. First, the hair on the back of her neck and her arms stood up, then her whole body tingled like electricity was running through it. Most shocking of all, her hands clenched into fists so tightly, they hurt.

"Who the fuck are you, bitch?" the guy demanded. "His mommy?"

In his late twenties at least, with tattoos covering his neck and arms, he was probably the leader of this little group and undoubtedly the one Ruben was here trying to impress. She bit down on her rising anger, ready to tell him that Ruben wasn't in his gang yet and could go anywhere he wanted. But before she could get the words out, one of the girls she knew from school spoke.

"This ain't his mom, Aaron." The girl smirked. "This is the teacher from Terrace Grove that got Wheels shot and arrested. The one always putting her nose into other people's business."

Aaron looked stunned, maybe expecting someone bigger or tougher looking, but then his face took on a dark, determined look, and Selena knew she was in trouble. But for some crazy reason, she wasn't as scared as she probably should have been. In fact, other than the fury flowing through her blood like acid, she felt incredibly calm.

"So, you're the crazy chica who thinks she can go up against my Locos, poking my boys in the eye day after day, and keep breathing?" he sneered. "Now you come here to my corner, trying to take Big Rube home to his granny? Bitch, you must be even dumber than everyone says."

He lunged for her, swinging his fist at her face.

Selena's first instinct was to back up and lift her hands in a useless effort to protect herself. But for reasons she couldn't explain, she met the gangbanger head on, anger rumbling from her throat in a low sound as she threw up her left arm and blocked the incoming punch.

She barely had time to marvel at how easy the move had been before her right fist whipped out in a straight jab.

The shot connected, and Aaron stumbled back a good five feet, jaw bones crunching and teeth clacking together with an audible sound. Selena waited for pain to explode through her small hand. She'd never punched anyone in her life and feared she'd done it horribly wrong. But as blood dripped from a gash near Aaron's mouth, she realized her hand didn't hurt. In fact, it felt fine. Like she hadn't hit anything at all.

Some part of her took note of the fact that absolutely nobody was moving, that everyone, including Ruben, was standing there staring at her like she was some kind of strange creature they'd never seen before.

Then Aaron was mumbling an endless stream of mostly unintelligible curse words as he charged at her. At the same time, another guy—a few years younger than Aaron—moved toward her back. There was a third one slightly off to the side headed her way, too.

The low growl that had slipped out when she'd punched Aaron escaped her lips again, louder and harsher this time.

Selena ducked under Aaron's first wild blow like he was moving in slow motion, growling again as she grabbed the front of his jacket and jerked him off his feet, spinning him around like he was nothing more than a bag of laundry and slinging him at the man behind her. Both gangbangers went down hard.

A tiny part of her wondered how she'd been able to move, much less throw a man who weighed so much more than she did. But then the third man—the one who had been moving slower—jumped over his two friends and came at her, and she had no more time to wonder about anything.

Selena rushed forward to meet the man even as she screamed at herself that this was insane. The man's fist grazed the side of her head, but she didn't slow down. Instead, she put her hands on his chest and shoved as hard as she could. He flew backward over his friends like he'd been hit by a truck, bouncing off the tall privacy fence and collapsing to the ground.

Even though the man hadn't even come close to hitting her jaw, her gums suddenly felt like they were on fire, and she tasted blood. She snarled, the metallic tang turning her anger into blazing white-hot rage as she turned to see if any of the other gang members were coming at her.

But they were all running away.

Selena started after them, stunned at how badly she wanted to chase them. The desire to drag them down from behind was like a physical need, but she stopped herself, teeth grinding together so hard, she heard them crunch.

Ruben looked over his shoulder at her, like he was thinking twice about leaving. But ultimately, he kept running, choosing to stay with his new friends. It tore at Selena to realize that, but at the moment, there was nothing she could do about it. Hopefully, she'd be able to find him later when his friends weren't around and talk some sense into him. But she couldn't help worrying it was already too late for that.

Noise from behind spun her around, and she saw two of the men who'd attacked her half running, half limping toward the street.

Selena glanced at Aaron, watching disinterestedly as

he stumbled to his feet. He looked a little unsteady, and his chin and neck were covered in blood.

His face was stiff with barely controlled fury, but Selena found she had very little interest in continuing the fight. It was like something inside had already decided going up against Aaron by himself was boring. Eyes never leaving hers, he yanked down the zipper of his coat and reached inside. Selena knew what he was going for, and while there was a part of her that wanted to run, the part in charge propelled her feet once more toward the threat. Suddenly, she wasn't bored anymore.

The taste of blood flooded her mouth again, but that only fueled her fire. She growled louder as excitement coursed through her body. She didn't know why, but she was almost eager for Aaron to pull out a weapon. An image suddenly popped into her head, of her leaping across the ten feet that separated them and crushing him to the ground, then taking the weapon from his hand and using it to beat the crap out of him.

Maybe Aaron sensed her anticipation, because his face suddenly paled. Pulling his empty hand out of his jacket, he held both of them up and slowly backed away.

"There's something wrong with you, chica," he said. "You're crazy." Turning, he ran after his two friends.

Selena watched him go, fighting that same urge to chase after him like he was some kind of prey.

The moment he was out of sight, it was as if all the adrenaline that had been holding her upright drained away at once, leaving her shaking and wrung out. She could barely stand, much less be sure if she could walk back to her car. That's when what she'd just done and how insane it had been finally hit her.

Selena replayed the last few minutes through her head, trying to understand how any of it had been possible. She'd beaten up three men bigger than she was, had thrown them around in a way that shouldn't have been possible. It seemed like a dream, making her wonder if any of the stuff she remembered had truly happened at all.

But the exhaustion in her arms and legs, along with the taste of blood in her mouth, confirmed she hadn't been dreaming. She'd gotten furious and gone crazy on those men like some kind of animal. She instinctively knew it was tied to the shooting in her classroom in some way but didn't understand how.

Turning, Selena slowly walked toward her car. She needed to talk to someone about everything that had happened. She just wasn't sure who.

Chapter 9

"WHY THE HELL IS CURTIS HERE?" BROOKS MUTTERED AS the Dallas chief of police joined Gage, who was standing with the prison warden, the Anderson County sheriff, and a collection of state troopers and U.S. Marshals by a large map board. There were mug shots of the seven escapees—Frasheri, Engler, Oliver, three omegas, and the truck driver—attached to the perimeter of the board, but at the moment, the group seemed more interested in the map itself, mulling over checkpoints and road-blocks the police had established around the prison and at nearly every major intersection connecting to roads leading south. Everyone except Gage assumed the escaped prisoners were heading for Mexico.

The board, along with a bewildering array of radios and computers, had been set up under a large pop-up shelter in the middle of the field where the prison truck had crashed earlier. The human driver, a contracted employee of the Texas Department of Criminal Justice, had been pretty messed up. He hadn't been wearing his seat belt when the vehicle flipped, so the guy was going to be in the hospital for a while before starting his prison sentence.

On the other hand, the two omegas who'd been in the back of the truck appeared to have come through the crash with hardly a scratch. Not true of course, but how was anyone to know their broken bones and wounds had essentially healed themselves before EMS arrived?

"I think the chief showed up because they're here," Zane said, motioning to the state and local reporters being herded into an area outside the crash site, a good fifty yards away from the command post. Most of the newsies were jockeying for space near the front where the microphones were set up. The rest were either doing sound bites in front of video cameras or taking photos of the overturned truck.

There was a snort from behind Zane, and Brooks turned to see Becker standing there, a sarcastic look on his face. "I'm disappointed you think so little of our esteemed chief. I'm sure he has a better reason for being here than getting his face on camera."

"Like what?" Zane asked. "It's not like he has any jurisdiction outside the Dallas city limits or even any valuable insights that might help with the apprehension."

Becker made a show of thinking about it for a second, then shrugged. "Okay, you're right. He's here for the photo op."

As if on cue, Curtis turned and headed for the press pool, a single U.S. Marshal accompanying him while everyone else stayed by the map board.

Brooks crossed the field to the pop-up shelter, Zane and Becker at his side. Zane grumbled under his breath as he stepped over the divots he'd made in his tumble when the bad guys had been shooting at them. He was still stewing over the way things had gone down, even if no one outside the Pack would ever know about it. As far as everyone else knew, the nearby truck had crashed on its own, and Brooks and Zane had barely gotten there in time to watch the other vehicle disappear after popping off a few shots. Thankfully, no one seemed to have noticed how fast—or how far—they'd run.

"And you have no idea who gave the order to transfer Oliver from administrative separation into the general population?" Gage asked the prison warden as Brooks and the other guys walked up.

The warden, an older man with more salt than pepper in his gray hair, shrugged as he flipped through a folder. "That's the problem. As far as I can tell, no one did. Everything in his record indicates he was still in solitary, but the guards told me he'd been in a cell in North Block for almost a week."

"The same cell block as Frasheri and Engler," Brooks observed.

The warden nodded, glancing his way. "Exactly."

"Have you figured out how they escaped?" Becker asked.

Another shake of the head from the warden. "We're still digging into it, but right now, it looks like the escapees got themselves transferred to the Trusty status. How, I have no idea, but it's possible someone hacked the prison record system to facilitate the change. Regardless, once their status was changed from G5 high-security offender to G1 Trusty, they had unfettered access to the minimum-security areas and the laundry trucks they used to escape."

Trusty status meant Oliver, Frasheri, and Engler were allowed even more freedom than prisoners in the general population. It wasn't like they could come and go from the prison when they pleased, but they didn't have to spend the majority of the day locked up in a cell.

Brooks crossed his arms over his chest. "Even if they were able to change their security status in the prison system, surely one of the guards would have caught on that something was screwed up. Prison guards know who the worst offenders are, and Engler and Oliver are both known killers. Nobody wondered why they were put on laundry duty?"

The warden's mouth tightened. "We're still looking into that."

The man didn't have to say what was on everyone's mind. This escape couldn't have happened without help from the inside, along with lots of people looking the other way.

"I'm more interested in the connection the escapees have to the Dallas SWAT team," one of the marshals said. A tall, wiry guy, he wore his hair military regulation short and had a slight New England accent. "It can't be a coincidence they ended up together in prison after getting arrested by Sergeant Dixon's team."

Brooks silently agreed. To say Frasheri and Engler came from two completely different worlds was an understatement. One was a wealthy mob boss, the other a cop from Oregon. Well, a deranged cop, but still law enforcement. They had nothing in common except their hatred for certain members of the Dallas SWAT team. If you threw Oliver into the mix, that angle made even more sense. They all hated SWAT and werewolves. Why not put aside their differences and work together?

The only thing Brooks couldn't figure out was where the omega werewolves who'd escaped fit in. The omegas had worked for Frasheri on the outside, so they would have been willing to work with him on the inside, too, especially to escape. But why agree to join forces with Engler and Oliver, men who despised werewolves with a passion? And why would Engler and Oliver be down with that? It made no sense at all.

They couldn't tell the marshal that, though. So Gage disclosed as much as he could about the men who'd escaped together—who they were, what their crimes had been, and how SWAT had taken them down.

The marshal frowned. "I know we're assuming the escapees are headed to Mexico, Sergeant Dixon, but it's entirely possible they could go after you and members of your team."

"That's very unlikely," Curtis said, stepping into the pop-up shelter.

Brooks resisted the urge to growl. Apparently, the chief was done posing for the cameras.

Curtis pointed at an area of the map on the board that was well south of Dallas. "We have confirmed sightings of the escapees in Round Rock and San Marcos. It's obvious they're making a beeline down the I-35 corridor straight for the border. I have no doubt we'll have them back in custody by nightfall."

Brooks wanted to point out those confirmed sightings could have easily been faked, especially considering Oliver and the others had outside help, but he bit his tongue. Curtis might have been a cop at one point in his past, but these days, he was a politician with aspirations for a higher office. He didn't care about facts. He wanted this situation cleared quickly simply because it would make him look good. Of course, if that didn't happen, Brooks had no doubt the man would make sure to point out this was actually a state and federal responsibility and had nothing to do with the DPD whatsoever.

A man in a suit whom Brooks recognized from DPD public affairs joined them then, a reporter in tow, asking Curtis if they could get some photos of the command center in operation. Nobody except Curtis looked thrilled with that idea, but no one complained.

Gage caught Brooks's eye and gestured to the side with his head, walking out of the tent. Brooks and his pack mates followed. Once they were too far away to be overheard, Gage spoke.

"Let's assume Curtis doesn't know what he's talking about when it comes to Frasheri and the others."

"Safe bet," Becker muttered.

"I'm not buying those convenient—and no doubt anonymous—sightings along I-35," Gage continued. "Engler's a former cop. He's too smart to let people see him that easily. Which is why we're going with the theory that Oliver and the other escapees might still be in the area and that they might be coming after us until we have real proof to the contrary."

"We need to put extra security on Jayna and her beta pack," Becker said, his face clouding with worry. "Khaki, too."

Brooks cursed silently. Becker's mate, Jayna Winston, and her small pack of devoted betas had been the ones who'd helped put Frasheri in jail. Likewise, Khaki was the reason Engler had been there. If those assholes came after anyone in the Pack, it would be them.

"I agree," Gage said. "But with Oliver involved, every werewolf in the city is a potential target. I don't want anyone going anywhere by themselves." He glanced at Becker. "Start snooping into the warden's investigation any way you have to. It's not that I don't trust him, but I want to know what the hell happened in there, since there's a good chance that whoever helped these guys break out of prison is also the man inside the DPD helping the hunters."

"I'm on it," Becker said, heading for the SWAT SUV he and Gage had driven and the computer inside it.

Brooks looked at Gage. "Do you think I have to worry about them going after Selena? We're supposed to go out tonight, but now I'm wondering if I should keep my distance from her for a while." His inner wolf rebelled at the notion even as he said the words. He wasn't a big fan of it, either. "I hate the idea of leaving her out there on her own, but at the same time, I don't want to put her in danger. If the hunters see me with her, they might realize she's one of us and go after her. I don't want to be the reason that happens."

Gage regarded him thoughtfully. "If I said yes, could you do it?"

Brooks automatically opened his mouth to say he'd stay away if it would make her safer but then stopped himself. The mere thought of not seeing Selena tonight twisted his gut into a knot. For a minute there, he could barely breathe. If there had been any doubts Selena was *The One* for him, they were gone now.

"Probably not," he admitted. "She's getting to me—fast."

"Trust me, I get it. It was the same with Mackenzie and me," Gage said with a smile. "Luckily, Selena just started going through her change two days ago. She won't show outward signs she's a werewolf for a while, so the hunters won't know she's not human."

"Actually, she's already shown outward signs," Zane said. "She bit Brooks last night."

Gage did a double take, his gaze locking on Brooks. "She bit you?"

"Yeah." Brooks reached up and pulled the collar of his T-shirt aside, showing Gage the fresh scars. "Selena and I were kissing when her fangs popped out."

Gage's eyes narrowed. "How big were they?"

Brooks shrugged. "I was a little preoccupied at the time, so I didn't see them, but probably at least half an inch. Maybe bigger. She was kissing my neck, and I guess she kind of lost control. It completely freaked her out, and the fangs were gone before she realized they were there."

"Huh." Gage was silent a moment as he considered what Brooks had said. "That's different. Apparently, Selena's going through her change faster than normal."

"Brooks and I thought it could have something to do with the hunters," Zane said. "You know, new werewolves going through the change faster to reduce the amount of time they're vulnerable?"

Gage nodded. "It makes sense. Regardless, the question of you staying away from her is moot. If Selena is going through her change this fast, she'll need you more than ever. Which means you're going to have to tell her what she is sooner rather than later."

Brooks let out a breath. "Yeah, I was thinking that."

"But while it's important for you to stick close to her, I don't want you out there on your own," Gage said. "I'll send someone to back you up."

"I'll go," Zane said softly.

The muscle in Gage's jaw flexed, an obvious sign he wasn't thrilled at the idea of an injured Zane providing backup. But after a moment, he nodded. "Okay. Just be smart. I don't want you taking any chances. Got it?"

Both Brooks and Zane nodded at that.

Gage's gaze went to the pop-up shelter where Curtis was in full politician mode as he spoke to the reporter. "I'd better get over there in case I have to do damage control."

After their commander left, Brooks turned to Zane. "I know there are probably a thousand things you'd rather be doing besides following me around on a date. So thanks."

"Sure." Zane shrugged. "Don't worry. I'll do my best to stay out of sight. But I'm warning you, if Selena starts nibbling on your neck again, I'm out."

Brooks chuckled. He and Selena were going on a double date with another couple. How wild and out of control could things get?

Selena parked in front of the Sovereign Row industrial building, then looked around to make sure she was in the right place. It would have been easier if there was a name on the structure, but most of the warehouses in this part of northwest Dallas had nothing more than a simple address on them. This was the place Ernesto had described to her, though she had no idea what he was doing with a warehouse this large. Maybe his custom car business was growing faster than she thought. Then again, he could be branching out into a completely new financial endeavor. He was always looking for the next opportunity.

Grabbing her purse from the passenger seat, Selena got out and made her way to the front door. After the fight with Aaron and the other gangbangers, she'd sat in her car in front of the liquor store trying to figure out who she should talk to. She was a little surprised that her first choice had been Jayden. They'd just met, after all. Yet something instinctively told her that he'd understand why she'd reacted like she had. But he was at work, and she didn't want to bother him. She would have talked to Becca, but her friend was in the middle of her fifth period history class right now.

That left her grandma, her priest, or one of the school board's counselors, but for reasons she'd explained to Jayden yesterday, she couldn't talk to any of them. So she'd turned to the one person who had always been there for her—Ernesto. She'd sent him a text, saying she really needed someone to talk to. He'd immediately texted back the address for the warehouse, no questions asked.

Ernesto must have been waiting for her, because he opened the door before she could even try the knob.

"Hey there, pretty lady," he said, flashing her a grin.

Selena returned his smile as he closed the door behind her. "Hey yourself, big guy. What's this place all about? A new custom car franchise?"

He laughed. "No. I have something new in mind. I'm diversifying my portfolio, I guess you could say."

"Well, color me impressed," she said and meant it.

She looked around the lobby area. There were two doors that led to small offices and another that appeared to lead to the warehouse itself. Besides a counter like the kind a receptionist would sit behind, there were a few chairs for customers, some fake potted plants, and the usual office equipment. The clang and rattle of heavy machinery echoed from the back of the building, and she caught the smell of some kind of sharp chemical odor that made her nose tingle. What the heck were they making in there?

"You going to give me a tour of the place or what?" she asked.

He gave her a sheepish look. "It's not exactly ready for the public yet. It's a mess back there, and I wouldn't want you getting all dirty walking around. How about a rain check?"

Something twinged inside her, and for a moment, Selena wondered if her friend was hiding something from her. But she quickly shook off the sensation. Ernesto was one of her best friends.

"Come on," he said. "Let's sit down."

She followed him across the lobby into the bigger of the two offices. It had a desk with a computer and not much else, unless you counted the expensive-looking leather couch.

"So, what did you want to talk to me about?" he asked as they took a seat. "It sounded important."

She forgot about the stuff Ernesto might or might not be hiding from her and let out a sigh. "I got in a fight with some Locos today."

Ernesto sat up straighter, his dark eyes narrowing. "What? Tell me who the hell it was. Did they hurt you?"

Selena shook her head. "I was out driving around, looking for one of my students. I found him over on Ferguson, hanging out with a group of Locos on that empty lot by the liquor store."

Ernesto gave her a pleading look. "Please tell me you didn't confront them by yourself? I told you to stop doing that, remember? Or at least to call me first, so I can confront them with you."

"It's not like I was planning to confront them. I was just going to talk to Ruben and get him to leave with me.

But one of the girls there recognized me as the teacher involved in Pablo's shooting, and it pretty much went downhill from there."

"Did they hurt you?" he asked again.

"No," she said. "In fact, it's kind of the other way around. I'm not sure you're going to believe this, but I came really close to killing some of them, and it's freaking me out."

Ernesto did a double take. "No way. You're a tough woman and always have been, but there's no way in hell you'd ever come close to killing someone. It's just not in you."

She stared down at her hands clasped in her lap. "Maybe before that shooting in my classroom," she said softly. "Ever since then, it's like I'm on the edge of losing control every minute of the day. I can feel the anger bubbling right below the surface, fighting to get out. And it got out today in that empty lot. I can't explain what happened. One second, the lead gangbanger was about to hit me, and the next, I'm punching him out and throwing guys all over the place. The details are mostly a blur, but I hurt them. There was a point, as they were all running away, when I swear I wanted to chase them down and kill them. It took everything in me not to go after them." She lifted her head to look at Ernesto. "It scared the hell out of me."

Even now, the memory made her so furious, she felt like punching a wall. Her hands started to tremble, and she clenched them more tightly together.

Ernesto reached out and covered her hands with his, giving them a gentle squeeze. "Sometimes, when we get put into impossible situations, we do what's necessary to survive. Those gangbangers were going to hurt you, maybe kill you. There was something inside you that stopped them. That part of you—the anger and violence—might be scary, but it kept you safe."

She gave him a small smile. "While I'm glad I didn't get hurt today, I still didn't like losing control like that. I don't want to do it ever again."

"I know," he said. "But the thing you have to remember is that while you might have thought about killing them, you didn't. You did what you had to do, then you let them go. That's what you need to focus on. In the end, you're still you."

When he said it like that, she believed him. She only hoped he was right. Leaning forward, she hugged him tightly. She still didn't know how she'd gotten so lucky to have someone like Ernesto in her life. If she couldn't have her brother, Ernesto was the next best thing.

A loud clanging noise from the back of the warehouse jarred her out of the moment, and she pulled back with a frown. "Maybe you should check and make sure nothing's wrong. It sounds like something is falling apart back there."

He frowned, wincing as the clanking in the warehouse came again. "You're probably right. You want to come over for dinner tonight so we can talk some more?"

She smiled and got to her feet. "Thanks for the offer, but I'll have to take a rain check on that. I'm Becca's wingwoman tonight. She has a blind date and doesn't want to meet him alone. Jayden is coming, too, so it's not all bad."

Ernesto lifted a brow as he stood. "Seeing this guy

two nights in a row. Sounds serious. Do I need to have a talk with him and see what his intentions are?"

She took a swing at his arm, but he skipped back out of reach. "Don't you dare say a word to him! Yes, I'm seeing him two nights in a row. And yes, it's serious. He's the nicest guy I've met in a long time, so don't mess it up."

He held up his hands in self-defense. "I wouldn't dream of it. But if he doesn't turn out to be the guy you think he is and you need to vent, call me, okay? You know I'm always here for you."

She swung her purse onto her shoulder. "I know." There was another clang, louder this time. Crap, it sounded like World War III was about to break out in the warehouse. "Go and fix whatever trouble is going on back there. I have to go home and get cleaned up for the club anyway."

Ernesto walked her to the door. "Before I forget. Did you catch the names of those guys who tried to attack you?"

"Why?" She frowned. "You aren't going to do anything stupid, are you?"

He shook his head. "No. Like you're always reminding me, I'm not in that world anymore. But I still know people. If I know who it was, maybe I can talk to someone and try to get them to leave you alone."

Selena felt that funny sensation in her stomach again but ignored it. "The only name I know is the one in charge—Aaron. Have you ever heard of him?"

Ernesto thought about it for a moment, then shook his head. "No. But there's no reason I should. Still, I'll see what I can do."

"Nothing stupid, right?"

He grinned as he opened the door for her. "Coming from you, that's funny. Go have a good time tonight, but don't do anything I wouldn't do."

"Is there anything you wouldn't do?" she quipped.

He laughed. "You're right. Don't do anything I would do, either. In fact, don't do anything at all."

Selena made a show of rolling her eyes as she left. Outside, her nose tingled from the chemical stench rolling out from the warehouse and filling the air. She got in the car and quickly closed the door so it wouldn't follow her. Whatever Ernesto's new business venture was, she hoped it was worth it, because it stunk like a chemical factory.

Chapter 10

"OKAY, I'M CONFUSED," ZANE SAID, EYES FIXED ON THE small TV positioned on the wall behind the bar. "The lean, athletic guys can move as much as they want, but the big guys have to remain bent over with their hands on the ground without moving at all before the one in the middle gives the quarterback the ball, right?"

Brooks glanced up at the TV. The club was too loud to hear anything the analyst on ESPN was saying—even for a werewolf—so all they could do was sit there and watch the highlights of the weekend's college football games. At that moment, the station was showing clips of the problems the Texas A&M Aggies were having with penalties, especially false starts.

He'd been trying to explain American football to Zane for years, but it was hopeless. Zane was overwhelmed by the number of rules, not to mention the endless penalties. Brooks supposed he couldn't complain. Zane had been trying to teach him soccer for years, and Brooks didn't understand a lick of it.

"It's a little more complicated than that," Brooks said. "The receivers, tight ends, and running backs are allowed to move before the center hikes the ball, but only one of them can do it at a time. Once everyone is set, they all have to remain that way for about a second prior to snapping the ball. The offensive linemen stand there motionless the entire time so they don't give anything away."

Zane looked at him. "Do you realize how stupid that sounds? Grown adults have to freeze like they're doing the mannequin challenge instead of playing football?"

Brooks chuckled. "Well, when you put it that way, I guess it does seem kind of silly. Like I said, it's a complicated game."

"That's one word for it," Zane muttered. "Not the one I'd use, but you go ahead if it works for you."

Brooks laughed again, taking a swig of beer as he glanced across the main dance floor to the club's other bar, which ran the length of the opposite wall. He and Zane had gotten there early for his date with Selena and had been surprised to find it packed, considering it was the middle of the week. An immense place, the interior was all black, right down to the Christmas decorations, but it was lit with purple, blue, and green lights that gave everything an almost luminescent quality.

He'd never been there before, since goth wasn't his thing. But apparently, they also held themed nights at the club, because the stuff coming out of the DJ's sound system seemed more like '80s pop than goth. Then again, he'd been a toddler for a good portion of the '80s, so he could be completely wrong about that.

The bartender came over with two more beers, even though neither he nor Zane had ordered them.

"Courtesy of the two ladies at the other end of the bar," the man said, gesturing with his head in that direction.

Brooks glanced over to see two women seated there. Like a good portion of the people in the club, they were dressed in goth clothes, but instead of the traditional jet-black hair he'd always associated with goth, one had bright-blue hair, while the other had purple streaks. They held up their glasses of red wine in a toast.

Zane tipped his beer toward them in thanks.

"You going to head over there and thank them in person?" Brooks asked.

"Maybe later," Zane said, setting his beer down on the bar.

That's when Brooks realized he'd barely touched the one he'd ordered when they'd first gotten there. Considering they had work early tomorrow, not drinking might make sense, but since it was essentially impossible for werewolves to get drunk, not drinking usually meant something else.

"You okay?" he asked, pointing at the bottle.

His friend shrugged. "Dr. Saunders has me on a new drug regimen to try to stimulate muscle growth in my arm. He's worried alcohol might inhibit the effectiveness of the drug, so I'm limiting my booze tonight."

"That's great!" Brooks sat up straighter. "I didn't know he had you on something. Is it working?"

Zane snorted. "Calm down. This is about the tenth different drug regimen he's tried, and none of them have worked so far. There's no reason to think this one will, either. Nothing has worked, not one damn thing. Not that I thought there was ever a chance they would."

Beside Brooks, Zane's heart thumped like a drum, his body tensing as gold flashed in his eyes. His claws were starting to extend, too.

Shit.

"Zane, you're losing it, man," he said softly. "Chill out."

His friend swallowed hard, his teeth grinding together as he took a slow deep breath, holding it for a moment before letting it out with a low rumble. It took a little while, but after some deep breaths, Zane's rapid heartbeat slowed a bit more with each one. The glow faded from his eyes and his claws retracted.

"What's going on, Zane?" Brooks asked after Zane had finally gotten it back together. "And don't try telling me it's about this drug regimen Dr. Saunders has you on. We both know that's a crock. Is this about the hunters and the other prisoners who escaped? If it is, you can relax. If we don't track them down, somebody else will."

"We shouldn't have to track them down," Zane snarled, looking sideways at him. "Nobody should have to do it. They should have never gotten away in the first place. And they wouldn't have if it wasn't for me. They got away because I'm too fucked up to do my job."

Brooks bit back a growl. "That's bullshit."

He should have seen this coming. After practically begging Gage to let him back in the field in some capacity, Zane had locked up the first time a hunter had shot at him with poison bullets. It was understandable, just not acceptable…for Zane, at least.

"I was useless out there today, Brooks. I could have gotten myself killed. Worse, I could have gotten you killed." Jaw clenched, he stared down at the label on the beer bottle. "I've become a liability to the team. I think it's time for me to walk away. Before it's too late."

Brooks did a double take. He didn't like where this was going. "What are you talking about? You'd leave SWAT?"

"More like leave the force completely." Zane shrugged. "I'm due for my department physical fitness test soon. You and I both know I can't pass it. The decision will most likely be out of my hands anyway."

Brooks's chest tightened. He didn't want to hear this crap. "Don't worry about that. You know Gage will cover for you. Hell, Deputy Chief Mason will, too. They'll make sure you have all the time you need to recover."

"I don't want them to cover for me," Zane snapped. "I'm nobody's frigging charity case. If I can't do the job, I don't want to be on the team."

"Shit, Zane. You almost died," Brooks growled. "Why don't you cut yourself some slack? You've been injured, and it's going to take time for you to heal, but you'll recover. You're getting better every day."

Zane shook his head. "No, I'm not. If anything, I'm getting weaker by the day. And I don't just mean my arm. I tried to go jogging over the weekend, and I couldn't make it a mile before I was on my knees coughing up blood."

Brooks ground his jaw, pissed his friend had kept all this shit from him. "But Dr. Saunders is working on something to help, right? He hasn't given up, so you shouldn't, either."

"Yeah, he's trying. Can't say he's not." Zane sighed. "But nothing he's tried so far has come close to working, and some has made it worse. He gives me something my human body can handle, and my inner werewolf metabolizes it before it can do what it's supposed to do. He gives me something designed specifically for my inner werewolf, and it nearly kills my human half. I'm getting tired of being his test dummy. Hell, I'm tired of all this."

Brooks didn't know how to respond to that. While he was trying to come up with something, another horrible thought hit him. "Wait a minute. When you talked about walking away, you don't mean you'd leave the Pack, right? Tell me you're not considering something that drastic?"

Zane didn't say anything.

Anger surged through him. There was no way in the fucking world he was letting his friend—his pack mate—walk away like that. But the moment he opened his mouth to unload on Zane, a delectable scent wafted across the crowded club.

Selena.

He inhaled deeply. Damn, her scent was even stronger and more powerful than it had been last night. He actually had to reach out and grab the edge of the bar to keep from falling off the seat.

Zane chuckled softly. "You really fancy this woman, don't you?"

"Don't try to distract me," Brooks said, even as he looked through the crowded club, trying to find Selena. "You can't drop a bomb like that about leaving the Pack and expect me to act like I didn't hear it." He looked at Zane. "Promise me you won't do anything stupid, not without talking to me first."

His phone dinged, letting him know he had a text, but he ignored it, his eyes locked on Zane's.

"Look, I don't know what I'm going to do. All I know is that I can't keep doing this," Zane said. "I promise to talk to you before I do whatever it is I decide. But in the end, it will be my decision."

Figuring that was the best he was going to get at the

moment, Brooks pulled out his phone. The text was
from Selena, saying she was there and waiting in a booth
near the left side of the bar with Becca. He sent a quick
text back, telling her he'd be there soon.

"You still worried about messing things up with
her?" Zane asked.

"Shouldn't I be?" He slipped his phone in his pocket.
"I don't have what anyone would call an impressive
track record when it comes to relationships or dealing
with a werewolf going through her first change. Throw
in the fact that Selena's change is coming on faster than
normal and the small issue of us likely being soul mates,
and there are about a dozen different ways this could go
bad. I'd prefer if that didn't happen."

"Then don't let it happen."

Brooks snorted as he picked up his beer and stood.
"That's the best advice you can give?"

Zane shrugged. "As complicated as you'd like
to make this, it's not. Selena is *The One* for you. It's
bloody obvious. As far as the rest… You're a good
person, a good cop, and one of the most capable alpha
werewolves in the Pack. You'll know when the time is
right to tell her."

Brooks wasn't so sure of that. "Catch you later."

Turning, Brooks headed toward Selena's table, following her scent like a homing beacon.

―∿∿―

His breath caught in his throat when he saw Selena.
She was sitting on the inside curve of the booth, the
sexy red dress she wore showing off a perfect amount
of cleavage. Becca sat beside her, next to a trim guy

with brown hair and glasses. They didn't see him right away, but Selena did. Or maybe she picked up his scent. Regardless, her eyes met his, and she smiled.

Brooks slipped into the booth and slid across, then leaned in and gave her a kiss. He'd intended it to be a light peck on the cheek since they were in public, but Selena turned her head and captured his lips with hers, her mouth opening and demanding he do this right. He kissed her back, immediately hardening in his jeans at the taste of her tongue. Damn, she tasted even better than she did last night. How was that possible?

Becca let out a polite cough, reminding him where they were. Even though it was the last thing his body wanted to do, Brooks broke the kiss and pulled away. While Becca was grinning from ear to ear, her date was nearly blushing.

"Jayden, this is Scott Llewellyn," Selena said to introduce them. "Scott, Jayden Brooks."

Brooks reached across the table, offering his hand. "Nice to meet you."

Scott took his hand, giving it a quick shake, then adjusted his glasses. If that didn't clue Brooks in that the guy was nervous as hell, the rapid heartbeat and unusually fast breathing would have. At first, Brooks thought it was because he was a cop. Some people got nervous around law enforcement. But then he caught the covert look Scott gave Becca and realized the guy was sweating the blind date.

Brooks's suspicions were confirmed a moment later when the waitress showed up with drinks. Both Selena and Becca had some kind of fruity drinks with umbrellas, but Scott had a Long Island iced tea, half of which he chugged while the server was standing there. The woman took one look at him and murmured something about bringing him another one. Brooks winced. This had the potential to go bad quickly.

"What do you do for a living, Jayden?" Scott asked.

Brooks hesitated. He hadn't been uncomfortable around the opposite sex since he was fourteen, but he still remembered what it was like trying to look cool in front of an attractive girl only to have some big jock mess everything up.

"I work for the city," he finally said, figuring that was a safe answer. "Pushing paperwork mostly. Pretty boring job to be truthful."

Selena and Becca looked at him funny but didn't say anything.

Scott seemed just as surprised. "You're…um…kind of big to push papers. I would have figured you for a job that was more…physical."

"Nah." Brooks took a sip of beer. "What about you?"

"I'm a tax accountant." Scott laughed. "I live to fill out forms, so I feel your pain carrying box after box of Xerox paper to the copy machine all day."

Selena gently squeezed his thigh, and Brooks glanced over to see her smiling. She mouthed a silent *thank you*, then they both went back to listening to Scott talk about tax preparation. Filing season was coming up, and he was positively giddy with anticipation over the new tax laws. Becca genuinely seemed to enjoy the conversation, which boded well for their relationship.

Scott slammed the rest of his Long Island iced tea and started on the next one, all but ignoring Brooks and Selena and focusing completely on Becca. The redhead must have thought the conversation was going well, because she gave Selena a subtle nod.

"Jayden and I are going to check out the dance floor," Selena said, nudging him out of the booth. "We'll be back in a little bit."

But instead of walking onto the dance floor, Selena led Brooks around it, heading for an empty highboy cocktail table. It was close enough for Selena to keep an eye on Becca and her date but far enough away to give them some privacy.

Out of the corner of his eye, Brooks saw Zane standing at another highboy table, drinking small sips from his beer and casually chatting up the two women who'd bought the drinks earlier. They gazed at Zane like they were hypnotized. That damn British accent of his did it every time.

"It was cool of you to downplay your job like that for Scott," Selena said. "How did you know that would make him relaxed enough to talk?"

Brooks chuckled. "Believe it or not, I've been in his shoes once or twice in my life. I figured he could use any help he could get. First dates can be tough."

Her eyes sparkled. "Was our first date tough?"

"Our first date was as easy as riding a bike." He grinned. "Actually, it was the best date ever."

"I'll have to take your word on that thing about riding a bike," she said. "But I agree with you about how amazing it was. Even if I did bite you. I have to admit, there was a minute there when I thought I might have to take you to the emergency room for stitches." She tucked her hair behind her ear, giving him an embarrassed look. "I still can't believe I did that. Or that you were so cool with it."

"It wasn't a big deal. Seriously," he assured her. "Look. You can hardly see the marks now."

He leaned forward and tugged the collar of his shirt aside, showing her his neck. She moved around the small table, getting close to take a look in the dimly lit club.

"Wow, they really are gone," she breathed.

She was so close to him that he could feel her warm, soft breath against his skin. Brooks expected her to step back, but she stayed where she was. That was when he realized she was sniffing him.

Her eyes were closed, and there was a rapt expression on her face as she breathed in his scent. Her nostrils flared as she moved a little to the right and left, taking him all in. At the same time, her tongue slipped out a little, like she was tasting the air.

Her change was coming at warp speed now, her sense of smell developing as fast as her fangs.

His inner wolf stood up and took notice.

A moment later, she opened her eyes and stepped back. Her arousal drifted toward him, making his mouth water. And his cock hard.

Brooks wondered if she could smell how turned on he was. The hungry gaze in her eyes made him think maybe she could. He half expected them to glow green, but they were still a dark chocolate brown.

While they didn't glow, he knew something had happened, because he saw it in her eyes. Selena knew exactly what she was doing to him.

They were still gazing at each other when a server appeared and asked if they needed fresh drinks. Brooks wasn't really interested in another beer but

ordered one anyway. Selena asked for another strawberry daiquiri.

"How'd your day go?" he asked after the man left.

"It was okay." She shrugged, concentrating on her
empty daiquiri glass. "I spent most of it driving around,
checking in with a few of my kids."

Her expression didn't give anything away, but Brooks
knew without a doubt she'd lied to him. Had she realized something was going on with her? Had she seen a
slip of fangs in a mirror or caught sight of her claws?

"I get the feeling something else happened today,"
he said. "You want to tell me what it was and why you
thought you needed to keep it from me?"

Selena jerked her head up at Jayden's question, those
seemingly ever-present waves of anger immediately
bubbling up inside her. She opened her mouth to tell
him she wasn't one of his perps and that he didn't have
the right to question her like one. But then she saw the
concern in his eyes, and the anger faded so fast, it left
her almost gasping. He was worried about her. That was
something Selena could understand. She worried about
a lot of people herself.

"Ruben Moreno, one of the kids from my fourth
period class, hasn't been home in two nights." She
sighed. "I went to look for him today and found him
hanging out with some Locos in an empty lot on
Ferguson." The bitter disappointment at losing Ruben to
a gang was still fresh in her mind, and she had to squelch
the anger threatening to take control again. "I tried to get
him to leave with me, but he wouldn't."

"I can't imagine the Locos were thrilled with you poking your nose into their business," Jayden observed.

Selena hesitated, not sure how much she wanted to tell Jayden. Ernesto had believed her, but that was because he'd known her forever. No way was Jayden going to believe her wild story about beating the hell out of three gangbangers.

"We got into an argument, and it got heated," she finally said. "By the time it was over, Ruben had run off."

Jayden frowned. "You know how crazy that was, right? Going face-to-face with a bunch of gang members by yourself is dangerous. Next time, call me for help instead of trying to take them on all by yourself, okay?"

Between him and Ernesto, she had quite the team of bodyguards. She smiled. "Okay. Next time I get ready to poke a hornet's nest, you'll be the first one I call."

The server brought their drinks, and while Jayden paid for them, Selena glanced over at Becca and Scott. It looked like they were still doing well. Selena couldn't help noticing he'd finished his second Long Island iced tea or the fact that Becca seemed to be doing most of the talking.

"They seem to be getting along okay," Jayden remarked after the server left. "I don't know Becca that well, but Scott doesn't strike me as her type. She seems way more outgoing than he is."

Selena couldn't help but think of Ernesto, who was exactly Becca's type. "Normally, I'd agree with you, but she's had a run of crappy dates lately with the guys she normally goes out with, so I guess she decided to try someone completely different."

He nodded. "Makes sense. I've never even considered

dating a teacher before, and now it seems like the best move I've made."

Her stomach did a crazy little flip-flop at his words. "If that was a blatant attempt to get on my good side, I should probably let you know it's working."

He flashed her a grin, his teeth white against his brown skin. "I guess I should keep doing it then."

Selena returned his smile. "I won't stop you. But before you start buttering me up with more compliments, maybe I should be polite and ask how your day went. You catch any bad guys?"

Jayden grimaced. "Unfortunately, my day wasn't so good."

"What happened?" she asked.

For reasons she couldn't explain, her fingertips began tingling like they had today in that empty lot on Ferguson. It felt like her fingernails were on fire.

"One of my teammates and I were down at Coffield Prison today to talk to a prisoner," he explained. "There was a jail break, and that prisoner, along with several others my SWAT team put in there, escaped. We tried to stop them, and we failed."

Selena blinked. With everything going on, she hadn't paid a lot of attention, but it had been impossible to miss the alerts about the half dozen psychotic killers who'd escaped and the men who'd almost died trying to stop them from getting away. She'd known there were some cops involved, but Coffield was so far away, she'd never dreamed it was anyone from Dallas, much less Jayden.

"You were the one trying to chase down the getaway vehicle? While they were shooting at you?" she asked, remembering that particular detail from the reports.

"My teammate and I," he said calmly, as if it was something he did every day. "Those men who escaped are dangerous and have a personal beef with the Dallas SWAT team. We had good reason to do everything we could to stop them, and they still got away."

Selena couldn't imagine trying to run down a vehicle full of escaped convicts, but Jayden talked about it like it wasn't even a big deal. "Are you in danger?" Her heart thudded unexpectedly hard at the thought. "Do you think they'll come after you?"

He opened his mouth to say something but then stopped himself. Selena could almost see the private battle happening in his smoky blue eyes, and she knew he was fighting over whether to tell her the truth or not.

"They probably won't come after me, but there are certain members of my team—and their loved ones— who are more likely targets," he finally said. "That really isn't important though, since a threat to any member of my pack is a threat to me. We take care of our own, and nothing is going to get in the way of that."

Selena gazed at him, fascinated as much by the determination she heard in his voice as she was at the way the club's colorful lights reflected almost gold in his expressive eyes. She wondered at the choice of words he'd used to describe his SWAT teammates as a pack, though. Regardless, there was no doubting the sentiment behind the term. Jayden and his team would do anything to protect the people they cared about. That resonated with her on a level deeper than she could have ever imagined.

Jayden took a long draught of beer, then looked at her. "This is probably going to seem like it's coming out of left field, but speaking of people who are important to me, one of the guys from the team is getting married on Saturday. I was hoping maybe you'd like to come?"

The question caught her off guard, and for a moment, she wasn't sure what to say. Ten seconds ago, Jayden had been talking about escaped prisoners possibly coming after the SWAT team. Now, he was asking her to be his plus one at a wedding. Selena was usually quick on her feet, but she hadn't seen this one coming. That didn't mean she didn't want to go with him.

"Are you sure it would be okay?" she asked hesitantly. "I've never met the bride or groom."

Jayden chuckled. "Don't worry about that. You'll be more than welcome. Max and Lana are really cool. They'd like nothing better than for you to be there, simply because it would mean a lot to me. Like I said, we're like a big family that takes care of each other."

Selena didn't have any experience with a big family, but she suddenly found herself wanting to be part of this one, as long as it meant being closer to Jayden.

"Okay." She smiled. "If you're sure. I'd love to come. Besides, I've been wanting to meet the other officers involved in my rescue, so I can thank them in person. This should be a perfect time."

His smile broadened. "Good."

Selena glanced at Becca and Scott again, who were deep in conversation. Glad to see Scott was actually talking now, Selena turned her attention back to Jayden, but not before her gaze lingered on the crowded dance floor for a moment. Even though it was '80s theme night, most people were wearing black leather, heavy boots, and trench coats, or some combination thereof. To say they made an interesting dichotomy was putting it mildly.

"Do you mind if I ask you something personal?" she said to Jayden.

His mouth quirked. "Even if we don't count the neck nibbling, I think we've been getting personal for a while now."

She couldn't help but laugh. "True, but this is a different kind of personal."

"Okay," he said. "Go for it."

"Have you ever been in a serious relationship? I mean one where you thought you might end up with the other person forever?"

He didn't say anything for so long, Selena got concerned she'd pushed too far too fast, but then he spoke.

"I dated a girl in college," he said slowly, his expression introspective. "For a long time, I thought it was real. I thought I was in love."

"What happened?" Even though Jayden was talking in the past tense, it bothered her that he'd been with someone. Which was silly as hell. They both had pasts. But she couldn't deny it or explain it. She'd never thought of herself as possessive, but when it came to him, she was.

"I met Sheri freshman year," he continued. "She came to every game, and we hung out all the time. When I blew out my knee and learned I wouldn't be able to play ball anymore, she was right there at my side. When I made the decision to become a cop after graduation, she moved to Gulfport with me. I thought we'd get married soon after that, but one day, I came home from a late shift and found her gone, along with most of my LSU collectibles."

Selena lifted a brow. "She took your old, smelly football jerseys?"

He laughed. "My well-laundered football jerseys, actually. Along with the five game balls I earned while I was there. Maybe she felt like it was her due for hanging with me all those years."

"Do you ever ask yourself why it didn't work out?" she asked curiously, wondering what kind of woman could walk away from a man like Jayden.

"Sure." He shrugged. "For years, I told myself it was because Sheri had gotten bored with the grind of being with a cop. You know, the long shifts, the phone calls in the middle of the night, the worries. I think I told myself that line so many times, I actually started believing it was true."

"But you don't think that now?"

He shook his head. "I came to the realization a little while ago that Sheri and I didn't work out because the spark that was supposed to be there wasn't. We were together because it was comfortable, but it wasn't special."

She felt a little tingle in her tummy. "When did you figure that out?"

His eyes met hers, his gaze almost hypnotic. "About two days ago. When I met you."

Her pulse skipped a beat. He hadn't known the spark was missing in his previous relationship until he felt the spark with her.

"How about you?" he asked casually. "Was there someone special for you that didn't work out?"

Selena ran her thumb along the stem of her glass. "No. I didn't date in high school, because my brother and Ernesto scared all the boys away. After Geraldo died and I went off to college, I was too busy with school to think about guys. I've gone out since then but can't say I've ever met anyone special."

"Haven't found that spark yet, huh?" he murmured.

She locked gazes with him. "If you had asked me that two days ago, I would have said no."

He didn't say anything, but it felt like hundreds of words passed between them as a smile curved his sensuous mouth.

"Do you want to dance?" he asked suddenly.

She returned his smile. She knew she kept asking herself this, but could he possibly get any better? The looks, the body, the personality, the perfect, open honesty. And now it turned out that he liked to dance? It was official now—Jayden Brooks was absolutely perfect.

"I thought you'd never ask."

Chapter 11

BROOKS PULLED SELENA CLOSER, THEN RIGHT BEFORE SHE collided with his chest, he stepped to the side and let her spin past under his arm. Her hand was tiny in comparison with his, but she held on to him easily as he guided her in a tight circle. Then he urged her back toward him, slipping them both into the salsa so fast and smooth, it felt like they'd been dancing together for years. Selena laughed, and Brooks was convinced it was the sweetest sound he'd ever heard.

The Whitney Houston dance beat they'd been moving to slowed, and the first few notes of a much slower song started filling the club.

"You want to take a break?" he asked over the music.

"Don't even think about it," she said as she tugged him close.

Despite their difference in height, her curvy body fit so perfectly with his, it was like they were two puzzle pieces. He couldn't help but wonder if they'd fit together this well in the bedroom, too. Something told him they would. In fact, he had visions of spinning her around in all kinds of positions right there on the dance floor just to see how many different ways he could fit the two of them together.

Selena buried her face against his chest as they danced, one hand near his shoulder, her other arm wrapped fiercely around him. He urged her even tighter to his body. The move pressed that delicious tummy of hers right into his hard-on, and he knew there was no way in hell Selena could miss it. He'd been aroused from the moment he'd smelled her walking into the club, but pressed up against her like this made the big guy stand up and take notice.

Selena slid her arm down his back, pressing her body against him, swaying to the music in a way that had his cock rock hard in seconds. Damn, she knew how to work it. He wondered if she could feel him throbbing, even through all the layers of clothes that separated them. If she could, she didn't give it away.

Instead, she breathed him in, a soft little moan slipping out with nearly every exhale. It had to be the sexiest sound he'd ever heard.

They were still swaying to the music when he realized he wasn't the only one getting rapidly turned on. If the scent of arousal coming from her and the way those little moans had turned to little growls was any indication, Selena was excited as hell.

Tipping her head back, she cupped his jaw and tugged him down for a kiss. He had to admit he got caught a little off guard when he felt her fangs brush against his tongue, not to mention the possessive growl she let out as her hand locked behind his neck and refused to let him move. Brooks knew this was dangerous, that Selena could be on the verge of a shift right here on the dance floor, but try as he might, he couldn't pull himself away. She tasted too damn good.

He deepened the kiss, letting her know he wanted this as much as she did. But when he felt her fangs extend farther and that growl started to rumble deep in her throat, he knew he had to get things under control before it went too far.

That was hard to do with her mouth firmly locked on his. Putting his hands on her hips and breaking the kiss so he could gently put some distance between them was one of the hardest things he'd ever had to do. His inner alpha howled in frustration as he did it, wanting to take her right there on the dance floor, to hell with all the people watching.

Selena looked almost dazed as she gazed up at him in confusion. He caught a quick glimmer of wild color in her eyes but figured it had to be the club's many strobe lights, since it sure as hell hadn't been green. He glanced at her hands and was relieved to see her claws weren't out. Even as he watched, the little bit of fang that was protruding over her lower lip disappeared before she even realized they were there.

Thank God.

Her eyes cleared but were just as quickly filled with confusion. "What's wrong?"

"Absolutely nothing," he said, pulling her in close again and dropping his forehead down to rest on hers. "I thought we might need to take a break and cool off a bit before you make me completely lose control and I end up doing something that's likely going to show up on YouTube."

Selena looked around, as if only then realizing they were in the middle of a crowded dance floor. A sultry smile curved her lips. "You have a problem staying in control when I kiss you?"

He grinned in return, knowing she could still feel his hard-on pressing against her urgently. "I think that's obvious."

She wiggled against him as if letting him know she was fully aware of his condition. "Okay, good call. But to be honest, I'm not too sure you would have been the only one losing control."

"At least you didn't bite me again," he pointed out.

She laughed. "Maybe later. Until then, let's check in on Becca and Scott."

Brooks took Selena's hand and led her off the floor, praying no one noticed the raging hard-on in his jeans as they weaved their way through the crowd of people between them and their booth.

They found Becca and Scott talking and laughing like they'd been dating for months. Jayden was kind of surprised...until he saw all the empty glasses on Scott's side of the table, along with three colorful metal cans that looked like something an energy drink would come in. Alcohol and caffeine. That was one way to loosen up.

Scott slid the glasses and cans aside, making room for him and Selena, laughing as one of the cans fell over and splattered a few droplets of clear liquid on the table. "Sorry about that. But I told Becca the only way she'd get me out there on the dance floor was to ply me with booze and energy drinks. I think she went a little overboard."

Brooks chuckled. Lots of guys hated to dance. They'd been indoctrinated since birth to avoid doing anything that might make them look silly or uncool. It was only alcohol—and the chance to get up close and personal with a good-looking woman—that usually gave them the courage to do it at all.

Brooks reached out and set the can upright, his nose wrinkling at the harsh chemical odor of whatever was inside it. He didn't recognize the container, but with the name BUZZ splashed across it in garish, lightning-bolt letters, it was obvious what the stuff was all about. It didn't smell like anything Brooks ever wanted to try, but Scott seemed to be cool with it.

"You two look so smooth out there," Becca said, grinning at Selena. "If I didn't know better, I'd think you've been dancing together for years."

While Selena and Becca talked about how great the music was, Scott leaned in and asked Brooks where he'd learned to dance.

"I learned most of the formal stuff in college," Brooks admitted. "I needed an elective, and ballroom dancing was an option. I picked up the rest here and there over the years."

Scott nodded. "That's cool. Where'd you go to school?"

Brooks was kind of surprised how easy it was, but before he knew it, he and Scott fell into an easy conversation about their college experiences. Brooks didn't mention the stuff about law enforcement, but other than that, he talked and had a good time doing it. On the other side of the booth, Scott drank another energy drink. Chill and excited at the same time, his feet were tapping like crazy in time to the music coming from the dance floor.

A few minutes later, Scott gave Becca a smile. "Want to dance?"

Becca nodded eagerly, smiling back at him. She started sliding out of the booth with Scott, only to stop and motion Brooks and Selena to join them. "Come on! It'll be fun!"

They hit the floor just as the worst dance song ever—at least in Brooks's opinion—started playing: "YMCA." Brooks felt like pointing out that the song wasn't even from the '80s, but he was pretty sure no one cared. He would have faked a hamstring injury, but it was obvious Selena loved the damn song. He threw a quick glance in Zane's direction, hoping he wasn't watching. Not only was his teammate watching, he was holding his frigging cell phone aloft, recording everything. Brooks gave him a covert finger. Zane smiled and waved back. This crap was gonna show up on the screen of the next SWAT training class for sure.

But when he saw how much fun Selena was having, he decided he didn't care. Beside them, Becca and Scott were laughing and dancing like crazy. Hell, Scott was actually jumping around with a completely euphoric expression on his face.

The floor filled with people dancing and singing, everyone bumping into each other and not caring a bit. But as the end of the song approached, Brooks's instincts screamed at him that something was wrong. At first, he was worried a hunter had slipped into the crowd, but after a moment, he realized that wasn't it at all. It was Scott. He'd stopped dancing. Not only that, but he was as pale as a ghost. And whereas his heart had been beating like a drum a minute ago, now it was thumping so slowly, Brooks could barely pick it up.

Suddenly, Scott's eyes rolled back in his head, and he started falling forward.

Becca screamed and tried to slow Scott's fall, but Brooks jumped in to catch him, lowering the man to the floor. Around them, everyone stepped back, gasping and murmuring in shock.

Out of the corner of his eye, Brooks saw Zane pushing his way through the crowd even as Scott's heart stopped.

"He's going under," Brooks said, starting CPR.

Zane dropped down to do the rescue breathing, coming up after his first two breaths with a stunned look on his face. "He's overdosing on fentanyl. I can taste it."

Shit. There were so many other frigging chemicals in the energy drink, he hadn't even smelled the fentanyl.

"Selena, call an ambulance," Brooks shouted.

He only prayed they weren't too late.

———

Selena sat at a table near the back of the club, watching Brooks talk to a group of other cops and paramedics. All the customers had left long ago, bailing after the music had been shut down and the lights had come up. Nobody had been interested in partying after seeing a person almost die on the middle of a dance floor. Half a dozen of the club's employees were quietly moving around, trying to clean up.

Brooks had suggested earlier she and Becca might want to call it a night since he had no idea how long he was going to be stuck there. But Selena had wanted to stay in case there was a chance he got done sooner than he thought, and Becca had been too freaked out to leave on her own.

"A paramedic just called the hospital for me," Becca said with a sigh as she sank weakly into a chair beside Selena. "She said Scott was conscious and aware when the ambulance brought him in. That's a good thing, right?"

Selena leaned over and wrapped an arm around her, giving her a hug. "Definitely. Jayden and that other guy got to him in time and kept his heart going. Scott's going to be okay. But you know, if you headed to the hospital and told them what happened, I bet you could get a nurse to give you some more details."

Becca nodded. "I know, and I'm going to go. But the paramedic suggested I wait at least an hour so the ER can get him stabilized."

That made sense.

"I get the feeling Jayden knows the other guy who jumped in to help him do CPR," Becca said. "They worked together too well to be strangers."

Selena had been thinking the same thing. Considering the other guy with the slight British accent was nearly as muscular and sexy as Jayden, she was pretty sure he was SWAT. The odds that two guys that hot—who both knew CPR—happened to be in the club at the same time was pretty slim.

"I think he's one of Jayden's coworkers," she said, watching the British guy casually chatting up the other cops like they all knew each other.

"I wonder what they're talking about," Becca said.

"Well, while you were talking to the paramedic, they were asking the manager where he got those energy drinks," Selena murmured. The guy behind the bar was still squirming at the looks the cops were giving him. "Narcotics officers tested the residue from the cans Scott had been drinking from, and it came back positive for fentanyl. But the manager claims he had no clue there were drugs in those cans, and he doesn't know where they came from, either. Some salesman showed up about a week ago and offered them a dozen cases at a good price, promising people would like it. The guy was right, too. The manager told the cops people had been begging for it. He'd been hoping the salesman would come back with more."

Becca stared at her open-mouthed. "I'm not sure what's more shocking, that a club like this one would buy drinks from some salesman they didn't know, or that you were eavesdropping on the cops."

"I was just sitting here minding my own business, waiting for Jayden to finish up." Selena did her best to look both hurt and innocent. "It's not my fault they were talking so loud."

Becca gave her a dubious look. "Right. And I'm sure it had nothing to do with you leaning in a little closer so you could hear."

Actually, it hadn't. Selena had been able to hear them fine from where she was sitting. She still could if she focused on what they were saying. But she didn't bother to point that out to her friend.

"Okay, if your hearing is so great, what are they saying now?" Becca asked.

Selena frowned. Becca really did have bad hearing. "The guy to the left of Jayden—I think he's from narcotics—is saying all the fentanyl on the street must be going into this energy drink. The older guy on the far right is named Ray. He's from the gang unit and insists the salesman is actually a front man for a local gang."

Beside her, Becca looked impressed. "You seriously heard all that? You're not making this up?"

Selena looked at the group of cops standing twenty feet from her and Becca, slowly coming to the realization that maybe it was a little weird she could make out what they were saying from so far away. From the concerned way Becca was regarding at her, it was obvious her friend had seen that thought flit across her mind.

"Are you okay?" Becca asked.

"Yeah. I'm fine," Selena answered. Suddenly, she didn't want to talk about her hearing anymore. "How about you? You're the one whose date OD'd right in front of her."

Becca shuddered as if reliving the memory of Scott collapsing to the floor. Selena reached out and tugged her friend into another hug, knowing it was a moment neither of them would ever forget.

"Seeing that happen to Scott was horrible," Becca murmured against her shoulder. "But you want to know the worst part?"

Selena pulled back enough to see Becca's face. "What?"

"Right before you and Jayden came back over to the table and we all went to dance, I'd been thinking the date hadn't really been going very well and how I wasn't sure if I'd want to see him again."

Yeah, thinking about dumping your blind date only to have him practically die five minutes later was bad. Guilt trip times ten.

"He was really nice," Becca said, like she had to explain herself. "And cute. But I don't think I've ever met a man so shy. He had to chug alcohol just to talk to me, and I swear he didn't look me in the eye the whole night. I couldn't even get him to stare at my boobs, and trust me, I was giving him every opportunity."

"He got up to dance with you," Selena pointed out.

"Only after downing a few of those spiked energy drinks," Becca muttered. "If not for them, I doubt he would have ever worked up the courage."

Selena sighed. "You probably don't want to hear this, but there's a good chance the reason he was so nervous was because he was attracted to you and figured someone like you probably wouldn't want to have anything to do with someone like him."

Becca snorted. "I'm not sure if I should take that as a compliment or an indication of how shallow I am."

Selena gave her friend's hand a squeeze. "Look, I'm just saying there's a good chance you're the most attractive woman Scott had ever gone out with, so he was probably a little nervous."

"There was no reason for him to be nervous," Becca insisted. "It was just a first date."

Selena lifted a brow. "I remember you were nervous on the way over here, and you had me flying backup with you. Just think what it was like for Scott, swimming all on his own."

Becca winced. "So, you think I should give him another chance?"

Selena shrugged. "You're the only one who can make that call. All I'm suggesting is that you don't make your decision based on how shy Scott was on this first date or what happened on the dance floor."

"He did try really hard," Becca admitted. "And he was cute as hell when he did get around to dancing. Maybe another date would be fun. Besides, I'd feel like crap if I dumped him after one date, especially after everything that happened tonight."

"So, is that a yes?" Selena asked.

Becca nodded.

Selena smiled. "Good, but maybe for the second date, you might want to try a place a little less intense than a night club. Maybe a coffee shop or a quiet restaurant. Scott might be a lot more relaxed in a different environment."

Becca thought about that for a moment. "Do you think Scott and I could ever have what you and Jayden have?"

"What do you mean?" She wasn't sure what her friend was getting at. "It's not like we're that far beyond you and Scott when it comes to dating. This is only our second date."

"It doesn't have anything to do with how many dates you've been on," Becca said. "You two have a connection that's blatantly obvious the second anyone sees you together. Hell, it's like watching magic happen. You probably didn't notice because you were a little busy at the time, but when you and Jayden were kissing on the dance floor, half the club stopped what they were doing and stared, mesmerized. Seriously, you have to know you two are meant to be together."

Selena blushed at the thought that everyone had been watching her and Jayden make out. Becca was right. She'd been so turned on right then she hadn't even noticed. But at the same time, she tried to think rationally about what Becca had said.

After only two dates, hearing Becca say she and Jayden were meant to be together should have made her laugh. It wasn't possible for two people to become so connected that fast. The really crazy thing was she couldn't say Becca was wrong.

Selena had been tense after her run-in with the gang-bangers earlier. She'd felt a little better after talking to Ernesto, but it wasn't until Jayden had slipped into the booth and kissed her that all the tension had really disappeared. And when they were on the dance floor, he'd made her feel like she was the most beautiful woman in the world.

"I'm falling for Jayden fast," she finally admitted. "So fast it's kind of scary."

Becca gave her a curious look. "He's hot, sexy, and awesome. What's scary about that?"

Selena laughed. "Don't get me wrong. Jayden is incredible. But when I'm around him, it's like I can't control myself. When we were dancing and kissing, it took everything in me to not jump him right on the floor and eat him up. That's not me. I'm always about being in control, you know?"

Becca nodded. "Yeah. But what are you worried about? That he's going to turn out not to be the guy you think he is? Because I have to tell you, I don't think that's going to happen."

"I know," Selena said. "Still, I don't want to wake up naked in his arms one morning and realize I've made a horrible mistake because I let things move too fast."

Becca made a face. "You offered me a suggestion a little while ago, so now it's my turn. Don't screw this up by overthinking it. If you close your eyes and try to imagine finding a man more perfect for you than Jayden, I'm pretty sure you won't be able to do it. So stop thinking so much, and let your instincts and your heart guide you. You're not making a mistake, and you're not going to move too fast."

Selena was still thinking about how incredibly right her friend's advice sounded when Jayden walked over with the guy who'd helped do CPR on Scott and the older guy she thought might be from the gang unit. Jayden introduced them as Zane Kendrick and Ray Porter, respectively, saying both men were good friends from the force.

Selena wanted to ask a ton of questions about the drug in the energy drinks, the gangs that might have sold it to the club, and whether there might be more of the stuff floating around the city. But she stopped herself, realizing she wasn't supposed to know any of that stuff.

She was trying to figure out if there was a sneaky way to wheedle out the information, but it seemed Ray was in a hurry, bailing shortly after shaking her hand, saying he wanted to get the unused cans of energy drink to the lab for fingerprinting. That left them with Zane, who was seriously attractive. Not as attractive as Jayden, but still.

"You're in SWAT too, right?" Selena asked.

The big cop with the British accent looked at Jayden.

"Yeah," Jayden said. "He's one of my teammates. It was just coincidence he was here in the club."

Selena felt that little twitch in her stomach and decided her boyfriend was definitely keeping something from her. She didn't call him on it, though. There was probably a good reason to keep the truth from her and Becca. Something that probably had to do with those men who'd broken out of Coffield.

They talked for a few minutes before Zane mentioned he needed to get back to the SWAT compound so he could check on their visitors. Selena couldn't imagine why there'd be people there at this time of night but didn't say anything. Then it hit her. *Crap*. Maybe it had something to do with the prison break. She really wanted to ask but resisted the urge.

Jayden pulled Zane aside before he left, and Selena heard him tell his teammate to be careful. "I don't think they'd come after us, but watch yourself all the same."

Selena glanced at Becca, but her friend didn't look

like she'd heard any of that. Okay, this was starting to get freaky.

"You want to hang out with Jayden and me?" Selena asked Becca as she waited for Jayden and Zane to finish up. "We can get something to eat if you want."

Becca shook her head. "Thanks for the offer, but it's late, and unlike you, I have class to teach tomorrow. Besides, I need to get to the hospital if I'm going to have any chance of seeing Scott tonight. I want to let him know I'd like to see him again. You okay catching a ride with Jayden?"

Selena nodded and gave her friend a hug. "Definitely. Tell Scott I hope he feels better soon."

"I will," Becca promised, giving Jayden a wave as she left.

"Did I hear you saying something about food?" Jayden asked as he walked over to join Selena.

She shook her head as she stepped closer to Jayden, breathing in his scent and realizing how glad she was she'd decided to wait for him to get done doing his police stuff. She wasn't ready for this night to end. Even if it was late as hell. "I just asked that for Becca's benefit. Truthfully, I'm not very hungry."

"That's too bad," he said. "I make a mean late-night PB&J with the crusts cut off."

She couldn't help laughing at that. It wasn't the line she'd expected. But she was already starting to realize Jayden wasn't the type to do the expected. "Well, if you're making them, maybe I'm hungrier than I thought."

He grinned. "Then let's get out of here."

Chapter 12

"YOU LIVE IN A WAREHOUSE?" SELENA ASKED IN DISBELIEF as Jayden steered his classic Chevy pickup truck into a small parking lot behind a metal-and-brick building with no windows and a distinctly industrial look.

"It's not a warehouse," Jayden said with a laugh that seemed to indicate lots of people asked the exact same question. "It was an electronics repair shop about ten or twelve years ago."

He shut off the engine, then got out and walked around to open her door, lending a hand to help her slide out of the high truck. His gaze immediately went to the length of thigh she exposed slipping off the seat. Okay, maybe she'd done that on purpose.

"Of course, nobody gets electronics repaired any-more," Jayden continued, dragging his eyes back up to her face as they walked toward the building. "They just replace them. Throw in the fact that this whole area got rezoned into a residential area about the same time, and the owner was sort of screwed. The place couldn't be used as a business anymore, and no one was interested in buying it for residential purposes, because the lot is too small. It went into tax foreclosure, and I ended up getting it for next to nothing. I got it into livable condition for barely over twenty thousand."

Selena tried to take that all in as Jayden led her to the back door. The tiny lot surrounding the building was well maintained, with more grass and hedges than one would expect from an industrial building. But still, it was obvious the place wasn't a normal house. Then again, Jayden wasn't a normal guy, so she wasn't surprised.

He unlocked the big metal door, then reached inside to flip on the light switch. Stepping back, he held the door open for her.

Selena stepped inside, steeling herself. She had visions of cinder block coffee tables, yard sale couches, and rust-covered walls. She was so ready to be underwhelmed that when she walked through the short entryway hall and into the big open space of the central room, she gasped. This was so not what she'd been expecting. She handed Jayden her coat and purse, barely paying attention as he hung them on a coat rack by the door, then tossed his keys on the shelf above it.

The main room had to be over a thousand square feet. There was still a very industrial feel to the place, with lots of concrete, brick, metal rafters, exposed lights, electrical conduits, and air vents. But the space was put together in such a way, it seemed like it was meant to look industrial instead of left that way by accident.

The concrete floor had been stained different colors as part of the effort to subdivide the big space into different functional areas. It was a creamy terra-cotta off to one side where the kitchen was and a relaxing caramel along the back wall where she saw a king-size bed, dressers, and wall units. The entire middle section, encompassing the living room and a sweet home gym, was a deep, glossy slate blue.

There was a huge TV mounted on the wall near the matching sectional sofas, with the rest of the wall space taken up with football memorabilia and pictures of cop-related activities. She had no doubt that most of those photos would be of his SWAT teammates or, as he called them, his pack. There were big potted trees positioned here and there around the space, and at first, she was sure they were fake. But then she saw the skylights in the roof and thought maybe they were real.

Besides the one they'd just come in, there were only two other doors in the entire place, one that looked like a second exit and the other leading into a walled-off corner area, the bathroom most likely.

"This place is amazing," she said, turning to face him. "If you tell me you decorated the entire thing on your own, I'm going to cry, because that would mean there isn't a single thing in the world you aren't perfect at."

Jayden chuckled. "No need to cry. My mom helped with a lot of it, but also some of the guys on the team. Zane is really good at decorating, though he'll deny it if you ever suggest it. How about we head for the kitchen and those PB&J sandwiches before I give you the fifty-cent tour?"

Selena nodded eagerly and followed him through the living room and gym to the kitchen, getting a good part of the promised tour on the way. This place was awesome. She couldn't wait to spend the night here. She immediately blushed a little at the audacity of that thought but then pushed the silly concern aside. Something told her she was going to be staying here a lot.

It wasn't until they walked behind the granite counter in the kitchen space that Selena saw the first thing that seemed completely out of place—two doggy bowls on the floor. She looked around, thinking she'd smelled a familiar odor when she first walked in, though she hadn't placed it as a dog's scent until now. It was very faint.

"You have a dog?" she asked, gesturing to the bowls as Jayden took the bread and peanut butter out of the cabinet.

"Technically, Tuffie belongs to the entire team." Jayden reached into the fridge for a jar of grape jelly. "She was shot by one of the men who broke out of prison today. Our team medics kept her alive until they could get her to a vet, and after that, there was no way we could let her go. So we adopted her. Now she takes turns staying with different members of the team each night."

"That's so perfect!" she squealed, pretty sure these SWAT guys might actually be angels in disguise and not just amazing cops.

As Jayden made the sandwiches, he talked about how they figured out who Tuffie got to stay with each night. Selena laughed when Jayden suggested some of the guys on the team tried to tweak the Tuffie duty roster so they'd get extra time with the unit mascot.

"They all try to act like they're big and tough, but when it comes to Tuffie, they're a bunch of pushovers."

"Might you be one of those pushovers?" she teased.

Jayden chuckled as he poured two glasses of milk. "Maybe. Not that you'll ever get me to admit it."

Normally, Selena never ate anything this late at night, but for some reason, she was nearly starving right then. And the peanut butter and jelly sandwiches were calling her name.

"Sorry about how the date turned out tonight," he said as they stood at the counter eating a little while later. "CPR and overdoses weren't exactly on my mind when I imagined how the evening would end."

Selena polished off the last of her sandwich faster than she would have thought possible. The scary part was that she couldn't stop eyeing the big jar of peanut butter, wondering if she should have another.

"While I agree the last part of the evening was something I never want to experience again, I wouldn't say the whole night was a waste," she said. "In fact, parts of the night were pretty nice. Actually, better than nice. And as for how the evening ends, I think that's still to be determined."

Jayden lifted a brow as he popped what was left of his sandwich in his mouth. "Are you implying our date isn't over yet?"

The heat in his gaze as he asked the question immediately reignited the fire that had been burning in her tummy earlier when they'd been dancing...and kissing. She gave him a smile while fighting the urge to reach out and pull him close, to press herself tightly to his muscular body and rub herself all over him like a cat.

"You really think the only reason I came here was for the PB&J?" she asked in a husky voice, taking a half step closer to him.

Selena was kind of shocked she was being so bold. It wasn't like her. She tried to tell herself Jayden was to blame for the change, but at the same time, part of her knew that wasn't the truth. This was all her...the new her.

Jayden laughed as he took a step toward her, closing the distance between them. She swore she could feel the heat of his body bathing her skin. "So, if it wasn't my amazing sandwiches that brought you here, what was it?"

Selena placed her hands on his abs, moving her fingers upward, feeling the ripples and indentations under his shirt of what could only be the most amazing set of six-pack abs on the planet. "Maybe it was because I wanted another chance to get close to you and feel you against me again. Like when we were dancing."

This time, she wasn't shocked at how bold she was being. It seemed this was the way things were going to be between the two of them.

Open.

Real.

She couldn't describe the sense of freedom that came with knowing that.

Jayden's eyes glinted so bright, Selena almost turned around to figure out where the reflected light was coming from. But she dismissed that concern when he rested one of his big hands casually on her hip for a few seconds before tugging her against him in the most delicious and possessive way.

"I guess you like to dance, huh?" he asked softly, his deep voice making the words vibrate in the air between them.

"The dancing was nice, better than nice, like I said." She swayed a little against him so she could feel his growing hard-on pressing against her belly. "But truthfully, the dancing was only an excuse. The touching was the part I really enjoyed."

Jayden growled a little, pulling her tighter. She felt him pulsing against her now, and knowing how excited he was made her crazy. Not only was her whole body tingling like mad, but there was a pleasant warmth between her legs too. And for some wild reason, her fingertips were throbbing.

"Do you know how amazing you make me feel?" he asked, his words rough and primal, like his throat was choking on emotions…or lust. "The way you make my body shake, just by touching me?"

She gazed at her hand on his big pecs, not remembering when she'd moved it up there. But all those muscles felt really good under her palm. It felt even better knowing that her touch did the same thing to him that his did to her.

She lifted her head to look at him, her lips curving into a smile. "You too, huh? And here I thought I was the only one feeling like I was about to lose control every time you got your hands on me."

He returned the smile, his gaze even hotter. "Sometimes losing control can be fun."

Selena felt a stab of electricity zip through her at the flirtatious words, her nipples tightening and the heat pooling between her legs turning into a throb. "I tend to remember the last time I lost control, it ended with me biting you and you bleeding."

Jayden snorted as he lowered his head, his lips hovering mere inches from her mouth as he regarded her with an intensity that was almost scary. "And I tend to remember telling you a few love bites weren't a problem for me... and I meant it."

Selena started to say something witty about Jayden's promise to bite her back, but his mouth came down on hers, making talking impossible. That was okay. Communicating like this was much more fun.

She wrapped her hand behind his neck, pulling him down and deepening the kiss, her tongue teasing his as he made those sexy growling sounds she loved so much. Damn, those animalistic noises were going right through her, making her want to do all kinds of crazy things to his hunky, muscular body. It was almost jarring when she realized biting was just one of the tamer ideas rolling around in her head.

She let her free hand roam over Jayden's body, moving from his chest down past those heavenly abs, stopping when it reached the bulge in his jeans. She rubbed her hand up and down the hard shape under the material, her mind filling in all kinds of details of what she was going to find once she had him naked. She smiled when he groaned to let her know what she was doing felt good. The sounds of his enjoyment were making one very particular place between her legs suddenly beg for attention.

Selena was getting into the mental image of where this was going, almost hyperventilating at the excitement filling her. She was so hot that her fingertips and gums were aching, even though it made no sense at all. She ignored all that, forcing herself to focus as she brought her hands to the buckle on his belt, ready to take this further.

Jayden pulled back, breaking the kiss so quickly, she almost fell over.

"What?" she asked, partly in confusion, partly in anger.

He smiled, his eyes bright. Like he knew exactly how ragged her control already was and exactly what he was doing to her. "I just realized I never gave you that fifty-cent tour I promised."

Selena's mouth fell open then. She was so stunned that words became impossible. Hell, thought was nearly beyond her, too. She had no desire for a guided tour of Jayden's place at that point.

But before she could tell him that, he grabbed her hand and tugged her out of the kitchen toward the living room area.

"Sixty-five-inch 4K HD," he said, motioning toward the TV mounted on the wall. "It's amazingly clear, and the sound system that comes with it is awesome, but I think the best part of the living room is the sectional." He glanced at her. "I really like how cushy it is, especially along the top. And the height is perfect."

Selena didn't have a clue what Jayden was talking about until he placed a big hand on either side of her waist and picked her up, setting her butt on the back of the couch. He perched her there on the cushy material, and she had no choice but to balance herself as he spread her thighs apart and stepped between them.

That's when she finally understood what Jayden had been babbling about. The back of the sectional really was comfy, and when he wiggled himself forward a little more, making her legs spread obscenely wide and her dress hike up to her waist, it brought his denim-covered hard-on right into contact with her panty-covered pussy. She realized then how perfect sex on the back of this couch would be…and why Jayden had taken the opportunity to lead her over here.

She was still thinking of the possibilities when Jayden slipped a hand into her long hair and tipped her head back, tilting her mouth up for his kiss. But within seconds, those magical lips of his trailed downward, tracing a line of searing fire along her jaw, then her neck. This time, she was the one growling, especially when she felt his teeth nipping at her jugular. It was light enough not to do any damage but hard enough to definitely feel.

The whole time he did it, all Selena could do was moan and wonder what it would be like if he bit down a little harder. Where the hell had that come from?

After the teasing went on long enough for her to think it might actually be possible to have an orgasm from Jayden nibbling on her neck, Selena somehow found the strength to shove him away long enough to grab the front of his shirt. The next thing she knew, material was ripping and buttons were flying everywhere. She was so surprised at what she'd done, she stopped and stared. She'd intended to open a few buttons so she could get her hands on some bare skin. Instead, she'd damn near ripped his shirt in half.

Jayden didn't seem to care. He grabbed the tattered remains of the button-down and yanked it off. He reached for her again, but she placed her hands on the big muscles of his chest, holding him at a distance so she could appreciate all that manliness. This was her first chance to see what he'd been hiding underneath that shirt, and she wasn't going to waste it.

"Not so fast," she ordered. "I want to look at you."

He obeyed her command, standing there while she got her fill.

The muscles of his chest, traps, and shoulders were thick and powerful. His lean abs rippled and flexed with every breath he took, and it required every bit of her control not to lean forward and lick them. He was absolute perfection. As in the kind of perfection that needed to be captured forever in a marble statute somewhere. Because he had the body of a Greek hero. Hell, maybe even one of their gods.

As she continued to drink him in, the first thing she noticed was the tattoo on the left side of his chest. It was difficult to miss the wolf head with the word *S.W.A.T.* underneath, imprinted forever right over his heart. She remembered him using the word *pack* earlier, and she almost asked if this was why he'd said it.

But then something else caught her attention...

several somethings in fact. Lines and marks that marred the otherwise perfect shape of her dark-skinned Adonis. The most obvious was a long thin line of lighter skin along the right side of his abs, stretching horizontally from his belly button and disappearing around his back. She traced a finger over the line, feeling a raised edge and realizing it was an old scar from what must have been a significant injury. It looked like someone had tried to cut him in half side to side.

"It was a big knife," he said softly. "A long time ago."

Selena continued running one fingertip along the raised line, not stopping even when her hand slipped around his side and kept going until it reached his spine in the back. She looked up at him, shock in her eyes.

"It was a really big knife," he added.

She nodded, taking her hand away from the scar as she spotted another—a shorter slash mark up near his left shoulder. She glided a finger over that mark too, the base of her fingernail tingling like mad at the curious but sensual movement.

"Box cutter," he murmured.

She touched her finger to another scar, this one an inch or so above the one left behind from the big knife he mentioned. Almost perfectly round, it looked as recent as the scar on his bicep that had come from a bullet.

She leaned close, exploring further, finding scar after scar hidden on the exquisite dark skin. Shotgun pellets, more bullets, barbed wire, even a shovel. Jayden had seen a tremendous amount of violence in his life, and it had left its mark on him.

But rather than disturb her, the scars only reminded her that Jayden was a tough man who stood up for what he believed in. He also seemed to be somewhat indestructible. For whatever reason, that made her find the marks rather sexy. She didn't realize how much until she found herself tracing her lips and tongue along a faint line near the wolf head tattoo on his chest, one that had been made with broken glass.

The growl that rumbled up from his throat vibrated through his chest, into her lips, and straight to the heat pooling between her thighs.

Oh, sweet cheese and crackers.

Excitement vibrated through her, making her heart pound, her gums ache, and her pussy clench with need. She'd never felt anything like that in her life, which was probably why she kept moving her mouth over his beautiful chest, even taking a moment to focus on his tattoo. That ripped another growl from him.

She was so lost in the sensations rushing through her body that she barely realized she'd stopped kissing and licking him until she tasted something slightly familiar in her mouth. She'd bitten him again. Right near his tattoo. Small beads of blood ran down the wolf's shaggy neck.

Selena started to apologize, but Jayden wrapped his hand in her hair and yanked her mouth in for a kiss so passionate, it stole her breath away. She kissed him back just as hard, nipping down on his lips and his tongue, wanting to taste all of him.

Jayden lifted his head long enough to drag her dress up and off. She vaguely sensed it ended up on the floor somewhere near the front door, but she wasn't sure. All she really knew was that she was sitting on the back of Jayden's couch in nothing but her bra, panties, and strappy heels, her legs wrapped around his waist and her body so hot, she thought she might burst into flames.

Selena squealed when he slid his big hands under her ass and picked her up. She wrapped her arms around his neck and locked her ankles behind his back as he strode across the room. Burying her face in his neck, she inhaled his delectable scent, moaning out loud at how good he smelled.

Just as she was becoming comfortable with the knowledge that she was getting incredibly turned on by the scent of Jayden's skin, two other scents hit her hard enough to make her head spin. Selena wasn't sure what she was picking up or how it was even possible to smell anything so strongly. Then she felt wetness soaking the crotch of her tiny panties, and some instinct inside told her that was one of the things she'd smelled.

The other was coming from the big bulge pressing against her tummy, and she instinctively knew she was smelling Jayden's arousal. This time, she didn't bother questioning how she could possibly smell such a thing. It meant he was hot for her. That was all that mattered.

Selena expected Jayden to carry her straight to his big bed—and in her opinion, they couldn't get there fast enough—so she was shocked and more than a little frustrated when he stopped in the middle of his home gym area and casually straddled a weight-lifting bench, sitting down with her in his lap. The position brought her panty-covered pussy down onto his jean-clad hard-on. The contact left her gasping. And wondering how much longer Jayden was going to tease her. Couldn't he tell she was already going insane?

"And this is my workout area." The amusement in his

voice was laced with no small amount of lust, and she realized that while he might be trying to draw this out for her benefit, it was definitely affecting him, too.

"The weight-lifting and cardio equipment cost almost as much as the entire rest of the house," he continued. "But this particular bench is one of my favorites. It's well-padded and wide enough to be comfortable but solid enough to take a real pounding."

The innuendo there didn't escape her notice, and Selena's heart rate began to ramp up all over again. Things only got hotter when he nudged her back so she was lying on the padded surface of the bench, her legs still wrapped around him. She lifted her arms above her head, the position leaving her back arched and her stomach stretched tight.

Right then, she couldn't think of a sexier position.

"Do you even know how beautiful you are?" Jayden murmured softly.

He slowly slid his hands along her thighs, over her hips, then up her abs, every move leaving a fiery trail of tingles in its wake. The combination of his touch and the heat blazing in his eyes made her squirm. She nearly begged him to move faster, to pull the rest of her clothes off and take her right there on that bench.

But she didn't. Instead, she closed her eyes and enjoyed it.

As for Jayden, he seemed content to keep teasing her, moving his incredible fingers back and forth from the top of her panties to the bottom edge of her bra. In between, he traced lazy circles around her belly button and along her ribs.

Selena was so enraptured by the touch of his hands, she

didn't realize he'd slipped off her bra until she opened her eyes to see him smiling, the black lacy garment dangling from his fingers.

"Oh, you are smooth," she said with a soft laugh.

Chuckling, he tossed her bra over his shoulder, then cupped her breasts, giving them a gentle squeeze. She'd never thought about it before, but she suddenly decided she liked a man with strong hands.

Her breath caught as he captured her nipples between his thumbs and forefingers, pinching and rolling them with just enough force to make her see stars. She arched her back, thrusting her breasts out, yearning for more.

Just when Selena thought she might scream from the pleasure, Jayden released her breasts and slid those wonderful fingers of his into the waistband of her panties. She was about to point out there was no way he was going to get them off her while her legs were still wrapped around his waist. But then there was a tug and a distinct tearing sound, and the remnants of her favorite panties went flying through the air. On one hand, she was annoyed, because Victoria's Secret didn't sell that specific style anymore, but on the other, having them ripped off was sexy as hell.

She opened her mouth to make a crack about him paying for them, but the moment she saw the blatant hunger in his eyes, words failed her. That's when it struck her that she was lying there in front of him wearing nothing more than a smile and a pair of high heels.

His gaze locked on hers as he glided his hands over her outer thighs, moving steadily inward as he reached her hips, then heading for the triangle between her legs. With her legs wrapped around his waist and her heels locked together behind his back, she was spread wide open, completely exposed to him. Her breath caught in her throat when his fingertips drifted through her downy curls, then exploded out in a gasp as he brushed his thumb across her clit before dipping into her wetness.

Selena whimpered, unable to believe how good that one little touch felt. She immediately steeled herself, expecting more teasing, but that wasn't the way this was going to go down. Instead, Jayden pulled his well-moistened thumb out and pressed it directly down on her clit, making a circular motion that had her hips wiggling like mad. He clamped one big hand down on her belly, holding her still so he could do exactly what he wanted to, which at that point seemed to be making her come.

It wasn't going to take very long. After all the dancing, kissing, and teasing, her body was primed to explode, and Jayden definitely knew what he was doing when it came to touching her. She threw her head back and moaned, running one hand through her hair and reaching the other down to grip the hand he had over her stomach. She had this uncontrollable need to hold him right then, just so she wouldn't fly off into space.

Her clit had been tingling before he'd even touched her, but now the sensation intensified rapidly, expanding out from her core in waves that made her tremble. She took little half breaths, expecting the pleasure to crest any second and the weightless fall to start, like a roller coaster going over the top of the first big drop. But it didn't happen that way. Instead, the pleasure continued to build until her whole body shook and stars flashed behind her closed eyes.

She heard loud growls and was shocked when she realized she was the one making them. But then the overwhelming pleasure finally reached its peak. Her orgasm hit her like a physical force, and she stopped caring about what sounds were coming out of her mouth. Her entire body clenched so tightly, it almost hurt, and wave after wave of perfect bliss rocked her to the core. Darkness mixed with the flashes of light in her eyes, and she wondered absently if she was going to pass out.

Her lover held her firm as she wiggled and squirmed, shoving the sensations of the climax higher and higher until she doubted her ability to survive it. There was a metallic taste in her mouth, and her gums were pulsing in time with her climax. She must have bitten herself in the throes of pleasure, but she couldn't bring herself to care.

Jayden brought her down from bliss slowly, touching her enough to keep her trembling but not going so far that it became uncomfortable. How did he know her body so well? She doubted she could ever make herself come this hard, even with all the technology available to a girl with a credit card and access to the internet.

The moment the last tremors faded away, Jayden swept her off the weight bench and into those powerful arms. She didn't open her eyes yet, too out of it to do more than rest her cheek against his powerful chest and pray they were heading to the bed.

She felt weightless for a brief moment as he tossed her onto his mattress, then she hit with a soft bounce. Immediately spinning around, she crawled toward the side of the big bed. Jayden already had his boots off and was unbuckling his belt by the time she reached him, but that still wasn't fast enough for her. After the orgasm he'd given her, all she could think about was getting him naked and between her legs—now.

She tossed her heels across the room, then got her hands

on the waist of his jeans. When the thick denim material stubbornly resisted her efforts to shove them down, she growled in frustration. She was shocked at the urge she had to rip the damn things off him like she'd done with his shirt.

Selena somehow kept herself in control, half growling, half moaning as she got his jeans down and the big bulge in his underwear came into view. The thin cotton of his boxer briefs was strained to its limit, and she knew without a doubt Jayden was as well-built below the belt as above it. Her hands started to shake in anticipation as she reached for his underwear, but before she got there, the scent of his arousal reached her, and she nearly lost it as a wave of hunger poured through her so hard and fast, it made her dizzy.

Any thought that she might take things slowly now and enjoy the moment quickly disappeared. Before Selena realized what she was doing, she had her fingers in the waistband of his briefs and had ripped them off. She vaguely heard a heated growl from him, but she ignored it as she finally got a chance to see him completely naked.

It seemed like she'd been using the word *perfect* a lot when it came to Jayden, but right then, it was the only word that even came close to describing him. His long legs were as powerfully muscled as the rest of him, and the ripped muscles of his abs blended into his waist with a sexy V-shape that naturally led her eyes downward. A faint happy trail pointed the way, too, starting directly above his navel and descending all the way down to the rock-hard shaft that seemed to be waiting just for her.

Her eyes locked on his erection, and she inhaled. It was long, thick, and as beautiful as the rest of him. Even better, it was hard as steel and throbbing with need, a glistening bead on the tip. Her mouth watered in anticipation at the thought of swiping her tongue across it and tasting him.

Selena reached out, fully intending to drag him close enough to get her mouth on him. But as her fingers brushed his rigid shaft, he grabbed her shoulders and spun her around so she was facing away from him. There was no resisting the move, no matter how much her inner cavewoman screamed that she wanted to lick him first.

"Stay," he commanded in that deep, rumbling voice of his as she threw a glance over her shoulder, wanting to ask him what he was doing.

She didn't like the idea of staying put simply because he said so, but all movement stopped when she saw him pull open the top drawer of his nightstand and yank out a familiar foil package.

Selena felt a surge of unreasonable jealousy that had her teeth and fingertips tingling as she realized there was a reason a man kept condoms in his bedside table. But she pushed that emotion aside as Jayden moved toward her with blatant hunger on his face, the gold blaze of lust in his eyes freezing her in place where she knelt on her hands and knees on the mattress.

Jayden was hers now.

And she was his.

"Stay," he ordered again, his voice more growl than words now. "Just like that."

She craned her neck, trying to keep her eyes on him as he touched a switch on the wall that dimmed the lights, then came back to the bed. Her breath caught in her throat when she felt his hand on her right hip, the sound turning into a low growl as he tugged her ass higher. If that wasn't sexy enough, the moment he had her hips right where he wanted, Jayden slid his strong hand along the center of her back, firmly pushing her down until her breasts and face were pressed down into the blanket-covered mattress. The position was so damn hot, she felt her pussy clench up at the mere thought of Jayden taking her this way.

He was like an animal.

Selena heard the tearing of the condom's foil package moments before she felt him grip her hip, then the head of his cock nudging at her wet opening. She gasped in pleasure, but the sound soon turned into a loud moan as he eased inside her.

That was when she realized how large Jayden really was. She worried for a moment he wouldn't fit. He did, of course, but his size had her gasping for air and grinding her forehead into the bed.

He moved slowly and carefully at first, his hands on her hips holding her firmly and controlling the pace. He must have realized she was ready for more, because he thrust harder, touching her in places that had never been touched before, making lightning skip and race through her whole body.

"Don't stop," she growled.

Her voice was so twisted with passion and need, she barely recognized it.

Who's the animal now?

His hips slammed into her, driving him even deeper. The sensations became nearly overwhelming, and all Selena could do was bury her face into the blankets and scream as the second orgasm of the night approached at the speed and intensity of a freight train. Her hands tore at the coverlet, her fingernails digging into the material as she shoved back against Jayden, urging him to go faster, to thrust harder, to make her come all over him.

When Selena's climax hit, she bit down on the blanket to keep from losing her mind. Between her teeth and nails, she knew she was probably tearing the bed to shreds. She was exploding from the inside out, bliss starting right where he drove into her over and over, then spreading out like wildfire. Her body shook and spasmed, her legs barely holding her up, and she knew she would have collapsed already if it wasn't for Jayden's strong hands on her hips holding her steady and yanking her back against him.

As her climax ebbed, she realized Jayden hadn't come yet. She managed to unlock her teeth from the blanket, absently noting that she really had ripped the material apart with her teeth somehow. She ignored that mystery for the moment as she twisted her face to the side.

"Come with me," she whispered.

She wanted—needed—for him to experience the same pleasure he'd just given her. But getting even those few words out was harder than it should have been. It was like her throat barely knew how to form any sounds other than those screams…and growls.

But Jayden apparently wasn't close to coming yet, at least not in this position. One moment, he was thrusting into her hard, his hips smacking up against her tender ass like he was spanking her, and the next, he slid out and flipped her over on her back, moving her into the center of the bed.

She had no time to even think about complaining before he moved between her legs and plunged right back in. Her legs wrapped around his waist instinctively, yanking him closer as her ankles locked together and refused to let him go.

"Harder," she commanded in his ear as she buried her face against his neck and bit down.

What he was doing felt so good that biting him seemed like a natural response to her now—as bizarre as that seemed.

The tremors inside her core started again, even though she couldn't imagine how she could possibly come again so soon. But there was no mistake. Having Jayden inside her like this, his weight pressing her into the mattress as he thrust, was like nothing she'd ever felt before. He could make her come as many times as he wanted.

She squeezed her legs around his waist tighter, urging him on, growling and nipping at his neck and shoulders. That's when she felt Jayden start to move faster, his breath against her skin becoming more ragged. He was close, too.

"Come with me," she murmured, the words urgent… begging.

He pumped into her, making her cry out in pleasure, pushing her closer and closer to that precipice. Selena tried to hold back, desperate to share this amazing experience with him this time. He must have somehow realized what she was trying to do, because he weaved a hand in her hair, yanked her head back to bare her throat…and bit her. Probably not as hard as she'd bitten him, but hard enough.

She exploded again.

Seconds later, she felt Jayden stiffen and explode with her.

It shouldn't have been possible, but this climax felt even more intense than the first two. She clamped her legs around him more tightly, then dug her nails into his back as hard as she could and sank her teeth into the thick muscles of his shoulder, tasting blood as she screamed through the most powerful orgasm she could ever imagine surviving.

Selena had no idea how long the orgasm lasted, but she vaguely remembered being on top of him for at least a few seconds of it. But finally, no matter how perfect it felt, the climax began to ebb and fade. She might have faded with it a bit, lying there on her back with his warm body pressed to hers, her eyes closed, and her breathing deep and steady.

"That was the most amazing night of my life," she whispered.

Her voice came out a little slurred, like her mouth had forgotten how to form words. Then she tasted the salty metallic taste that was becoming way too familiar, and she worried she'd bitten him too hard. She was about to sit up so she could check when she felt movement on the bed. Then Jayden was between her legs again, his mouth moving down from her breasts, along her abs, then lower.

Her breath caught. There was no way he could be doing what she thought he was going to do.

"Who said this amazing night is over?" he murmured.

Before she could say anything, his tongue flicked out to touch that most sensitive place on her body, making her throw her head back and growl again.

Chapter 13

BROOKS WOKE UP TO THE SENSATION OF SUNLIGHT BEATING on his face, the annoying little beams sneaking under his eyelids and reminding him that he'd overslept. He turned his face away from the light, groaning as he tugged Selena a little closer.

Moving didn't help much, since the reflective material he'd installed around the inside of the skylights had been designed to light up almost every part of the building, even at this time of the morning. He'd done it on purpose so the windowless building wouldn't feel like a cave. Since he rarely, if ever, slept much past sunrise, it had never been a problem. But now, after the night he'd had with Selena, maybe he'd need to install automatic shades of some kind. Because he sure as hell wasn't ready to get up.

He shifted slightly so he could look down at Selena where she slept peacefully on his chest. She was so beautiful, it almost hurt to look at her. A few stray hairs had fallen across her cheek, and he absently reached to brush them back behind her ear. He traced his finger gently along her jaw and down her graceful neck, then back up to the corner of her sweet, captivating mouth.

The longer he gazed at her, the stronger the feeling in his chest became. He was in love with Selena. He'd accepted she was *The One* for him, but those were words that barely carried any meaning for him. It was like saying she was an Aries. What he felt now was real, powerful, and all consuming. He finally understood what it had been like for the other guys in the Pack who'd found their soul mates. Selena had stolen his heart in the span of four days. And he was completely fine with the idea that she was never going to give it back.

All this would have been a lot easier if he'd figured out a way to tell her that she was a werewolf already. He'd secretly been hoping he'd have a little more time to find the perfect way to tell her, but after last night, delaying any longer wasn't an option. The completely shredded bed, the bite marks marring the perfect skin of her neck and shoulders, the scratches and welts that covered his chest and back, and the dried blood was all stuff that would need to be explained. There would be no avoiding the truth.

Brooks only hoped he'd be able to say the right thing when the moment came. For both of their sakes. It wasn't the kind of thing he could figure out how to explain by rehearsing in front of the bathroom mirror.

He sat up a bit, keeping Selena tucked comfortably against his chest as he leaned against the headboard. He felt the twinge of pain as he moved, reminding him of how wild she'd been last night. He smiled, reliving some of the more vivid moments.

While he'd never gotten a chance to see her eyes glow, because Selena had a habit of shoving her face into the bed or the crook of his neck when she orgasmed, there was no doubt in his mind she'd shifted several times last night. Her claws had come out in a big way, and she'd used him like her own personal scratching post.

Those claws of hers were damn long—and damn sharp.

When he'd first learned Selena was a werewolf, he'd assumed she'd be a beta. He wasn't sure why he thought that, other than because she was so petite and angelic looking. But after seeing her claws, it was obvious she was an alpha. No beta he'd ever met had claws that long.

Then there were the fangs and the blatant aggression. Betas didn't have canines an inch long, and he was pretty sure they didn't throw guys Brooks's size around like a play toy while in the midst of orgasm. Selena had given as good as she'd gotten last night. While she was much smaller than he was, she was just as strong and tough.

Selena stirred in his arms, her eyes drifting open and fluttering a few times. She lifted her head, pushing her long hair back from her face with her hand. Her gaze came to rest on him, and she smiled.

"Hey, there," she murmured, running her fingers up his arm to his bicep, lingering on the barbed wire tattoo encircling it.

"Morning, baby."

His breath caught as her warm thigh glided along his, making a tremor of excitement run through him. Selena must have felt it, too, because she laughed softly.

"Didn't get enough last night?" she teased.

He grinned down at her even as he told his cock to behave. They had other stuff to do this morning besides make love.

"Did you?" he asked.

"I guess not." Her lips curved. "Though I have to admit some parts of last night are a little hazy, which I blame completely on you, by the way."

"Yeah?" He lifted a brow. "How's that?"

"It's hard enough remembering details after a half dozen normal orgasms," she said. "But after what you did to me last night, I'm lucky to remember any of it. I didn't do anything to embarrass myself, did I?"

He shook his head. "Not a chance. You rocked my world a few times."

That answer must have satisfied her, because she sat up a little straighter, her hand moving down his abs to his slowly stiffening cock. He might have told it to behave, but it wasn't listening.

As Selena's eyes traveled in that same direction, she caught sight of a set of four parallel scratches that ran left to right across his body from just under his pec to his hip flexor. She'd given him these particular gouges rather early on in the evening, so they were almost healed up completely already.

Selena shot upright on the bed, her eyes wide.

Brooks cursed silently as he heard her heart rate kick into high gear. "Relax," he murmured, holding up his hands.

She might have done just that, if it wasn't for the bite marks along his neck and shoulders. Unlike the scratches on his chest, some of the bite wounds were from later in the evening, so they were fresh and probably kind of scary looking.

She freaked, jerking away and scrambling all the way across the bed until she was close to falling off the side. He held up his hands again, trying to calm her with the gesture. It didn't work. Her heart hammered even faster. Her eyes were starting to glow a little, too.

"Selena, I need you to calm down," he said, keeping

his voice low and as soothing as he could make it. "I know this is all crazy, but I can explain everything. If you just give me a chance."

She shook her head. "There's no explanation for this. I bit you. I hurt you."

He shook his head in return. "Yeah, you bit me. But you didn't hurt me. I can promise you that. Last night was the most amazing night of my life. There's nothing you did that won't be healed up by tomorrow."

"Jayden!" she said in a loud voice, like she was trying to shock some sense into him. "Those wounds in your neck are deep. They'll probably need stitches. Don't tell me they don't hurt."

He took a deep breath and let it out in a sigh as he sat up higher against the headboard. "You don't want me to tell you they don't hurt? Then I suppose I should ask you the same question. Anything hurting on you at the moment?"

Selena looked confused for all of ten seconds before slowly looking down at her own body. She gasped, climbing completely off the bed this time. Her eyes widened to saucers as she caught sight of the light scratches tracing her shoulders, abs, hips, and thighs. They weren't anywhere near as deep as the ones she'd put on him, but they were there, and Brooks could see her trying to understand how she hadn't noticed them until now.

Then she lifted her hand to her neck and felt the bite marks. Her face went pale. "You bit me?" she asked, her voice filled with disbelief. "Bad enough to leave open wounds?"

He nodded. "We both got a little crazy last night. I get

the feeling it's always going to be like that for us. But like me, every mark on you will fade by tomorrow and be completely gone in a few days."

She looked down at her body—her beautiful, sexy, smoking, passion-marked body—then looked at him in confusion. "What are you talking about? I look like I've been in a fight with a rabid mongoose. It will take weeks for all this to heal up. These marks on my neck will probably never go away."

He sighed again and moved across the bed until he was sitting on the side of it. This was going about as badly as he could have imagined. But on the not-really-bright side, it wasn't like he had to worry about dealing with a hard-on anymore. It was completely gone.

Selena took a few steps back but stopped when she realized he wasn't going to come after her. He couldn't miss the way her eyes darted around his place until she positively ID'd the location of her dress, bra, and shoes.

"I'd hoped I'd be able to find a better way to tell you this, but that option is off the table now," Brooks said. "So I'm just going to dump it all on you and pray you're able to deal with it. But you have to promise to stay calm and let me get it all out."

She took a step closer to her dress, her eyes never leaving him. "You're starting to scare me a little. I've never heard you babble like this."

He was babbling? He'd hadn't done that since he was five. Then again, he'd never had to deal with a situation like this before. Bad guys with guns were simple compared to this.

"When Pablo shot at you in your classroom, it started a genetic change in your body." Damn, he wished

Gage—or even Cooper—were here to tell him what to say. But in their absence, he went with his gut. And his gut told him Selena wasn't the kind of woman who liked to beat around the bush. "That's why you've probably been experiencing some strange stuff that doesn't make a lot of sense to you. Like being able to smell things you shouldn't or hearing conversations when there's no way in hell you possibly could. You've also probably found yourself getting upset, emotional, and even angry for no reason."

She stared at him, the confusion in her eyes painful to see. "How can you possibly know all that?"

The urgency of the question was displayed more in the tension on her face than in her words. It made him wonder what kind of crap she'd been dealing with over the past few days that he didn't know about.

"Because I went through the same confusing time after I lived through my own incredibly painful and traumatic episode in Gulfport," he explained. "I couldn't control my emotions, I smelled my neighbors baking weed four blocks away from where I lived, and I overheard my beat partner telling the shift sergeant he thought I was having a nervous breakdown. Which was probably what it looked like from the outside. Of course, I happened to hear that particular conversation from the far side of a pistol qualification range, which obviously shouldn't have been possible."

Selena didn't say anything. Instead, she stood there naked and vulnerable. He wanted to take her in his arms and hold her. But he couldn't. Not yet. There was more that needed to be said.

"This genetic change is also why you bit me on our

first date and again last night," he added. "Part of it is because you've just started the process, but the biggest part is that you haven't gained control over your body yet. Your fangs and claws are going to pop out whenever you get angry—or aroused—until you gain control."

He was about to follow up with a promise to help her gain that control. To be there with her through the whole thing and then some. But he didn't get the chance.

"Fangs and claws?" she growled. "What the hell are you talking about? You make it sound like I'm turning into some kind of monster."

Damn, he was doing a crappy job explaining this.

"You're not turning into a monster," he said quickly. "But you are getting claws and fangs. They're part of the package when you become a werewolf."

Selena stared at him, her expression unreadable. Bending over, she picked up her dress and yanked it over her head, ignoring her bra completely as tears filled her eyes. Brooks stood up to follow, knowing he was blowing this. She either didn't believe him, or she thought he was insane. Both were equally bad.

"Selena, stop. Please!" he pleaded, walking around until he was in between her and the back door. He didn't want to pen her in, but she needed to understand what the hell was happening to her. For her own safety and for the safety of every werewolf out there in the world. "I know this sounds crazy, but I promise it's true. You're turning into a werewolf, and all this stuff that's happening to you will only get worse until you learn how to control it. If that isn't enough, there are people in the world who will hurt you if they know what you are. You need to let me keep you safe."

She didn't say anything as she dragged her heels on, the move unbelievably graceful even in her anger.

Brooks reached for her, intending to pull her into his arms for a kiss. He needed to make her see that all of this was a big mistake. But then she spun around and stabbed him with a glare that stopped him in his tracks. Dark eyes flickered with a color deep in their depths. He wasn't sure what color it was, but he knew it sure wasn't green.

"Stop it right now!" she shouted. "I don't know whether you think this is funny or if you really believe this crap. Either way, just stop. I don't want to hear anymore."

Brooks heard Selena's heart thudding at a thousand miles an hour. He could smell the fear coming off her in waves. She was terrified and confused, and the way he was handling this situation was making it worse. His gut twisted as she shoved past him, heading for the door. The protective alpha instinct in him started to panic, warning him that if he let her go, he may never get her back. She might be *The One* for him, but that wouldn't mean anything if he let her get away before she knew what the hell being *The One* even meant.

He wanted to reach out to grab her, to somehow keep her here with him until he could get her to listen to him. But he knew that would never work. He remembered the strength she'd shown last night while they'd made love. If she wanted to leave, it would take a lot of physical force to even attempt to stop her. Brooks wasn't ready to do something like that to her. Not even to keep her safe.

So he decided to do the one thing that might get her to understand he wasn't making this up.

"Selena, wait!" he called out, running to catch up to

her as she reached the door. "If last night meant anything at all to you, I'm begging you to stop and look at me for a second."

She hesitated, then slowly turned to face him. There was doubt, fear, and sadness in her eyes. But there was anger, too. So much frigging anger. He didn't have much time to do this.

"Don't freak out," he said softly.

Holding up his right hand, he let his claws slip out to their maximum length.

Selena's eyes widened, and she stumbled back, hitting the door, fear and shock overcoming every other emotion.

"Please don't be scared," he begged, taking a step closer and moving his hand this way and that so she could see it. "They're just my claws. The same kind of claws you have. The same claws you used to scratch my stomach and my back."

Selena's gaze was locked on his claws, until he'd said the part about his back. Then she moved so fast, he could barely follow the movement, her hand grabbing his shoulder and spinning him around.

He'd known his back was scratched up, but he didn't realize how bad it was until he heard her sharp intake of breath. He spun back around to see her standing there with both hands covering her mouth, an expression of pure horror on her face.

"It's okay," he whispered, taking a step closer. "You just got a little carried away last night. That won't happen once you gain more control."

"I really am a monster," she whispered.

Her claws extended as the stress and fear of the moment overwhelmed her. At the sight of them, her whole body began to shake, and he could see the tips of her fangs peeking out from behind the hands she still had over her mouth. She must have felt the sharp tips against her lips and realized what they meant, because her eyes widened in near total panic.

Brooks closed the distance between them, not able to stand the sight of her so scared. But that turned out to be the very worst thing he could have done. He swore it sounded like her heart was going to explode as more fear ripped through her.

"Stay back!" she sobbed, her fangs and claws on full display as she tried to push him away. "I don't want to hurt you again!"

He tried to resist, but that only made it worse. One moment, Selena was growling in fear, and the next, she was snarling in uncontrolled rage, her eyes flashing vivid blue. The next thing he knew, he was flying across the room like he'd been hit by a truck.

Brooks landed on the floor hard enough to knock the air out of him, but it wasn't the impact that stunned him nearly senseless. It was the image of Selena snarling at him with those vivid blue eyes. He'd only seen blue glowing eyes like that one other time in his life...and he'd almost died then.

The sound of a heavy metal door slamming pulled his attention back to the present, and he scrambled to his feet as fast as he could to follow after her. But he wasn't even halfway to the door when he heard the engine on his old truck rumble to life. She must have grabbed his keys as she'd left.

Brooks kept going anyway, running outside in time to see his truck spinning out onto the road behind the building, rear tires smoking as it sped away. He took about ten steps after her before he remembered he was still naked. He slowed to a standstill. If he chased her, she'd only run faster. Besides, it wasn't like he was going to tackle his own truck, especially with Selena driving it.

All he could do was stand there buck-ass naked in his backyard, howling in frustration as Selena drove away, wondering how the hell he'd missed the fact that the woman he loved was turning into an omega werewolf.

Chapter 14

IT WAS AFTER TEN O'CLOCK BY THE TIME BROOKS WALKED into the bullpen in the admin building later that morning. He stopped short, groaning when he realized that, with the exception of Becker, the entire Pack was there. Like they'd been waiting for him. From the way they were looking at him, they knew exactly what had happened to him that morning, too.

He turned and glared at Zane as his pack mate strolled in behind him. "You told them?"

Zane made a face and walked past him, heading for his desk. "What, that you're so bad in the sack Selena woke up screaming this morning and left you, taking your truck with her?" He pulled out his chair and sat. "I might have mentioned it."

"Damn, Brooks." On the other side of the room, Cooper chuckled. "What is it with you dating women who steal your stuff? First, the one in Gulfport took your LSU gear, then the one from the narcotics division swiped a bunch of your dress shirts, and now Selena jacks your ride? Maybe you need to find a different type of woman to hang out with, because if you keep going like this, before long, you won't own anything."

Everyone laughed at that. Remy even leaned across the aisle from his desk to fist-bump Cooper.

Muttering under his breath that they were all degenerates, Brooks walked over to his desk. That's what he got for calling Zane to pick him up. At least his teammate hadn't told everyone Selena had shifted and completely lost control. Or that Brooks had only made it worse when he'd tried to calm her down.

"Since Brooks has finally decided to join us, maybe we can finally start the morning briefing," Gage announced from the doorway of his office, his tone suggesting he wasn't happy Brooks was late.

Brooks stifled a groan when another round of laughter swept through the room. He dropped into his chair as Xander and Mike moved to the front of the bullpen and began conducting after-action reviews on each of their recent response calls before transitioning into updates on any ongoing missions. Gage held these meetings at least once a week—sometimes more—as a way of making sure everyone on the team knew what their teammates were working on and also so they could hopefully learn from each other's experiences.

Brooks tried his best to pay attention, but within minutes, his head was a million miles away, scenes from last night and this morning replaying through his mind over and over. But no matter where he started, he always ended up in the same place. With Selena totally losing it and running out of his house with tears on her terror-stricken face.

He had alternated between calling and texting Selena for nearly an hour after she'd left. He'd left countless messages, saying he was sorry he'd scared her and that everything was going to be okay…if they could just talk. When Selena hadn't responded after the twentieth text, he'd finally stopped, afraid he was only going to freak her out even more.

On the way to the SWAT compound, he and Zane

had driven past Selena's apartment to see if she was there. Brooks was smart enough to know trying to see her would have been a complete catastrophe, but he'd wanted to make sure she'd gotten home okay.

Unfortunately, his Chevy hadn't been in the parking lot. He'd immediately had visions of his truck ending up in a ditch somewhere because she'd been too far gone to even control it. He was so damn worried, he'd actually considered putting out a BOLO on his pickup. Thankfully, Zane had talked him out of it. The last thing they needed was a DPD patrol car pulling Selena over because they thought she'd stolen the vehicle. In her condition, she'd probably attack the officer.

"Brooks, what's the status on the joint gang task force?" Gage asked from the front of the room.

He looked up to see not only his boss staring at him, but everyone else, too. Brooks stared back. His head was so completely trashed, he had no clue how to answer Gage's question. He had the intel from last night at the club, but that info was more than twelve hours out of date. Ray and the rest of the task force could be working a dozen new angles by now.

Knowing how bad it was going to look but not having any choice, Brooks opened his mouth to admit he was completely out of the loop on the task force operation. But before he could get the words, Zane spoke.

"I talked to Ray about an hour ago," his friend said, throwing him a pointed look before turning back to Gage. "The energy drinks we confiscated from the club last night came back laced with high levels of fentanyl. According to the lab, the concentration in a single can is enough to put the average person on a pretty good ride.

Drink more than one—or add in alcohol—and you get the overdose scenario we had last night."

"Did the lab get any usable fingerprints from the cans?" Gage asked, eyeing Brooks for a second before looking at Zane. "Any way to ID where this stuff is coming from?"

Zane shook his head. "Unfortunately, no. The cans came back covered in prints, but it's going to take a while before the crime scene unit sorts them out. Ray and his people spent the morning hitting the other clubs in town and found five other places selling the energy drink. They all told the same story—they were approached by a sales rep they've never met before who provided them cases of Buzz at low cost in an attempt to build a market for it."

"That doesn't make a hell of a lot of sense," Connor pointed out with a frown. "Whoever is making this crap has to know they won't be able to sell it in legitimate clubs much longer, even if they build up a demand for it. Once word gets out this drink has synthetic heroin in it, no one is going to touch it with a ten-foot pole, no matter how much people might want it."

"They won't care by then," Brooks said, still playing catch-up. "Once word hits the streets that someone has figured out how to make heroin you can drink, the dealers can move it to the underground market. Think raves, college parties, and private clubs. Hell, they can sell it on street corners or out of the back of a truck in a parking lot somewhere. It won't matter, because this crap will move like crazy by that point."

Connor shook his head. "That's a nice frigging thought. Throw in the fact the dealer can probably change the appearance of the cans anytime they want, and this has all the makings of a whole new direction in drug distribution."

Gage crossed his arms over his chest. "Is anyone working on ID'ing the sales reps who dropped the cases off at the clubs? With six different clubs targeted, someone has to recognize them."

"Ray has police sketch artists working with people in every club, and he's got the employees looking at mug shots," Zane said. "He's still working on the theory this is connected to the new gang boss."

Brooks grimaced. Unlike in the movies and on TV where it took cops five minutes to find someone in their fancy computer database, it took a whole lot longer in the real world.

He was still musing about the probability of Ray's crew finding a connection when Cooper asked if there'd been anything new on the prison break.

Gage grunted. "There's crappy news and less crappy news. Which one do you want first?"

"Less crappy," the entire room said in unison.

"Becker was able to successfully hack into the personnel records for Coffield. He also broke into the security system that monitors and tracks prisoner movements, along with the warden's computer and those of the Marshals Service."

At the desk beside Brooks, Rachel looked a little uncomfortable that a fellow SWAT cop hacked into other people's computers. That was only because she didn't know Becker yet. While the guy was younger than almost all of them, he'd been a scary good computer geek even before he'd worked for the Secret Service back when he was human. He'd only gotten sneakier after that. That he'd been able to break into both the state prison system and the marshals' computers wasn't a big shock to any of them.

"What did he find out?" Brooks asked.

"He's come up with a detailed outline of how Frasheri and the other inmates were able to break out, right down to when their security status was downgraded and which checkpoints they passed through on their way to the laundry area."

"That has to narrow down the list of possible suspects," Zane pointed out.

"It has," Gage agreed. "He's working through a list of twelve prison guards and five members of the administrative staff at the facility as we speak. The guards work the gates, doors, and checkpoints. The civilians work in either the admin services department or IT. Any of them could have slipped in and changed the security status of the escaped inmates. The crazy thing is that half of those suspects used to work for the Dallas PD."

Brooks frowned. "That can't be a coincidence."

"I don't think so either. That's why Becker's focusing his attention on them first," Gage said. "With any luck, whoever helped those inmates escape will lead us to the traitor in the DPD who's working with the hunters."

The idea of finally coming face-to-face with the asshole in the department who'd sold them out to the hunters sooner rather than later was almost enough to make Brooks forget what a shitty morning he was having.

Cooper picked up his mug and took a swig of coffee. "If that was the less crappy news, what's the crappy news?"

Gage's brow furrowed. "About an hour ago, I got a

call from the U.S. Marshal in charge of the manhunt. They found two of the prison escapees in a house just south of Waxahachie. Both of them have been dead since yesterday afternoon."

"Please tell me one of them was Seth Oliver," Max growled, his blue eyes flashing gold. "I don't give a crap who the other one is, as long as Oliver is dead."

Considering Oliver almost killed Max's bride-to-be, Brooks didn't blame him. He wasn't the only one. Zane looked just as interested in the answer. Brooks wouldn't shed a tear for the man either, that was for damn sure.

Gage shook his head. "Unfortunately, it wasn't Oliver. It wasn't Frasheri or Engler either. It was two of the omegas. They'd been shot in the back of the head, execution style."

"Damn," Brooks said.

His pack mates seemed just as disturbed by that as he was. A bullet to the head was the fastest way to kill one of their kind. While those omegas had gone to prison for their involvement with Frasheri's Albanian crime family, that didn't mean anybody wanted to see them murdered like that. It tended to remind a werewolf of its own mortality.

"What about the third omega?" Zane asked. "There were three of them in the back of the truck that got away. Are the marshals sure there were only two?"

Gage nodded. "They searched the woods around the house. Even used a K9 team. They found a lot of blood and some broken branches in the undergrowth but no body. The marshals think the inmates were arguing over the escape plan and turned on each other."

"Like hell they did," Brooks muttered. "Frasheri doesn't give a damn about werewolves any more than Engler or Oliver do. They included the omegas in the escape in case they needed muscle. Once they were out, there was no reason to keep them around."

"Likely," Gage agreed. "But with the executions happening so close to Dallas, the marshals are now concerned Oliver and the others are hanging around to take a shot at one or more of us. They're assigning some of their people to keep an eye on us, though they wouldn't be specific about it." He looked at Max. "They suggested you and Lana put your wedding on hold until the escapees are back in custody. Or," he added when Max opened his mouth to argue, "that you at least move the ceremony and reception to a more secure venue than the compound."

Max snorted. "Like where? The frigging prison? Oliver and his new buddies sure aren't going back there." He shook his head. "If we aren't safe on the SWAT compound with more than fifty werewolves around us, where the hell are we safe?"

No one had an answer to that. Was there any place in this city that was safe for any of them at this point?

"Which omega got away?" Cooper asked. "Becker will want to know who it was. He got to know a lot of them when he was undercover in Frasheri's organization."

"Caleb Lynch."

Brooks couldn't remember which werewolf Caleb was. Not that it mattered. It wasn't like an escaped convict would come to the Pack looking for protection from the hunters.

The briefing broke up a little while later. Afterward, Gage, Mike, and Xander went into Gage's office and closed the door. Most of his pack mates disappeared to other parts of the compound to handle various administrative responsibilities while Cooper, Diego, and Connor went back to the reports they'd been working on. Brooks had some paperwork he should be doing, too, but he couldn't concentrate. Now that the meeting was over, all he could think about was Selena. Not knowing if she was okay was making him nuts.

Brooks got up from his desk to slip outside so he could try her cell again when Connor's cat strutted into the bullpen. Tuffie padded along behind her, a completely happy doggy smile on her face.

"Hey there, Kat." Connor chuckled as the cat jumped gracefully up on his desk and rubbed her head against his hand. When he ran his fingers over her fur, she immediately began to purr. "You and Tuffie having a good morning?"

Brooks stared, not sure what was crazier—the fact that Tuffie and the cat seemed to be BFFs, or the name Connor had given her.

"You named the cat…Cat?" he asked incredulously. "That's the best you could come up with?"

Connor snorted. "I didn't name her. She named herself that. And it's not Cat with a *C*. It's Kat with a *K*."

Brooks lifted a brow. "You're saying that furry little critter told you her name?"

"Not exactly." Connor shrugged. "We were hanging out at my place last night when I realized she didn't have a name. So we worked through a long list of possible names until we got to the one she liked."

"You're shitting me, right?"

Connor shook his head. "No way. Kat's easy to read. When I suggested a name she didn't like, she had no problem letting me know."

"Oh yeah?" Brooks said. "How does she do that?"

"Watch and learn, brother." Reaching out, Connor gently caressed the cat under her chin. "Is your name Whiskers?"

The cat stopped purring and immediately swatted his hand away with a seriously unhappy look on her face.

Connor sat back. "See? She obviously hates that name. She reacted the same way any time I called her anything other than Kat…with a *K*."

The moment he said her name, the cat stepped forward and rubbed her head against his hand again.

Brooks was still trying to come up with something rational to say about how bizarre the whole thing was when Gage opened the door to his office and stuck his head out. "Brooks, we need to talk."

Out of the corner of his eye, Brooks saw Zane look at him. He ignored his pack mate as he headed for Gage's office. His boss had obviously noticed something was going on with him this morning and finally decided to find out what it was.

Brooks was so not looking forward to this.

Mike was sitting in one of the chairs in front of Gage's desk while Xander leaned against the wall. Both squad leaders regarded Brooks thoughtfully as Gage took a seat behind his desk.

"Sit," Gage ordered.

Brooks dropped into the empty chair beside Mike, bracing himself for the ass chewing that was almost certainly coming his way.

"What the hell is going on with you?" Gage demanded. "You've always been one of my most dependable officers, the guy I ask to take over when Xander or Mike are out of pocket. I know you just met the woman who's probably *The One* for you, but that doesn't explain why you stumbled in to work three hours late this morning."

Mike and Xander looked interested in that answer, too.

Brooks opened his mouth to reply, but Gage cut him off, his dark eyes swirling with gold—a sure sign he was on his way to getting pissed.

"It also doesn't explain why Zane had to fill us in on the status of your gang task force operation," Gage continued. "And it sure as hell doesn't explain the call I got from a friend over in the Northeast Division asking why someone saw one of my officers standing outside his house buck-ass naked this morning."

Shit. Brooks hadn't thought about anyone seeing him when he ran after Selena. He hadn't been thinking about much of anything except her. Even now, his gums and fingertips tingled as his wolf half tried to come out.

"Selena shifted last night and clawed me up pretty good," he explained as calmly as he could. "When she woke up this morning and saw what she'd done, she completely lost it. I tried to tell her what she is—what I am—and she threw me across the room. Then she grabbed the keys to my truck and took off. I started to follow her but figured I'd only scare her even more." He shook his head. "I've been calling and texting since, but she isn't answering."

Gage exchanged doubtful looks with Mike and Xander.

"You're telling us a woman who can't be more than 115 pounds soaking wet threw you across a room?" Mike looked at him in disbelief. "I'm having a hard time buying that, especially considering she just started turning into a werewolf four days ago."

Brooks ran his hand over his hair, frustration making

his inner wolf even more restless. "I know it sounds crazy, but I'm telling you, she has claws and fangs an inch long and is as strong as one of us."

"That's not possible," Mike insisted.

"No shit." Brooks shook his head. "I don't know. Maybe the blue eyes have something to do with it."

Mike did a double take. "Blue eyes?"

"Yeah. When she shifts, her eyes glow blue instead of green."

Gage cursed. "Xander, find Carter and tell him to get in here."

Brooks frowned. "What the hell does Carter have to do with this?"

His boss leveled his gaze at him. "He's an omega."

There might have been an audible thud as Brooks's jaw hit the floor. Carter Nelson was an omega?

Omegas were violent and out of control.

Not like Carter.

Besides, what did that have to do with Selena? Unless… *Shit.*

Brooks opened his mouth to ask if that was what Gage meant, but Zane leaned in the open doorway. "Ray just called. They have a lead on one of the guys distributing the spiked energy drinks to the clubs. They're getting ready to arrest him, and Ray wants SWAT there ASAP."

Gage muttered another curse. "Brooks, take Carter with you and the other guys. Tell him Selena is an omega and that you need him to bring you up to speed on what that means."

Brooks's head spun as he raced outside. Selena couldn't be an omega werewolf. Gage had to be wrong.

Omegas were violent and out of control.

Exactly like Selena.

Double shit.

—∿∿—

Selena knew Becca was home long before she heard the rattle of keys in the door of the apartment. It had been impossible for her to miss the echoing slap of low heels on the concrete stairs at the far end of the complex. How she'd somehow known those footsteps could only belong to her friend was something she didn't like thinking about. The implications were too scary.

The door burst open, and Becca ran in, slamming it behind her. "Selena? Are you okay?"

Selena didn't move from the throw she was huddled underneath on the couch in the living room. "I'm here."

Thankfully, she and Becca had keys to each other's apartments. If not, Selena wouldn't have had anywhere to go. Her own apartment was out of the question. Jayden would almost certainly look for her there.

Becca hurried into the living room, dropping her purse on the overstuffed chair as she came around the couch. She stopped and stared, her mouth open.

Selena knew she probably looked like hell. Her eyes were red from crying, her face was streaked with tears, and her hair was a complete train wreck. The funny thing was that she felt even worse than she looked. She couldn't explain it, especially since she'd felt fantastic when she'd woken up this morning in Jayden's arms. But from the moment she'd attacked him, she'd felt crappy. Stealing his truck and running away had only made it worse.

If it hadn't come on so suddenly, she would have thought she had the flu or something. But after what

had happened this morning, she knew the horrible sensations twisting up her insides were yet another symptom
of the drastic changes taking place. The changes that
were slowly turning her into a monster.

"This is even worse than I thought," Becca said, sitting on the edge of the couch and wrapping Selena in a
warm hug. "I knew there was something wrong when
you texted and said you needed me in the middle of a
school day. I'm just sorry it took me so long to get here.
Eva had a hard time getting a sub for my class." She
pulled away. "What's wrong? Did you and Jayden have
a fight or something?"

Selena shrugged, the throw slipping off her shoulder.
"I guess you could say that."

Becca frowned, her eyes locked on Selena's exposed
shoulder. Reaching out, she yanked the throw down,
exposing the sleepshirt Selena had nabbed out of her
friend's dresser.

"What the hell did he do to you?" Becca asked, her
face going pale at the sight of the half-healed bite marks
peeking out from the collar of the shirt. "Oh my God.
He bit you." Cursing, Becca stood and grabbed her purse
from the chair. "I'm calling the police."

Selena shoved off the throw she'd been huddled
under for the past few hours and jumped to her feet.
"You can't!"

Becca didn't look at her as she dug through her
monstrous purse, coming out with her phone. "Why?
Because he's a cop? I don't care. He can't treat you like
that. I won't let him."

Selena reached out and gently took the phone from
Becca's hand, surprised at how easy it was. Then again,

she seemed to be a lot stronger than she used to be. "You can't call the cops, but it's not because Jayden is in SWAT."

"Then why?" her friend demanded angrily.

"Because if the cops got involved, they'd see that the bite marks I put on Jayden are ten times worse than the ones he put on me. The claw marks alone would probably land me in prison for assault."

Becca stared at her in confusion. "What are you talking about? You're too tame to even give a guy a hickey. There's no way you could ever scratch a man up that bad."

Selena sighed. Dropping Becca's phone in her purse, she moved over to the couch and sat down. "Before this week, I would have agreed with you. But since last night, everything is different. I don't really know what I'm capable of anymore. All I know is that I'm dangerous now."

"I don't understand." Becca sat beside her. "What happened last night to make you think you're dangerous?"

"I don't really know. It's kind of hard to explain," she admitted. "But it's why I called and asked you to come home. If I don't talk about this with someone, I think I might go insane."

Becca regarded her silently. "Okay, you needed me to come home to talk, so talk. But start from the beginning, because right now I'm confused as hell."

Selena opened her mouth to start, then closed it again, not exactly sure where the beginning of this story really was. She was as confused as Becca. Finally, she took a deep breath and began at the place that seemed to make the most sense.

"Jayden and I got a little carried away the night he came over to my apartment for dinner," she said softly.

"While we were making out, I…well…I bit him. Hard enough to make him bleed."

Becca looked at her like she was waiting for a punch line. "Look, I have to ask this now so we can get it out of the way. But this whole thing isn't going to turn out to be some weird, kinky sex game, is it? If so, I don't think I'm the person you should be talking to about it. I'm as vanilla as a Starbucks Frappuccino. I don't do kinky."

Selena laughed despite herself. Part of the reason she'd come to Becca was because her friend always knew how to get her to calm down. "No. As much as I wished this was some kind of sex game gone wrong, it isn't."

Becca nodded. "Okay. Well, if it wasn't some kind of sex kink, why'd you bite your hunky boy toy hard enough to make him bleed?"

"It's not like I planned it," Selena said. "I was on his lap, kissing his neck, and the next thing I knew, I had blood in my mouth and four fangs in his neck. He didn't seem concerned by it, but I freaked."

Becca held up a hand. "Wait a minute. Did you say fangs?"

"Yeah. Four long, really sharp fangs. Though I didn't realize what they were at the time."

"You're joking, right? Please tell me you're joking."

Selena's stomach twisted at the horrified look in her friend's eyes. "I know it sounds bizarre. But there's more."

"Go on," Becca said hesitantly.

"Yesterday, I found Ruben hanging out with a bunch of Locos on that empty lot on Ferguson." Selena had replayed the entire scene through her head over and over again in light of what had happened that morning with Jayden. What she'd been able to do to those gangbangers made a lot more sense now. "When I told Ruben I wanted him to leave with me, three of the Locos attacked me."

Becca gasped, her hands coming up to cover her mouth. "Were you hurt?"

Selena shook her head. "It was the reverse. I beat the crap out of them."

Becca looked even more stunned at that, but Selena couldn't stop now. She could already feel the tips of her fingers tingling and knew she needed to get the rest of this story out before it got worse.

"Last night, Jayden and I made love," she said. "It was amazing, powerful, and overwhelming. I came so many times that some parts of the evening are little more than a blur. But I vaguely remember biting and scratching Jayden. I thought it was my mind playing tricks on me, but when I woke up this morning, I knew it wasn't."

"What did Jayden say?" Becca asked, leaning forward on the edge of the seat like she was watching an episode of *Game of Thrones*.

Selena took a deep breath. "He told me that I'm turning into a werewolf. That I have been since that day in the classroom when Pablo tried to kill me."

Becca stared at her for a moment, then bolted to her feet, her face suddenly red with anger. "That's not funny, Selena. I came home because I was worried about you. I almost called the cops because I thought your new boyfriend abused you. I sat here and listened to what you had to say because I thought you were honestly in trouble. But if you're going to make a joke out of all this, I'm going back to work. You can deal with your own problems." Becca grabbed her purse and started for the door.

Selena swallowed hard, tears stinging her eyes. Why

would anyone—even her best friend—believe a tale this unbelievable when Selena barely believed it herself?

Selena stood. "Becca, wait!"

Her friend turned, her hand on the doorknob.

"I can prove it to you," she said. "Just...don't freak out, okay?"

Selena didn't wait for her friend to answer. Instead, she held up her hands, palms facing her, and focused on the fear that had been growing inside her the entire morning. Hours alone in Becca's apartment had already taught her that being scared made the claws come out. Anger did it, too, even easier than fear.

Becca stumbled and almost fell over when Selena's claws came out. Her eyes went so wide, Selena thought for a second her friend might pass out. She resisted the urge to run forward to be there to catch her, just in case. That would only terrify Becca more.

She moved her hands behind her back, hoping that would help. It didn't at first, but after a few moments, Becca's breathing slowed to normal. Setting her purse on the floor, she walked over to stand in front of Selena, then put out her hands, palms up.

Selena slowly brought her hands out from behind her back, carefully resting them on top of Becca's.

Her friend stared at the inch-long claws for a long time without saying a word. While Selena had quickly figured out that fear and anger made the claws extend— and sometimes her fangs—she'd yet to figure out how to make them go away as fast. They'd usually retract after she calmed down, but at the moment there was little chance of that happening.

"So, you're a werewolf," Becca finally said.

Selena nodded. "Yeah. At least, that's what Jayden told me."

Becca lifted her gaze, her expression concerned but not necessarily scared. "How did you turn into one?"

"I don't know for sure." Selena's voice cracked a little as the waterworks threatened to turn back on. She'd spent a good portion of the morning reflecting on this same subject. It hadn't gone well. "Jayden said something about this being related to Pablo shooting at me."

Becca seemed to consider that for a moment. "I can't believe I'm going to ask this, but how did Jayden figure out you're a werewolf?"

Selena closed her eyes for a second, thanking God he'd given her a friend so good at dealing with this kind of stuff. "He recognized the signs because he's a werewolf, too."

"Of course he is." Becca sighed. "Did you turn because he bit you?"

Selena had already considered that possibility. It was one of the first irrational conclusions she'd leaped on after getting to Becca's apartment. "I don't think so. I was acting weird long before last night."

"I'm not going to argue with you there," Becca agreed. "What about when you bit him the night before? Maybe you got it through his blood."

She shook her head, taking her hands away from Becca's. "Nope. I already had the fangs then, remember. I'm pretty sure I was already turning into a werewolf when you saw me in the hospital after the shooting. It's probably why my vitals were so wacky."

Becca blew out a breath. "Okay, that's the end of my bright ideas then. What about Jayden? What else was he able to tell you about being a werewolf?"

Selena winced. "Unfortunately, I didn't give him a chance to say very much."

"I'm almost afraid to ask," Becca said.

"Remember when I said I freaked out when Jayden told me I was a werewolf?" Selena's stomach clenched at the memory. "Well, saying I freaked out might be a bit of an understatement. I attacked him."

Becca nudged Selena over to the couch, sitting her down, then taking a seat beside her. "What do you mean you attacked him? Because I refuse to believe you could hurt anyone, especially Jayden. It's not in you, werewolf or no werewolf."

Selena wondered if Becca would say that if she'd seen her earlier. "When Jayden first told me I was turning into a werewolf, I got mad. I thought he was trying to be funny about something that wasn't funny at all, like you did with me a minute ago. But then he showed me his claws, and I lost it. That's when my claws and fangs came out, which only freaked me out even more."

"That's understandable." Becca gave her a small smile. "It's sort of a lot to take in."

"Yeah, I guess." Understatement there. "Jayden tried to get me to calm down, but when I saw how much I'd clawed him up while we'd made love, it scared me so badly, I was convinced I was a monster. The look on Jayden's face when I flipped out only made it worse. It was like he was seeing a monster, too."

"Honey, Jayden does not think you're a monster." Becca took Selena's hand, not caring that her claws were still out. "He thinks you're a werewolf like him."

"I know what you're saying, but you didn't see the look in his eyes when it happened."

Becca squeezed her hand. "No, I didn't. But I saw the way he looked at you in the club last night. The man is in love with you. A few days after meeting you, and he's crazy about you. I'd bet my life on it."

A part of Selena desperately wanted to believe that, because she felt the same way about him. Running away from him had been the hardest thing she'd ever done, and if she hadn't been so damn scared, she probably wouldn't have been able to do it. But the longer she sat here now staring at her claws and remembering how badly she'd hurt the man she was already in love with, the harder it was for her to believe Jayden could ever forgive her. He might be a werewolf, but she was a monster.

"Even if you're right about Jayden being in love with me last night, he's not now," she said miserably. "Not after what I did to him this morning."

Becca frowned. "You keep saying you attacked him. What exactly did you do?"

"I shoved him—hard," Selena said. "I didn't even realize what I was doing. One second, I'm standing there freaking out, and the next, Jayden is flying ten feet through the air and bouncing across the floor."

Her friend's eyes went wide. "Wow. I guess this werewolf thing comes with more than claws."

Selena nodded. "Then after I threw him across the room, I stole his truck and left him standing naked in his driveway."

Becca didn't say anything. Selena wondered whether it was because her friend was trying to come up with something or she was simply picturing Jayden naked in his driveway.

"No matter how bad it was this morning, you know

you're going to have to talk to Jayden again, right?" Becca finally said. "I don't think this is a problem you can deal with on your own, so unless you know another werewolf you can talk to about it, Jayden's the only one who can help you with this."

Selena sighed. "I know you're right, but I don't know how I can face him again after what I did to him. It feels like I'm going to lose control just thinking about it."

Becca leaned over and hugged her. Selena felt tears burn her eyes as she returned the gesture. Knowing her friend was still able to touch her like this after realizing what Selena was meant a lot.

"There's no reason to rush out and see him right now, you know." Becca pulled back to look at her. "You're more than welcome to stay here with me as long as you want. We can run by your place and pick up some of your clothes, then we can crash here together until you're ready to talk to him. I'll even be right there with you when you do, if that makes you feel more comfortable."

"Thanks. You're the best friend a girl could ever ask for," Selena said. "Which is why I hate asking, but could you do me another big favor?"

"You know there isn't anything I wouldn't do for you. No matter what you need, I'm there for you. I mean, if you need five pounds of raw steak or a gallon of pig's blood, all you have to do is ask."

Selena laughed, unable to help it. "Thanks, but fortunately, it's nothing that drastic. I was wondering if you'd be willing to text him and let him know where his truck is? I feel horrible for stealing it."

Becca looked almost disappointed. "Oh, okay. I can do that."

Chapter 15

BROOKS SMELLED THE BLOOD AND GUNPOWDER LONG before he, Carter, and Diego reached the back door of the East Side Collision Damage Repair Shop. He hesitated, not sure if he could trust his nose. His head was spinning from all the crap Carter had told him about omegas on the drive over and what it all meant for Selena. To say he was distracted was an understatement.

But after taking another deep breath, he no longer doubted he was picking up the scent of fresh blood from inside the building they were about to raid. A lot of it, too. Combine that with the fact that he didn't hear a single sound coming from a shop that should have been full of noise at this time of day, and Brooks was pretty sure he already knew what they'd find once they went through the door.

"No sign of movement from the back side," Brooks whispered into his radio, pushing aside any thoughts but those related to the raid. He couldn't think about Selena being an omega right now, as difficult as that was to do. "Ready when you are."

He would have liked to pass along the info on the blood and gunpowder, but with Ray, José, and half a dozen other officers from the task force sitting in the ops van with Zane, he simply couldn't. It would lead to questions he didn't want to answer.

"We're in position," Trey announced from the front of the building. "Thirty seconds to entry. Still seeing no movement from this side, either."

"Roger that," Brooks said. "Count it down."

Ray and his gang unit had put in a long night trying to get fingerprints off the confiscated cans of spiked energy drink. When that hadn't panned out, they'd shown mug shots of the gang members Ray thought might be involved to every employee from the clubs where the cans had been distributed. One of those club employees had identified the man who'd sold him the cases as Aaron Perez. He was a member of the Terrace Grove Locos and had a long history of assault, burglary, and drug distribution. An hour later, Ray had a location and a warrant for the place where Aaron liked to hang out—this collision shop on south Ferguson. The place looked legit from the outside, but according to Ray, it had a reputation for being a gang hangout and the kind of place cars went to get chopped down for parts.

Hopefully, it was also a storage and distribution location for the fentanyl-laced energy drink. Hell, if they were lucky, Aaron might even be the new gang leader they'd heard about. Assuming Ray was right and this new gang boss was the one behind Buzz.

Due to the limited amount of time they'd had to come up with it, the plan for raiding the shop was a basic one. The back of the building had no windows and was shielded from the street out front, so Brooks and his team would make a direct entry from that direction— nothing sneaky or covert about it. At the same time, Trey, Connor, and Remy would go in the front. But since that side of the shop had a wall full of windows that would put Trey's team at risk, they were making their approach in the back of an unmarked moving van. That way, they could pull right up to the door without anyone seeing them.

"Five seconds," Trey said.

Brooks grabbed the doorknob to check it, expecting it to be locked, but it wasn't. He yanked it open, making way for Diego and Carter as Trey called out his own team's entry.

They all stayed tight and alert as they moved into the back of the shop, covering each other and checking every corner and blind spot, even though Brooks could already tell they were the only ones in the place.

"They're up here," Trey said from the front of the shop, his tone confirming what Brooks had feared.

Brooks moved past a half dozen metal racks full of car parts, a heavily customized Monte Carlo in need of a paint job, and more tool boxes than he could count to find Trey and the other guys on the team standing around three bodies. There was a partially crushed case of Buzz energy drink off to the side.

He recognized Aaron, but just barely. The gangbanger and the other two men had been shot in the head but only after they'd been beaten to hell with the assortment of wrenches, hammers, and other bloody tools on the floor nearby. For whatever reason, they'd been tortured before being executed.

"We're all clear, Ray," Brooks said into his radio. "But we're too late."

—◦◦◦—

"That from Selena?" Carter asked, gesturing with his chin at the cell phone in Brooks's hand.

Brooks didn't answer. This was the first chance he'd had to check his phone since the raid, and he just about freaked when he'd seen the text from Becca. Outside the operations truck he and Carter were in, cops and crime scene techs were digging for clues. He ignored them, focusing his attention on the text and trying to read between the lines for any hidden messages.

After determining there was no ongoing threat at the auto shop, Brooks had sent everyone except Carter back to the SWAT compound. They probably didn't need to be there, but Brooks didn't feel right leaving. He owed it to Ray to hang around in case the techs turned up something that might be helpful. Besides, staying there gave him a chance to talk to Carter in private about Selena.

"No, it's not from Selena," he finally said, slipping his phone in a side cargo pocket on his uniform pants. "It was from her friend, Becca. She said I could pick up my truck in front of her apartment building. Becca wanted me to know Selena is okay and that she's staying with her. She thinks Selena needs a little space, though."

Carter lifted a brow. Two years older than Brooks, his blond-haired pack mate had been a U.S. Marine before joining SWAT. "You think she knows Selena is a werewolf?"

Brooks shrugged. "I don't know. Maybe. Either way, Becca seems focused on protecting Selena. That's the important thing."

"What are you going to do?" Carter asked after a long silence. There'd been a lot of those lately. "This thing Selena is going through isn't something she should handle on her own. Trust me. I tried to do it on my own for a long time, and I wouldn't wish it on my worst enemy."

Brooks's chest tightened. From the moment he'd realized Selena's glowing blue eyes meant she was an omega, he'd feared the worst. All he knew about omegas was that they were unpredictable and on the verge of going psychotic at the best of times. The idea that Selena—and Carter—were omegas was hard to wrap his head around.

"How come you never told any of us you were an omega?" he asked, ignoring the question his pack mate had asked about Selena for the moment, since he had no clue how to answer it. "Up until the Pack mixed it up with the omegas who worked for Frasheri, most of us didn't even know they existed. You could have let us know what we were going up against. Hell, you could have at least clued us in that when an omega's eyes glow blue, it means they're on the edge. That info sure as hell would have helped this morning."

Carter stared at the TV mounted to the wall of the ops truck, watching the news conference Chief Curtis was holding at that very moment. Curtis was talking about the current murders and the recent rise in gang-on-gang violence in the city. No doubt, the moron was making sure everyone knew it wasn't his fault.

"And how would that conversation have gone, Brooks?" Carter said, abruptly turning to lock eyes with him, his jaw tight. "What would you and the others have said if I casually dropped the fact that I know all about how out of control omegas get because I've been there myself. That I spend a good portion of my waking hours worrying about keeping it together? That if I lose it the least little bit, I can go from growling to completely mental in ten seconds flat? Would you and the others have been comfortable having me cover your backs during a high-threat entry? Would you have wanted me on the team? Would you have wanted me in the Pack?"

Brooks opened his mouth to say of course they would, but Carter cut him off.

"Before you answer, seriously ask yourself whether you'd consider letting one of the omegas who worked for Frasheri in the Pack after seeing what they were like. By the way, you don't have to answer. We both already know what the answer would be."

"That's a stupid question," Brooks insisted. "Those omegas we fought were crazy, like they were on some kind of drug."

Carter regarded him thoughtfully. "Crazy. Drugged. Yeah, that's pretty much what it's like to be an omega. And none of those omegas we fought that night were actually out of control, which is why you never saw their eyes glow blue. Still want to ask why I never told the Pack?"

Brooks thought about that for a few moments, then shook his head. "Has Gage known all along?"

Carter nodded. "Yeah. When Mike and Xander became squad leaders, we had to tell them, too, so they'd know how to calm me down if I start to lose it."

Brooks frowned. "That's still something you have to deal with? Losing it, I mean."

Carter's gaze went to the TV again. "The urge to give in and let the omega wolf inside me come out is always there. I've been working on control for a long time, so as far as completely losing it, that hasn't happened in a while. But I'm like a heroin addict. I'm one slipup from starting all over."

Damn. Brooks couldn't even imagine what it would be like to have a constant battle going on with his inner wolf. Knowing Selena might be going through that while he sat there in the ops truck made his own wolf want to howl.

"Is that why I've never seen your eyes flash blue?" Well, bluer than Carter's eyes naturally were, Brooks silently amended. "Because you've never completely lost it around me?"

Carter nodded. "Pretty much. Most of the time, a male omega's eyes glow gold like any other male were-wolf's. When they slip over the edge because they're angry, afraid, or even extremely sexually excited, they glow blue instead. The bluer they glow, the further gone they are."

Brooks remembered how scared Selena had been that morning and how her eyes had glowed bright blue. It only made him feel worse about letting her run away. She must have been so damn terrified.

"Do you think it's possible for an omega to become an alpha the same way Jayna went from being a beta to an alpha when her pack needed her to be one?" Brooks asked.

Carter shrugged. "I've never seen it, but I guess it's possible. Lots of weird crap has been happening lately, so who's to say what we see next? It's not like this were-wolf thing comes with a user's manual, you know?"

For some reason, the possibility that Selena might get better gave Brooks a feeling of hope. But then he immediately felt like shit for letting his mind even go in that direction. Selena didn't need to *get better*. She was perfect and amazing just the way she was.

But as perfect and amazing as she was, there was no escaping the fact that Selena was facing the same constant uphill battle Carter did. She'd have to fight to stay in control, always terrified she'd lose it and hurt someone. While she seemed so gentle and angelic, the claw marks on Brooks's back were evidence of how dangerous she could be when her omega side took over.

Brooks bit back a growl. Selena had already dealt with so much crap in her life. On top of her parents taking off when she was a kid, her brother had been murdered. Throw in the day-to-day burden of watching one kid in her class after another lose their futures to the gangs, and it was more than any person should ever have to face. Now, in addition to dealing with claws and fangs, Selena had to deal with uncontrolled rage, all because she was an omega werewolf. It all seemed so unfair.

"I still don't get why Selena became an omega," Brooks mused. "She risked her life to save a whole classroom full of students. Why isn't she an alpha? For that matter, why aren't you? You turned because you saved people from a burning vehicle."

Carter didn't say anything for a long time. Instead, he gazed off into the distance like he was reliving something from his past. After a moment, he looked at Brooks. "Was Selena angry when she stood up to that gangbanger in the classroom?"

Brooks didn't even have to think about it. "I know she was. She hates the gangs and anything to do with them. After what they did to her family and the kids in her class, can you blame her?" That's when it hit him. "Shit. That's it, isn't it? She's an omega because she was so filled with hate and anger when she turned."

His pack mate nodded.

"Is that why you're an omega?" Brooks asked.

"Yeah," Carter said.

There was a story there, Brooks was sure about that, but now wasn't the time or place to get into it.

He sat back in the swivel chair, rubbing his hand along the neat beard edged along his jawline and trying to get his head around what all of this meant.

"Selena's going to lose control more often and with less provocation," Carter continued. "This morning, it was because she thought she'd hurt you. In a week, it might be someone cutting her off in traffic or bumping her in a crowd. In a month, it could be someone looking at her the wrong way. If she's lucky, the claws and fangs you saw this morning are as far as she'll be able to shift. I don't know about that for sure, since I've never seen a female omega. But still, the chances of her exposing what she is to someone—or killing them—is high, and it'll get worse the longer she's on her own."

Brooks let out a low growl, refusing to even think about any of those possibilities. "Selena won't be on her own. She'll have me."

His pack mate studied him, a look of sadness in his eyes Brooks had never seen before. It made him wonder when Carter had become so solemn. Oh yeah, maybe a couple of hours ago, when Gage had decided it was time for his big secret to come out.

"Do you love Selena?" Carter asked.

"Yes. More than I ever thought possible."

Brooks said the words without hesitation, for the first time putting what he felt for Selena into words. He'd known there was a connection with her from the moment he'd seen her, and he'd been more than ready to accept she was *The One* for him. But this was the first time he'd allowed himself to truly consider what all that meant. He only wished he'd told Selena how he felt before this morning. Considering they'd only been on two dates, it probably would have been way too fast, but maybe it would have kept everything from going so bad.

"I'm not talking about her being *The One* for you," Carter said. "That's obvious. What I want to know is whether you're ready to do anything necessary to help Selena, even if that means watching her walk away."

The question caught him off guard. "Walk away? What the hell are you talking about?" The words came out sharper than he intended, his fangs extending slightly. "I'm not letting her walk anywhere without me. I want to help her control this thing."

"I know that." Carter's mouth curved up in a small, mirthless smile. "Look, learning how to stay calm enough to control their claws and fangs is a long-term project for an omega. I worked on it by myself for almost two years before Gage found me. It's still hit and miss, even after all this time. The best thing you can do for Selena is be there for her when she needs you. Introducing her to the Pack might help, too."

Brooks scowled. "Might help?"

"You're going to have to take this at her pace," Carter said. "Some omegas, like me—and the ones that have moved into the area since the hunters showed up—can live in a pack environment. But others never get to that point. As a rule, omegas are loners. If you try to put a wall up around Selena for her own protection, you might chase her off."

Brooks opened his mouth to say he wouldn't let that happen to the woman he loved, but Carter interrupted him. "Ray's coming. I'll let you two talk."

Carter was out the door before Brooks could stop him. Ray stepped in a moment later. He grinned when he caught sight of Brooks.

"You know you didn't have to hang around, right?" Ray grabbed the chair Carter had vacated. "It's not like we're going to need any doors kicked in at this point."

Brooks couldn't help but smile at the little groan of pleasure Ray let out now that he was off his feet. The guy acted like he was eighty even though he was the fittest cop in his midfifties in the department. "I know. But I wanted to be here in case you found something worthwhile."

Ray snorted. "Hope you haven't been holding your breath then, because we haven't found much of anything."

"Nothing?"

"Nothing of substance. We confirmed the other two victims were members of the Hillside Riders. Put that together with the fact that Aaron is a member of the Locos, and it confirms the new gang boss was behind this. It's the only thing that explains members from different gangs being in one place."

"You think this new boss is still clearing out gang members who refuse to follow him?" Brooks asked.

Ray crossed his arms over his chest with a shrug. "Maybe. José and the others from narcotics are leaning that way. Most of my people think the boss caught

Aaron and those other two skimming some of the spiked energy drinks for themselves, either to drink or sell to make some money on the side, and made an example of them."

"But you don't buy either of those explanations?" Brooks prodded, knowing his old friend well. "You think there's another reason for the murders?"

Ray nodded. "That beating put on Aaron and the other guys wasn't someone sending a message. That was personal. Those men did something to piss off the boss, and he came after them himself. I don't think it was something as minor as swiping a box of drugged-up energy drink."

"Like what?"

"No clue," Ray admitted. "But if we figure out what the reason was, it will point us straight at the man we're after."

"Any chance the techs can get prints off the tools the killers used to beat those men to death?" Brooks asked.

"They're trying. But it could be weeks, even months, before we find a match. If they find any prints at all."

Ray was right. Even though Dallas had its own lab, matching fingerprints was a painful process. Not necessarily because it was technically difficult but simply because there was such a backlog of cases for the lab to work on, not just for this county, but also for the surrounding counties that used the local institute to process their evidence. The truth of the matter was that three dead gangbangers likely killed by other gangbangers didn't rate very high on the department's priority list.

"How'd you guys swing getting a TV signal routed to your ops truck?" Ray asked suddenly, drawing Brooks's attention back to Curtis's press conference. "I'd have thought the budget cuts would keep you from doing something like that."

Brooks chuckled. "Becker did it. Which means it's extremely techie, probably shady, and possibly illegal. We've learned not to ask too many questions."

Ray nodded, apparently understanding. "Have you been listening to what our esteemed chief of police has been saying this time?"

Brooks shook his head. "I avoid listening to Curtis whenever I can."

"That's generally a wise outlook, but in this case, I thought you might have heard him announce who the next sergeant for the gang unit might be. I'm hoping it's one of my people, but with the way he likes to play politics, there's no telling who it will be."

Brooks did a double take. "You're out already?"

Ray's smile was sad. "I told you it would happen. Curtis made it official this morning. He's replacing me. He told me I could either retire or move to a desk job in range services or the evidence property warehouse."

Talk about being put out to pasture. Ray was a good cop. He didn't belong in the evidence room. "What are you going to do?"

"Put in my retirement packet. I'll be out in a few weeks. I'm hoping I can close this case first, but that might be tough. Whoever this new gang boss is, he's smart. If I don't get him, it will be up to whoever takes my place."

"Damn," Brooks muttered. "I'm sorry about this."

Ray shook his head. "Don't be. It's time. But enough about me. Tell me about that girl I saw you with last night. Selena, right? I didn't have a chance to talk to you much, but I got the feeling she's someone very special. Any chance I'm going to see some little baby SWAT cops running around anytime soon?"

The idea of having children with Selena made him smile. "I don't know. I'd like that, but it's complicated."

Ray laughed. "I have no idea what's going on between you two, but I doubt it's as complicated as you're making it out to be. It never is. Like Curtis replacing me. There are a hundred different ways I could react to the situation, but there's only one way that'll get me what I want, so that's what I have to do. Same for you. All you have to do is figure out what's important to you and what you really want, then do what you have to do to get it."

Brooks didn't say anything. Ray could always make the most complex problem simple. Even when it involved love and out-of-control werewolves.

Chapter 16

"I KNOW I DON'T HAVE ANY RIGHT TO ASK YOU FOR A FAVOR, Jayden," Selena whispered into her phone, pushing herself deeper into the shadows of the alley, hoping nobody across the street could hear her. "But I really need your help. You're the only person I can turn to."

"I'll be there in five minutes," he said.

No argument. No complaint about the fact that she hadn't responded to any of his earlier texts or phone messages. Instead, he'd said the exact words she needed to hear. The gentle, confident tone was almost enough to calm her racing heart all on its own. Thank God, she'd had the courage to call him.

"I'll always be there for you," he added. "Just keep out of sight until I get there, okay?"

"I will," she said. "But please hurry. Marguerite just sent me another text. She thinks Ruben might have taken some kind of drug in addition to all the alcohol he's been drinking. She said he's not acting like himself."

"I'm already out the door," Jayden said. "Just... promise you'll wait for me...okay?"

Selena looked across the darkened parking lot at the raucous crowd of partygoers moving in and out of the three-floor apartment building, knowing there was no way in hell she was going in there by herself...not in her current condition.

"I'll wait. I promise."

She heard the sound of a truck door slam closed over the phone as Jayden hung up. She leaned against the brick wall of her hiding place, fighting for control as her body continued to react to the wild energy pouring out of the building on the other side of the street. Merely being here had her claws and fangs extending and retracting in uncontrollable spasms. That should have been enough to make her turn around and go back to Becca's apartment. But the idea of abandoning Ruben to whatever kind of trouble he was in was more than Selena was willing to live with. She took a deep breath and let it out slowly. She was going into that apartment building to rescue her student—as soon as Jayden arrived to make sure she didn't go nuts and tear someone apart.

Selena's claws and fangs hadn't slipped out on their own since yesterday, and she'd almost begun to think maybe she might have this thing under control. It had been enough to convince Becca it was okay for her to head out for the evening to spend some time with Scott.

"Don't worry about me," Selena had insisted. "I'll just hang out here and watch Netflix."

That truly had been her intention. Then Marguerite had sent a text, saying Ruben was in trouble. It had been tricky getting all the details through texts, but somehow the girl had found him at a Locos party, getting drunker by the minute. Selena had panicked, not sure what she should do. Putting herself in a situation like the one Marguerite described was asking for trouble, but in the end, she didn't have a choice. She thought she'd be okay, that she'd be able to handle it.

She'd been wrong. Within seconds of reaching the apartment complex Marguerite had given her the address for, Selena's claws and fangs had slipped out. Even worse, she'd found herself already heading for the entrance of the building before she'd consciously decided going in was the plan. It was like she had no control over her own body anymore. That was when she'd accepted she couldn't do this on her own and had called Jayden.

Calling him had been one of the toughest things she'd ever done, but now that she had, it was like a huge weight had been lifted from her shoulders. She was still terrified she'd hurt him again, but knowing he was on the way was enough to help her calm down. Still holding onto her phone, she slid down the wall of the building and sat there waiting for him.

Selena heard Jayden approaching from farther down the alley long before she smelled him. Not surprising, since she'd already accepted that her werewolf ears were better than her werewolf nose. Crazy what you come to accept when you don't really have a say in the matter. Still, his scent was both mouthwatering and comforting as he dropped to a knee a few feet away from her. Staying out of her reach until he knew what kind of shape she was in was smart, she supposed.

"Are you okay?"

"I'm good," she said, surprised at how calm her voice sounded. Ignoring the urge to throw herself into his arms, she got to her feet. "I haven't heard anything from Marguerite in nearly ten minutes, so we need to get in there."

She started for the entrance of the alley, only to find Jayden blocking her path. She pushed down the growl that immediately rumbled up in her throat, forcing herself to calm down. He wasn't trying to stop her from going. He simply wanted to talk to her first.

She eyed him up and down, noticing he hadn't worn his uniform. That was good, since a cop's uniform wouldn't go over well in a gang hangout. But Jayden didn't need a uniform and police gear to look the part for what they were about to do. With all those muscles bulging and flexing under that T-shirt, he looked intimidating enough to convince most people to stay out of his way.

Selena suddenly realized she probably shouldn't have been able to see him so clearly in the darkness, but she was grateful she could. His ruggedly handsome face, so full of concern, was enough to almost make her cry. It was exactly the same way he'd looked right before she'd shoved him across his apartment and stolen his truck.

"I know you're worried about Ruben," he said softly, stepping close enough to touch her but refraining. His gaze traveling over her body was almost like being grazed by his touch, and she found herself leaning forward, his presence and scent calming her as much as his touch would have. "But are you sure you're okay to go in there? Say the word, and I'll do it myself."

She swallowed hard. "This time last week, I wouldn't have thought twice about charging in there and dragging Ruben out." She wanted like crazy to reach out and hold Jayden. But she'd lost that privilege when she'd attacked him. "After what happened yesterday, I'll admit I'm scared. I want Ruben out of there, but I don't want to hurt anyone. Ruben doesn't know you, though. If you try to bring him out, it'll probably get physical. In that kind of place, that could be really bad."

She expected an argument, but Jayden merely nodded. "I understand. But if you start feeling like you're about to lose it, you have to tell me. I'll get you out of there before you hurt anyone, then we'll figure out another way to get Ruben out. Okay?"

"Okay," she agreed. "But I'm hoping it doesn't come to that."

As she followed Jayden across the street, she shot off a quick text to Marguerite, asking the girl where she and Ruben were.

> Second floor. End of the main hallway.
> Haven't seen Ruben in a while. Worried.

"Marguerite's waiting for us at the end of the hall on the second floor," Selena told Jayden as they began skirting through the cars in the parking lot, heading for the crowd of people hanging around the stairs leading up to the front door of the building. "She can't find Ruben."

"Can you track him by his scent?" Jayden asked.

Selena wasn't sure why the question was so jarring. Considering how good her sense of smell was now, it only made sense she'd be able to pick up on a particular person's scent. But the idea that she could track any scent through a crowd like this still seemed crazy.

"I don't think so," she admitted. "I don't know what he smells like."

Jayden looked like he would have answered, but they had already reached the crowd of people standing on the stairs. Instead, he took her hand and started up the steps. Some people complained, but the moment they caught a glimpse of his size, most backed off.

As they neared the landing, two large guys stepped out and put their hands on Jayden's chest. Both men had a hand behind their backs, and Selena had no doubt they were carrying some kind of weapons. "Private party, and you're not invited."

Selena tensed, wondering what Jayden would say to that. But instead of trying to talk his way in, Jayden grabbed the guy on the right by his throat, picking him up and walking up the last few steps, then slamming the man's body into the double doors. Some people screamed, but most just scattered as the glass in the doors broke and fell out of the frames. The second bouncer seemed stunned, but he recovered quickly. Yanking a gun out from behind his back, he headed after Jayden.

Selena froze at the sight of the pistol. But when she saw the man aim it at Jayden, a snarl ripped from her throat.

One moment she was on the fifth step from the top, and the next she was in the entryway, one hand wrapped around the gunman's throat while the other crushed the fingers holding the gun. She heard a shout followed by small cracking sounds, only vaguely realizing it was the man in her grasp screaming in pain as she broke the bones in his hand.

She panicked as her fangs came out. *Crap*. She was going to lose it right in the main entryway of the building with people all around. But then Jayden was by her side, his hand on her shoulder, his scent filling her nose.

"Selena," Jayden said softly. "He dropped the gun. You can let go now."

A part of her wanted to growl at Jayden for getting in her way, but then she felt one big hand massaging her shoulder, the other pressing gently against her lower back. It was the distraction she needed to regain control, and she released her grip on the second bouncer. The guy dropped to his knees, cradling his broken hand for a moment before scrambling to his feet and running out the door and down the stairs. She noticed he'd left the handgun where it had fallen.

"Breathe, Selena," Jayden entreated, his voice still low and calm. "Just breathe."

She did just that for a few seconds, letting her heart rate slow.

"You okay?" Jayden murmured, his mouth close to her ear, his warm breath stirring her hair.

She nodded, surreptitiously sliding her tongue across her teeth, checking for fangs. They were there, but just barely. Maybe she hadn't lost it enough for anyone to see anything. She glanced down at her fingertips, relieved to see her claws hadn't come out.

"Yeah," she said. "Sorry. I thought that guy was going to shoot you."

Jayden nodded, then led her toward the middle of the loud, music-filled building and the stairwell they found there. On the way up, they passed by dozens of people, an alarming number of them carrying those familiar colorful energy drink cans, glazed looks in their eyes.

"I'm the one who should apologize. Not you," Jayden said, glancing at her over his shoulder. "I thought I'd be able to finish off the first guy, then get to the other one before he could get his weapon pointed in my direction."

"I almost killed him," Selena said when they reached the top of the first set of stairs and headed down the long hallway in the direction she hoped they'd find

Marguerite. She'd been worried about hurting someone, and she'd almost done worse than that.

"No, you didn't," Jayden said, stopping to look at her. "You broke his hand and kept him from shooting me. Those bullets wouldn't have hurt me much, unless he got a lucky shot off to my head or heart, but you didn't know that. You could have ripped out his throat easily, but you never even squeezed. You only hurt him as much as you had to, and you kept yourself in control. The wolf inside you can make you violent, but it can't change who you are. You shouldn't be upset at yourself. You should be proud."

Some of the tension in Selena eased as she realized maybe she wasn't the monster she'd feared. She was still considering that when she heard a familiar voice calling her name. She looked up and saw Marguerite squeezing through the crowded hallway, tears in her dark eyes.

"Thank God you're here, Ms. Rosa. I've been looking for Ruben everywhere and was starting to think maybe he'd left, but a friend told me they saw him heading up to the roof with a bunch of Locos and Riders. My friend said Ruben looked really out of it. Like he was high."

"Was he drinking that energy drink in the colorful can?" Jayden asked.

Marguerite looked up at him in suspicion, but then her eyes widened in surprise. "You're that cop who saved Ms. Rosa."

They really didn't have time for this.

"Yes," Selena said. "He's here to help. But before he can do that, we need to know if Ruben was drinking the stuff in the cans."

Marguerite nodded. "Yeah, I saw him drinking a couple of them. He's probably had a lot more since then. I can't imagine how many. There are coolers full of them all over the building."

Jayden turned and headed for the stairs, Selena right behind him. She thought about yelling back to Marguerite to call the police and let them know there was a kid about to overdose. Probably more than one. But before she could even consider getting the words out, she heard shouting coming from somewhere overhead.

Crap. The roof.

By the time they reached the last flight of stairs heading to the roof, they had to fight through a stream of humanity coming down, most of them looking freaked out and a few commenting about the whacked-out guy on the roof trying to kill himself. Selena didn't know what they were talking about, but her insides were screaming it had to involve Ruben.

She and Jayden came out onto the roof to find more than a dozen guys standing around, laughing and pointing as Ruben walked precariously along the parapet of the roof. The men shouted at him to jump, accusing him of being a coward for being too scared to do it. Even from halfway across the roof, Selena could see Ruben was completely out of it as he moved along a concrete coping that couldn't be much more than six inches wide. Her heart nearly jumped out of her chest as she saw him stumble over his own feet, almost going over.

Between seeing Ruben on the edge of the roof and the jackasses shouting at him to jump, Selena was already on the verge, her claws threatening to extend at any second. She fought for control, but then she saw a group of men converging on Jayden as he tried to reach Ruben, telling him to stay out of it. That's when she stopped worrying about controlling herself and decided those assholes deserved anything she did to them.

When one of the men pulled a knife, Selena growled and tore across the roof after him. There was a thud as she slammed into the man's chest. She felt a dull pop in her shoulder, but it didn't hurt, so she didn't care. She snarled at the man as he tumbled away, his knife skipping across the rooftop. Dismissing him, she then turned toward the next man. That one must have seen something he didn't like, because his eyes widened to the size of golf balls as she leaped on him and drove him to the edge of the roof. She slashed his face once with her claws, wanting to do it again but knowing she didn't have the time. Jayden was fighting at least ten drunk gangbangers by himself, and Ruben was barely staying atop the parapet.

Selena jumped up just in time for the first man she'd knocked down to come running at her, the knife once more in his hand. She felt the tip of the blade slice through her right forearm, instinctively knowing the stinging wound was deep. But she ignored the pain, reaching out with a claw-tipped hand so fast, it was nothing but a blur, and grabbed a wrist that snapped easily under her grip. Then she was slinging the man aside. She saw Marguerite's wide-eyed expression as the man crashed into the doorframe the girl had just run through. Marguerite looked terrified, but Selena didn't have time to worry about that, either.

"Get Ruben!" Jayden called out to her.

He wasn't fighting as many men now, but the ones

still standing looked furious. Something in Selena urged her to go after them first, to protect her mate at all costs. But she fought those instincts, turning toward the edge of the roof where she'd last seen Ruben.

He'd stopped dancing around on the parapet now, standing in one place, swaying back and forth like there was a breeze moving him. His eyes were so glazed over, Selena doubted he even noticed her approach. His skin was ghostly pale, and his heart was thumping like a tiny bird. Selena knew he was about to die.

His knees collapsed, and Selena threw herself forward to grab him as he tumbled over the side. She was stronger than she'd ever been in her life, but Ruben was a big kid. On top of that, he was unconscious and falling fast. She got an arm around his chest, growling in frustration and anger as his weight pulled her over with him.

She grabbed the coping of the roof with her free hand, getting her elbow locked over the edge as his weight snatched at her, trying to rip her off, too. She looked down at the pavement three stories below, wondering if she could live through the fall, knowing Ruben couldn't.

She fought for a better grip, sure they were both going to fall, when a big arm looped around her, dragging her and Ruben back to the safety of the rooftop. She knew without looking it was Jayden. Even if his scent hadn't filled her nose, no one else would have been strong enough to lift two people up like this.

They all thumped to the graveled roof hard. Then Jayden was doing CPR on Ruben, yelling for Marguerite to call 911, to tell them they had a fentanyl overdose.

Marguerite did as he ordered, her terrified eyes locked on Selena the whole time. Selena knew her fangs were out, but there was nothing she could do about it. She only hoped the paramedics would get here in time for Ruben, to somehow make everything that was about to happen worth it.

—∿—

Ruben looked confused as hell when he finally came around, his glazed eyes darting around the hospital triage room like a man desperate to understand what was happening to him. When he saw Brooks standing beside the bed, he looked relieved.

"You're that cop who saved Ms. Rosa the other day in school, right?" the kid croaked out, his voice dry and rough. Then he frowned, as if remembering something else. "You were on the roof, too. Fighting with the Locos and Riders."

Brooks nodded. Luckily, Ruben had come out of the overdose with his memory intact. That wasn't always the case. He was about to ask the kid what else he remembered about tonight, but before he could, Ruben lifted his hand to his chest and groaned in pain.

"Shit. What the hell happened? I feel like an elephant sat on me."

"I gave you CPR until the paramedics showed up and got your heart beating again," Brooks told him. "You have a few cracked ribs that are going to hurt like hell for a while, especially since the doctors can't give you any pain medication."

That seemed to catch the kid by surprise, and he stared at Brooks in confusion for a second until a light-bulb flickered on. Ruben's face crumpled, and he closed his eyes. "I overdosed, didn't I? Up there on the roof."

Brooks sat on the side of the bed. He would have preferred a chair, but they didn't have any in the triage cubicles in the emergency room. They were trying to find Ruben a room, but that was going to take a while. The paramedic had transported fifteen patients out of that party—nine ODs in addition to the six gangbangers with broken bones and concussions from the fight on the rooftop. People were lined up in the hallways of the emergency room, waiting to be seen.

"Yeah, you overdosed," Brooks said softly. "Your heart stopped beating on its own multiple times. There was synthetic heroin in those energy drinks you were downing. If Selena and I hadn't been there..."

Ruben looked up sharply, another frown crossing his face. "I kinda thought there were drugs in those cans, but I drank them anyway. Everything was like a dream—a bad dream. I remember you fighting the guys I'd been hanging with and Ms. Rosa grabbing me as I fell off the roof."

There was silence for a time, and Brooks let it linger so Ruben could process the memories and deal with what happened. "Any chance you heard who put those cans on the street? How they got into that party?"

Ruben shook his head. "I heard a bunch of guys from the gangs talking about the stuff, saying they were making a lot of money off of it. But I didn't hear anything specific."

Brooks cursed silently. If they didn't get this drink off the street, it was going to kill a lot of kids just like Ruben. But there was nothing he could do about it right now. They'd have to keep digging for a clue that would lead them to the person making this crap.

"Did I really fall off the roof?" the kid asked. "Did Ms. Rosa catch me? Was that real?"

Brooks nodded.

"It's all so blurry, but I swear Ms. Rosa had fangs when she lunged at me. Her eyes were glowing, and at the time, I thought she was a monster or something." He looked at Brooks. "Pretty crazy, huh? The drugs I guess."

"You had a lot of drugs in your system," Brooks agreed, glad there was a reasonable excuse for what the kid had seen. "Your memories are going to be a mess for a while. But that's okay. The important thing is that Selena was there to save you. That's the only part you need to remember clearly."

Ruben nodded, his eyes closing again and his big body crumbling in on itself once more. Brooks thought the kid was going to start crying, but he didn't, somehow holding it together. "Is Ms. Rosa here at the hospital?"

"She's in the cafeteria with Marguerite, getting something to eat."

Ruben opened his eyes, chagrined. "Marguerite knows I OD'd, too?"

"Yeah. We would never have been at that party looking for you if it wasn't for Marguerite," Brooks said. "She knew you were in trouble and did what she had to do to get us there. I think she cares about you a lot, something you might want to keep in mind when you get out of here. It's not a stretch to say you owe your life to both of them. You're lucky to be alive."

Ruben winced as he tried to sit up. "Grandma. Damn, does she know? Did anyone call her?"

Brooks gently nudged the kid back down. "Yeah, Selena called her. But she downplayed the worst of it and made sure your grandma knew you were okay. Selena convinced her to wait until morning to come see you. I'm not sure how she cleared all the paperwork with the doctors, but she did."

"Grandma. Ms. Rosa. Marguerite." Ruben sighed. "I guess I really let everyone down, didn't I?"

Brooks got the feeling Ruben wasn't the kind of kid who wanted the truth sugarcoated. "Yeah, you did. I guess the big question though is why you did it. You saw what getting involved with the gangs did for your friend Pablo. Why go down the same road unless you want to end up in prison just like him? Why go to that party and let them give you drugs?"

Ruben shook his head. "I don't know."

"I'm pretty sure you do," Brooks pressed. The kid needed to hear this, even if he didn't want to. "Why did you start hanging out with the Locos and Riders all of a sudden?"

Brooks didn't think the kid was going to answer. In fact, he thought Ruben might retract into a ball and shut down completely.

Instead he sighed, shoulders slumping in defeat. "I just wanted to belong. To be part of something. For people to stop laughing at me all the time. Is that so bad?"

"No, it's not bad to want to be part of something or have that feeling of knowing where you belong. And nobody likes being laughed at," Brooks said. "Your only mistake was thinking the gangs would give you what you needed. That's not how gangs work. They don't give you anything. They take from you until there's nothing left."

Ruben was silent for a moment. "What do I do instead?"

Brooks remembered a time in his past when he'd been looking for someone to tell him which way to go. Jack Walker had changed his life. Now he hoped he could change this kid's.

"You decide who you want to be and if you want to be something more than you are now," Brooks said, telling Ruben the same thing Jack had told him all those years ago. "Then you find people who will help you be that person. If you're looking for a place to start, I'd suggest Marguerite. Because something tells me she's seen something more in you all along."

Ruben seemed to consider that for a while, then nodded. "I think I'll do that, but I'd like to do more. To pay everybody back for helping me."

"Like what?" Brooks asked, wondering if maybe he was talking about apologizing to Selena or something like that.

"I could find out who's making those energy drinks," Ruben said slowly. "Ask around the gang people I already know, and get that info to you."

"No way," Brooks said. "It's too dangerous."

Ruben winced as he pushed himself up higher in the bed, dark eyes determined. "I'm not going to do anything stupid, and it might keep somebody else from overdosing."

Brooks opened his mouth to argue, but Selena and Marguerite chose that moment to walk in. Brooks gave Ruben a pointed look, making sure he realized the conversation was over, then he slipped off the bed, making room for Marguerite as he motioned Selena toward the doorway.

"Everything okay between you and Marguerite?" he asked softly.

The girl had taken a seat on the edge of Ruben's bed, and the two of them were already deep in conversation. Brooks had been a little worried when Selena and Marguerite had gone to the cafeteria. The girl had seen Selena's claws and fangs. The drunk, high gangbangers on the roof had seen them, too, but nobody was going to believe them. Marguerite was different.

Selena nodded. "Yeah, it's good. As far as Marguerite is concerned, she saw me save Ruben's life. That's all she cares about. And the only thing she ever plans to tell anyone."

"You believe her?" he asked.

"Yes." Selena glanced at her students. "Did you and Ruben get a chance to talk?"

"Yeah. I think he's going to be okay," he said as Marguerite leaned forward and shyly kissed Ruben. "Now that he's got someone to keep him straight."

He and Selena stood there for a few more minutes before she smiled at him.

"We should go," she whispered. "They're okay on their own now, and I think it's time the two of us had a long talk. Without me freaking out and running away."

Brooks let out a soft chuckle. "I'm good with that. And if we can avoid the part when I run after you naked, that would be good, too."

Selena laughed, taking his hand and tugging him close as they headed for the exit.

Chapter 17

Brooks opened the back door of his place and flicked on the lights, then stood back so Selena could enter. She stepped inside, hanging up her coat and purse on the rack by the door as if it was the most normal thing in the world. Like the fiasco from the other day hadn't happened at all.

"I'm going to leave the keys right here on the top of the rack. In case you need to grab them again, okay?" he said softly, closing the door and locking it. "And the truck has a full tank of gas, so no worries there either."

She turned and gave him an exasperated frown. "I'm not going to steal your truck again. We already talked about that. We're going to sit here and have a nice calm, intelligent conversation about what it means to be a werewolf. There won't be any claws, fangs, or drama. You have my word on it."

He moved over to one of the wall switches to turn down the lights. It was nearly three in the morning. They didn't need it to be so bright in there, especially considering the conversation they were about to have.

When they'd left the hospital, he thought they were heading to her apartment. But they'd stopped at Becca's building just long enough for Selena to park her car in her friend's visitor space, then she'd jumped in the passenger seat of his truck and said she wanted to go to his place again.

"You sure?" he had asked.

She'd nodded. "My apartment has thin walls. Talking about werewolves there is definitely a bad idea. And while Becca already knows about my situation, I'd prefer to keep the rest of the details from her for now."

Brooks hadn't been shocked to discover Becca knew about werewolves. Obviously, Selena had needed someone to talk to after the crap that had happened the other day, and Becca struck him as a really good person. She'd been there for Selena at least, and that meant a lot to him.

"You want something to eat?" he asked as he followed her over to the big sectional in the living room area.

Her gaze lingered on the back of the couch where they'd made out. A moment later, she shook her head, as if clearing the memories, but not before he caught a whiff of her arousal. His thoughts immediately went *there* at the scent, but he pushed it away fast. They needed to talk without the complications of sex.

"Thanks, but I'm good," she said as she sat down. "I ate a muffin when I had coffee with Marguerite. Let's just talk, okay?"

Brooks grabbed a seat at the other end of the sectional, putting some space between them. He wanted to sit beside her and drag her into his lap so he could kiss her for the rest of the night. But this was important, and the distance would make it easier. At least for him.

"I guess the best way to start is with an apology," he said. "So, this is me saying I'm sorry for not figuring out a better way to tell you that you're a werewolf. Springing it on you after a night of wild sex was definitely the very worst way I could have possibly handled it."

Selena tilted her head at that, as if considering

whether she should disagree. "I can't say you're wrong, even if the sex was mind-blowing, since the evening did end in catastrophe. But if we're being truthful here, I can't imagine any way you could have brought it up that wouldn't have freaked me out."

"Probably true," he agreed. "Still, I wish I'd done better."

"Ditto." She smiled. "Losing control and slinging you across the room wasn't my finest moment, either."

"Don't forget stealing my truck." He grinned. "That ended up getting me called into my boss's office because someone in the neighborhood saw me run after you completely naked."

She clapped her hands over her mouth with a laugh. Jumping up, she joined him on his end of the couch, curling her legs under her and staring at him with big, wide eyes. "You're kidding, right? Did someone really see you?"

"They did. Fortunately, one of Gage's friends on the force took care of it. Still, having to explain to my commander why I was chasing after you naked wasn't fun. Not that I'm blaming you for anything that happened. It wasn't your fault. Some of it comes from you going through your change so fast. The rest is part of you being an omega."

"What do you mean, going through the change so fast?" she asked, still smiling. "And what's an omega?"

"Okay, Werewolf 101 time." This was why they were sitting on the couch at three o'clock in the morning and not buried in a tangle of arms, legs, and sheets. "The period of time between the traumatic event that triggers the change and the first tangible evidence of that change—claws, fangs, and glowing eyes—is usually three or four weeks. But in your case, you did it in about three days. The speed of your change almost certainly made everything a lot rougher on you than it normally would be. And in my defense, it also forced me to tell you what was happening a lot sooner than I wanted to."

Her heart beat faster. "This just got real—fast. But let's start there. Why is my change happening more quickly than it should?"

"A lot of rules are changing for werewolves lately," he explained. "From what we can tell, it's because our pack has been discovered by hunters—people who kill werewolves like us because they hate us for what we are. We first became aware of their existence back in June, but they didn't come at us directly until a month ago. We dealt with them, but it was costly. They know how to hurt us."

"Those inmates who broke out of Coffield," she said.

He lifted a brow. "How'd you know?"

"Your heart only beat hard like it is now a few times," she said. "When we were fighting on the roof of that gangbanger apartment, when we were making out the other night, and when you talked about those men escaping from prison. The first two obviously aren't in play now, so that leaves the men from the prison break."

It was his turn to sit and stare. Damn, she was good.

"Yeah. There's a chance they left the country, but it's also possible they stayed around to take another shot at us. Regardless, from the moment we first heard of these hunters, strange stuff started happening to the Pack."

"Like what?"

"Some new abilities for one thing," he said. "But the biggest difference is finding our mates when we'd always been on our own before."

"And new werewolves going through a three-week process in three days," she added slowly. "It makes sense, I guess. Like animals in the wild learning how to run within hours of their birth so they don't get eaten by predators."

Brooks hadn't thought of it that way, but the analogy was a good one. "We've pretty much come to the same conclusion. Sorry it makes it tougher for you, though."

"It's not your fault," she said, waving off his concern. "What about the omega thing? Does that have something to do with the hunters, too?"

He hesitated. This part was going to be more complicated. "No, being an omega has nothing to do with hunters. It's strictly a werewolf thing."

Selena sat there waiting patiently.

"There are three kinds of werewolves that we know of." Man, he hoped he didn't screw this up by saying something wrong and messing up everything. "There are alphas, which are big, strong, aggressive werewolves. They can take a lot of damage and heal very quickly, and they're generally in control of their inner wolf all the time."

"You're an alpha," Selena announced.

He nodded. "Yeah, I'm an alpha. Along with nearly every one of my SWAT teammates."

"Your pack!" She grinned, her face lighting up. "Cooper and the other guys who helped rescue me. They're all werewolves. And nobody knows?"

Brooks returned her smile, forcing himself to stay on topic. "The second kind of werewolf is the beta. They're smaller and not as strong as an alpha. In fact, they're not aggressive at all. They don't heal as fast as alphas, but in return, they have zero control issues and a strong instinct to bond with other betas. It helps them form tight, supportive packs."

She considered that. "Okay. So, alphas, betas…and omegas are obviously the third type of werewolf. I'm an omega. What are my defining characteristics?"

His heart started to thud hard as hell at the question.

Selena frowned, obviously picking up on it. "What is it? Is there something wrong with being an omega?"

Brooks shook his head, taking a deep breath at the same time, both to control his heartbeat and make sure Selena didn't take what he was about to say the wrong way. "There's absolutely nothing wrong with being an omega. I'm only talking in generalities, okay? And for every rule in the werewolf world, there's an exception. Like a few months ago, a beta ended up turning into an alpha because her pack was threatened. Just yesterday, I learned that one of the alphas in my SWAT pack is actually an omega, too. So, nothing I'm talking about is etched in stone, all right?"

Her heart pounded as hard as his now. "Jayden, you're starting to scare me again, and I don't think either of us wants me to be scared. What is it about omegas you don't want me to know? Is being an omega why I freaked out so badly the other morning?"

He nodded. "Omegas are a lot like alphas. They're big, strong, and fast. They can take as much damage as an alpha and heal just as quickly. But they generally have aggression issues and tend to lose control when exposed to strong emotions, like anger or fear. It can take a real effort on their part to bond with other werewolves."

She didn't say anything for a long time. He wished he knew what she was thinking, but unfortunately, werewolves couldn't read minds.

Brooks took her hand in his and gave it a gentle squeeze. "I'm not saying it's going to be like that for you. Like I said, there's an omega in the Pack who doesn't have any of those issues because he figured out how to overcome them. If it's okay with you, I'd like to introduce you to him, so he can teach you how to stay in control. Would you be okay with something like that?"

He spoke the words so softly, he wasn't sure Selena could even hear him over the thundering of his heart. Hers was still beating nearly as hard. He wasn't sure what that meant.

All at once, Selena climbed onto his lap. Brooks shifted on the couch, making it easier for her to straddle his thighs. She tugged his head down, resting her forehead against his.

"Jayden, I know you're freaking out right now, but there's nothing you just told me about omegas I didn't already know about myself," she said softly. "I'm fine meeting your teammate and talking to him. But when it comes to learning how to be in control, I'd rather learn that from you. Because at the end of the day, you're the man I care about, the man I trust."

Brooks opened his mouth to tell Selena there wasn't anything he wouldn't do for her, but she kissed him. Not a crazy kiss from an omega. A warm, inviting kiss from the woman he loved.

—⁂—

Jayden's tongue slowly played with hers, his hands resting lazily on her hips as they made out on the couch. Selena could tell he was trying to keep things chill. Like that was possible with a guy as hot as he was. As her fingertips tingled and electricity zipped through her body, she had the urge to nip, bite, and claw.

To rip both their clothes off.

To take and be taken.

She knew now that was the omega inside her. There was a certain amount of power—and relief—knowing where that intense desire came from. Maybe now, she could control the wolf inside her a little better.

Moreover, Jayden had poured his heart out to her, revealing his darkest fear that the omega would take over and leave him with the creature who'd nearly clawed him to shreds, thrown him across the room, then run away like a wild animal. Leave him with a werewolf that had no interest in bonding with anyone—even him. It had been humbling to be gifted with that much honesty, and Selena promised herself the gesture wouldn't be wasted. If that promise meant going slowly and carefully when they made love, she was fine with that.

So, when Jayden pulled back to gaze at her, she forced herself not to complain, even if there was a part inside that wanted to growl and snatch his mouth back down on hers.

"I'm okay," she said softly, lifting her hands. "See… no claws."

His sensuous mouth curved. "I wasn't stopping because I was worried about your claws coming out. I wanted to ask if you still wanted to go to the wedding tomorrow. I understand if you don't, but there'll be a lot of other werewolves there I'd like you to meet, including the omega I mentioned—Carter."

She caught her lower lip between her teeth, hesitating.

"Do they all know about me? That I'm an omega, and that I attacked you? Your teammates, I mean."

He nodded. "We're a pack. It's almost impossible to keep secrets from each other, so we usually don't try. So yes, they know what happened, and yes, they'll likely rib the both of us about the whole thing, but they don't care that you're an omega, and they certainly won't treat you differently because of it. Everyone in the Pack has had to deal with tough issues at some point in their lives, either as a result of the trauma they went through to become a werewolf or because of the problems they faced when they found their mates. In one way or another, they've all been where you are, so you won't catch them throwing rocks. In fact, you're going to find more than a few of them willing to help you out with what you're going through."

She considered his words for a moment before taking a deep breath and nodding. "Okay, I'll go. But you're going to stick close, right? Because getting nervous probably isn't good for me, and something tells me this is going to be a completely new experience."

He slipped a finger under her chin, tipping her face up and kissing her so gently, it almost brought tears to her eyes. "I won't leave your side for a second," he murmured against her lips. "Promise."

That was good enough for her. Of course, with everything going on, she hadn't given even a second thought to what she'd wear tomorrow. On a teacher's salary, it wasn't like she had a closet full of fancy dresses and shoes to choose from. She only had a few to work with, and without knowing the bride's color scheme, it was going to be tricky.

But then Jayden slipped his hand in her hair and captured her mouth in another kiss, his tongue easing inside to play. Her body immediately responded, and she forgot about dresses, shoes, and how she was ever going to get her hair done in time for a wedding the next day. Instead, she focused on how good it felt to kiss him. She could gladly do this for the rest of the night...what was left of it. And from the hard-on in Jayden's jeans, he was thinking the exact same thing.

Caressing his bearded jaw, she opened her eyes ever so slightly and saw him looking at her with a smolder that took her breath away. But the thing that captured her attention even more than the passion in his eyes was the glow there. The gold was impossible to miss. Until she realized she had missed it before—lots of times—when she'd assumed it was nothing more than the reflection of a nearby light. How could she have possibly thought something so remarkable was simply a funny bounce of the light?

Selena pulled back, gazing at him in awe and fascination. "Your eyes are gold. Do all werewolves' eyes glow like that? Do mine?"

He chuckled. "Werewolves' eyes only glow when they're really riled up, like with anger, fear, or arousal. When it happens, male werewolves' eyes turn gold, while female werewolves' turn green."

She tried to imagine what she looked like with eyes that were a different color but couldn't. "Do I look strange with green eyes?"

"Actually, yours don't turn green."

"They don't?"

He shook his head. "When we were dancing at that club a couple nights ago, I noticed something that almost looked like a blue-white lightning dancing around in the depth of your eyes, but I thought it was the strobe lights. It wasn't until you freaked out the other morning that I saw your real color. When you're on the edge, your eyes turn vivid blue."

Selena didn't know how she could be excited and bummed at the same time, but she was. It was cool that her eyes turned blue. In fact, it sounded kind of sexy. But finding out it only happened when she was on the verge of going psychotic kind of ruined the moment.

"Is the blue unique to me?" she asked. "Or is it the in color with all the crazy werewolves this season?"

"Stop that." He scowled at her. "You're not crazy. You're a brand-new omega who's just learning how to control her abilities. Cut yourself some slack, okay?"

Face coloring, she nodded. "Okay. Sorry to wallow like that. So, only omegas have blue eyes?"

"According to Carter, yeah. I've only seen it one other time in my life, so it's got to be rare. Which is a good thing. If other omegas out there are controlling themselves, you can, too."

She supposed she could see his point. "But if I stay in control, you'll never get to see my eyes glow when we make love. That kind of sucks."

He shrugged. "I wouldn't be so sure of that."

"What do you mean?"

"I mean that it might be okay to let your control slip a little, as long as we're in a carefully controlled environment, so you don't go too far."

"Carefully controlled environment?" she repeated, confusion making her scrunch up her brow. "Like where?"

Grinning, Jayden leaned forward to kiss her again.

"Like here in my place for example. When it's just the two of us moving slowly like this and being careful."

A rush of heat spun through her as she suddenly realized what he was talking about. "Are you sure that's a good idea? Isn't that what made me freak out before?"

"No. You freaked when you thought you'd hurt me. If we take precautions and keep your claws and fangs away from any place they shouldn't be, I think we'll be okay."

She kissed him again, liking the sound of that plan—a lot. But then she remembered something he'd said earlier, and she pulled back to look at him. "You said you've only seen a werewolf with blue eyes one other time in your life. When was that?"

The cringing face he made right then spoke volumes, and she suddenly decided maybe she didn't want to know about this other omega. "Hey, if this isn't something you're comfortable talking about, that's okay. I didn't mean to pry."

"You're not prying," he said. "But the story doesn't exactly paint a very flattering picture of omegas. I'm not sure it's something you need to hear right now."

She smiled. "Jayden, I'm an omega. The word doesn't define me, but I can't hide from it either. It's a big part of who I am now. And if I'm ever going to learn how to control it, I'm going to have to own it. That means learning everything I can about being an omega—the good and the bad. If this is a story that involves you and an omega, I want to hear it."

He gazed at her with what could only be called wonder on his face. "You're amazing, you know that?"

She grinned. "Yeah, I know. Now, stop stalling and tell the story."

Jayden was silent for a long time, as if collecting his thoughts. "It was right before I left Gulfport," he finally said, his voice soft, his eyes taking on a distant look. "I was on patrol that night when I got a call on the radio about a suspicious person at one of the local high schools. Volleyball practice was just finishing up, so there were still kids hanging around. I was on the scene less than a minute after the call, but a big guy with a knife had already sliced up a couple of the students and a teacher by then. One of the students thought she could lure him away from her classmates because she was a fast runner, but the guy caught her. By the time I got to her, she was bleeding really badly. I didn't see the psycho with the knife, so I picked her up and ran like hell."

He swallowed hard, like he was reliving the memory. "The guy came out of the darkness growling and swinging a machete. I couldn't protect the girl and myself at the same time, so I protected her. The guy cut me."

"The scar from the machete on your side?" Selena murmured, even though she knew that had to be it. "The one that wraps all the way around your back?"

"Yeah. I was sure I was done for. I had to keep fighting so he wouldn't hurt the girl. That's when I saw the fangs and glowing blue eyes. I had no idea what the hell it meant at the time. I just thought I was hallucinating from blood loss. I definitely didn't think I was fighting a werewolf."

The wolf inside Selena stirred restlessly, wanting to kill the omega who had hurt her mate. *Her mate*. The words made her feel warm all over. "What happened?"

"I killed the guy, then lay there on the ground and watched his fangs retract while the paramedics did everything they could to keep me from joining him. I

would have died if I hadn't turned into a werewolf."
Jayden shrugged. "A few weeks later, Gage showed up
and recruited me for his SWAT team."

"How did he know you were a werewolf?" she asked.

Jayden's mouth edged up. "He's good at reading
news stories and finding people who just went through
their change."

Selena wanted to ask for more details, but that could
wait until later. Right now, she was more interested in
the werewolf who'd tried to kill Jayden.

"So, getting attacked by the omega was what turned
you, the same way Pablo's attack changed me?"

Jayden nodded. "Yeah. I didn't find out the guy had
been a werewolf until Gage told me. I never made the
connection between the blue eyes and the fact that he
was an omega until your eyes turned blue, and Carter
told me what it all meant. I guess Gage didn't think it
was something I needed to know."

She sighed. "No wonder you looked so freaked out
when I attacked you. Seeing my eyes change must have
made you relive the trauma that happened all those
years ago."

"A little," he admitted.

"Is that what you're worried is going to happen to
me?" she asked. "That I'll go crazy and attack someone
like that omega did?"

Jayden wrapped his arms around her, pulling her
close. "I'll never let that happen to you. That omega was
a complete loner who totally separated himself from all
human contact. You'll never have to know what it's like
to be alone, because I'll always be there for you. If you
get worried and think we need to get away from people,

say the word, and I'll drop everything and run off to the middle of Siberia with you, okay?"

Selena closed her eyes and snuggled against him, smiling despite how horrible that story had been. "Thanks for offering to run off to Siberia with me. It really means a lot. But if it's all the same, I'd rather stay here. I hate the cold weather."

He chuckled, his arms tightening around her. "Deal."

They stayed like that for a long time until something occurred to her. She pushed away to look at him. "What happened to the girl you saved? Did she make it?"

"Yeah." He grinned. "She made a total recovery and went on to play for the U.S. volleyball team at the Rio Summer Olympics in 2016. She even got a therapy dog to help her with the bad memories. Named him Brooks."

Selena laughed. "I love it."

Jayden pulled her in for another kiss, this one as tender as the ones that had come before it. She moaned and ran her hands down the T-shirt he wore, exploring the muscles hidden underneath. She'd been wrong earlier. She didn't want to make out like this all night.

She dragged her mouth from his with a groan. "What do you think about moving this into the bedroom?"

He didn't answer, but instead, picked her up and carried her over to his bed, where he gently set her down before slowly taking off her clothes. Then he gazed down at her naked body, his eyes molten gold.

"If we're going to make love, we're going to do it my way," he said huskily. "Slow, gentle, and without any biting, clawing, or growling. You think you can deal with that?"

Selena nodded, unable to do more than that as he

yanked his T-shirt over his head, then shoved down his jeans and underwear. The sight of him made her body tingle all over—her fingertips especially.

"I'm not sure I can keep my claws from coming out," she said breathlessly. "They're close already."

"That's not a problem." Nudging her a little farther back into the middle of the bed, he climbed between her spread legs. "Just keep your hands down by your sides, and I'll make sure they behave themselves."

Selena didn't have a clue what he meant by that until he settled between her thighs, then slowly and teasingly ran his tongue up and down her pussy. She gasped, her claws extending. Not wanting him to stop but terrified she'd hurt him, she opened her mouth to tell him, but before she could get the words out, Jayden wrapped his long fingers around her wrists, pinning them to the bed and keeping her from shredding anything.

That turned out to be an excellent plan, as his teasing tongue quickly began to drive her wild. The worst part was that he refused to lock his mouth on her clit. If he had, she would have exploded in seconds. Instead, he seemed more interested in getting her hot—and wet.

When her orgasm was so close, she began to growl with need, he moved up her body with that sexy gold smolder in his eyes. Taking a condom out of the bedside table, he rolled it on without ever breaking eye contact, then grabbed her wrists again, pinning them to the mattress over her head this time.

She growled when he lodged the thick head of his cock in her opening and pushed the first few inches inside. He kept his eyes on hers, making soft shushing sounds.

"Relax," he murmured. "We're going to do this slow

and gentle, okay? It's all about control, not rushing to the finish line."

Selena wanted to ask him whose control they were talking about, because it seemed like he was doing a good job of keeping all the control for himself. But she wasn't going to complain. What he was doing felt too damn good.

Jayden moved slowly the whole time, occasionally dipping his head down to kiss her neck. He kept her wrists trapped gently against the bed, careful to stay out of reach of her fangs too. Good idea, she guessed, since they were definitely out at the moment.

She begged him to go faster and thrust harder, but he maintained that same slow, perfect pace, his groin pressing against her clit and making her wild with need every time he went deep.

The orgasm she ended up having was like nothing she'd ever experienced. It was like a slow-motion tidal wave that didn't crash over her but instead washed along her body until she thought she was drowning in it.

Her climax seemed to last forever. She screamed and moaned softly. She squealed a bit and growled a lot too. But she never broke eye contact with him the entire time. Not even when she felt him come, too, and thought she might pass out from the pleasure of the moment.

The experience was completely unique, but oh so worth it, especially when he rested his forehead on hers and smiled at her after they'd both come back down to earth.

"There are those beautiful blue eyes I was looking for," he said softly as he continued pumping gently into her and rocking her to sleep.

Chapter 18

"TRUST ME, IT WON'T BE LIKE THIS FOR LONG," CARTER SAID as the gentle evening breeze swirled in through one of the immense tent's open door flaps, sending a hundred overwhelming scents Selena's way. "After a while, you'll be able to ignore the scents you aren't interested in and focus on the one or two you care about."

Selena groaned as the combined aromas from the caterer's chafing dishes lined up along the far wall nearly made her gag. It wasn't because the food was gross. On the contrary, it was delicious. Altogether, however, the aromas were a little much to take.

"Is it that obvious?" she asked.

Carter looked like he was fighting to keep from laughing. "Between the watering eyes and the way you keep trying to breathe through your mouth, yeah, it's obvious. It would be worse if you were a newly turned alpha or beta. Their sense of smell is probably twice as good as ours. If you weren't an omega, you'd be outside hyperventilating by now."

She breathed a sigh of relief for small miracles and took a shallow breath through her mouth until the person who'd been holding open the door of the huge tent moved away, cutting off the breeze and finally slowing the avalanche of scents. It was cool that Max and Lana had rented what could only be described as a circus tent for their reception. Even cooler was the fact that they'd had it put up right in the middle of the SWAT compound. But after a night of dancing and partying, the place had gotten a little warm, even though it was a chilly December evening. That had made the already strong scents even more powerful.

Selena glanced around the tent, easily finding Jayden in the crowd. He wore a dark suit that had been perfectly tailored for his broad shoulders and powerful arms. If she thought he'd looked good in jeans and a button-down, it was nothing compared to how much she swooned when he'd picked her up at her place in that suit. After dancing with her most of the reception, he still looked cool and relaxed. And smelled even better. His was one scent she'd never get tired of.

He was currently chatting with some of his SWAT teammates as he got her a fresh drink from the bar. True to his word, he'd stuck close to her side throughout the wedding and the reception. He'd taken her around and introduced her to his pack mates, the significant others in their lives, and an incredible array of betas and omegas who lived in the area. Sort of like an extended pack. The Pack mascot, Tuffie, and a cat named Kat had been in the tent earlier but had gone into the admin building a little while ago. Everyone was warm and welcoming and made her feel like she belonged.

But while she was comfortable with his friends, she was sure Jayden wouldn't have slipped away for more drinks if she hadn't felt comfortable with Carter. There was no doubt in her mind he was a person she could trust.

"How long did it take for you to get control of your nose?" she asked, turning back to him.

"Not long," he said. "About a year and a half."

Selena did a double take. "What?"

He chuckled, his blue eyes twinkling. "Just kidding. Truthfully, it did take a while for me to get the hang of it, but that was because I didn't have anyone to help me, and I was doing it all wrong. Fortunately, you won't have to learn it the hard way like I did, because you'll have a lot of people in your corner."

She considered that. "Were you on your own a long time?"

Selena could only imagine how horrible coming to grips with being a werewolf would be if Jayden hadn't been there for her.

Carter shrugged. "About two years. It seemed longer at the time though. Gage saved my ass when he finally found me."

She was considering if it would be okay to ask Carter what that time on his own had been like when Jayden came back with their drinks.

"Carter isn't scaring you with all his horror stories about being an omega, is he?" he asked, setting her strawberry daiquiri on the table in front of her, then trailing a hand teasingly over the part of her back left exposed by the dress she wore as he took a seat beside her.

Selena's pulse skipped a beat at his touch. "No. We were talking about an omega's sense of smell and how certain scents seem to be so overwhelming right now." She leaned in close to give Jayden a light kiss. "Not your scent of course. I could never get tired of smelling your hot, hunky body."

Carter groaned. "Okay, I really didn't need to hear that. I'm going to check with Max and Lana and see how much longer they want to hang around."

"Hold on," Jayden said as Carter got to his feet. "Who's pulling security at the hotel with you?"

Selena lifted a brow. "Hotel security? Are you working another job?"

Carter shook his head. "No, nothing like that. Lana and Max didn't think it was a good idea to go on a honeymoon with the hunters out there, but they still wanted to do something special on their wedding night, so we all chipped in to get them a honeymoon suite at the Ritz-Carlton for the weekend. Trevor, Hale, and I are going to keep an eye on them."

"The place has good security," Jayden added. "But Gage wants some of the Pack there just in case."

She and Jayden had spent some time talking about the hunters today, so she could understand why Gage would be worried, even though it was difficult to believe they'd attack somebody in the middle of a fancy hotel. Still, the fact that the team had done something like that for Max and Lana was really sweet.

"Honeymoon suite at the Ritz, huh?" she mused. "Pretty romantic."

"It was all Brooks's idea," Carter said. "We were going to buy them a Kitchen-Aid, but he insisted we do something more personal." He gave Jayden a nod. "Later."

Selena smiled at Jayden as Carter walked away. "How'd you come up with the idea for the honeymoon suite?"

"It wasn't a big deal." He shrugged almost sheepishly. "I thought they'd like to do something official to start off their marriage. Make it seem more real, you know."

Selena practically melted right there in her chair.

What the hell had she ever done to deserve a fantastic guy like Jayden? He was so far beyond perfect, it was all she could do to not tell him she loved him.

Her breath caught as she realized what she'd just admitted…even if only to herself. *She loved him?* That was crazy. They'd just met. You couldn't fall in love with a man you'd only met five days ago. It was impossible.

Or was it?

While she'd never been in love before, she was definitely feeling something amazing, something that made her heart beat fast all the time. And as for what was impossible, it was difficult to ignore the fact that until a few days ago, she'd thought being a werewolf was impossible, too.

Selena gazed at Jayden, wondering if he could possibly feel the same way about her. She opened her mouth to tell him she was falling for him—that maybe she'd already fallen—but movement out of the corner of her eye caught her attention. She found herself looking that way, not knowing why but following her instincts.

At first, she didn't see anything unusual. Max and Lana were making the rounds, talking and laughing with their friends as guests slowly streamed out of the tent into the night, heading for the cars parked all over the place outside the perimeter fence.

Then a gray-haired man stopped in front of the newlyweds to wish them well. Lana's face paled, her body going rigid, and Selena heard the woman's heart suddenly begin beating like crazy. Whoever the guy was, Lana clearly didn't like him.

Jayden had introduced Selena to a lot of people today, but the gray-haired man hadn't been one of them. She supposed he could be a cop, but with that fancy suit, he looked more like a politician.

Halfway across the tent, Lana was shaking the man's hand. Knowing it was probably a horrible thing to do, Selena turned her head a little, straining to hear what they were saying. She'd been able to eavesdrop easily in the club after Scott had OD'd, but unlike her nose, which seemed to work all the time whether she wanted it to or not, her ears were a little tougher to control.

She was able to pick up enough to hear the man congratulating Max and Lana and wishing them well as they started their life together. While it seemed sweet, Lana looked like she'd swallowed a lemon.

Selena turned to Jayden, expecting to see him staring at Max and Lana as hard as she had, but instead, he was focused on the entrance of the tent and the two werewolves who'd just walked in. Becker and the woman with him weren't exactly dressed for a wedding. In fact, the jeans and T-shirts they wore looked like they'd slept in them. Becker and the blond woman, on the other hand, looked like they hadn't slept in days.

"Why wasn't Becker at the wedding?" Selena asked.

"He and his mate, Jayna, have been digging into the prison break nonstop since Wednesday, trying to see if someone in the Dallas PD might have been involved. Come on."

Taking her hand, Jayden led her across the tent to intercept Becker and Jayna. They caught up with them in the far corner where Gage, his human wife, Mac, Zane, and Lana's parents were all talking.

"It's Curtis," Becker said to Gage.

Selena didn't know who Curtis was or why he was

important, but everyone else did if the stunned disbelief
on their faces was any indication.

"Are you sure?" Gage demanded, his dark eyes
intent on Becker. "I mean, positively-absolutely-you-
can't-be-wrong-about-this sure?"

Becker nodded. "It's him. Remember those suspects
I was looking into who work at the prison? It took
some time, but I narrowed it down to three guards and
one IT specialist. The three guards were on duty the
morning of the escape and were assigned to the security
checkpoints Oliver and the other inmates went through.
More incriminating than that, though, was that someone
with serious computer skills had gone out of their way
to make it look like those three guards were working
somewhere else in the prison that day. He changed
duty rosters, altered the entries in the security system
that records when and where guards swipe their ID
cards, even snipped out small sections of various security camera footage to make sure you couldn't see the
inmates on any videos they shouldn't have been on. It
was actually some high-quality work. It took over a day
for me to figure out what was missing, but once I realized I was dealing with a top-of-the-line hacker, it led
me straight to the computer geek in IT."

"Becker," Gage growled, making Selena jump. "Stop
all this damn techie talk, and get to the point. You found
the four people responsible for the prison break—great.
What the hell does any of this have to do with Curtis?"

Becker made a face at being interrupted. "Jayna and
I have been going nonstop for the past eighty hours
straight, living on nothing but Doritos and Mountain
Dew, probably breaking hundreds of state and federal

laws, and you want me to skip the best parts and get to the point?"

Gage glowered at him. "Yes."

Crap. Jayden's boss definitely had an intimidating voice when he wanted to.

"Who's Curtis?" Selena whispered close to Jayden's ear, interested in knowing but not wanting to interrupt the others.

"Randy Curtis," he whispered back, not taking his eyes off Becker and Jayna. "Chief of police."

Selena's eyes widened. Sweet cheese and crackers. The chief of police was involved with the hunters? And he'd broken them out of prison? How was that even possible?

"Fine," Becker grumbled. "It turns out all four of these guys used to work for the North Central Division Investigative Team about ten years ago. That's quite the coincidence, but not nearly as interesting as who their lieutenant was."

"Curtis," Gage said.

"Yup," Becker said. "Real long story short, most of the team was dirty, skimming stolen property from residential and business burglaries. Nobody ratted on Curtis, so he came out looking clean and ended up getting a promotion out of it. In return, he got the guys hired on at Coffield. They've been loyal to him ever since."

"Do you have anything solid pinning Curtis to the prison break?" Gage asked. "Beyond the fact that these dirty prison employees used to work for him a decade ago?"

It was Jayna who answered. "Curtis was careful to avoid calling any of the men himself, and apparently, he wouldn't let them call him, either." She tucked her long

hair behind her ear. "We know that for sure, because
Eric tapped his home phone and cloned the SIM card
on his cell. The four guys from the prison weren't as
careful. They've been calling, texting, and emailing
each other for the past two weeks." She shook her head.
"You'd think a bunch of ex-cops would be smarter than
to put stuff out there like that, but then again, they did
get caught for stealing stolen property from their own
evidence room. So I guess they're not that bright."

"Regardless," Becker added, "we have more than
enough evidence to directly connect these four—and
Curtis—to the prison break. I've already made sure the
U.S. Marshals stumble across everything we found in a
way that will make it completely legal in court. As soon
as those four guys are picked up by the feds, one of them
is going to flip on the others and hopefully on Curtis, too."

"That's all great," Zane said. "But did you find anything that will lead us back to the hunters?"

Jayden had told Selena that Zane had been injured
by the hunters. He wouldn't give her any details, saying
that was Zane's story to tell, but she knew the British
werewolf hated the hunters and wanted them to pay for
what they'd done.

"Not yet." Becker's voice was rueful. "I'm still working on it."

"Or we could talk to someone who obviously knows
all about the hunters and see what he's willing to tell
us," Gage said, his voice low and menacing.

Selena followed Gage's gaze to the older man still
talking with Max and Lana. Besides the werewolves
from the Pack, a few other wedding guests were still
in the tent as well, along with the caterers, who were

currently cleaning up the place. A moment later, the older man started toward the exit.

"That's Curtis?" Selena asked.

"Yes," Jayden said, giving her hand a squeeze before releasing it and falling into step beside Gage as his boss headed across the tent.

Selena hurried to catch up with him. Jayden didn't slow as he caught her hand and tugged her protectively behind him. Zane slipped ahead of her, so that they were both shielding her. She knew Jayden was doing it because he cared about her, but her werewolf side didn't like it. He was her mate, and she had a crazy urge to be the one protecting him, even though he was obviously much stronger and a more experienced fighter than she'd ever be.

Max and Lana met them halfway, their faces tense.

"Curtis is the one I heard over the telephone talking to the hunter during the attack at the clinic," Lana said quickly. "I'm sure of it."

Gage nodded, not bothering to tell her they already knew that, and continued after the man. "Chief Curtis."

The man stopped and turned, his eyes narrowing at Gage and the rest of them. "What can I help you with, Sergeant Dixon?" He glanced down at his watch before locking eyes with the SWAT team leader. "I was just leaving."

"We know you helped those men break out of Coffield," Gage said.

Curtis's heart sped up, but his expression never changed. "I don't know what you're talking about. I had nothing to do with those men escaping custody."

Selena's instincts told her the man was lying his ass off.

"Really?" Gage said. "That's funny, because the marshals already have phone and email records from your four buddies. You know, those former cops who used to work for you in the North Central Division? You should have hired people smart enough to not mention your name over and over online."

Curtis regarded them thoughtfully. "If that's true, why are you the one talking to me instead of the marshals?"

"We wanted to ask you a few questions first," Jayden said. "Who knows? Maybe we can put in a good word for you with the marshals."

"And what could I possibly tell you?" Curtis asked.

"The name of the man in charge of the hunters," Gage told him.

Selena expected him to deny it like he had the previous accusation, but Curtis snorted. "Now why the hell would I ever tell you that?"

"Because after we bite you and turn you into one of us, you're going to need our protection when they come after you," Jayden growled.

Selena knew the threat was an empty one. Jayden had told her a bite from a werewolf wouldn't do anything except hurt. You'd never know that from the threat of violence in Jayden's voice, though.

Curtis laughed, not even a little bit frightened. "Thanks, but no thanks. I don't want to be one of you mangy mutts."

Pulling a pistol out of his jacket, he pointed it at Jayden and squeezed the trigger before any of them could so much as blink.

Selena opened her mouth to scream when an explosion from outside shook the tent. A split second later, a man in a caterer uniform stepped into the open doorway of the tent with an automatic rifle and started shooting.

––––––~~~––––––

Brooks knew he'd been hit with a poison bullet before he even stumbled back. The odor of the synthetic wolfsbane was impossible to miss. Ignoring the pain he knew was coming, he twisted himself around to protect Selena.

Everything went insane as he grabbed her, automatic weapons fire coming from all around them as another explosion rocked the compound. The softer pop of pistol fire immediately followed. Brooks had no idea who was shooting at whom when another round slammed into the back of his thigh as he dragged Selena down to the ground and shielded her body.

A voice in the back of his head noted that while the hunters' bullets definitely burned like hell, the pain wasn't nearly as excruciating as it should have been. It also wasn't getting worse like it had with Zane. Dr. Saunders's vaccine must be working. That was a relief.

Instinct demanded he grab the small-frame .40 caliber he had strapped to his right ankle, find out who was shooting at them, and kill those people. But he couldn't. While the synthetic wolfsbane in the bullets wouldn't kill him or any other werewolf there, Selena hadn't gotten the vaccine yet. He couldn't leave her unprotected and risk her getting hit. He heard her growling under him, her heart thumping in near panic as she tried to work herself free. He held onto her more tightly. He needed to protect her from the omega inside her just as much as from the hunters.

Zane suddenly appeared, crouching at his side. "Let me have her. The hunters think you're the alpha of the

Pack, which means you're putting her in more danger. I can't fight them, but I can protect her."

The idea of letting Selena go ripped a growl from his throat, but when he saw the number of armed men pointing weapons in his direction, he realized his friend was right.

"Stay with Zane," he told her, yanking his Glock out as he jumped to his feet.

As he ran, Brooks heard Selena snarling, trying to escape Zane's hold, but his pack mate refused to let her go. More importantly, the moment he started moving, the hunters, dressed in the white-and-black uniforms of the catering crew, adjusted their aim to follow him. Zane was right. He was their primary target. The faster he got away from Selena, the safer she'd be.

Popping off shots in the hunters' direction, Brooks took in the situation as he ran across the tent toward the main entrance, ignoring the sting as several more bullets hit him. The human wedding guests who'd been trapped in the tent when the shooting started were either hugging the floor or trying to hide under the tables, including Lana's parents. Gage was down on the floor as well, protecting Mac with his body. Curtis was long gone, far enough away that Brooks could no longer pick up an active scent. Trevor, Hale, Carter, and Max were standing guard over Lana, slowly and carefully putting down one target after another with their own backup weapons. All four of his pack mates had been hit multiple times, but that didn't slow them down.

Smaller explosions echoed outside the tent as two more hunters ran in, their rifles held high as they assessed the situation. Brooks didn't recognize the first guy, but the second one through the door was very familiar—Seth Oliver.

Oliver's eyes widened when he saw that Brooks and his pack mates were alive. The same couldn't be said of his fellow hunters around the tent. Those men wouldn't be getting back up again. Brooks didn't know if Oliver was more surprised their poison bullets didn't work this time or that the Pack had been carrying backup weapons during a wedding reception.

The man locked eyes with Brooks for half a second, then he turned and fled. Brooks chased him outside only to slow a bit as he took in the violence going on around the rest of the darkened SWAT compound.

Brooks had never been in the military, but he imagined this was what a war zone looked like. Wedding guests were running all over the place, trying to get out of the compound. There was the flash and pop of automatic weapons fire coming from the direction of the main admin building and growling and shouting from over near the volleyball court. In addition, a bomb had taken out the front side of the armory building, which was currently on fire. The hunters had tried to destroy the armory, probably hoping to keep them from reaching any of their weapons.

Brooks ignored all of that as he caught sight of Oliver running toward a line of SUVs parked outside the front gate of the compound. He threw a quick look at the fighting going on over near the main building, noting the gunfire had already slowed drastically. The battle there was almost over. He only hoped the Pack was winning it.

He took off after Oliver, refusing to let the asshole get away this time. But as he got closer to the vehicles,

Brooks realized Oliver wasn't the only hunter beating a retreat. There were four other men heading toward the SUVs, the one going for the driver's side limping badly. Brooks smelled the scent of blood and fear pouring off them, and he changed course slightly, turning aside to go after the four random hunters instead of Oliver. He hated Oliver, but taking down four hunters made more sense from a mathematical point of view.

But then he saw Rachel loping after the four men, a small double-action .380 handgun held low at her side, her eyes glowing vivid green as she tracked after her prey. Baring her fangs, she lifted her weapon and aimed for the injured driver.

Brooks turned his attention to Oliver, running faster as the hunter jumped behind the wheel and gunned the engine to life like his life depended on getting away— which it did. The SUV started to pull forward, but Brooks didn't care. He was stopping the man, no matter what.

Just as he tucked his shoulder and prepared to ram the SUV off the road, he caught Selena's scent, quickly followed by Zane's. He glanced over his shoulder to see Selena coming toward him, her eyes glowing blue. Zane was right behind her, trying to catch up.

A growl to his right caught Brooks's attention, and he looked over to see Rachel standing near the perimeter fence, her weapon still aimed at the injured hunter. Brooks waited for her to pull the trigger, but she didn't. Instead, she and the hunter stared at each other, confusion on both their faces. A split second later, the hunter leaped into the SUV and took off. Brooks didn't know why, but for whatever reason, Rachel hadn't taken the shot.

It was too late for Brooks to change course and go

after the vehicle with the four hunters now. He was committed to Oliver's SUV.

Brooks hit the front quarter panel right behind the wheel at full speed. The impact was so violent, he felt multiple bones crack, but he ignored them. The vehicle was big, but he'd hit with a shitload of force, and the nose of the SUV went up and sideways, almost going over as it slid across the narrow street along the front of the compound and into the ditch on the far side.

He punched through the glass of the driver's window, gripping the frame and ripping the door off, then pulling Oliver out and throwing him to the ground.

"I can tell you stuff about the hunters," Oliver said urgently, scrambling to his feet and trying to back up even as he attempted to line up a shot at Brooks's head. "I know who the man in charge is. I know where you can find him."

Brooks reached out to smack the gun from Oliver's hand when Selena arrived in the form of a growling blue-eyed blur that slammed into Oliver's chest so hard, Brooks heard bones crack.

Oliver bounced off the front of the SUV, his weapon coming up again but pointed at Selena this time.

Shit.

Heart pounding, Brooks lunged, grabbing Oliver and snapping his neck before he could pull the trigger. Gage almost certainly would have preferred letting the man live long enough to tell them about the hunters, but that simply hadn't been an option.

Brooks pulled Selena into his arms, making soft shushing sounds as he attempted to calm her down. She held on to him tightly, her face pressed against his chest.

"It's okay, baby," he whispered. "I've got you."

He glanced at Zane, who shook his head.

"She wiggled loose," Zane said. "She's a lot stronger than a werewolf her size should be, and she was freaked out worrying about you."

"It's okay," Brooks murmured again, using the same calming tones on Zane as he had on Selena. "It's all going to be okay now. No harm, no foul."

Zane nodded, even though he still looked embarrassed as hell.

Brooks sighed, listening to Selena's heartbeat slow to normal as the tension drained from her body. He couldn't see her eyes, so he wasn't completely sure, but something told him they were no longer blue. That was good. She'd gotten herself under control quickly.

He looked around, realizing the shooting had stopped. He could make out a few members of the Pack moving about, checking on wedding guests. The hunters had come at them again, with a coordinated, targeted assassination attempt, and Curtis had been a part of it.

But while the assholes had done a lot of violence and made one hell of a mess, the Pack had come out on top. Some of the hunters had gotten away. In fact, Rachel was still where she'd been watching the other vehicle's taillights disappear into the distance. Oliver was dead, though, and there were a lot less hunters in the world than there used to be.

The battle looked like it was over for tonight.

Then Brooks heard the sound of approaching sirens, and he realized this evening was just getting started.

Chapter 19

"THE REAR LOADING DOCK IS ALL CLEAR," BROOKS whispered into the radio, as he, Connor, and Diego slipped between the three tractor trailers parked behind the Sovereign Row industrial building and headed for the big roll-up doors that lined the side of the place. Two of those doors were wide open, but it didn't help much. Between the awful rattle and clank of conveyor belts and the harsh, burning stench of chemicals, Brooks couldn't say if there was one person in the warehouse or twenty.

"Front lobby is clear, too," Trey said into his earpiece. "Ready to move when you give the word."

Trey, Remy, and several members of the small task force entry team had headed for the main entrance a few minutes ago. They all assumed there'd be at least one gang member there standing guard, but apparently, the new gang boss was getting cocky.

"Side door is locked," Ray said over the radio. "Give us a second."

Brooks motioned his teammates behind the trucks, glancing at his watch as they waited for Ray to give the word. As they crouched down beside a trailer up close to the loading dock, where it was unlikely anyone would see them, he glanced at his guys, noticing how tired they looked. The attack on the SWAT compound last night had taken a lot out of everyone.

Trey and Alex had spent hours digging bullets out of

every member of the Pack and each other. The synthetic wolfsbane wasn't deadly to them any longer, thanks to the vaccine, but that didn't mean it was fun getting shot with it. Their bodies still had to detox the crap out of their systems, reminding Brooks a lot of what it used to feel like to be hungover. He decided it wasn't anything he missed.

Beside him, Connor leaned against the trailer and closed his eyes. Brooks moved a little closer in case he had to catch his pack mate before he face-planted on the concrete. Connor was functioning on little more than adrenaline fumes at the moment and probably shouldn't have even been on the raid, but there was no one to take his place. The truth of the matter was that everyone on the team was just as exhausted right now.

Last night had been filled with a steady stream of questions from Internal Affairs, the city manager, half the city council, and the U.S. Marshals. As if that wasn't enough, then the frigging FBI had shown up. Because apparently the whole thing had looked like a terrorist attack to them.

Not that Brooks was surprised to see so many high-ranking people on the scene. It wasn't every day the chief of police of a major U.S. city attempted to assassinate members of his own SWAT team. Then there was Curtis's alleged involvement in the prison break. That didn't go over well with the city officials either.

And everyone from each of the aforementioned agencies had wanted to know what the hell had happened at the compound. Why would the chief of police want to kill them? What did SWAT know about the prison break? Who the hell were all the dead people with automatic weapons? How did Oliver end up with a broken neck? Why was there so much blood everywhere but so few wounded cops?

Brooks and his teammates had dealt with situations like this before—maybe not on this scale—so they had experience covering for the strange things that happened to them. They kept their stories simple and to the point and never elaborated on anything. That had earned them a lot of dubious looks, but it wasn't like anyone was going to suspect they were werewolves.

The marathon interrogation session hadn't ended until around nine o'clock that morning. Even then, there'd been no rest for any of them. Half the team had been sent out to provide SWAT support to the cops responding to all the hotline tips coming in claiming to know where Curtis, Frasheri, Engler, and the four hunters who escaped might be. The other half of the team had started digging out the armory building, recovering as many weapons and pieces of equipment as they could. It had been miserable, dirty, smelly work, but it had to be done. Without the weapons in that armory, they were nearly worthless to the department. By the time they were done, Brooks had reeked. Even after showering twice, he still smelled like smoke and ashes.

The sun had been going down on a really long day, and he was looking forward to getting home—and Selena, who'd finally agreed to go to his place and get some rest after spending the night along with Lana and his other pack mates' significant others in the small dorm room of sorts in the admin building where the team could catch some shut-eye if they needed to—when his cell had rung. It had been Ruben, giving him this address on Sovereign Row, saying it was where the gang was making the spiked energy drink. According to the kid, the man who'd taken over and consolidated most of the local gangs would be there overseeing the movement of several truckloads of the stuff. Apparently, they were shipping it out of state.

Gage had offered Brooks half the team, but instead, he'd stuck with the four guys who'd been with him on this from the start. And Zane.

"Side door is open," Zane's calm voice murmured over the line. "We're ready to go."

Brooks had told Gage he needed Zane along to handle task force coordination. He'd said Zane wouldn't be going in with the entry team, but that had been a lie. One Gage had almost certainly seen right through.

Zane had risked his life for Selena, and there was no way in hell Brooks was ever going to forget it. If that meant taking a risk on this raid and letting Zane take part, he'd do it in a second. That said, he'd put Zane with Ray's team, figuring his friend wouldn't be able to get himself into any trouble if he was stuck with the slower moving team of human cops.

Brooks nudged Connor. His eyes snapped open immediately, a light gold ring around the edges of his pupils.

"We go in five seconds," Ray called out.

Brooks gave his pack mates a nod, then led them around the trailer and onto the loading dock.

"Three…two…one…go!" Ray shouted.

The moment they were through the door, Brooks and his team spread out slightly as they moved toward the center of the building. The chemical smell was even worse inside the warehouse, making his eyes water. The scent of fentanyl was predominant, and Brooks wondered briefly if he and the others could get high from breathing in the fumes.

The mechanical noise coming from the endless miles of moving conveyor belts was unreal, too, and as they slipped deeper into the building, weaving around the belts, heavy equipment, and half-stacked pallets of Buzz energy drink, Brooks realized their greatest were-wolf advantages—namely their senses of smell and hearing—were completely neutralized in there. They'd be forced to do this the old-fashioned way, depending on their training and instincts like every other cop in here.

He was surprised how uncomfortable he was at that thought. He hadn't been forced to deal with a situation like this without access to his enhanced senses in a long time. Not since Gulfport in fact. And he didn't like to think about how that had ended.

They were nearly to the middle of the warehouse before they saw a guy pushing a pallet of shrink-wrapped cans toward the locking dock. The gangbanger took one look at them and reached for the handgun shoved in the waistband of his pants. The moment he yanked it out, everything went crazy, as shooting and shouting immediately filled the cavernous space.

Connor took a round in the shoulder, but they got the gangbanger down and zip-tied without killing him. Then they were moving, Brooks calling out updates over the radio as he came to grips with the sheer scale of this drug operation. There were dozens of pallets loaded with the spiked energy drink, not counting what had already been loaded into the trucks outside. If they distributed the drink like they intended, the number of overdoses would be mind-boggling.

Random shots continued to ring out around the building. Based on those and the number of hostile contacts getting announced over the air, there had to be at least twenty or thirty gangbangers in there. That was a lot more than Brooks and the other members of the task force had expected. But there wasn't anything they could do about that now.

He and his teammates kept moving through the warehouse, arresting those who made that an option, doing what was necessary in the other cases. It wasn't a choice he preferred, but getting into long, drawn-out confrontations would only put other members of the task force at risk. Fortunately, more of the gangbangers gave up instead of fighting.

Brooks thought the raid would actually go down easier than he'd feared, but then he heard heavy weapon fire coming from the right, in the direction of Ray's team and the side exit.

"Need backup on the east side of the warehouse," Ray said calmly over the radio. "We're pinned down by four men with automatic weapons."

Brooks threw a quick look at Connor and Diego, who simply nodded and kept moving forward without him.

"On the way," he called out over the radio. "Keep your heads down."

Luckily, Brooks didn't have to engage with any other gangbangers on the way. Mostly because there weren't many left. He followed the sounds of heavy gunfire, the stench of chemicals getting worse as he ran past several large industrial kettles, each bigger than a car. This must be where they made the energy drink. The odor alone was enough to make him wonder why anyone would drink the crap. It smelled like scented battery acid. While the noise wasn't as bad in this part of the building, he still wished someone would shut down the damn conveyor belts. The constant clank and rattle was digging right through his sensitive ears and giving him one hell of a headache.

Brooks liked to think his werewolf instincts led him directly to Ray, but that would probably be pushing it. The truth was that one second, he was running down an alley between two long rows of cardboard boxes, and the next, he saw Ray on one knee behind a heavy steel support column, facing a guy with an automatic rifle. The gangbanger was walking right toward Ray, keeping him pinned down with a hail of bullets.

"Dallas PD!" Brooks shouted, instinct and training forcing him to give a warning he knew would be ignored. "Drop the weapon!"

The man spun, the cheap knockoff M4-style automatic rifle spraying the walls and ceiling with bullets as he tried to change his aim point and take Brooks out.

Brooks didn't give him the chance.

He scanned the area to make sure it was clean but didn't see anyone, even though Ray had said there had been four men with automatic weapons here earlier. He sniffed the air, hoping that would give him a clue, but the odor of fentanyl was so strong, he almost got dizzy from it. He kept going, approaching the downed suspect and kicking the rifle away as Ray moved to join him.

"Where are the other shooters?" Brooks asked as he dropped to a knee to see if the man he'd shot was still breathing.

A flash of movement from the corner of his eye

caught his attention, and he snapped his head around to see three men step out from the walkway between the boxes. Everything seemed to freeze as he recognized the big man in the middle of the group, even as his head tried to tell him what he was seeing couldn't be right.

Ernesto.

Selena's friend, the man who'd become like a brother to her after Geraldo had been murdered. What the hell was he doing here?

Before Brooks could even try to answer that question, Ernesto and the two men with him lifted their weapons and started shooting. Brooks whirled around as he got to his feet to return fire, knowing he was probably going to be hit at the same time but not caring.

Suddenly, a blur passed in front of him. Brooks had only a second to shout in warning as Ray went down, hit multiple times with a spray of bullets as he attempted to protect Brooks from the incoming rounds.

Brooks brought his weapon up, firing an entire thirty-round magazine at Ernesto and the other two gangbangers. They moved fast for humans, diving to the side and slipping away down a corridor between the conveyor belts. He knew he should chase them, but he couldn't. Ray had been hit. There was no way Brooks was going to leave him.

Shit, it was bad. Blood leaked through a hole in the center of Ray's tactical vest, right where a bullet had punched through it. More poured from an abdomen wound, well below the bottom of the vest. There was another wound in Ray's left thigh, but that was minor compared to the other two.

"Officer down!" Brooks shouted into the radio as he

kneeled by his old friend. "I need EMS support ASAP to the east side door, two hundred feet inside the building."

He didn't hear anymore shooting in the building, which was a good thing. Someone had finally turned off the conveyor belt, too.

There was a clang as someone shoved the nearby door open. Brooks knew it was Ernesto and the other gangbangers getting away, but he ignored them as he ripped Ray's tactical vest off, exhaling a little when he saw the bullet hole to the right side of the sternum. The round had clearly missed the heart, but it had sliced through Ray's right lung, and the bleeding was severe. He quickly rolled Ray to that side, so his left lung would stay clear of blood. At the same time, he pressed a firm hand to the wound on Ray's abdomen.

Ray let out a hiss of pain, his eyes starting to glaze over. "You should go after them," he said weakly. "They're getting away."

"We'll get them later," Brooks said.

Ray opened his mouth like he wanted to argue, but Trey and Zane showed up. Zane stood there, a devastated look on his face, while Trey immediately went into his medic role, checking Ray's pulse and calling to alert EMS for a severe chest wound.

"Two fucking weeks," Ray whispered, his voice getting weaker as one of his lungs began to fill with blood. "I haven't even sent in my paperwork yet. Was gonna do that tomorrow. Can you believe that shit?"

"Stop worrying about that." Brooks swallowed hard. "You're going to make it through this. You're too damn tough to die. Besides, didn't you hear Curtis is a criminal piece of shit who's currently being hunted by half the law enforcement agencies in this country? You don't even need to retire now. You can keep working until you're a hundred. You just have to hang on."

Tears stung Brooks's eyes. *Shit.* He was saying some of the same stuff Jack had said to him all those years ago when Brooks had been the one lying on the ground dying at that high school.

"I just wanted to always do the right thing," Ray said, the words so soft, Brooks had to lean over to hear them. "I guess in the end I did that. I saved your life."

Brooks had to fight not to let out a howl, not having the heart to tell Ray that his life had never been at risk.

Ray's eyes started to slip closed, and Brooks felt a moment of panic. Then he heard his friend's heart continuing to beat, and he relaxed a little. Ray was still holding on.

By the time the paramedics came in with the gurney a few seconds later, Ray was completely unconscious. Trey nodded at Brooks as if to reassure him the old guy was going to make it. Brooks wasn't so sure, but he nodded in return, then followed the paramedics so he could ride with them to the hospital.

He needed to be there with Ray.

Just in case.

———

"I can't believe the chief of police tried to kill you," Ruben said as he used a broom to sweep up another pile of glass. "And at a frigging wedding! How fucked up is that?"

"Language," Selena murmured, not looking away from the poster she was repositioning on the wall. When it was straight, she shoved a few tacks into the corners to keep it there. Once done, she looked around, sighing at all the work left to do.

The windows had been replaced, the bullet holes in the wall patched, and the blood cleaned up, but that was it. Broken glass was still scattered everywhere, the chair/desk combos pushed against one wall, the literacy posters either lying on the floor or torn apart. What a mess. If Eva hadn't called earlier to confirm everything was set for classes to restart tomorrow, Selena would have thought the room needed another week of work. But she guessed they expected her to do most of the cleanup. Shocking—not.

She hadn't been sure if she was ready to come back, especially after the way she'd lost it last night. But after waking up in Jayden's bed after a solid seven hours sleep, she realized her kids needed her. It was time to get back to her job, her passion.

Fortunately, she had Ruben there to help her clean up, even though she still had no idea how he'd known she'd be here. But within minutes of her getting to the school, he'd shown up at the door, holding the key to the janitor's closet and asking what she needed him to do. She supposed it was his way of repaying her for saving his life. She was just glad to see he was out of the hospital.

"Were you scared?" Ruben asked suddenly, and she glanced over to see him regarding her curiously. "When those men were shooting at you at the SWAT compound, I mean."

Selena's thoughts drifted back to last night's events. The evening had started out almost magical. Dancing, laughing, meeting all the other werewolves, and coming to realize how many others like her were out there. But then the shooting had started, and everything had gone insane.

"I was scared," she admitted slowly. "But not for myself."

"Officer Brooks?" Ruben asked, his knowing expression somewhat out of place on his otherwise youthful face. "You were worried about him getting hurt?"

She smiled, hearing someone call Jayden that. He wasn't Officer Brooks to her. He was simply Jayden. Ruben was right, though. She'd been worried about him getting hurt. Actually, that was an understatement. When Jayden had been shot, she'd nearly lost her mind to the degree that she had a hard time remembering the details of what had happened right afterward. The only thing she remembered clearly was Jayden running out of the reception tent and trying to follow him. Zane had slowed her for a few moments, until her fear had pushed her shift to the point that nobody, not even another werewolf, could slow her down as she'd raced out of the tent after the man who was more important to her than anything else in the world.

"I know he's a cop. And that he's strong and really good at his job," she said. "But knowing that doesn't make me worry any less about him. The idea of him getting hurt…" She shook her head. "It's hard to even think about."

"Are you two going to get married?" Ruben asked, not looking up from the pile of glass he was scooping up and dumping into a metal trash can.

Selena laughed. Leave it to a kid like Ruben to dismiss the silly stuff about having only known Jayden for a week, or how you shouldn't rush into any important decision, or how true love takes time. He knew how much she cared about Jayden and wondered aloud when the wedding might be.

"Maybe," she admitted. "We haven't actually discussed it, but I really like him, and I think he likes me just as much. I can see us being together."

Ruben smiled. "That's cool."

Then he went back to sweeping up glass, like everything she'd just said was obvious. In some ways, maybe it was.

"What about you and Marguerite?" Selena asked as she moved over and pulled a chair/desk out of the pile along the wall and slid it across the floor that Ruben had already cleaned. "What's going on with you two?"

He laughed. "I don't think we're ready to get married yet. I mean, we haven't gone on our first date yet."

Selena made a face. "Very funny. I meant when are you guys going to go out and where are you going."

His shoulders lifted in a shrug. "I'm not too sure. She got in trouble when her mom and dad found out she'd been at a party at a gang hangout. Her parents also know I OD'd there, so I don't think they're going to be down with us going out together."

It was Selena's turn to shrug. "That simply means you need to win over her parents."

"Yeah, but how do I do that?"

Selena grabbed another chair/desk combo and slid it across the floor. "Find out what kind of food her parents like, get a big bag of takeout, then put on the nicest clothes you own and show up at their door on a Friday night. Have your first date with Marguerite and her parents. And if you have to, do the same thing every week until her parents realize they can trust you to be around their daughter."

He winced. "That could get really expensive."

"Getting the girl you want takes work," Selena said. "Which in this case means you might have to get a J-O-B. Trust me, if Marguerite is the right girl for you, it will be worth it."

They were still talking about how he'd know if Marguerite was the right girl for him when Selena heard footsteps by the door. She looked over to see Ernesto standing there, a tired smile on his face. The two men with him appeared just as haggard. Selena had never seen either of them before, but the way they stood in the hallway, looking left and right like they expected someone to jump them at any moment, was kind of weird. Selena felt a twinge of worry. Was Ernesto in danger? But that was crazy. He was a businessman now, not a gangbanger.

"You'd better listen to her, kid," he said as he walked into the room. "This is one teacher who knows what the hell she's talking about when it comes to appreciating true love when you get a shot at it."

Selena laughed and crossed the room to hug Ernesto. "Not that I'm not glad to see you, but what are you doing here?"

"I need to talk to you." He pulled away and glanced at Ruben. "In private."

That request for privacy, not to mention the tension coming off Ernesto in waves, made her inner wolf suddenly wary. The feeling only got stronger when she saw the concerned look on Ruben's face. Something wasn't right. But Ernesto was her friend. She was going to trust that fact over some strange werewolf instincts she didn't understand yet.

She smiled at Ruben. "I'll see you tomorrow, okay? First thing in the morning, so don't even think of sleeping in. And thanks for the help cleaning up."

Ruben stared at her for a long moment before darting a quick look at Ernesto with what could only be called suspicion in his dark eyes. But then he nodded and gave her a weak smile.

"Okay. See you tomorrow, Ms. Rosa."

Leaning the broom against the wall by the door, he walked out, casting nervous glances at the men standing in the hall before turning right and disappearing out of sight.

"Ernesto, is something wrong?" she asked as he closed the door, leaving his two companions outside. "Because you're acting all kinds of freaky."

Her friend ignored her question as he moved over to look out the windows, something that was a lot easier to do now that there weren't any blinds in the way. Ernesto's heart was beating fast as hell, and if the scent coming off him was any indication, he was also sweating like crazy. She didn't understand what that meant, but it couldn't be good.

When he still didn't answer, she walked over and put her hand on his arm, trying to get his attention. "Ernesto, talk to me."

"Leave town with me," he said suddenly, the words coming out in a rush as he turned to her with what looked like panic in his eyes. "Tonight."

Selena found herself stepping back defensively, tingles running all over her body, the hair standing up on her arms. "What are you talking about? I'm not going to leave town with you."

There was a spike in his heartbeat as he took a step forward, closing the distance between them again. "I need to leave the country, and I want you to come with me. Just think of it as a vacation. You've always talked about seeing other countries. So, let's do it."

Now her heart started pounding hard, too, anger slowly taking the place of the worry she'd been feeling. "Why do you need to leave the country?" she demanded, tipping her head back to look up at him. "And don't give me that crap about a vacation. What the hell did you do?"

Ernesto glanced out the window, his Adam's apple bobbing nervously. "I didn't do anything. It's not like that. I just need to leave. If you feel anything for me at all, you'll stop asking me questions and come with me."

Selena opened her mouth to tell him she wasn't going anywhere with him, but he grabbed her wrist before she could say anything, like he thought he could physically drag her out of the room. Her fingertips and gums immediately ached, a sure sign her claws and fangs wanted to come out. With a growl, she drove the heel of her hand into Ernesto's chest, knocking him back a half dozen steps.

"Don't touch me!" she snarled.

Crap. Her fangs had slipped out a little. She tried to hide them as much as she could with her lips, because they sure as hell weren't going away. She wasn't sure she wanted them to. Her inner werewolf told her there was danger here, and she was starting to believe it.

Ernesto stared at her in shock, his hand absently coming up to rub his chest where she'd thumped him. "I didn't mean..." He stopped, took a deep breath, and began again. "Selena, I love you. I've always loved you. And you've always loved me. Let's stop playing games. I'm in trouble and need to leave the country, and I'm asking the woman I love to come with me."

Selena blinked. Who the hell was this jackass and what had he done with Ernesto? Because this wasn't the friend who'd been right there at her side through most of her life. "Yes, I love you, Ernesto. But as a friend and a brother. I can't love you any other way. That place in my heart is taken by another man. Someone special I want to be with forever."

Ernesto turned his back to her, and for a moment, she thought he was going to walk out without another word. But then he spun around and grabbed her arms, yanking her off the floor and shoving backward until her shoulders slammed into the wall.

"You mean that fucking cop?" he shouted, shaking her so hard, her head bounced off the wall. "You'd rather be with that piece of shit instead of me? What the hell did he ever do for you, huh?"

Hearing him talk about Jayden that way made her want to claw him to pieces. "Ernesto, stop! I don't want to hurt you."

Even as she said the words, her claws extended. If she let the wolf out, she had no idea what she'd do.

Ernesto shook her again. "Was he the one who kept the gangbangers away from your tight little ass all through high school? Was he the one who paid your bills and kept a roof over your head before you went to college? Was he the one who kept the Locos and Riders from popping a cap in you every time you stuck your nose into gang business and got in the way of their recruiting? Was he the

one who put a bullet in the back of Aaron Perez's head for
daring to lay a finger on you? I don't fucking think so. I've
been there for you. Every time you needed me, I was there.
And if you think I'm letting a fucking cop have you now,
you're crazy. You've been mine from the moment I first
saw you, and if I didn't let Geraldo get in the way of that,
I sure as hell won't let an asshole cop come between us."

Selena's control was almost gone by the time Ernesto
admitted to killing Aaron, so she'd barely paid attention
to the rest of his rant…until he'd mentioned her brother.
When he said he refused to let Geraldo get in the way,
had he meant…?

Her vision blurred in rage as her fangs came out the
rest of the way. Lifting her feet, she kicked Ernesto in
the stomach, catapulting him away from her so hard,
he slid across the floor and into the desks still stacked
against the wall.

She started toward him before he'd even managed to
crawl his way out of the pile of furniture. She growled
long and low, making him glance up. His face turned
white, and he almost fell backward again. She probably
looked like a monster to him, but she didn't care. He was
the monster, not her.

"What did you mean you didn't let Geraldo get in
the way?" she growled, her claws flexing and clenching.
"What did you do to my brother?"

Eyes wide, Ernesto backpedaled, shoving some of the
desks in her path to slow her down. "I didn't mean it that
way. I didn't."

"Stop lying!" she roared, tossing them out of the way.
"Tell me what you did."

Ernesto kept retreating until his back finally hit the

wall. He glanced left and right, but there was nowhere for him to go. "I don't know what happened to you, but we can fix you. We can take you to a priest, or a doctor, or someone else who can help you. I know you're still in there, and I still love you."

Selena grabbed the last chair/desk combo in her way and slung it across the room so hard, it bounced off the wall and smashed through one of the new window panes. Eva was going to be so pissed.

"Tell me what you did to my brother," she snarled, halting in front of him.

Ernesto reached behind his back and came out with a handgun, his hand shaking like a leaf as he pointed it at her. She knocked the weapon away, gouging three shallow lines across the inside of his wrist with her claws.

He jerked his hand back, staring at her in terror. A noise from somewhere outside almost distracted her, her wolf sense telling her there was something going on out there. But she ignored it, focused only on the man in front of her.

"Last chance," she warned.

"I wanted to go out with you," Ernesto shouted. "I'd wanted you for a long time, but I waited until you were old enough. Geraldo said no. He said no gangbanger—not even me—was going to touch his sister."

She stopped. The omega inside screamed at her to kill Ernesto, to shove her claws into his chest and rip him apart. But the human part of her wanted to hear the rest.

"So you shot him?" she demanded. "Because he didn't want you going out with me and dragging me into the gangs? What about the whole gang war after that? Getting out and going straight? Was that all a lie, too?"

He nodded, taking a deep breath to get himself

together. "I didn't mean for it to happen, but when everyone assumed Geraldo's death was gang related, I went along with it. When it was all said and done, both of the old gangs were pretty much wiped out anyway. So I swept up the pieces and used them to grow my custom car empire. I got rich doing the same shit I always did. I just did it while wearing a suit."

She shook her head. He'd lied to her the whole time. The man she'd thought of as a brother had taken away the only other family besides her grandmother she'd had left in the world.

"Why leave the country now?" she asked, fighting to control the urge to kill him. "If you had it all figured out, why run?"

"I got greedy and became personally involved in my latest business venture. The profit potential was huge, but things went to hell when that damn cop boyfriend of yours showed up."

At first, Selena thought Ernesto was talking about the hunter's attack on the SWAT compound, but then she realized what this was about. "The energy drink spiked with drugs? That was you?"

He shrugged. "I was set to make millions on that stuff. With the way kids love energy drinks, it would have started a whole new wave in the drug trade."

The casual way he justified selling drugs to kids sickened her.

"Ruben almost died drinking that stuff," she said. "Two other people at that same party did die."

He smirked. "You know the saying…*drink responsibly*."

Selena bared her fangs in a snarl. "I should just kill you and do the world a favor."

Chapter 20

"CAN'T YOU DRIVE ANY FASTER?" BROOKS GROWLED AS Zane's BMW slid through a curve, fishtailed a bit, then straightened up and accelerated…still moving too damn slow.

"Not unless you want to arrive at the school with a long string of patrol cars on our arse, lights flashing and sirens blaring."

Brooks responded with another growl, longer, lower, and much more frustrated.

"She's going to be okay." Zane slowed down to something that vaguely resembled a stop as they passed through a busy intersection. "She's more than capable of taking care of herself. She's a bloody omega, remember? If Ernesto is dumb enough to try to hurt her, she'll likely kill him."

Brooks knew that, too, but it didn't necessarily make him feel any better. Selena was everything to him. The idea of her being scared, even if she could protect herself, tore his insides into pieces.

He and Zane had been at the hospital waiting with the rest of their task force members for Ray to come out of surgery. The older cop had only gone into the operating room an hour ago, and they'd all known they were in for a long night, but no one was going anywhere. The doctors had said all the right things about Ray being stable and in good hands, but everyone had still been worried. Ray was no spring chicken.

Then Ruben had called.

Brooks had moved off to the end of the hallway out-side the waiting room to take the call so he didn't disturb anyone. That turned out to be a good thing, because he'd just about lost it when Ruben told him Ernesto Lopez was at the high school with two gangbangers.

He'd told Ruben he'd be right there, then motioned to Zane and walked out without saying a word. He hadn't even told his other pack mates. He'd wanted to move fast and not talk. Zane agreed to drive. For all his com-plaining about speed, Brooks was glad his friend was driving. He was too freaked out.

The front end of Zane's car scraped the asphalt as they pulled into the high school parking lot, and Brooks couldn't help but remember the last time he'd been there, when he'd saved Selena from Pablo. He prayed to God this visit would have the same happy ending.

Ruben waved them down before they were halfway across the lot, panic on his face. "Ms. Rosa is in there with the asshole who's making those energy drinks," he said as they both jumped out. "She seems to know him, but I'm pretty sure they're arguing. I've heard a few shouts already, and a chair/desk came through the window just before you got here. I know this is going to sound crazy, but I think I heard growling, too."

Zane threw Brooks a quick look. The shouting, growl-ing, and airborne furniture meant Selena was pissed.

"Any idea what they're talking about?" Brooks asked as they ran across the parking lot toward the building Selena's classroom was in.

Ruben shook his head. "Those two muscle heads are parked in the hallway right outside her door, so I can't get anywhere close to the classroom. And listening at the windows doesn't work. But I think I heard him say something about her leaving with him."

Brooks bit back a growl and moved faster. What the fuck? Ernesto thought Selena would go on the run with him? Was the man that frigging stupid?

"If you plan on storming in through the front door, don't you think we should have a plan to deal with the guards Ernesto set in the hallway?" Zane asked. "If he hears us coming, it might provoke him into doing something stupid."

Brooks slowed, knowing his friend was right. He needed to stop thinking like a freaked-out werewolf and start thinking like a SWAT cop.

"Can you distract them?" He glanced at Zane. "Get them out of the hallway? I'll come in the far door of the building and go for the classroom while you deal with them."

Zane looked at him dubiously. "The moment they see me in this uniform, they're going to warn Ernesto or shoot, neither of which is really what we're looking for."

"I could distract them," Ruben said. "Get them outside so you can deal with them."

That was a horrible idea, and Brooks opened his mouth to tell him so, but then he heard a shout from inside the building. Selena screaming for Ernesto to stop lying. The raw anger and rage in her voice were enough to decide the matter.

"Go," Brooks said. "Get those two gangbangers out of that hallway now."

Then he was off and running for the far side of the building, his head imagining all kinds of horrible shit. Selena would never voluntarily go anywhere with

Ernesto, even if he was a longtime friend. But if he had a gun...

Brooks heard the sounds of fighting on the other end of the building as he reached the door on his side. True to his word, Ruben had gotten the gangbangers out of the hallway. Brooks only hoped Zane was up to the challenge of quickly and silently dealing with two armed men.

But as he shoved open the door and raced for Selena's classroom, he heard something that made him stop worrying about Zane and refocus on the more serious issue of stopping the woman he loved from doing something she'd regret for the rest of her life.

"I should just kill you. And do the world a favor."

Cursing, Brooks opened the door and found Selena a foot away from Ernesto, her eyes vivid blue, her claws and fangs out, murder in her gaze.

"I really don't think you want to do that, Selena," Brooks whispered softly. He needed to pull her back from the edge—fast. "And I don't want you to do it, either."

Brooks ignored the terrified look Ernesto gave him, walking over to her even as she snarled at him. Like she was warning him away from her intended prey. He ignored that, too, only stopping once he was beside her.

"I'm here now, Selena," he said softly. "It's okay. I'm here."

She didn't even look his way, her gaze locked on the rapidly beating pulse throbbing visibly in Ernesto's neck. Her fingers flexed, claws retracting and extending. No doubt, she was picturing what it would be like to rip out the man's throat.

Brooks didn't give a damn if she shredded Ernesto to pieces. After what he'd done to Ray, the guy was officially scum. But Selena would be devastated if the omega inside her ever killed someone, even if that someone deserved it. She simply wasn't the kind of person who could deal with doing something like that.

"He killed my brother," she whispered, still not looking away from Ernesto. "Because Geraldo wouldn't let him bang his little sister. Ernesto shot him, then used his death to take over the gangs and turn them into his custom car empire."

Ernesto shook his head, like he thought Brooks wasn't going to believe what Selena said. This asshole was a grade A piece of shit. Brooks had never really liked the man from the moment he'd met him. But you don't get to pick other people's friends. You just have to deal with them.

Brooks ignored Ernesto and gently put a hand on Selena's arm, making a soothing, shushing sound. "You need to let him go, Selena. He needs to be punished for what he's done, but you don't need to do it. He killed your brother, and he'll pay for that. I promise. But killing him isn't the answer."

She continued to glare at her brother's killer for so long, Brooks was afraid she hadn't even heard him. But then she turned her gaze on him, blinking until the blue began to fade. The second she stepped back from Ernesto, the son of a bitch crawled away like the piece of crap he was.

Brooks pulled Selena into his arms, hugging her as she buried her face in his chest and cried. He wished he'd heard the entire story Ernesto had given her, because maybe that would have helped. But even without the full story, he knew Selena was going to need a lot of time to deal with it. She was completely wrecked.

Because he couldn't do a damn thing about what was

making her cry, he turned his attention to the problem he was going to have to fix, namely explaining what the hell had happened here. A broken window, a crying teacher, and a gangbanger ranting about monsters. This was going to be damn tough to cover up, but he was sure as hell going to try.

. Brooks was so focused on Selena, he didn't realize how far Ernesto had crawled until he heard a slight creaking sound and looked up in time to see the man pointing an automatic at them, already squeezing the trigger.

Brooks didn't think. He just slung Selena around in a circle and tossed her behind him, then lunged toward Ernesto. The automatic went off before he got there, and he felt a punch as the first round took him in the shoulder and the second one got him in the gut.

It said something about how bad the hunter bullets had felt when he realized traditional 9mm ball rounds didn't even feel like a bee sting in comparison. But still, getting shot and having another uniform messed up by the man who'd killed Selena's brother was enough to piss anyone off.

He hit Ernesto hard, knocking the gun out of his hand and slamming him to the floor. On the way down, they toppled over one of those industrial metal trash cans, which made a shit ton of noise as pieces of glass large and small flew out.

They landed in the glass and fought for a dominant position. It should have been laughably easy for Brooks to slam the asshole through the floor, but it had been a shitty past few days, and he'd just been shot twice. Not to mention the fact that Ernesto was a big guy raised on the street and taught to fight since the day he was born.

They rolled back and forth in the broken glass, cutting the shit out of themselves, punching and shoving. Brooks could have finished this quickly if he'd wanted to, but he was still trying to take Ernesto down alive. For Selena's sake.

He just about had the man pinned until Selena landed on top of them, growling, clawing, and biting like the out-of-control omega she was.

Brooks was trying to shove Selena aside without hurting her when Ernesto's hand came up in a blur. That's all he saw before a long shard of glass slammed into his throat and snapped off. The pain was intense, and blood went everywhere. But the worst part was that Selena completely lost her mind. She let out a snarl, not caring Ernesto had another piece of glass in his hands and was aiming for her neck this time.

Brooks forgot the pain and the blood pouring down his windpipe, which was choking the hell out of him, as he threw himself forward to protect Selena, lashing out with his claws and ripping out Ernesto's throat.

Brooks turned and looked at Selena to see her growling and snarling as she stared down in blue-eyed rage at the man dying on the floor. Then a movement caught his eye, and Brooks glanced over to see a stunned and silent Ruben standing in the doorway, staring at a scene he couldn't understand.

It didn't help when Brooks stood up, a glass shard in his neck and bleeding like a stuck pig as he moved over to Selena to pull her into his arms and calm her down all over again. She continued to stare at Ernesto's body but didn't resist the comfort Brooks gave her while she sobbed like crazy.

Brooks looked past her to Ruben, who still stood there gawking like this was the most extreme thing he'd ever seen in his life, which it probably was. Damn, this was going to be difficult to explain.

Zane walked up behind Ruben a few seconds later. He looked like he'd been in a pretty good fight. He was holding his injured arm stiffly, like it was hurting him, but he had a satisfied look on his face that Brooks hadn't seen in a long time. Maybe that fight with the two gang-bangers had finally proved something to him.

His friend took one look at the scene and winced, then put a hand on Ruben's shoulder.

"Come on, kid," he said. "Let's go talk about this."

Brooks thanked him with a nod, then went back to comforting his mate. He tried to make the same shushing sounds as before, but his throat wouldn't work. He pulled back a little from Selena, hoping she wouldn't notice, and tried to get a grip on the piece of glass still sticking out of his throat.

He couldn't do it without being able to see what he was doing. He tensed, knowing the wound would heal while the glass was still in there. He wondered if he needed to go get Zane when Selena realized what was going on. Reaching up, she gently tugged the shard out.

Brooks sighed in relief the moment it was out, wrapping his arm around her and urging her into the hallway where he hugged her to his chest again and let his body have time to heal itself.

After a moment, Selena pulled back to look up at him, her brown eyes filled with concern. "Are you okay?"

He nodded, because it was all he could do at the moment, asking her the same question with his eyes.

She glanced back at her classroom, then nodded. "Yeah, I'm okay. But I'm not sure if I'm processing everything that happened. I just found out my brother didn't die because he was in a gang. He died because he was trying to protect me from someone he thought wasn't good enough for me. I also found out my best friend, the man I spent years leaning on, was the person who killed him. And now that Ernesto is dead, I don't feel anything but relief."

Brooks tried to say something, but the words still wouldn't come out. *Dammit*. So instead, he hugged her again, trying to say everything he felt with nothing more than his touch.

"I love you," she said against his chest. "I've known since we first met but couldn't seem to find the time to tell you. It's probably not the best time to say it now, but you came and saved my life…again. The least I can do is muster the courage to tell you how I feel."

Brooks swallowed experimentally, relieved it didn't feel nearly as painful now. "I'll always be there to save you," he whispered in a rough voice. "I love you, too."

Selena leaned against him, squeezing him tightly. "I know, and it feels really good."

They stood there like that until Brooks heard the sounds of approaching sirens. No doubt Selena heard them, too.

"We need to figure out what we're going to say to them," he whispered. "But once this is over and we're home, I'm going to tell you about the werewolf legend of *The One*. Okay?"

She smiled up at him. "You get me home before midnight, and you can tell me any legend you want."

Chapter 21

"You sure you don't need some help with the cooking?" Jayden asked, even though Selena knew it was a waste of time. She'd only known Zane for two weeks, but she'd already picked up on the fact that he was one stubborn Brit.

"No, I don't need help," Zane growled, managing the thirty or so burgers on the grill with only his right arm, the other still a little sore from the fight he'd gotten in last Sunday. "The food is almost ready, so go play volleyball with the others. Or go pet Tuffie and Kat if you want. Just go away and stop distracting me."

Jayden looked like he was about to insist, so Selena hooked her arm in his and dragged him away from the line of grills and tables groaning under the weight of all the food that had already been set out and closer to the volleyball courts and the people playing and laughing over there. Jayden had said it himself the other day. Zane was doing a lot better now. His arm still wasn't working, but he'd had some kind of epiphany during the fight at the high school. It was like he'd concluded his injury wasn't going to define him. It was one of the reasons he'd volunteered to cook today.

They stopped by the sand-filled volleyball pit, watching the combination of kids, teens, and adults run around trying to smash a poor little ball that had never done a thing to them. Ruben and Marguerite were out there giggling their heads off with a bunch of younger kids as the adult members of the Pack let them play the game any way they wanted, even if that meant kicking the ball, which Selena was pretty sure wasn't in the formal rule book.

Scott, Becca, and Marguerite's parents were chatting with a small pack of beta werewolves on the sideline of the game. Becca had spent a good portion of the day looking around curiously, no doubt trying to figure out which people were werewolves and which ones weren't. Every once in a while, her friend would subtly point in someone's direction, silently lifting an eyebrow. Selena would only laugh and refuse to indicate one way or the other.

While the weather was chilly today, the SWAT compound was packed with people having an incredibly good time, even though it wasn't hard at all to find signs of the recent battle there. New bricks had been laid along the front of the armory, and nearly all the various bullet holes in the admin building had been patched. But there were still a lot of scorch marks all over the place, because it was apparently too cold right now to paint. Nobody seemed to care about any of that, though. If she had to guess, she'd say it was because the damage was a reminder to everyone that they'd won. It hadn't been a pretty win, with everything tied up in a nice pretty bow, but everyone was safe and unharmed. They'd confirmed the wolfsbane vaccination worked, there were a lot less hunters in the world than there had been before, and while no one had found Curtis yet, they would soon. His face was plastered over every news outlet and social media platform in the world.

Even Jayden's friend, Ray, was doing fantastic. He'd

wanted to come to the cookout, but his doctor shut that idea down. Now that Deputy Chief Mason was acting chief of police, Ray wouldn't be retiring anytime soon, something that pleased Jayden immensely.

"Food's ready, people!" Zane called out.

The game ceased immediately, and everyone ran for the tables to grab something to eat. Plates piled high, they disappeared inside the training building where tables and chairs had been set up. Selena waved and hugged people as they passed, still working hard to learn everyone's name. She and Jayden ended up at a table with Gage, Mac, Zane, and some of the other Pack werewolves.

"Is everything getting back to normal in your classroom?" Mac asked as she loaded her fork with barbecue chicken.

"Pretty much." Selena had been planning to go with a single cheeseburger, but when she'd seen the fish and chips—Zane's specialty—she couldn't help grabbing those, too. Her appetite was crazy since she'd become a werewolf. "Some of the kids are still having a hard time walking into a classroom where there's been a shooting, but the counselors are helping with that."

She didn't mention the part about how some things were much easier now than they'd been before. Gang activity was at an all-time low at the school, now that so many gangbangers were dead or in prison. Then there was the matter of her reputation. After word had gotten out about her beating up those gangbangers at that party and how she'd faced down Ernesto, classroom management wasn't an issue for her anymore. Nobody wanted to get on her bad side.

"How about with you?" Gage's dark-haired wife

prompted gently. "You doing okay walking into that room?"

A big, strong arm slipped around her, and she looked over at Jayden to see him regarding her warmly. They'd had this same talk earlier in the week when she'd stayed over at his place, which she did every night now. He'd been worried about how she was handling Ernesto's death.

"That's a work in progress, too, but it's going well," she admitted. "Cooper introduced me to a friend of his—Dr. Delacroix—and I've been talking it over with her. I guess I had a lot of anger issues tied up along with my brother's death. Finding out how he died and that the person responsible for it is dead, too, seems to have helped me. As hard as that is to understand."

Mac shook her head. "It's not that hard to understand at all."

In a way, letting go of all that anger was helping her control the omega wolf, too. Her eyes had even glowed green for the first time last night when she and Jayden had made love.

"Did anyone have a problem with the story you gave about how Ernesto died?" Diego asked from the end of the table, his voice soft so no one around them would hear. Well, no one who wasn't a werewolf at least.

"I said his throat got slashed with some broken glass during the fight," Jayden said. "I'm not sure the ME bought it, but no one tried to second-guess us."

As they ate, the conversation centered around more family-friendly topics, like how well Tuffie and Kat got along, or how cool it had been for the Ritz to offer Lana and Max a free suite there this weekend since their previous plans had been ruined by the hunters. The newlyweds were headed there right after the cookout.

"Still no word on where the hell Curtis disappeared to?" Jayden asked. "It's hard to believe no one has seen him yet. The guy isn't that good at blending into a crowd. I thought they'd catch him by now."

"Funny you should mention that," Gage said, grabbing a handful of fries from his plate. "I didn't mention it before because I didn't want to get any hopes up, but in addition to cloning the SIM card on Curtis's cell, Becker also installed a parental snooping app. We hadn't gotten anything out of it since Curtis disappeared, but it popped up this morning long enough for our former chief to send and receive a text message. The phone disappeared again immediately after that, but Becker was able to grab the phone's location and the two texts. Curtis was arranging a meeting location."

Everyone around the table sat there in stunned silence.

"Where is it?" Rachel asked urgently, a forkful of potato salad halfway to her mouth. "Please tell me he's here in Dallas?"

Gage shook his head. "Unfortunately, no. He's in LA. He requested a pickup from someone. Whoever it was told him to go to the Griffith Observatory."

More silence reigned.

"What are we going to do?" Jayden asked. "Turn the info over to the marshals or the FBI?"

"I was thinking we'd send some people out there to look around and see what they can find," Gage said softly. "If he went to the effort of going all the way to California, it's probably because that's where the other hunters are."

"I'll go," Zane offered. "I've done undercover work before, and I know a few people out there who owe me some favors."

Selena barely knew Gage but could immediately see he wasn't thrilled at the idea. But before the Pack leader could say anything, Jayden interrupted.

"Plus, Zane could pretend to be a tourist or something," he said. "He already has the accent."

Gage glowered at Jayden, and Selena held her breath, wondering if a growl was on the way. But after a moment of locking eyes with her mate, the SWAT commander finally looked at Zane.

"Okay," he said. "But there's no way in hell you or anyone else is going without backup."

"I'll go," Rachel said. "I've never been, but I've always wanted to see LA."

"Count me in," Diego murmured. "I got family in LA, and I know a lot of cops there."

Gage considered that, then nodded. "Okay, that's the plan then. Zane, you take lead. Rachel and Diego, you go in as a couple. Observe and act as his communications link to us unless he needs backup. I'd like to send Becker out there with you, but he needs his computer to be useful. Besides, he'd end up taking Jayna, which means her whole beta pack would want to go, too. That would be a catastrophe. So, any hacking you need, you're going to have to work with him long distance."

Zane exchanged looks with Jayden, giving him a small nod. Jayden nodded back.

The party didn't wind down until hours later, after more food, a few games of volleyball, and some seriously delicious desserts. Selena even brought several trays of brownies, much to Cooper's delight.

"You about ready to get out of here?" Jayden asked after Becca and Scott took off.

Selena nodded. "Yeah. Is it okay if I crash at your place again tonight?"

He chuckled. "Of course, it's okay. I don't know why you don't just move in and save rent money."

She smiled. "Is that your really romantic way of asking me to cohabitate with you?"

"That depends on your answer." Jayden flashed her a grin. "If your answer is yes, then it's definitely my attempt at romance. If the answer is no, then consider it a clumsy attempt at humor."

Selena kissed him long and slow, then grabbed his hand, pulling him toward the exit, keenly aware of all their pack mates watching them. "The answer is most definitely yes."

Acknowledgments

I hope you had as much fun reading Brooks and Selena's story as I had writing it! I knew Selena was going to be a werewolf when I first came up with the story. What I didn't know was that she was going to be an omega. But up until now, I hadn't explored what it's really like to be an omega werewolf, and I realized Selena would be the perfect character to do that with. It gave me a chance to show an omega in a completely different light.

This whole series wouldn't be possible without some very incredible people. In addition to another big thank-you to my hubby for all his help with the action scenes and military and tactical jargon, thanks to my editor and go-to-person at Sourcebooks, Cat Clyne (who loves this series as much as I do and is always a phone call, text, or email away whenever I need something); and all the other amazing people at Sourcebooks, including my fantastic publicist and the crazy-talented art department. The covers they make for me are seriously droolworthy!

Because I could never leave out my readers, a huge thank-you to everyone who has read my books and Snoopy Danced right along with me with every new release. That includes the fantastic people on my amazing Street Team, as well my assistant, Janet. You rock!

I also want to give a big thank-you to the men, women, and working dogs who protect and serve in police departments everywhere, as well as their families.

And a very special shout-out to my favorite restaurant, P.F. Chang's, where hubby and I bat story lines back and forth and come up with all of our best ideas, as well as a thank-you to our fantastic waiter, Andrew, who takes our order to the kitchen the moment we walk in the door!

Hope you enjoy the next book in the SWAT: Special Wolf Alpha Team series coming soon from Sourcebooks, and look forward to reading the rest of the series as much as I look forward to sharing it with you.

If you love a man in uniform as much as I do, make sure you check out X-Ops, my other action-packed paranormal/romantic-suspense series from Sourcebooks.

Happy Reading!

About the Author

Paige Tyler is a *New York Times* and *USA Today* best-selling author of sexy, romantic suspense and paranormal romance. She and her very own military hero (also known as her husband) live on the beautiful Florida coast with their adorable fur baby (also known as their dog). Paige graduated with a degree in education but decided to pursue her passion and write books about hunky alpha males and the kick-butt heroines who fall in love with them.

Visit Paige at her website at paigetylertheauthor.com.

She's also on Facebook, Twitter, Tumblr, Instagram, tsu, Wattpad, Google+, and Pinterest.

Also by Paige Tyler

SWAT: Special Wolf Alpha Team
Hungry Like the Wolf
Wolf Trouble
In the Company of Wolves
To Love a Wolf
Wolf Unleashed
Wolf Hunt
Wolf Hunger
Wolf Rising

X-Ops
Her Perfect Mate
Her Lone Wolf
Her Secret Agent (novella)
Her Wild Hero
Her Fierce Warrior
Her Rogue Alpha
Her True Match
Her Dark Half
X-Ops Exposed